**For Dan Alderson and Gary Hudson,
with many thanks**

KING DAVID'S SPACESHIP

JERRY POURNELLE

BAEN BOOKS

KING DAVID'S SPACESHIP

This is a work of fiction. All the characters and events portrayed in this book are fictional, and any resemblance to real people or incidents is purely coincidental.

A Baen Book

Baen Publishing Enterprises
P.O. Box 1403
Riverdale, NY 10471

ISBN: 0-671-72068-6

A substantially different version of a portion of this work appeared in *Analog Science Fiction* under the title *A Spaceship for the King*, copyright © by Condé Nast Publications, Inc., and was published by DAW Books, copyright © 1973 by Jerry Pournelle.

Cover art by David Hardy

First Baen Printing, February 1987
Second Baen Printing, July 1991

Printed in the United States of America

Distributed by Simon & Schuster
1230 Avenue of the Americas
New York, NY 10020

CONTENTS

PART ONE
Colony

PART TWO
Loyalties

PART THREE
Prince Samual's Hope

CHRONOLOGY

1969: Neil Armstrong sets foot on Earth's moon.
1990: Series of treaties between United States and Soviet Union creates the CoDominium.
2008: First interstellar drive tested.
2020: First interstellar colonies. Great Exodus begins.
2110: Coronation of Lysander I of Sparta.
2111: Formation Wars begin.
2250: Leonidas I proclaims Empire of Man.
2250–
2600: Empire of Man enforces interstellar peace.
2273: Prince Samual's World becomes Member Principality of Empire.
2603: Secession Wars begin.
2627: Prince Samual's World drawn into conflict.
2632: First bombardment of Prince Samual's World.
2637: First battle off Makassar.
2640: Secession Wars continue. Dark Ages in many systems. Effective termination of First Empire.
2658: Second battle off Makassar; remnants of loyalist fleet take refuge on Prince Samual's World.
2680: Battle of Prince Samual's World. Loyalist officers deposed.
2681: Brief occupation of Prince Samual's World by secessionists.
2694: Loyalist-engineered coup on Prince Samual's World.
2711: Bombardment of Prince Samual's World; effective end of high-energy civilization.
2723: Last starship visits Prince Samual's World; many loyalist families evacuated by remnant of Empire.
2740: Prince Samual University founded to preserve knowledge.

Part One

COLONY

1

The Blue Bottle

The crowd was noisy in the Blue Bottle, although it was early in the evening. Tavern girls squealed as customers pinched them, gaily clad waiters brought round after round of drinks, and throughout much of the room everyone was shouting merrily.

The reason was not hard to find, for in one corner of the crowded room three officers of the Imperial Navy held court, buying drinks for anyone on Prince Samual's World who would sit with them and laugh at their jokes. Some of the regulars held back, their distaste for the enforced association more evident with every round, but for each of them there were four others from Haven City more than willing to share the Emperor's humor and liquor. Before the night ended the officers would doubtless have new recruits for the Royal and Imperial Marines, young lads suddenly sobered to find themselves in an iron service out among the stars, never to see their homes and discovering that Imperial officers were not such jolly good fellows when you were under their command.

For the moment the whiskey, brandy, and grua—distilled from a cross between a berry and a peach grown only on Prince Samual's northern continent—flowed freely, the jokes were new to the locals even if they had been told a century before in the barracks at New Annapolis, and His Imperial Majesty's crimson-and-gold-jacketed officers were relaxed, feeling as at home as they ever did on a barely civilized planet.

The three of them were classmates, not six years out of the Academy, the gold and silver stripes of lieutenants only recently sewn on their sleeves. Closer inspection would have revealed that one of them was a year younger than his friends, a school prodigy admitted early to midshipman status as much because of his talents as his family influence, and that young-and-only-just-lieutenant Jefferson was very, very drunk. His classmates had discreetly opened the top clasp of their stiff tunic collars, but Jefferson's was half unfastened, revealing a none-too-fresh shirt and a tiny breast-pocket computer beneath.

His natural shyness overcome by countless thimble-sized glasses of grua, Lieutenant Jefferson basked in the esteem of the flatlanders. He had almost forgotten that they were barbarians, and that he and the tiny Navy outpost on Prince Samual were the only representatives of true civilization within ten light-years. The others were singing, and when his turn came he added a verse so obscene it shocked the tavern girls. He grinned and looked about for approval, then tossed off another glass.

Across from Jefferson a young native, browned by

field work, too young to be in the Blue Bottle if he were not sitting with the Emperor's overlords, beamed at his new friend and shouted approval of the song. "Great, Lieu—uh, Jeff, great. Tell us more about what it's like out there. Tell us about other worlds. Are we the most backward place you've ever seen?"

Lieutenant Jefferson belched loudly, murmured an automatic apology, and focused dizzily on his admirers. "Oh holl, no, Simom, not by a full broadside. Samual's got guns, and factories, and—and long-distance communications, and hydroelectric power; man, you've got nothing to be ashamed of. You've got no world government, and those wars you're always in stomp you down or for sure you'd be Class Two status in the Empire instead of a colony. When I think how bad you got torn up in the Secession Wars, it's amazing you got this far in a few centuries . . . standard centuries, that is. You're doing fine here. That right, laddie?" he asked, digging his elbow into his classmate's ribs.

Lieutenant Clements turned his black face to Jefferson and grinned, his teeth sparkling. "Sure that's right, Jeff, you tell 'em this is the best duty we've had since we left the capital. Maybe better," he shouted, turning back to the tavern girl beside him.

"Hear that?" Jefferson asked his companion. "Simom, we've been to places where they don't even have hydro-carbon power, no electricity, no pellet guns, nothing but horses and men running around in iron pants the way you see—well, the way *we* see in Imperial history books, books about the time when Earth was all there was to it. Friend, you almost have space travel. Another hundred years, another fifty years even, you'd have found us instead of the other way around. Too bad you didn't," he added, his voice changing. "Been better for you if you had.

Class Two status for sure, maybe Class One, if you'd had real space flight before we got here. Not your fault; the survey ship just happened by looking for a gas giant to scoop some fuel from and decided to look you over. A real pity." He looked at his empty glass. "Host! Host! More grua!"

Two of the regulars of the Blue Bottle made a point of walking past the officers as they stamped out of the tavern, their kilts swirling, but Jefferson did not notice them. As the headwaiter brought more drinks, Simom asked, "What was it like, that place where they wore iron pants? Is it far from here? Have you colonized it? Can we go there?"

"Ho, one at a time," Jefferson shouted. "Far? Not more than twelve light-years, one jump from here, I think. Let's see, yeah, there's nothing between the two suns and theirs is a big one; hell, it's that thing you people call the Eye of the Needle; you could see it right now if you went outside. And no, no colonies there, not enough to make it worthwhile yet. And we're spread so thin. Keep a little observation post there to watch for outies, a first lieutenant and a couple of middies, few Marines. Not even a ship in orbit. Detection gear, observation satellite, that's about all. Nothing important there, except, of course, their Temple."

Jefferson had allowed his voice to drop for a moment, a note of weariness creeping in as he thought of the immense task of the Imperial Navy trying to reclaim the pieces of an Empire lost and shattered in the Secession Wars, the capital itself only reaching for the stars decades ago. His Majesty hoped to knit together the fragments before another war could send mankind staggering back to primitive conditions. There had been no winners of the last war, and the next would be worse. There must not be a next one, he said to himself. Never again. Then he brightened as the raucous humor and obvious friendship of the natives washed over him. Best enjoy it now, he thought. They wouldn't be so friendly to the Navy after the colonists arrived—but that was years away, and the night was young.

"The funny part, Simon, is that the Temple is worth more to them than the whole bloody planet, if they only knew it! They were right to make it a holy place and preserve it, but if they only knew! Why, there's a whole Old-Empire subsection library in that rabbit warren they've built up around what used to be the Viceroy's Palace! The Service librarians almost went out of their minds, some of the history books and things they found there. Even a few science books, operating manuals for old Imperial Fleet stuff; you name it, it's there, or bits and pieces of it are.

"They don't even know what it all is! Wouldn't do them any good if they did, no technology to understand it anyway. And my sweet Savior, how they guard that stuff! Thought we'd never get any of it copied for the archives. If we'd taken just one of those cubes out—yeah, cubes, the library was geared to a computer. Not much like your books. Took a lot of work to get *that* fixed, I'll tell you. And those priests watched every second we were there. Never did make copies of most of the stuff; we'll get it some day. Be a great job for some historian. We had to sneak in, convince their bishops we were from the stars—they still haven't told the people in the city about us. And the chaplain had to get in on the act, convince them we were religiously orthodox, gave them some song and dance about how we, too, believed that God spoke from their archives. The chaplain said it was all right, the first thing they copied was a Bible, so he didn't lie about it. Couldn't harm a thing copying the stuff or they'd have boiled up so thick it'd take a battleship to kill them all. Can't do that, they're good people. We'll need everyone in this sector one day. Whoosh, I talk too much, pour me some more. That grua's the best thing about this planet. Well," he added, looking at the tall blond girl who stood at his elbow, "*one* of the best, anyway."

Lieutenant Jefferson was not the only drunken officer in the Blue Bottle, but he would hardly have recognized the gray-eyed man in a plain kilt two tables away as a member of the officer class. Colonel Nathan MacKinnie, lately cashiered from service to the Committee of Public Safety of Orleans, preferred whiskey in large glasses, and had had almost as many of those as Jefferson had of grua. MacKinnie was tall, centimeters taller than usual for Samualites, but without the remarkably broad shoulders typical of the planetary dwellers. With his straw-colored hair silvering at the temples, he looked more akin to the senior Imperial Navy officers than the natives. He sat quietly, motioning effortlessly for a new drink from time to time, and smoking countless pipefuls of 'robac. At intervals a particularly loud shout from the Imperial table would bring a grimace to his face, but for the most part he sat emotionlessly, giving no sign of the enormous quantities of whiskey he poured down his gullet.

Hal Stark, MacKinnie's one-time sergeant, now servant, companion, and comrade, watched his colonel anxiously, mentally computing the amount of whiskey Nathan had drunk, the time since they had eaten, and the earliness of the evening, before he turned to his own drink, his second of the day. He was allowing the amber grua to roll back over his tongue when MacKinnie snapped his pipe against the heel of his hand so hard that the stem broke.

"Damn!" he muttered. "Hal, look at those drunken excuses for officers. And those sots are the rulers of Prince Samual's World, the 'representatives of civilization' as they call themselves, the men who can decree what will be done and snuff out the independence of Orleans like a candle in a hurricane. Babbling, shouting, the overlords of everything we've ever known."

"Yes, sir. Begging the colonel's pardon, but I seem to recall a young lieutenant some years ago couldn't hold his liquor no better than them, if it's all right to say so." It was difficult to tell just how much of Stark's apologetic air was genuine.

Colonel MacKinnie frowned for a moment, then burst into a loud guffaw. "I sure didn't, did I, Hal?" He looked at the ruined pipe in his hands, then signaled for the barmaid and bought cigars of genuine Earth Stock tobacco for a price he couldn't afford. "There were a few times when you had to roll me back to barracks, weren't there? You never missed, either. What are you best at, Hal? Batman, sergeant, or unemployed striker to a colonel with no command?"

"Best at whatever the colonel wants me at, that the right answer? Where are we going next, Colonel?"

MacKinnie shook his head slowly and looked around the room as if there might be some answer to the question. "They haven't stopped the fighting on South Continent. Maybe we can pick up something there." He reached into his pouch, and added, "We'd better find something soon, or we starve. But it won't be the same, Sergeant. Just something to fight over, get the bills paid. What we do won't matter anymore. The future here belongs to them." He waved his cigar at young Jefferson, who held the blond girl on his lap, her hands deep inside his open tunic, while he tried to force a glass of grua between her body and his lips. She squealed.

"Worse for you than for me, Colonel. I never did know what we were after, not really anyway, not the way you did. Long as you know, it's good enough for the troops." Stark tossed down the last of his drink, then looked back at his officer. "Drink up, Colonel, there's plenty to do somewhere. We could raise up a fair-sized regiment of men who'd follow you to hell. Tomorrow, I'll round up some of the old headquarters company and we'll go show the Southies what war's really like."

MacKinnie grinned momentarily as he methodically warmed his cigar before lighting it. The bar was pleasant, the company was good, and for a moment he forgot the hopelessness, even ordering a small grua to dip the end of his cigar into. He inhaled the strong smoke and leaned back in his chair, his feet stretched out under the table. Stark looked at him again, saw the lines leave Nathan's face, and ordered another round.

It was no good, MacKinnie thought, but there was no point in upsetting the big man next to him. He'd have to play the game out to the end, but, by all the Saints, he was tired now; tired in a way that the sleep and rest and soft duty they'd had for the last weeks could never cure. It was strange, he thought. Colonel of his own regiment at forty local years, a full citizen of Orleans, inevitably to be senior colonel and then general before his last parade. Not bad for a wandering mercenary soldier whose city-state had been extinguished only months before his graduation from its tiny war-academy, set to wandering in search of a living until he'd ended in the ranks of Orleans's army. Promotion, merit, recognition, citizenship, a

good career. And it was all over when the landing
boats came down from the ship that still whirled in
orbit above Samual.

Ten years of brilliant campaigning had ensured
that Orleans would not suffer the fate of his native
Samand. No power or likely combination of powers
could annex the Republic—but in a week the Imperial
Navy had accomplished it, so that Orleans was now
the Duchy of Orlean, subject to His Majesty King
David Second of Haven, and no Orleanist officers
wanted in the Royal Service, thank you. Honor, of
course, and an inadequate pension to the hero of
Blanthern Pass whose regiment had defeated the
best that Haven could put in the field. Well done,
old chap! Of course His Majesty has his own colo-
nels, but we have a pension for you sir. No hard
feelings, and of course no retaliation against the
Orleanists. Well, not much, anyway, and only against
a few of the political officers. You were never in
politics, were you, Colonel? No, of course not. Too
good a soldier. Yes, you can go now. And Colonel
Nathan MacKinnie was suddenly an old man, feeling
his campaigns and ready to drink far too much. He
had left the palace and walked aimlessly before he
noticed that Stark was behind him.

He could have fought, of course. Even after the
Committee bowed to the inevitable power of the
Imperial Navy, he could have taken MacKinnie's
Wolves to the fields, wandering in the forests, cutting down Haven soldiers, fighting tiny actions with
formations too small for the Navy to find and blast
out of existence with their space weapons. But for
how long? And what would the Imperials do to Orleans? How long would the people of the Republic
have supported him? How long before the romantic
gesture turned stale and the admiration of the citi-

zens turned to hatred and disgust as town after town was bombarded from space, turned to a blackened cinder as Lechfeld was? MacKinnie inhaled his cigar, letting the warm smoke drift over his tongue, out his lips, and into his nostrils, tasting the incredibly pleasing combination of real tobacco and grua before destroying the delicate flavors with the harsh tang of whiskey.

Across the next table, a couple rose and staggered toward the door, leaving him a clear view of Lieutenant Jefferson. The young naval officer was telling an admiring peasant about a strange planet, a place where they had no guns, only swords, and they worshiped Christ in a temple which once was an Old Empire library. Both of us drunks, MacKinnie thought. But the boy's one up. He's going somewhere, and what he does won't be undone by something you couldn't fight, couldn't understand. Stark was right. The young man did resemble the old Nat MacKinnie, but not this one. The old one was going somewhere, and what he accomplished would be his. And so the same would be true for that boy. Cursing bitterly, Nathan MacKinnie realized that he felt envy for the young men who had conquered his world.

2

Gentlemen Robbers

The evening wore on. The first round of entertainers finished their acts. It was too early for the late performers, and for many of the customers it was several drinks too late for anything else. The room became less noisy as the early festive crowd departed, leaving the Blue Bottle to serious drinkers and tavern girls. Only the voice of Lieutenant Jefferson, punctuated by the giggles of the girls at the Navy table, was heard above the low buzz of conversation. MacKinnie decided that it was time to go.

He stood in sudden decision, but when he swept his hand behind him for the cloak he had left on a nearby chair he lost his balance and lurched heavily into a small, round-faced man with a tiny mustache. The little man jumped backward with rabbit agility and began to mumble apologies.

"Not at all, sir," MacKinnie told him. "My fault entirely. No offense intended," he added unnecessarily. The little man was unarmed, and the thought of his issuing a challenge to Colonel MacKinnie was humorous. With an effort Nathan suppressed the laugh that the image generated.

"None taken, of course," the man said. "Would you join me in a drink?" He extended his hand. "Malcolm Dougal," he said apologetically.

The grip was firmer than MacKinnie would have expected. He took a long look at the chap. He saw nothing out of the ordinary. A kilt of some family plaid, a muted version of a much bolder tartan no longer worn in public, well suited for business. Expensive jacket, minor jewelry in excellent taste, a heavy signet ring on his left hand, probably Prince Samual University although there were other places that copied the design. Except for his small stature you could see a hundred like him in businessmen's dining clubs anytime you cared to.

On closer inspection, though, Dougal wasn't really so small. He just appeared to be such a rabbit that you took him for a small man, and of course anyone standing next to Stark would seem tiny. There was something else about Dougal, an air that was faintly threatening when you looked at him closely, but that was ridiculous. MacKinnie shook his head to clear it of whiskey.

"Thank you, I've had more than enough," Nathan said. "Nathan MacKinnie. I'm sorry, I'm forgetting my manners. Too much whiskey. No offense intended."

"And none taken. Perhaps we'll meet again. Good night."

"And a good night to you, Citizen Dougal." MacKinnie bowed and faced the exit, leaving Stark to collect their cloaks and pay the bill. Outside, they turned toward the harbor, walking slowly to the waterfront hostel where they had rooms more compatible to MacKinnie's meager pension than the brick and stone district around the Blue Bottle. MacKinnie had no objection to staying in cheap lodgings, but he was still sufficiently a colonel to want to drink in a gentleman's tavern.

A light rain began to fall, causing the few citizens out on the street to scurry for cabs. An alcohol steam car whirred quietly by, slowing momentarily as the driver gazed at their faces before deciding they would not be customers. Then a horse-drawn two-wheeler clopped alongside.

The coachman shouted at them. "Good rates, sirs. Anywhere you want to go. Anything you could want to find in Haven, I know where it is. Good rates. You'll get wet out there, sirs, you will."

MacKinnie nodded, and the coachman jumped from his bench to hold the canvas doors open for them. "Where will it be, sirs? Blackfriar? Hellfire? Want to meet some ladies? Not like the ones in the Blue Bottle, though there's plenty that likes them, too, but I mean real ladies, maybe not welcome back home no more but well brought up, you know." Examining Stark with an expert eye, he added, "And my ladies got real handsome young maids live right there in the house with them for your man there, sir."

MacKinnie snapped his fingers, ending the chatter, and the coachman climbed back to his seat. He started the team and leaned down to the window. "Where to, sirs?"

"Waterfront," Stark answered. "Imperial Landing Wharf." He was damned if he'd give this garrulous old coachman the name of the cheap hotel they were forced to live in and let him someday say he'd taken Iron MacKinnie to a flyblown flophouse.

The rain came down harder, forcing the old man to raise the dodger on its elaborately carved wooden braces. "Wonder if he gets many customers in this rig?" Stark mused.

The old man leaned down and cackled. "More than you might think, chum. Lots of gentlemen want to visit my ladies. And lots of real ladies still think cabs are better than steam buggies. We aren't as fast as those things, but plenty of people remember the good old days when there weren't nothing but us and they don't forget old Benjamin, no, they don't."

MacKinnie snapped his fingers again, and the coachman turned back to the road, muttering to himself, but after a few moments he again leaned down to his passengers. "Even those Imperial Navy lads, they like the cabs. You hardly see nothing else around Empire House but cabs. Oh, they keep a few steam cars waiting by just in case they're in a hurry, but you watch, them young officer kids, they never rode in a cab with real horses before. Get the biggest thrill out of it, so they tell me."

"I expect so," MacKinnie said absently.

"Been a big lift for the cabbies, the Imperials," the coachman said. "Just them being here, that's better than taking over Orleans, not that the Kingdom's not going to do right by itself out of the Duchy, no, sir." The old man whistled to himself and looked to the road again, guiding the team through the twisting, narrow streets of the old waterfront town until they emerged on the broad Dock Street, deserted except for a few drunken sailors reeling perilously close to the water's edge.

Across the narrow protected bay which had given Haven its name, brilliant lights, brighter than anything seen on Prince Samual's World for three centuries, played on Empire House and the hundred-meter-long landing boat the Imperials used to ferry their people from the destroyer in its orbit. Another city block housed a complex of strange machinery the Imperials used to support their base. Pipelines extended into the harbor. Their power plant had warmed Haven's waters, making fishermen happy with their catches, but outraged at the rapid growth of shipworms and other vermin.

The brilliant lights also played across the hemisphere that was Marine Barracks, but none was reflected from that sheer black surface. Imperial Marine Barracks was protected by what the Navy people called a Langston Field.

MacKinnie knew little about the Field. Artillery shells fired at it were slowed to a halt, and the explosion was absorbed by the black shield, or perhaps by the metal walls beneath; certainly they did no apparent damage. The Navy proclaimed that resistance was useless: nothing short of an Imperial cruiser would be able to penetrate Marine Barracks. MacKinnie had reason to know that whatever weapons a cruiser might carry, nothing MacKinnie's Wolves had been able to fire would harm the fortress. It was one reason the Wolves surrendered.

The landing boats were vulnerable, though. In the short fight around Lechfeld he had damaged one badly and killed several of the Marines aboard—then fire came from the skies, a flaming death that scorched the village and baked half a battalion of Wolves in an instant.

But the Imperials could be hurt. They were only men. If they hadn't had Marine Barracks . . .

Wishful thinking, MacKinnie told himself. Even if he captured the barracks and destroyed the last of the landing ships the destroyer up there in the sky was safe from anything the entire population of Prince Samual's World could do. Some of the professors at Prince Samual University were experimenting with rockets which might, built large enough, go so fast they would never come back to ground. They might get to the destroyer. The professors had built one great war rocket which used liquid fuels and went more than two hundred kilometers, but there had only been the one—and even if they had another, how could they make it hit the destroyer?

The Imperial Navy said the destroyer was also protected by a Langston Field. Even if the rocket hit, there would be no more effect than MacKinnie's howitzers had had on Marine Barracks. The Imperials were right. Resistance was useless. A feeling of helplessness settled over Nathan MacKinnie. He closed his eyes and felt the whiskey reel his head around and around.

He was awakened by shouts. He had no idea how long he had dozed miserably, hoping to get to a rest room and then to bed before the full effects of all that whiskey did their worst. It could not have been long, he knew, because they were not yet around the bay to Empire House.

It took MacKinnie precious moments to rouse himself from the stupor of half-drunken sleep and realize that the coach had been stopped by several men. Robbers? Here in Haven, near Empire House? Bold robbers, then, desperate men indeed.

He snatched open the door and tumbled out in a fighting stance, his pistol in his hands for a moment before a heavy cane struck his wrist and sent the big service pistol spinning into the dark. On the other side of the coach he heard Stark growl deep in his throat, the enraged sound of a deadly fighting man, and he heard the sharp *chunk!* as his big sergeant's hand, arched into a blade that could easily crack baked clay, snapped into flesh. Someone over there would not get up for a long time.

He hoped Stark was giving a good account of himself. Whatever Hal could do, MacKinnie was helpless. A pistol pointed at him from the shadows, and on either side were men with shortswords. With a shrug, MacKinnie raised his hands. There was nothing else to do.

He heard Stark strike again, then a dull sound which he could not recognize. Moments later three men carried his sergeant around the coach. One dangled a sandbag from his fingers and looked to the dim figure of the man with the pistol. "He's only out for a little while as you ordered, sir. I wish I could say the same for two of my men. They may never get up again."

"That will do," the voice from the shadows said. It seemed strangely familiar to MacKinnie, but he could not recall it. "Bring Colonel MacKinnie and the others with us, if you please." The figure vanished into a side street.

MacKinnie felt the point of a sword at his back. The weapon was similar to those carried by the Haven police, and as he thought about it, MacKinnie remembered that shortswords had been standard equipment for Haven soldiers until the present king had increased the length of the bayonets his troops carried and relegated swords to dress uniforms. The men at either side of him seemed quite familiar with their weapons. Very useful skill, MacKinnie thought. Very useful indeed if you wanted quiet work.

They walked on in silence for the better part of a kilometer, twisting through deserted streets and getting soaked by the rain until they entered a multi-storied building no different from the others they had passed. They descended two flights of stairs in utter darkness before one of the men struck a light and another produced an electric torch, and MacKinnie could see three more men carrying Stark.

They had to be military, MacKinnie thought. Their discipline, silent and efficient, was excellent, and it was obvious that this was no simple robbery. There had been ample opportunities to cut their throats and take what little remained of his monthly pension. Besides, the leader had known MacKinnie's name and rank, and had even insisted on personally examining Stark before they started off. Thieves did not take such good care of their victims.

At the bottom of the stairs they entered a dank stone tunnel which seemed to stretch nearly a hundred meters before it turned, twisted, and ended at the bottom of another flight of stairs. MacKinnie was now genuinely interested in where he was being taken, and needed no prodding from behind to climb vigorously, each step working off more of the whiskey until he was better able to handle himself. Without the fog of drunkenness he felt more in control of the situation, ready to take any opportunity to free himself.

He was halted in a wood-paneled hallway. The only light was from the small electric torch of the guard behind him. They stood for several minutes before a door was opened from the inside and bright light spilled out to blind him. Then he was ushered into a large office. Around the walls hung red drapes of rich material, and over the desk was a large painting of King David Second.

Sergeant Stark was draped on a woolsh-hide couch along one wall of the office, his shoulders so broad that nearly half of him was spilled over, one arm

dangling to the elaborately patterned carpet. Mac-
Kinnie saw that his companion was breathing stead-
ily, although he was not yet conscious.

Under the copper-edged painting of the king was a
rich wood desk, fully two and a half meters by two,
its gleaming top bare of papers or any other object,
and behind the desk stood Malcolm Dougal, still
resembling a rabbit, a nervous smile on his lips as he
spoke.

"Welcome, Colonel MacKinnie. Welcome to the
headquarters of His Majesty's Secret Police."

3

Citizen Dougal

MacKinnie looked slowly around the room. Two young men dressed in kilts as plain as Malcolm Dougal's stood against the door behind him, their pistols held carefully across their chests in a guard position. Plain kilts or not, they were soldiers, and under their dispassionate expressions MacKinnie detected a slight twitch, nervousness perhaps, at the presence of the secret policemen, or, more likely, hatred for Nathan MacKinnie who had defeated their army three campaigns running.

The room gave the general impression of opulence. The only furniture was the desk, two chairs, and the couch, but there might have been anything behind the red drapes which ran from floor to high ceiling along two walls. When Nathan said nothing, Dougal motioned toward one of the woolsh-hide chairs.

"Please be seated, Colonel. Can we get you anything? A drink, perhaps? No, I suspected not. Something else? Earth Stock coffee, or chickeest?"

There was a visible tightening to Dougal's lips as he offered Earth coffee, something which told MacKinnie the offer was a test. Without hesitation Nathan said, "Chickeest, thank you. Black, and lots of it."

Dougal relaxed. He waited until MacKinnie was fully seated, then motioned to the guards. "That will be all, Corporal. Remain on call." MacKinnie heard the door close quietly behind him. "They will bring the refreshments in a moment, Colonel," Dougal said. "And now, you are wondering why you are here."

"I'm more interested in who you are. I've never seen or heard of you before, and I know of most of His Majesty's officers."

"The two questions are not unrelated. Malcolm Dougal is actually my name. My position is rather vague in the budgets presented to Parliament, but as it happens, I am the Director of His Majesty's Secret Police Service."

MacKinnie nodded. "I suspected that Lord Arindell was too stupid to operate as efficient a service as Haven's. So Inspector Solon reports to you when he wants his real orders."

"Yes. You see, I am being honest with you, Colonel. I expect you to be so with me. Had you taken my offer of a drink at the Blue Bottle, I might have brought you here in a more pleasant manner, but I could not take the chance of your refusal. Or of the Imperial Navy noticing either of us. Everything depends on their not becoming suspicious. Everything."

He leaned forward and regarded MacKinnie intently. "I now ask your word of honor that nothing said here tonight will ever be repeated to anyone without my permission except as it may conform to duties I have assigned you and you have accepted. Please," he said urgently.

MacKinnie longed for a cigar, but thought better of displaying the Earth tobacco he had in his pouch. The warning had been plain in the way Dougal had pronounced the words "Earth Stock" when offering the coffee. Dougal leaned back in his chair, but his manner was alert, expecting an answer. MacKinnie said the only thing he could under the circumstances. "You have my word, Citizen Dougal. My word of honor."

"Thank you." There was a tap at the door, and one of the guards brought in a platinum tray with copper pots of chickeest, pewter mugs, and cigarettes of a popular Haven brand. MacKinnie noticed that everything he had seen since he entered the room was native to Samual.

Behind the guard, the tall, thin figure of Inspector Solon, dressed in the midnight-blue undress uniform of the Royal Haven Police, stood silently in the doorway. He made no move to enter, and Dougal did not speak to him. When the guard left, Solon went out behind him, closing the door.

"You saw the inspector, of course," Dougal said. "There are two reasons for his being here. First, I wanted you to see that he obeys me so that you know I am who I say I am. But more important, I trust no one else to guard that door until we are finished." He smiled pleasantly. "I trust I have impressed you sufficiently. Enjoy your chickeest; you will be here for some time."

"What about my sergeant?"

"He has already been examined by Inspector Solon, and the man who struck him was an expert.

There is no permanent harm. He should be joining us in an hour, perhaps less."

"Then get on with it." MacKinnie sipped the bitter stuff, never as satisfactory as Earth Stock coffee. Only a few things were that you found among the stars. Men had colonized Prince Samual's World nearly a thousand standard years ago, but they had lived on Earth for millions.

"Tell me what you know of the plans the Imperial Navy has for Prince Samual, Colonel MacKinnie."

"Precious little. They appeared less than a year ago, and almost immediately settled in Haven. At first they didn't interfere with the planetary governments, but then they made an alliance with your King David—"

"Your king also, Colonel," Dougal interrupted.

"With King David. They helped you conquer the other city-states around Haven, and finally did for you what no Haven army had ever been able to do. They gave you Orleans. I don't know who's next, but I presume this goes on until Haven takes all of North Continent. After that . . . who knows, the Southies, I suppose."

"And then what will they do, Colonel?"

"Your newspapers keep telling us they'll help us, give us all kinds of scientific marvels, but I've yet to see any of them. You Havenites have kept them all."

"We haven't, because there have been none. Every assistance the Imperials have given us has been direct, with their Marines operating the weapons and none of my people even allowed to see their new technology. Go on, what after that?"

"Once you have conquered the whole blasted planet, I guess they take you into their Empire, with David Second as planetary king."

"And you find that unpleasant?" Dougal smiled.

"What do you want me to say, Citizen Dougal? You've told me you head the secret police. You want me to say treason out of my own mouth?"

Malcolm Dougal poured more chickeest, carefully, not spilling a drop, and took a long sip before replying. "Appreciate your situation, Colonel. If I meant you harm, it would happen to you. I need no evidence, and there would be no trial. No one knows you're here but my most trusted men, and if you never leave this room, why, who will know it? I'm interested in what you think, Iron Man MacKinnie, and it's damned important to Haven and the whole planet. Now stop being coy and answer my questions."

It was the first spark of emotion MacKinnie had seen in Dougal save for the slight tightening of the lips when he mentioned Earth. MacKinnie paused for a moment, then answered.

"Yes, I find that unpleasant. I can think of more unpleasant things, such as domination of the planet by one of the Southie despots, but after what you've done to Orleans, damned right I find it unpleasant."

"Thank you." Dougal was speaking in his normal tone, an apologetic note to his voice, but the resemblance to a rabbit was gone. Now he merely looked like a businessman. "Would you find absolute domination by an Imperial Viceroy even less pleasant?"

"Of course."

"And why?" Dougal waved in an imperious manner. "I know why. For the same reason that you drink chickeest, bitter as it is. Because he is an outlander, a foreigner, not of Samual at all, and we belong here. This is our world and our home, and I tell you, Colonel MacKinnie, that we will never be slaves to that Empire. Not while I live and not while my sons live."

"So you hope to escape that by using the Imperial Marines and Navy to conquer the planet?"

"No. I had hoped to do so, but it won't work. Colonel, once their colonists and viceroy land here, King David will have no more influence over this planet than your sergeant. I thought you knew little of them. Few know anything at all." He reached under the desk for a moment. Within seconds, MacKinnie heard the door open behind him.

"Yes, my lord," a flat voice said. Before he turned to look, MacKinnie knew it was Inspector Solon. The voice fit him perfectly, cold and toneless, like a voice from a tomb.

"Bring that book, Inspector," Dougal said quietly.

"Yes, my lord." The door did not close, and seconds later Solon crossed the room carrying a sheaf of papers held by a strange clasp.

"Thank you." Dougal dismissed Solon with a wave and pointed to the papers. "This is the only Imperial artifact we have been able to obtain. It appears to be some kind of work of fiction, about the adventures of a naval officer on a newly settled planet. But it also gives us much information about the structure of the Imperial government, just as one of Cadace's best-sellers would tell them a lot about the government of Haven even though there's not a line in it intended to do so. Do you understand?"

MacKinnie nodded.

"Then," the policeman continued, "understand this. The Empire has several kinds of planetary governments within it. There is Earth itself, which is the honorary capital, but is mostly uninhabitable because of the aftermath of the Secession Wars. For their own reasons they keep some institutions including their naval and military academies there, but the real capital is called Sparta, and is in another planetary system entirely. After the capitals there are what they call Member Kingdoms, which are planetary governments strong enough to give the Imperial Navy a good fight if the Empire tried to interfere with their internal affairs."

"All monarchies?" Nathan asked.

"There is at least one republic. Many are monarchies." Dougal sipped at his chickeest. "Then there are Class One and Class Two worlds. We can't tell the difference between them, but they have less authority over their own affairs than the Member Kingdoms. They do have representation on the capital in one house of a multi-house advisory council, and some of their people are officers in the Imperial services. The two classes refer to some difference in technology which we do not understand, but the relevant factors are the technology levels when admission to the Empire takes place. They both seem to have something called atomic power which fascinates the physicists at the University, and their own spaceships."

MacKinnie nodded, recalling some remarks made by the drunken lieutenant in the Blue Bottle. He mentioned this to Dougal, who nodded.

"Good," Dougal said. "You are here because you overheard him. You see, Colonel, after the Class One and Class Two worlds, there's nothing left but colonies. And that's what we'll be."

"What's the status of colonies?" MacKinnie asked.

"They have none. Imperial citizens are imported as an aristocracy to impart civilization. A viceroy governs in the Emperor's name, and the Navy keeps a garrison to see that no trouble develops. The colonists end in complete control of everything, and the locals do as they're told or else."

"How can they govern a whole planet against everybody's will? What good does it do them to burn half the world to ashes like Lechfeld?" MacKinnie drank the last of his now cooled chickeest, then answered his own question. "But of course they don't have to fight their own battles, do they? There's always a local government ready to toady to the Imperials. Someone to do their dirty work for them." He looked significantly at Dougal.

Malcolm Dougal pretended not to notice. "Yes. There is always one. If not King David, then one of the Southie despots. But it won't happen, MacKinnie I've found a way to win this fight and get Class Two status for Samual. I've found a way, a chance, but I can't do it alone. I need your help." Dougal leaned across the desk looking intently at Nathan MacKinnie.

Colonel MacKinnie stood slowly, stretching to his full height before lifting the copper pitcher and pouring another mug of chickeest. Still moving very carefully, he strode to the couch, examined Stark for a moment, then returned to his chair. "Have you a pipe and 'robac, my lord?" he asked. "This promises to be quite a night . . . Why me?"

"I hadn't intended it to be you until tonight. I had no real plan before, merely studied a series of actions I might be able to take, made preparations for an opportunity, any opportunity, but now that young fool has told us how to save the state. You heard him, of course."

"If I did, I didn't understand. What are you going to do?"

"But you must have heard him. You were there when he babbled about the Old Empire library on a planet at the Eye of the Needle."

MacKinnie thought for a moment, then said. "Yes, but I don't see how that can help us."

"You haven't thought about this for months, as I

have. We found that book not long after they landed, Colonel. It took only a few weeks to understand most of the language. It's not all that different from ours, at least the written forms, which is why the Imperials get around Haven so easily."

The policeman lit a 'robac cigar, leaned back in his chair, and glared at the ceiling. "Ever since I could read that thing, I've thought of little else but ways to escape this trap. There's no way to avoid being part of the Empire, but by the Saints we can make them take us in as human beings, not slaves!"

"If you had the book so early, you must have understood what they wanted before Haven made the alliance with them."

"Of course. It was on my advice that His Majesty entered the alliance. Unless we consolidate Prince Samual's World under a planetary government, we have no chance at all of escaping colonization. And unless it's under King David, I won't have any influence over the planetary government, and you will pardon me if I think I may be better at this kind of intrigue than some of the, shall we say, more honorable men of the other city-states?"

"All right," MacKinnie said. "So you're a master of intrigue. I still don't see what we can do."

Dougal laughed. "You've drunk too much whiskey, Iron Man MacKinnie. Tonight and other nights. You're not above a bit of duplicity yourself. You used several very clever dodges on us. Your record, Colonel—I have it here—your record says you are more than just a simple combat soldier. But it's pleasing to be able to instruct you."

Dougal poured more chickeest. "That library is the key to it all. If we had the knowledge that must be there—our people at the University, and the industrial barons of Orleans and Haven, and the miners of Clanranald—what couldn't they do? We could build a spaceship. A starship, perhaps. And by their own rules the Imperials would have to admit us as a classified world, not a colony. We'd still have to knuckle under to them, but we'd be subjects, not slaves."

MacKinnie took a deep breath. "That's quite a plan."

"It's the only possible plan."

"I don't know— Look. Suppose it's true. With knowledge, construction plans even, with a planetary government to bring together the technology of North Continent and the resources of South Continent, perhaps it could be done. Perhaps. But we haven't the time. It would take years."

"We'll have years. The Imperials won't move until we consolidate the kingdoms. They're in no great hurry. They've made it clear they want as little bloodshed and destruction as possible. I can see that it takes time to bring in all the city-states. That will give us time to build the ship. It won't be easy, building a thing like that under their noses, but they won't have very many people on this planet, and they won't suspect a thing until it's done."

MacKinnie shook his head. "I don't see how you can keep them from finding out, but you're better at that than me. But you can't get at the library without a ship, and we can't build a ship without the library. Even if we had one, we couldn't operate it. There's been nobody on this planet who ever saw the inside of a starship for hundreds of years. Until the Imperials came, most of the population thought that history before the Secession Wars was just a lot of legends. How in hell do you propose that we get to the Eye of the Needle?"

"That's the simplest part of the plan, Colonel. The

Imperials have already offered to take us there." He smiled at Nathan's startled look. "They're not all Navy and Military, you know. Some Imperial citizens are Traders. There's one batch of them right now negotiating with King David over the rights to grua. They think our brandy will be worth a fortune on their capital.

"They want platinum and iridium, too; those metals seem to be very useful to them and in short supply. But there isn't much they can give us in return, because the Navy won't let them sell us what we really want—technology. The Navy rule is, you can't trade anything more technologically advanced than what your customer already has without special permission from the Imperial Council. We offered to buy those little devices they all carry around like notebooks. 'Pocket computers,' the Navy men call them. They seem to be machines. They can't sell those."

"What can they sell?"

"Not much, it appears. But they have offered the king transportation to a world less advanced than ours, someplace where we can try our luck at selling. They suggested a planet at the star we call the Eye of the Needle as the closest, and we are already discussing an expedition to go there and try to organize trade. . . ."

"The Navy will permit this?" MacKinnie asked.

"Under conditions. Stringent conditions, I might add. We can't take anything more advanced than the natives already have. The Navy inspects our trade mission and goods before we go to the planet. But they will let us go. It appears that the Imperial Traders Association has a good-sized block of votes in the Imperial Council. I don't pretend to understand capital politics, but the ITA seems very influential.

They can force the Navy to let us trade with that planet, Makassar, it's called."

"Won't they be watching to see that we don't get near the library?" MacKinnie asked. The whiskey fog was gone from his mind now, but more than that, he felt useful again, as if there were something he might do which could not be taken away by a whim of fate. He listened to Dougal with keen interest, not noticing that Sergeant Stark was stirring on the couch to his right.

"They have never mentioned the library," Dougal said. "Until that young lieutenant babbled about it in the Blue Bottle, I never knew it existed. I think the library's an anomaly in their records, not listed as an advance artifact because it's so old and the people on Makassar don't know how to use it. That's only a guess. I do know they've been willing to let us go there."

Dougal paused and again looked intently at MacKinnie. "That leaves me with the problem of one Colonel MacKinnie, who knows about the library. I decided when I heard about it that we'd have to try to get the knowledge there, and since you know about the library, I'd either have to kill you or send you on the expedition. I don't know how to get those books, and I'm not sure that anyone on this planet does know. But I'd rather have you on our side than dead. You were very resourceful against Haven, Colonel. Will you swear allegiance to King David and work for Haven now?"

4

Trader

MacKinnie woke to the stale taste of 'robac and the sick feeling of whiskey in his stomach. He lay for a few moments on the caltworm-silk sheets, slowly recalling where he was. There were no windows to the room, and the only light was from a soft glowplate on one wall. To his right there was a rest room with marble appointments, and through it was a connecting door to a room similar to the one where he was lying. He knew it was there, because Sergeant Stark had lumbered unsteadily into it when they left Dougal's office. They were in the same building, but beyond that MacKinnie had no idea of his location. The only doors leading outside the suite were locked, and he had no doubt that Dougal's guards stood watch in the hall.

He raised himself on one elbow. To his left a

closet stood open, revealing racks of rich clothing. His own kilt and jacket, freshly cleaned and pressed, hung neatly on the door, and with them hung his service pistol. MacKinnie wryly slipped from the bed to examine it, not surprised that there were no cartridges. His watch was in the pouch hanging with his clothes, but it had stopped. He had no idea of the time.

Now that ho was up, he decided he might as well stay up. He took his time in the rest room, using luxurious shaving equipment and treating himself to a double dash of the most expensive lotions and powders he had ever seen. If all guests of King David's secret police fared as well as he, there would be long lines of people hoping to be arrested for high treason, but he suspected there were more dungeons in the building than guest suites.

As he finished shaving, Stark knocked at the door, then waited for MacKinnie to finish. The sergeant had shaved and dressed by the time Nathan had put on his kilt and was buttoning his coat. Stark seemed no different from the hundreds of mornings they had spent in garrison as he expertly straightened MacKinnie's jacket and made tiny adjustments in the kilt and fall.

"What have we got ourselves into, Colonel?" Stark asked. As he spoke he made tiny signals with his hands, indicating the walls, then his ears.

MacKinnie nodded. "I'm not sure, but it beats chasing Southies. This could be a job worth doing. Tell me, can you round up some of the Wolves who can keep their mouths shut and act like Traders' guards?"

"Many as you want, Colonel. How many do you think we need?"

"All of them, but I don't think the Imperial Navy will let us take a regiment to Makassar."

"We'll get as many as you want. Going to be funny calling you Trader, but I reckon I can get used to it." Stark looked around the chamber, noting the carved wooden furniture, and the crystalline rock formation patterns in the parts of the floor not covered by carpets woven in the Archipelago. "Fancy quarters, uh, Trader, sir."

"Yes. Well, I suppose we might as well get on with it. We wouldn't want to keep Dougal and Inspector Solon waiting."

"Yes, sir. Begging your pardon, sir, I hope he won't go with us to that crazy place. Going up high like that, off the world even, that's enough without that walking corpse to give me the creeps."

"He won't be coming along. Nervous, Hal?"

"No, sir, not if you say not to be. But I am having a little trouble getting used to the idea."

"That's two of us. All right, Hal, tell them we're ready for breakfast."

"Yes, sir." Stark found the speaking tube in a small recess under the dim light, uncapped it, and whistled. After a second there was an answering note. "Our respects, and the colonel and I are ready for breakfast." Stark listened for a few moments, then returned to MacKinnie. "He says someone will be with us in five minutes, sir. Seemed polite, anyway." When there was no answer from Nathan, Hal capped the tube.

Four guards were visible when the door opened. At least two of them were from the party which had captured MacKinnie and Stark the night before. Their weapons were holstered, and they were extremely polite as they invited MacKinnie and Stark to accompany them, but Nathan noticed that as one led the way the other three fell in well behind, eyeing Stark nervously as they walked stiffly along.

They were ushered into the big office MacKinnie had seen the night before. The curtains were drawn back along one wall to reveal a walled veranda beyond where Solon and Dougal sat at a glass-topped table sipping chickeest. As MacKinnie approached, Solon stood, nodded to Dougal, and left without speaking to them.

"Good morning, Trader," Dougal said. He stood, waited for MacKinnie to be seated, and indicated a place at a table a few feet away for Stark. "Your breakfast will be here shortly. I trust you enjoyed your sleep?"

MacKinnie smiled pleasantly. "A great deal more than I thought I would when I was first invited here."

Dougal nodded. "There have been others who did not enjoy their stay in this building at all." He dismissed the guards with a wave, then turned back to Nathan. "The subterfuge starts this instant, Trader MacKinnie. We will use your proper name, although we will change your first to Jameson. MacKinnie's common enough in Haven, and there is a great Trader family by that name."

"Are you sure the Imperials won't recognize me?"

"Reasonably. Besides, they aren't looking for a dead man. Colonel Nathan MacKinnie was killed at Lechfeld. Died of his wounds a few weeks after the battle. Tough old soldier, too proud to say anything when he turned over his sword to the Haven General Staff. The records already show that."

"But there was a young officer who interviewed me . . . and the paymaster will know my pension has been paid for months. Then there's the landlady at our flop."

"There *were* those people, Trader. Unfortunately, they all died last night in a series of tragic accidents. The Blue Bottle had another accident, I'm afraid. It burned to the ground, everyone in it killed shortly after the Imperial Navy men had left. Nothing the Watch could do, the fire was so fierce. It almost seems as if someone deliberately set it, but I'm sure His Majesty's Police will catch the scoundrels if that's true. More chickeest?"

"And my men? My former officers?"

"They're being recruited for an expedition to the Archipelago, with offers so generous I'm sure no one will turn them down. If anyone does, well, Traders' expeditions have been known to have reluctant members in the past."

Before MacKinnie could reply, the corporal arrived with their food, and Dougal insisted that they eat before resuming the conversation. When they had finished, the policeman signaled, and the corporal brought MacKinnie a pipe. It was one of his own from the rooms where he and Stark had been living. It did not seem necessary to comment on it.

"You haven't been very active since you left the Service," Dougal said. "It won't be difficult to cover your tracks, at least enough to keep the Imperials from looking too closely at you."

"All right, what's the drill for today?" MacKinnie asked.

"Mind your aphorisms, Trader. We wouldn't want your military background to show through, although we will have your records show that you served honorably as a company commander in His Majesty's Home Guard during the Theberian War. You won't have to play a part for long; I intend that you leave as soon as posssible. We'll send for the other members of the expedition now. Remember, this is a trading mission, and you are Trader MacKinnie. You've met none of them before. Here." Dougal held out a small box. On opening it, MacKinnie found it full of rings, brooches, and other personal jewelry, all in good taste and the kind of thing he might have worn if the military habit were not so strong in him. He selected a ring, brooch, and earring and put them on.

"Now you look more like a Trader. I have more for your man." Dougal held out gaudier jewelry, flashier but less expensive than Nathan's, and waited until Stark had put it on before beckoning to the corporal.

As the others approached, MacKinnie asked quickly, "What are you to these people?"

"A high officer of the secret police. They are all trustworthy servants of the crown, but they do not know the real purpose of this expedition." Dougal stood, smiling expansively. "Welcome, gentleman, freelady. This is Trader MacKinnie, who will manage King David's shares of this expedition. He has financed much of it, I might add. Trader, here are your crew and advisors."

They sorted themselves out and stood expectantly, waiting to be presented. The first was broad-shouldered, of medium height, and stood stiffly erect. Dougal said, "Trader, this is Shipmaster MacLean of the Royal Merchant Service. He is qualified in both sail and motor vessels."

"Honored," MacLean mumbled, looking straight ahead. His grip was firm, testing MacKinnie's, and Nathan was pleased to note the surprise in the officer's eyes before he let go. The man was so obviously from the Haven Navy that MacKinnie could not understand how the Imperials would be expected to be deceived, but he said nothing.

"And this is Academician Longway, who studies

social organization and primitive cultures as well as ancient history." MacKinnie studied him closely. The man was broad and short, typical of the people of Prince Samual's World, dark hair and light eyes, and could have been a miner if it were not for the thick spectacles. His kilt was scholarly, dark with a thin red stripe, but the grip was firm and the voice steady.

"Honored to meet you, Trader, and I must say, pleased to be selected for an expedition as important— important and rare—as this. It's not often a scholar gets the chance to visit a really strange culture. I've been to the Archipelago, to many of the islands there, but of course it isn't the same. I can't say how pleased I am to be going with you. It's an historic event."

"Let's hope you feel that way when we return." MacKinnie said. He kept his voice as pleasant as possible, and found that easier than he had thought it would be. He had never liked men who chattered, but the enthusiastic friendliness of the scholar was infectious all the same. Longway motioned to the man who stood behind him.

The man was young, not more than twenty local years. He stood shuffling his feet nervously, his long gangling arms hanging loosely at his sides. He was of very slight build and stood with a stoop that made him seem even shorter than he was. He also wore thick spectacles, and his kilt was plain, smudged with ink and foodstains. He carried a large book under his left arm, and the end of a bulky notebook protruded from his pouch.

"This is my assistant, Scholar-Bachelor Kleinst," Longway said. "Most brilliant student at the University, I might add. Does very good work."

"Honored, Trader," Kleinst mumbled, holding his hand out perfunctorily and withdrawing it limply as soon as possible. His voice matched his appearance, and MacKinnie instantly disliked him. Nathan turned expectantly to the last member of the group.

"Allow me to present Freelady Mary Graham," Dougal said. "She will serve as your assistant and secretary. I might add that she is a graduate of the University."

MacKinnie hid his surprise. There were few women in the universities, and fewer still graduated.

He had seen lovelier girls, the city of Haven being noted for the beauty of its women, but there was nothing wrong with Mary Graham's appearance. She had the typical brown hair and light eyes of the Haven population, but she was considerably smaller than most of the city women; not so small as to be tiny, and well formed for her height. She wore rather severely tailored clothes which did not quite hide a pleasing figure, and Nathan noted that she stood attentively, waiting for him to speak, her nervousness betrayed only by a slight motion of her fingers drumming against her skirt. Nathan guessed her age at something more than twenty, but almost certainly below twenty-five.

"Honored, freelady," he said, nodding slightly.

"My honor, Trader."

Her voice was not unpleasant, MacKinnie decided. But her presence annoyed him. There was no need for women in an expedition as important as this, and he was surprised that Dougal would suggest it. In Nathan's world women were divided into two groups: freeladies to be protected, and camp followers who served no less useful a purpose but who were more or less expendable. Mary Graham did not seem to fit into either category.

He was certain that he was again being tested, because a more unlikely group for saving the state would be hard to imagine. Dougal had explained the night before why MacKinnie himself should command the expedition. The Imperials were likely to know of any of Haven's really competent officers, yet a military background seemed required if anything were to be accomplished on Makassar. Still, MacKinnie did not look or act exactly like a Trader, and the crew assembled here contained an obvious naval officer, a talkative scholar of uncertain abilities, a weakling of almost effeminate appearance, and a girl. Surely, he thought, the Imperials would suspect—but even if they did not, what would be gained by sending this group to Makassar?

Dougal ushered in two more young men wearing battle dress without insignia. "MacReedy and Todd, guards," Dougal explained.

MacKinnie looked them over carefully and decided they were the most authentic in appearance of any of his expedition. He indicated Hal. "This is Stark, your guard leader. We'll have a few more guards for the expedition when we find out precisely how many we can take. Guard Leader, please take your men to your table and get to know them."

"Yes, Trader." Stark led the men to the other side of the veranda.

MacKinnie turned back to the policeman. "My lord, I am sure the others will excuse us a moment while we discuss the cargo. There are some difficulties about financing which I am sure would only bore them, so perhaps they can be working on equipment lists while we discuss finances in your office?"

"Certainly, Trader." The others bowed, and MacKinnie led Dougal through the veranda doors to the office beyond.

Once inside, MacKinnie exploded. "How in hell do you expect the Imperials to be stupid enough to pass that crew? This is a thin enough plan to begin with, Dougal. I can't begin to accomplish the mission if you saddle me with incompetents. My Saviour! You give me an obvious naval commander itching to learn anything he can about their starships, a weak-eyed little intellectual, and I don't know, maybe the Academician will do, but where did you find that girl? In your freshman spy classes?"

Dougal hold up his palm briefly, stopping Nathan's tirade. "Sit down, Trader, and have something to drink. Calmly, now."

Still fuming, Nathan sat and stuffed his pipe. "And another thing, I don't appreciate murder. How many people did you kill last night, anyway?"

"As many as necessary, Trader," Dougal said coldly. "Think of them as martyrs to Prince Samual's World, and we'll erect statues for them when this is over. If it works. What would you have had me do with them after they heard the most important secret on this planet?"

"Swear them to secrecy—" MacKinnie was stopped by the policeman's laughter. "I suppose not," Nathan said. "Hide them? Lock them up—"

"So that if one escaped we would really have lost the secret. Tell me, Colonel Iron MacKinnie, do you recommend that the military do things by half measures?"

"No—"

"Nor can we. I am not proud of what was done last night, but in my judgment it was needed. Tell me, did you ever consider guerrilla war against the Imperials? I know that you did. Would not innocent lives have been lost in your war? How many more will be killed in futile resistance to the Imperial colonists if we fail? I wish to hear no more about it." He lit a cigarette, calmly inhaled, and continued.

"As to your crew. First, of course MacLean is a naval officer. The Imperials will know we intend to send a spy on the expedition. It might as well be a clumsy try so that they don't suspect you. They will probably be careful to keep MacLean away from their ships' engines and controls, but I doubt they will object to his going.

"Academician Longway has been on several expeditions to the Archipelago, and he knows as much about primitives and ancient civilizations as any man on this planet. He has fought his way out of tough situations in the past, too. He may be of more use to you than you think."

"All right," MacKinnie said. "I didn't object to him anyway. What about the scholar? A strong wind would blow him away."

"Kleinst is just what he appears to be, except for one small deception. He's not an historian, he's a physicist. The best we have who isn't prominent enough to be known to the Imperials. The boy is sharp enough to learn Longway's patter sufficiently well to fool anyone not an expert. I admit his appearance is against him, but we can't be choosy. You'll need someone who understands what science we know if only to tell you what to bring back."

MacKinnie lit his pipe. "And the girl?"

"The daughter of one of my officers. She really is a graduate of the University, she's reliable, and no one expects a girl to be intelligent. She may have an opportunity to learn something you don't. Pretty girls often do; they have methods not available to men."

MacKinnie started to interrupt, but Dougal gestured him to silence. "You may keep your shocked proprieties to yourself," the policeman said. "She is loyal and reliable, if somewhat young, and secretaries are not that uncommon on trading expeditions. We know that, among the Imperials, women often accompany men. There are even women officers in the Imperial Navy—oh yes, I'm quite serious."

MacKinnie tried to digest that thought, but couldn't. It was just too alien. "And which one is your agent watching me?" he demanded.

"All of them. But you won't betray us. I have enough information on you to fill a small library. The Service has had you in mind as a possible servant to King David since we took Orleans. When you overheard that conversation, I already had more than enough to act on. I don't waste good men, MacKinnie. Haven will need everyone we can find for the great task ahead of us. We're saving a planet from slavery! You won't violate your oath."

"Thank you for the confidence." MacKinnie stood. "Just how much do they know?" he asked, indicating the group on the veranda with a wide sweep of his hand.

Dougal smiled faintly. "Enough. They know this to be an expedition to a primitive world, with the ostensible purpose of establishing a trade mission, and an ostensible secret mission of filling the war chest for planetary conquest. They think the real purpose is to learn all they can about Imperial science, customs, military power, and that sort of thing— that this is a straight intelligence mission. They've been ordered not to violate Imperial regulations without specific orders from you, but to keep their eyes open whenever they're around Imperial ships. You and your sergeant know about the library. You can tell them about it when you've reached Makassar." Dougal lit another cigarette.

"I suppose they'll have to do," MacKinnie said. "All right. Now what about my cargo?"

"Primitive weapons, in large quantities. Axes, swords, and the like. Armor. Some gold and platinum, but not much because we can sell those to the Imperials directly. Cloth. Good tartan woven from winter-sheared woolsh. Grua. Spices. Some trinkets. You'll have the list soon enough, and if you think of something primitive the Makassarians might buy, or something you will need, let me know. But don't try to smuggle in anything the Imperials would object to."

"Not likely," MacKinnie said. He sighed and stared at the ashes in the bowl of his pipe. "Ever head a military force?" he asked.

"No. Only police. Why?"

"Old maxim. No plan survives contact with the enemy. This one won't either."

"Probably not, but what else have we?"

MacKinnie shrugged. "I don't know. But it's insane. Oh, it's probably the best we can do, but you'd better have a Plan B, because I think your main battle plan has about as much chance of working as I have of swimming the Major Sea."

5

Empire House

MacKinnie sat alone on the veranda. The others were off on their various errands, leaving him as the only member of the expedition with nothing to do. He had finished his chickeest, and was wishing mightily for a good cup of coffee when Stark arrived.

"Find any of the Wolves?"

"Yes, sir. We can get our pick of the noncoms. The officers are a little harder to find. But are you sure you want any of the men? Being as how you're supposed to be dead? They're good at fighting, but they aren't so long on keeping that kind of secret. Don't know how good I'll be, for that matter."

"What about those two that Dougal furnished? Any use?"

"MacReedy's typical, si—uh, Trader. Served a hitch in a trading expedition guard unit on South Continent, another on a sea passage through the west end of the Archipelago. He'll do. Todd's another case. Officer cadet, I expect. Seems a good lad, probably make colonel some day, but his speech and manners don't come from the barracks. Keep him from talking too much and he'll pass."

"About what I expected," MacKinnie said. "No point in complaining. Dougal has his own ideas of how this ought to go, and we won't be able to change anything until we're off-planet. Maybe not even then. I'm not completely sure who's in command."

"I am," Stark said.

MacKinnie grinned. "Well, let's be sure of it." He thought for a moment. "Hal, get us Dunston and Olby, and pick a couple of available corporals. I have a hunch we may need some steady noncoms, and I'd as soon not have all the fighting men come from Haven. Uh—there's no need for them to advertise that they're Wolves."

Stark grinned knowingly. "Yes, Trader." The grin faded. "Think we'll have much fighting?"

MacKinnie shrugged. "I don't know. Dougal does, or he wouldn't be sending me. I don't do a lot else. I'll find out more when I meet the Imperial Traders Association reps, I suppose."

"Yes, sir. When do we get rolling?"

"Soon as possible. There's nothing to wait for. Not enough time for proper training of the troops, and not much idea of what to train them for anyway. There's one hell of a job waiting for us if we do get back with what we're after, but that's Dougal's problem. His and Solon's, and the Magnates." He looked up to see Mary Graham and Academician Longway approaching.

"That was prompt," he told her. His smile was forced.

Graham gave a thin answering show of teeth and said, "As soon as you approve the cargo list, Trader, I'll have the goods taken to the Imperial wharf for loading. It's all in the warehouses. Have you any other instructions?"

"Yes. Get someone who knows how to make body armor and find out what dimensions are needed. I want a full suit of chain mail for each of us, and that includes you, freelady. And have a variety of swords of the best quality obtainable, all types available, brought for our inspection. We'll want to choose personal weapons. Guard leader Stark will instruct you on how he wants his men equipped."

"Yes, sir." She took a notebook from her pouch and wrote with tiny precise motions. "Is that all?"

"No. Join me for lunch."

"Yes, sir," she said in the same tone, then turned to follow Stark to his table.

MacKinnie turned to Longway. "Academician, is there any special equipment you will need?"

"I'm afraid not, Trader. There are many items we could use, but they are all technological and forbidden. I would suggest you have breastplates made for yourself and your men. If the Makassarians have developed archery to any extent, you will need them."

"An excellent suggestion." MacKinnie lit his pipe. "Of course we don't expect to fight pitched battles. I hope we'll only need armor to protect ourselves from thieves and the like. Still, some decent plate might be useful, if it can be made in time. I'll tell the freelady."

"As for the rest," Longway said, "we know so little about Makassar that it is hard to tell what we should take with us. Notebooks and paper, of course. A few drafting instruments for making maps. Some standard reference works would also be useful. Do you think the Navy will allow books? Does Makassar have movable type?"

"No books," MacKinnie said. "And don't ask the Navy about them. Take only handwritten material, and don't ask the Navy about any specific item without my permission."

Longway nodded thoughtfully. "If you say so, Trader. I still have some of my personal clothing and trading items to assemble. Am I excused?"

MacKinnie nodded dismissal and went to the table where Stark sat with his men. Todd and MacReedy were quietly drinking ale while Stark issued instructions to Mary Graham. She wrote furiously in her book as he spoke.

Hal had a look of concentration and drummed his fingers against the table as he spoke. "I'd like crossbows, freelady. Good spring steel ones. There's an armory sergeant, Brighton, in the Orleans garrison who knows how to make them—he used to supply them for our special forces teams. Thirty of those, I'd reckon. They ought to have that many in stock somewhere."

"Crossbows," Graham said. "And quarrels?"

"Yes. As many as they have." Stark paused thoughtfully. "For underneath the armor we'll want suits of woolsh-hide with the hair left on, good thick stuff. If a man's going to pound on me with a sword, I want some padding under the chain mail. You go order all that, and I'll have more for you by the time you get back."

She nodded and left. MacKinnie sat at the table and poured ale for himself. "She seems to get the job done," he said. "Maybe she'll be useful."

"Never had much use for women on campaign, Trader." Stark said. "But she doesn't miss much. I'll make up my mind when I see the gear, but she's got it all down in that book of hers and seems to know where to find things in a hurry."

"Why are we in such a hurry, sir?" Todd asked.

"The Imperial Trader ship is leaving soon," Mac-Kinnie answered. "We have to be on it or wait for another."

That's the official reason, MacKinnie thought. But there's a better one. If those Navy kids start talking about that library again, to the post commandant, or the Traders, or anyone, eventually somebody's going to connect us and the library. The sooner we get out of here the better.

It's a fools' errand, but it's worth a try, and the quicker we get back the quicker the Magnates can work on that ship. If we can get them anything, and if they can build one at all.

He knew that Dougal had already suggested that some of the University scientists work on life-support technology, using hints from the stolen novel to guide them. Others could investigate hull designs. But first Dougal would have to secure their loyalty; Prince Samual University was located in Haven, but had been independent, its independence guaranteed by treaties, for centuries. Now that Haven had conquered so many neighbors the University's independence wasn't likely to last long, but the rector would hardly take direct orders from King David's secret police. . . .

That would be Dougal's job.

But none of it would mean a thing until the secrets of the engines and their energy sources were discovered.

And that's my job, he thought.

Mary Graham returned for her luncheon engagement, her notebook bulging with subsidiary lists and scraps of paper. MacKinnie held her chair, then examined her with frank curiosity.

She's pretty enough, MacKinnie thought. And she knows how to dress so as not to emphasize her looks. She gave a lot of thought to that outfit, which means she wants to make a good impression. Why does she want to go on a tomfool expedition like this? There's only one way to find that out. "You look as if you have some sense," he said. "Why do you want to come on this insane trip?"

"I think it's my duty, Trader." It was obvious that she was choosing her words carefully. If that was an act, she was very good at it. "Citizen Dougal says this could be one of the most important missions in Haven's history, although he wouldn't say why."

"You're a patriot, then?"

She shrugged. "Not a vehement one. I would like to be part of something important. There's not much opportunity for that. Not for women."

True enough. Which was the way things should be. Women on campaign were a nuisance. Although there had been one—he quickly pushed that thought away. He couldn't think about Laura without pain and anger, and he'd brooded too much anyway. Now he had a job to do, and it was important to keep his mind clear. "And just what do you think you can do for us?" he asked.

"I don't know, whatever is necessary, I suppose. Many trading expeditions do have secretaries, and my education may be useful to you."

Nathan laughed softly. "I doubt it." And I doubt further if you'd do the only thing I think of that might really be useful, he thought. Or will you? She could be a highly trained agent. Haven was said to employ women in their secret-police forces, but the few that Orleans's security forces had encountered had been obvious, lower class women pretending to be from good families. This girl wasn't like that. She had the manners of the aristocracy. Like Laura. And Laura had been small, like this girl—Once again he pushed that thought away. "Just what was it you studied at the University, and for that matter whatever possessed you to go there in the first place?"

"I studied a little of everything, Trader. Since there are so few girls in the University, I could study almost anything I liked. My professors didn't know what to make of me, anyway. Such serious old men, you could almost hear them clucking their tongues when they discovered they were expected to listen to a girl read them papers. But since they didn't take my efforts to get an education seriously, I could study what I wanted to and go to the lectures that interested me. Really, it's a wonderful way to study."

"You still haven't said why you went, freelady."

"Please call me Mary. After all, I do work for you. Don't I?" She sipped cold wine, and MacKinnie noticed that she did so gingerly. A telling point; girls of her class wouldn't be accustomed to drinking wine in the afternoon. "Now. Why I went there," she said. "I don't know, it just seemed the thing to do. Shocked all my friends . . . the few friends I had, anyway. They're all married now, and I'm a terrible old maid. You can just hear them, 'Poor Mary, she can't catch a man and hold onto him!' But I wasn't interested in that. There's so little for girls in Haven, anywhere on North Continent, I guess. No adventure. It was explained in one of Academician Longway's lectures, that the war left so few women on Samual that men kept them at home so no one would see them, and it's only recently we were allowed to go out on our own. I don't know if I believe it, but that's what he said. Certainly I'd like to do something more than just raise children and help my husband get promoted by flirting with his superiors. I thought the University would help, but it just made people think I was a frimp. That's why I wanted to go on this expedition so badly." She stopped, out of breath, and smiled nervously.

"So you have no romantic attachments?"

"Not now. I was engaged once. To the son of one of my father's friends. But that's all over."

"What does your father think of your entering the Service and going off to another planet?" MacKinnie appeared to be relaxed, but he watched the girl closely. He was fairly sure that she was just what she seemed to be, which meant that she would probably be more hindrance than help. By her own account, her education at the University didn't seem to be anything useful to the expedition.

"He gave his approval, Trader," she said stiffly. "I have all the necessary permissions duly notarized. Are you afraid he might challenge you?" Her eyes flashed briefly, then she thought better of what she had said. "Oh, I didn't mean that. Please don't be angry with me, but I get so tired of having to ask Father's permission for everything I do."

"I take it you would prefer some such equality-of-sexes nonsense like Therean."

"Not that equal, Trader. I've no wish for the life of a camp follower or a tavern girl. But—surely there's a place for us in some honorable work. Not all of the secretaries in Haven were born in the charity wards. If freeladies can manage affairs for Magnates and Traders, why can't they own property themselves? Academician Longway says they did in the Old Empire. Why, there were even women in Parliament and nobody thought anything of it."

"Do you believe that?"

"Well, it seems a little strange, but why not? We're not brainless, you know. Not all of us, anyway. Who managed the estates when the men were off on campaign? You know as well as I do that not all of the wives and companions had guardians . . . if they could manage their property as long as the men were alive, even when they were away for months, why couldn't they do it after their men were killed?"

MacKinnie laughed and turned his attention to his pipe. "Management is one thing, ownership is another, freelady Mary. If you own something, you can sell it." And there were city states where women owned property. Often enough, given the casualties in war, the result was that most of the land was owned by heiresses, and the men sought good marriages as a route to wealth.

None of which was important. It was obvious that Dougal was sending Mary Graham for reasons of his own, so MacKinnie might as well make the best of it. She might even be useful. "How far along is the cargo?" he asked.

She reached into her pouch and shuffled through papers until she found a bulky sheaf. "Here is the list. The items checked off have already been moved to the Imperial landing dock."

"And the armor?"

"Citizen Dougal has arranged for the Haven armory to prepare the chain mail. They seem to have found something which works, and one of their people will measure us this evening. The tanners will be along to measure us for the underpadding as well. And Duncan and Larue are forging swords to various patterns, and have sent over all the varieties they make. We've located crossbows, and they're making bolts for them."

"Duncan and Larue," MacKinnie mused. "I can

remember when I was younger, there were whole regiments of cavalry armed with sword and pistol. Battles decided by them." But then, he thought, everything changed. Suddenly there was a new military technology, new tactics based on self-loading rifles and quick-firing guns with multiple barrels, breech-loading field pieces light enough to be towed at a gallop. The whole manner of war changed, to become more impersonal and a great deal uglier.

I learned the new ways, he thought. Learned them well, when a lot of my brother officers wouldn't. They couldn't change. Insisted that elan and military spirit were more important than weapons and tactics, and they got their regiments butchered for their pains. I learned the new ways, but I never liked them. He looked up from his reverie. "That's one company that will profit by this expedition. Assuming we find something worth importing."

Dougal arrived an hour later. "You will meet the Imperial Traders shortly," the policeman announced. "We have fresh clothing ready for you in your quarters. When you get changed, we'll go to Empire House." The policeman fell in beside MacKinnie, walking with him to his suite. "Be careful with these Imperial Traders. There are two of them, and they both look soft. Don't believe it; they didn't get rich by being stupid. Of the two, Trader Soliman is probably the actual leader although they claim to be equals. There is antagonism between the Imperial Traders and the Navy, but I wouldn't count on it too much. We don't know the real story, but the Traders seem to be with us against the Navy."

"Yes," MacKinnie said. "You told me that the Navy wouldn't let us go on this trip if the Traders hadn't pushed them into it."

"Exactly. The Traders are eager for us to go. Quite generous in their terms. I'm not sure why."

"When a businessman wants to do you a favor," MacKinnie said, "I've found it a good policy to watch your pocketbook." They arrived at the door to his suite, and Dougal waited outside.

MacKinnie found a dress kilt, doublet laced with gold and silver piping, and jewelry in the style of the great merchant princes of Haven. When he lifted the clothing, he found cartridges for his pistol had been laid discreetly on the bed. With something approaching relief, Nathan loaded the large-caliber revolver and buckled it on before he realized how out of keeping it was with the rest of his clothing. A quick search of the small leather case he found on the bed with the clothing revealed a smaller dress pistol, its dragonwood handles inlaid with pearl and jade and thin copper strands. He unloaded it and squeezed the trigger several times, pleased with the smoothness of its action. The proofmarks showed it to have been made by the Brothers of St. Andrew, reputedly the best gunsmiths on Samual and certainly the most expensive. Although he hesitated to carry a weapon he had never fired, MacKinnie buckled it outside his doublet, sadly leaving the big service pistol hanging in the closet.

Two sets of guards were on watch at Empire House. Outside the large, walled courtyard, soldiers of King David's personal guard stood rigidly at attention. A junior officer in a tiny office inside the gates examined their passes, collected their weapons apologetically, and directed them across the lava stone courtyard to the building itself.

Two huge doors swung open as they arrived. The Imperial Marines inside the entryway wore full dress, scarlet and blue uniforms with gold trim, a blaze of color; but the weapons the sentries carried were incomprehensible to MacKinnie. Their rifles looked very functional, but the knobs and dials along the stocks were meaningless—and there were no visible openings in the barrel ends.

MacKinnie expected to be searched again, but instead the Marine noncom looked at a panel of lights and meters and a screen that showed shadowy figures; MacKinnie got only a glance at it, but he thought he saw the outline of his cigar lighter on the screen. In some way the Marines could see through the leather of his pouch. . . .

They waited in silence while the noncom spoke into a handset.

Very efficient, MacKinnie thought. It would be difficult to penetrate this place. Not that it would do any good to take Empire House. The fortress would still remain, and so would that ship in orbit above Prince Samual's World. No. Dougal's way was best— except that Dougal's way doomed Orleans to rule by Haven. . . .

An inner door opened and a young naval officer came in. He had small badges made of a curious substance, not metal but not anything else MacKinnie had ever seen. He gave one to MacKinnie.

"You are to wear these at all times inside Empire House," the officer said. "My name is Lieutenant Akelian, and I will take you to your appointment."

"This has my picture," MacKinnie said.

Lieutenant Akelian looked up in surprise. "Of course. We take photographs of everyone who visits Empire House. This way, please."

MacKinnie glanced at Dougal. The policeman's lips were set in a tight line. And no wonder, MacKinnie thought. Akelian was one of the three who had been at the party in the Blue Bottle. But he doesn't seem to recognize us. Given the amount he drank that night, it's no wonder. . . .

Akelian led them through brightly lit hallways. MacKinnie had never seen an inside room so well lighted. Electricity, someone had told him. Electric lights. But not from a carbon arc like a military searchlight. The professors at Prince Samual University were experimenting with a new kind of light, as they had experimented with long-distance communications using electricity, but electrical equipment took miles of wire, too expensive to be very practical on copper-poor Samual. They were ushered onto a moving stairway, then at the top led to another door. Akelian opened it to show them a large room.

Two fat men in plain clothing, wearing trousers rather than kilts, undecorated coats, and only a few jewels, their almost drab appearance contrasting strongly with MacKinnie and Dougal, rose languidly as they entered a large, plainly decorated room. Akelian waved MacKinnie and Dougal in, looked sternly at the civilians for a moment, and left without speaking.

As soon as he had left the room, one of the Imperials laughed. "God bless the Navy," he chuckled. "But may He grant that their lieutenants come of age soon. Good evening, gentlemen."

Dougal returned the greeting, then said formally, "Imperial Trader Soliman, I have the honor to present Trader Magnate MacKinnie, His Majesty's servant and manager for this expedition. Trader MacKinnie, Imperial Trader Soliman of the Imperial Capital, and as I understand it an officer of the Imperial Traders Association."

MacKinnie watched them narrowly and noted that the fat man made no movement to offer his hand.

MacKinnie bowed slightly, was rewarded with an even smaller bow, and turned to the next man.

"Imperial Trader Renaldi, I present Trader Magnate MacKinnie," Dougal purred.

"My honor," Renaldi said. When Nathan began his bow, Renaldi matched him, bending to within a degree of MacKinnie but not quite as deep. The difference might have been measured with calipers.

"Gentlemen," Soliman said, "this room is at our disposal for the time. Let us sit and enjoy ourselves like civilized beings." He indicated couches drawn up in front of an open fire. As they sat, he continued, "Remarkable how peaceful it is to have a fire in the room with you. We haven't used them in the capital for a long time now. There are very few houses with fireplaces, and I can't remember when I last saw one lighted. I will have to have one installed on my return, a great aid to contemplation. Right, Chasar?"

"It would be pleasant," Renaldi said.

"They are not quite so pleasant when they are your only source of heat," Dougal said.

"No, I suppose not," Soliman said. He looked thoughtful. "When the Navy permits trade in such things, Imperial Autonetics will bring factories to make better heating systems. I expect we could sell many of them." He sighed. "But the military departments never act quickly. It will probably be some time yet."

MacKinnie noted that both men spoke the language of North Continent almost perfectly, but with the careful pronunciations that indicated that it was a recently learned foreign tongue. Having never heard the Imperial language, he was not sure how close it would be to that used on Samual, although it would obviously be similar if Dougal were able to read the book his agents had stolen. Still, it must require some study, he thought, and therefore it followed that the Imperials either had some method of learning languages quickly, or that the Traders thought it important enough to spend the time and effort learning the local tongue. Either alternative seemed interesting.

Soliman hovered around them, offering refreshments which he poured himself at a small stand at one side of the room before finally joining them before the fire. They sipped chilled wine from one of the islands of the Archipelago, and Soliman praised it highly. "I hope it travels well," he told them. "This will be worth a fortune on the capital. It is as good as real Earth wines, or nearly so, and they command a price you would never believe. This is a very fortunate world, gentlemen, your wines and brandies can make you rich. And your grua—do you think the peach plant would grow elsewhere? Ah, but it would never thrive as it does here. If only Earth had not been so devastated in the Secession Wars."

He lowered his voice confidentially. "That is why the Navy is so stern, you know. Their academy is there, and they grow up with the results of the wars. They are determined that it will never happen again, even if they must enslave the entire galaxy to see to it. And now that it is traditional for the Emperor to send the heir apparent to New Annapolis, the whole government is infected with their dedication." He sighed deeply.

"Have you visited Makassar yourself, Traders?" MacKinnie asked.

"Briefly, briefly," Soliman replied. "A desolate place, with little of value to us. Yet I am certain you will find many things useful there," he added quickly. "Not so desolate as all that, and of course we are accustomed to more comforts than you. Copper abounds there, but perhaps the costs of shipping will prevent you from importing it on any really large scale. There may be little for us, but we believe you will find the voyage profitable. And of course we did not venture far from the city where the Navy has its base."

"Has the Navy decided on the details of the voyage?" Dougal asked. "Will Your Excellencies accompany us? A naval officer, perhaps? Who will command the ship?"

"I have business beyond Makassar, but I will go with you there," Renaldi told them. "I am looking forward to the voyage, and Trader Soliman will guard my interests here." Renaldi's tone indicated that he and Soliman had tossed coins for the privilege, and Renaldi had lost, although he was attempting to act in good humor. "As Soliman and I own the ship, it will be commanded by our own merchant captain and crew. One of the Imperial Navy officers will be aboard as observer, to ensure that none of their silly regulations are violated. We must caution you, Trader," he said, turning to MacKinnie, "they are very stern about their rules. Do not attempt to violate them, or you will never see your charming planet again. The Imperial prison world is not a pleasant place."

"No need to speak of such depressing matters," Soliman interrupted. "Better to think of the profits that can be earned. And, of course, this will be the first time any of your people have been off this planet since the days of the Old Empire, will it not?" His offhanded manner could not conceal his interest in the question.

Before MacKinnie could answer, Dougal asked, "And the language of Makassar? Will Trader MacKinnie find it difficult to deal with the natives?"

"The language is much like your own, or ours," Soliman answered. "Degenerate forms of Old Empire, with some local words. It requires study, but there will be no great difficulties. Tell me, Trader Magnate MacKinnic, are you looking forward to going off-planet?"

"With some anticipation," MacKinnie answered. "It will be a new experience for me." He emphasized the last word slightly, receiving an approving nod from Dougal. "But what are the conditions on Makassar? Are they likely to be friendly? Will we be allowed to wander about their cities, or must we remain in one place and let them come to us?"

"The Navy has no objection to your traveling about," Rendaldi replied, "provided you take nothing more advanced than they already have on Makassar. Journeys on the planet with primitive equipment can be dangerous, you understand. The planet has no political system as even you on Samual might know it. Here, you have a few strong governments and many city-states in a complex of alliances—at least on North Continent. On Makassar, there are dozens of kingdoms, free cities, small republics, leagues, and such, none very large by your standards. The kingdoms themselves are more fiction than fact, with independent baronies scattered about them. No doubt this is the result of their lack of technology, coupled with their primitive military organizations. All of this is huddled together on the coast of the one large continent. But it all comes to an end on a great grassland plain that stretches east for over three thousand kilometers. You will find none but barbarians there. No one knows how many of them there are; they move around at will and raid the edges of the civilized lands. There are also island kingdoms of barbarians off the coasts of the civilized regions, and these stage raids on even the largest cities. You are welcome to wander the countryside, Trader MacKinnie, but do not be surprised if you are killed. The only safe place is in one of their large cities, and they are not entirely safe. The Imperial Navy maintains a fortified observation post, but no warships, so that even if you were able to signal the Navy, there would be little they could do to rescue you. Makassar is not altogether a healthy place."

"Ah, but there are never profits without danger," Soliman purred. "And who knows what you may find out among the kingdoms of the east? The Navy post is on the western coastline, and we know so little about the planet."

MacKinnie nodded. "We will be very careful if we leave the Imperial fortress. Gentlemen, what I do not understand is why Makassar is so primitive. Why did they not retain any basic technology at all?"

"Ah," Soliman answered, "this is something we have speculated about without final answer. From our records, it was relatively unpopulated when the Secession Wars began. The planet seems to have served mostly as a rest area for the Old Empire Navy and Civil Service . . . a park world, kept uninhabited and unspoiled. Little machinery. Few power installations. Then, as the wars continued, for some reasons of strategy we do not know, parts of the plant were fortified. The fortifications were destroyed, and with them, much of the only city, although the old palace seems to have survived. Then the wars boiled on past Makassar. Perhaps there were not many people left on it. Many of them would be civil servants. Few artisans, and of the native inhabitants most would have been dedicated to service professions. Pleasure-house operators. Prostitutes. What kind of civilization would you expect them to build, given the destruction of most of the machinery?" He paused thoughtfully, sipping his wine.

"And then, too, much of the vegetation on the planet is native to Makassar. Not edible by us. Hardy stuff. A form of our wheat grows across the plains, but it is straggly and more fit for horses and cattle than men. Most of the crops of Makassar are Earth Stock; they have a very wide variety of such food-stuffs but getting an edible crop takes constant attention. How natural for some of the population to become raiders, living off the cultivators! And so the cultivators divert part of their efforts into maintaining a warrior class. The warriors become an aristocracy. The warriors must have something to do in times of peace, and they will not toil in the fields. . . . Indeed, they can't, because the barbarians may sweep over them at any time, and the warriors must know their business if they are to do their job. The planet has known constant warfare, between the civilized people and the barbarians, among the warriors within the civilized area, between civilized cities and baronies. At least, we think that is what happens. Certainly they are fighting all the time."

"There was a period much like that on old Earth," Renaldi observed. "It would seem to have been ended by the development of scientific farming, which was a discovery of the Church. But Makassar has developed its own ideas of a church, not altogether to the satisfaction of New Rome."

"Ah, yes," Soliman added. "In addition to yourselves and the Imperial Navy observers, you will find one other group on Makassar. His Holiness has sent a bishop and a small group of missionaries to win these people back to the state religion. They are not having notable success."

Dougal finished his wine and set the glass down.

In an instant, Soliman hauled his great stomach off the couch and gathered the other glasses on a copper tray, taking them to the cabinet to fill them. As he did, Dougal observed, "I am sure that Trader MacKinnie will be careful not to fall afoul of His Reverence the Bishop. May we here on Samual expect a similar visit soon?"

"Doubtless," Renaldi answered. "Of course, you seem to have developed along more orthodox lines than the people of Makassar, although the Church will find the multiplication of sects distressing. Still, you will find New Rome tolerant and willing to compromise. Do you anticipate much resistance to unification of the churches?"

"Not much," MacKinnie answered. "We had religious wars, over a hundred standard years ago. Not much zeal left on Prince Samual's World. The orthodox churches have been proclaiming their obedience to New Rome since the Imperial Navy landed, and the others don't know quite what to make of it. How much will the Empire interfere with local matters like religion anyway?"

"Oh, hardly at all, hardly at all," Soliman assured them. He served the wine carefully, and MacKinnie caught a stern look which Soliman passed to Renaldi. The latter quickly changed the subject, and the next half hour was passed discussing trade goods and the proposed cargo. They were interrupted by a knock at the door and, when Renaldi answered it, two Imperial Navy officers entered the room and walked stiffly over to stand in front of MacKinnie. Their manner was anything but friendly.

6

Regulations

The contrast between the two officers could not have been greater. One was young, tall, of slight build, his hair an indescribable brown something like damp straw. The other was much older, with lines of care etched around his expressionless eyes, his hair gray where there was hair at all. He was heavy and short, but he had in common with the younger man a look of hardness and dedication; yet, again in contrast to his junior brother in service, there was none of the air of expectancy and anticipation the boy displayed.

"Trader MacKinnie." The older man said it factually. "I am Captian Greenaugh of His Imperial Majesty's Navy. I command the garrison here and *Tombaugh* up there in orbit. This is Midshipman Landry, who will be my observer on this stupid voyage of yours."

MacKinnie stood and bowed slightly to Captain Greenaugh, even less to Landry, making no move to extend his hand when the others did not.

"Won't you sit down, Captain?" Soliman asked softly. "Some wine, perhaps? Grua?"

"No. Mr. Landry and I are on duty."

The midshipman's face was impassive; or had there been a hint of a smile? It was hard to tell.

"Then please be seated," Soliman insisted.

"I prefer to stand." He turned his attention to MacKinnie. "As you are to be the local in charge of this expedition, sir, it is my duty to caution you that any infringement of Imperial regulations on the part of any member of this expedition will result in trial and punishment of both the crew member and you personally. Is that understood?"

"Yes, Captain," MacKinnie said. He elaborately inspected the large ring on his left hand, then looked up. "I understand perfectly. Tell me why you are so unhappy with me, if you would, please."

"I am not unhappy with you, sir. It is understandable that you would wish to travel in space. I am unhappy with Mr. Soliman for browbeating me into letting you do it."

"Browbeating, Catpain?" Soliman said in an amused tone. "Why, I merely indicated—"

"You merely indicated the relevant passages in the Imperial regulations and reminded me of your influence. I don't give a damn about your influence, but I can't ignore the regulations. However, I warn you, MacKinnie, if Mr. Soliman can be sticky about regulations, so can I. You'll get a copy of the pertinent sections before you go, but I decided to see you personally to try to talk you out of this venture."

"If you please, Captain," Dougal asked, "why are you so opposed to our simple trading expedition? I thought it was Imperial policy to encourage trade among the worlds of the Empire. Your ambassador promises that Prince Samual's World will profit highly through joining the Empire."

"Sir—" The captain paused and snapped his fingers.

"Citizen Dougal, sir," the midshipman answered. "In the service of King David."

"Citizen Dougal, I have all too few officers on this station. I am responsible for the protection of this world from all interference with its development and assimilation into the Empire. There's a nest of outies not twenty parsecs away; your King David is in one hell of a hurry to unify this planet against stiff opposition; the survey team keeps borrowing my people; and thanks to this expedition I have to send a junior officer off for the Saints alone know how long. There'll be reports to file, inspections to conduct. And for what? So Mr. Soliman here can add another megacrown to his bank account, and you people can bring some kind of gimcrack new luxuries to absorb what little capital there is on Prince Samaul's World. I don't like it and I don't have to like it."

"Sorry you feel that way, Captain," MacKinnie said. Inwardly he knew all too well the plight of a military man caught up in the details of government. He would have felt sympathy for Greenaugh, but the memory of Lechfeld was too strong. The Imperials were the enemy. "But you have admitted that you understand our motives for wanting to go. I hope we can get our work accomplished without causing you any trouble."

"You're damn right you will," Greenaugh snapped. "But before you make your final decision, let me acquaint you with the regulations. Item: you will be supplied with a basic naval study of the planetary languages found in the chief city of Makassar. You will at no time teach any native your own language or Imperial speech. All negotiations will be conducted in one of the planetary languages. Is that understood?"

MacKinnie nodded, suddenly realizing why all the Imperials he had met spoke a variant of the language of Haven. If you used a man's own language, you weren't likely to tell him anything he didn't know about. He wouldn't even have the words for most advanced concepts.

"Item: as Imperial subjects," Greenaugh continued, "you would ordinarily be entitled to protection from barbarians and arbitary imprisonment. In your case we can't extend it. The garrison on Makassar is too small and there's no ship. If you get in trouble, you're on your own."

The captain took a small notebook-sized object from his pocket, touched a stud on the side of it and glanced at its face before returning it to his scarlet tunic. MacKinnie recognized it as one of the tiny Imperial computers, supposedly equivalent to hundreds of the best mechanical calculators in use in Haven's banks; equivalent and more. The Imperials used them for everything, as notebooks and pocket clocks, for communications and diaries.

"Another thing, MacKinnie. Any technical innovation traced to you directly or indirectly can result in a charge of interference. If it results in any severe disruption of the development of that planet, you can get life imprisonment. Assessment of the effects of innovations and your responsibilities for them are up to the Emperor's Lord Judges."

"Why are the regulations so severe, Captain?" Dougal asked. "It is our understanding that the Empire intends only peace and friendship for its member worlds."

"Damn right. And sudden technical changes destroy both. I've seen worlds where some smart guy used a little technology and a lot of guts to set himself up as a planetary king. Half the population out of work, the other half in a turmoil. Took the better part of a fleet and a division of Marines to keep order on the place. Mister, it's not going to happen in my sector."

"The regulations are severe for a purpose," Renaldi added. "There is no telling what the effects of even the most innocent technical revelations can be. Even something as inherently benign as medicines can change the whole pattern of life. There is a famous case, from the early days of the New Empire. The Church went in and with the best of motives taught practical medicine to primitives. The missionaries were particularly concerned with saving children from infant diseases. They intended to give them some new agricultural and industrial techniques, but the people were not ready for them. They rejected the agriculture and industry, but they adopted the medicine. Within fifty standard years, there was famine all over that world. The results were horrible."

Greenaugh nodded. "Still were when I was young Landry's age. I served a hitch on an escort vessel convoying a provisions fleet. Silliest thing you ever saw. You ever think of how futile it is to try to ship food to a whole world that's starving? If you took every ship in the Navy and merchant service and put them on it, even if the food was free and waiting in the same star system, it wouldn't do any good. But the Emperor's sister got interested in the place and they had to have a try at 'helping.' Did no good at all. Population's thinned out a bit now on Placentia, but the planet'll never be the same."

"So you see," Soliman said softly, "it is important

not to interfere. No matter what the reason. You can always say that things would have been worse if you did not interfere, but you can't know." He sipped his wine. "Besides, people will have adjusted to the evils they are accustomed to. Your attempts to help may introduce evils they don't know, which are always worse to bear and will probably retard their natural development."

"Thank you," MacKinnie said. "We will be very careful. What else must I know?"

"Still determined," Greenaugh said. "Thought you would be. Well, if I can't persuade you to give it up, I can't. Bring your crew here tomorrow for inspection. Midshipman Landry will tell you the rest of the details." He strode to the door, then paused and turned back. "Just remember, MacKinnie you were warned. The hell with it." He went briskly out, followed by his midshipman.

MacKinnie started to speak to Dougal once they were in the cab and drawing away from Empire House, but Dougal motioned him to silence. They returned to the Royal Guest House, where Dougal invited MacKinnie to shower, insisting that he do so in a manner that told MacKinnie it was an order. When he finished, he found fresh clothing, the elaborate Trader's kilt and doublet gone. Dougal joined him as he finished dressing, and MacKinnie noted that the policeman had changed as well.

"Sorry, Trader," Dougal said, "but we have found by bitter experience that the Imperials have devices, so small you would hardly notice them, which in some manner allow them to hear over long distances. Our engineers did not believe it at first, but I tested the hypothesis by feeding them false information when we had reason to suspect. I proved it, and now my people have found one of the things. Not as big as the end of your thumb."

MacKinnie whistled. "Was there one attached to our clothing?" he asked.

"No, not this time. But the cab stood outside Empire House while we were there. They had ample time to do as they liked."

"Any idea of the range of those things?" MacKinnie asked.

"None. And as we do not know how they work, there is no guess. Some of our best physicists insist they have a theory how one might be built, now that they know it is possible, but they say any such device would have to be very large and use much power. Still, it is a start." Deprived of a place to sit, the policeman locked his hands behind his back and paced the room nervously.

"By the way," MacKinnie asked, "what will our churches really do if their New Roman Church decides to take over here? I notice King David's bishops are thick as flies in Orleans."

"Better ours than the outlanders'," Dougal snapped. "And all the more reason for the success of your mission, MacKinnie. Perhaps they are not as severe on the Classified worlds."

"Yeah." Nathan stood against one wall, patiently watching Dougal stride back and forth. "But after that interview I don't know any more about how to get those books—but they aren't books, are they? That Navy kid, the night he babbled about it all, said they were spools, whatever that might be. That they could be made to print books, if we knew how to do it. Only we don't know how, do we? We don't really know much of anything."

"Giving up?" Dougal asked.

"No, by God!" MacKinnie grinned. "And the sooner we start, the better chance we'll have. It's still a fool's errand, but at least I can feel useful again, win or lose!"

7

The Burden of Empire

Lieutenant Alphonse Pavlovnicek Jefferson was in love. It had happened very suddenly, but he had no doubts about it; he had all the signs he'd been led to expect from romantic novels. His previous affairs seemed laughable or disgusting in recollection; he had no desire at all to go tavern-crawling with his classmates; he wanted only to get back to Elaine. It had to be love.

He'd met her on the street when he'd lost his way and asked for directions. Of course he'd been glad for an opportunity to speak to a local girl; getting acquainted on Prince Samual's World wasn't as easy as it was on more civilized worlds. Since he was more lost than he'd thought, she had to draw a map, and it seemed natural to offer to buy her a coffee at a sidewalk restaurant that seemed so conveniently located that it made Jefferson believe the fates approved of his meeting Elaine. She said later she'd accepted because she had never talked with an Imperial before. Her parents didn't encourage that.

Hours went by. He couldn't remember anything significant they'd said. It was just talk, at the coffee house and then walking in the park and along the waterfront, a pleasant stroll on a pleasant afternoon, with nothing important said, but there it was: he wanted nothing more than to see her again, and she'd agreed. Of course he would have to call for her at her home, and meet her father, and ask his permission to see her. He'd been warned that local customs were very strict, and Captain Greenaugh had made it clear that any officer causing problems would be handed his head.

Jeff wasn't exactly looking forward to the interview with Elaine's father, but surely all would be well. Fate couldn't play him such a trick as to let him find Elaine and then be forbidden to see her. Her father was a Haven civil servant, and the Empire was allied with Haven. He couldn't openly dislike Imperial officers, and he might even welcome the opportunity to get to know one. Jeff told himself that several times.

For the moment, though, he had another appointment. High Commissioner Sir Alexei Dmitrivitch Ackoff was holding his weekly seminar on colonial government, and it was strongly suggested that all junior officers attend. Presumably there was a difference between a strong suggestion and an order; if Elaine hadn't already been late getting home for dinner, this might have been the day Lieutenant Jefferson found out. However, she had insisted on going home, and even in his euphoric mood Jeff knew it wouldn't be a good idea to test Ackoff's patience.

He was very nearly late. The others had already gone into Ackoff's spartan conference room. Jeff hurried inside and as he did the opposite door leading into the Commissioner's office opened and the others stood respectfully.

Sir Alexei nodded and waved them to their seats around the big conference table as he took his place at its head. He was not a tall man, nor was he large; from his looks no one would have guessed that he was the most powerful man on Prince Samual's World, the only man there who could give orders to the Navy and make them stick. He did have an air of importance, of speaking in a tone that indicated he expected to be obeyed, but even that wasn't permanent; he was, after all, a diplomat, skilled in persuasion. This was his first assignment as top authority on a planet, but he'd been deputy commissioner twice before, and was said to be highly competent.

Jeff's father knew Ackoff slightly, and in his last letter to Jeff had mentioned the Commissioner as an excellent example of the best—and worst—of the Imperial Civil Service. "Give him a policy, and he'll enforce it. Even have sense enough to grant exceptions. But you have to give him a policy. He's not likely to come up with one on his own." The dry voice went on to suggest that Jeff erase that portion of the letter, lest Sir Alexei find it. "Your brother will inherit the family title, my lad," his father's image had said with a wink. "And you'll need friends like Sir Alexei if you intend to found your own branch of the family. You might even think about staying on Prince Samual's World. Not a bad place from what I hear, and they'll want colonists. Shouldn't be surprised if you managed a barony out of it. So it's worth keeping Sir Alexei happy. Besides, he's not a bad sort if you deal with him on his own terms."

"Gentlemen," Ackoff began. "I find myself falling further behind in necessary work, so we will have to cut this short today."

Midshipman Landry was seated across the table from Jeff. Landry looked relieved. Jeff hoped that his own face wasn't quite as obvious, but it probably was, because Ackoff looked directly at him.

"You are amused, Mr. Jefferson?"

"No, sir."

"You shouldn't be. As of tomorrow you will be assisting the survey team. So will most of the rest of you. And you needn't groan, gentlemen. The work is important."

I suppose it is, Jeff thought. But . . . "Sir?" he asked.

"Yes?"

"I—do you know where I will be assigned?"

"Near Haven for the moment," Ackoff said. "At the University." His lips curled slightly, perhaps in a smile, perhaps something else. "We must fully understand the capabilities of the industrial base here. Get a total picture of their energy budget. Assess their ability to maintain complex technologies. Without that information we can't know what to license for import."

Midshipman Landry raised his hand.

"Yes?" Ackoff said.

"Trader Soliman says he already knows what he wants to import, and if he's wrong the market place will show him up soon enough."

"Yes. He would say that," Ackoff said. "I don't suppose he gave you the benefit of his thoughts on what he would import?"

"No, sir."

"You may be certain that Mr. Soliman's ideas will be considerably different from mine," Ackoff said.

"Luxury and convenience items, no doubt. And imbecile acts like this expedition to Makassar. It's quite natural that Mr. Soliman wants profits for Imperial Autonetics, and it doesn't take genius to imagine ways to accomplish that. Our task is to bring this planet smoothly into the Empire, and that may be a bit more difficult. Consider our situation, how very few we are, how expensive it will be to bring *anything* here. We cannot afford mistakes. The market may show up Trader Saliman, but the worst disaster he faces merely costs money. Our mistakes will cost lives—and do not deceive yourselves, we *will* make mistakes."

The officers around the table looked at each other significantly. This was Ackoff's favorite lecture, and once started it was unlikely that he'd change the subject. More importantly, he wasn't likely to ask many questions. You could safely relax and daydream when Ackoff took that tone and spoke of the burdens of Imperial office. . . .

"For example," Ackoff said, "any fool knows that energy systems are the key to industrialization. Make energy cheap and plentiful, and people will figure ways to use it. But what energy systems? Satellites? This planet hasn't the industrial base for that, and we haven't the personnel to build either the orbital or the ground components. We're unlikely to get enough skilled people. Scratch power satellites for a generation or more.

"Small fusion plants? Who will operate them? Who will maintain them? How many engineers do we bring in, and who will train others here? And how is the power to be distributed on a world where metals are dear and copper so scarce it's used as jewelry? We'll have to use organic conductors. That's a very sophisticated technology, far too complex for a world this primitive, but I suppose we'll have to do it even so.

"And once we begin, when we've made electricity cheap and plentiful—how do we control industrial developments? No matter what we do, we're going to change the class structure of this planet. Power relationships will shift and flow in unpredictable ways. Mister Jefferson. What is our primary mission?"

"Sir?" Jeff looked up with a start and tried to recall the question. "To keep the peace."

"Precisely. Which means that when this planet does develop an industrial base, it *must* be governed—*well* governed—by people loyal to the Empire. Governors both able and popular, at least popular enough to retain their offices without constant revolt. Yet consider this. If we are to bring them industry, we must bring in the personnel to build and operate the primary systems. How do we induce them to come here? What can we offer highly skilled people so that they will colonize a primitive world?"

"Wealth," Landry said.

"Precisely," Ackoff agreed. "Wealth. Opportunity. The chance to found an aristocratic family. Power indeed. But whenever you bring in an alien governing class you will inevitably breed resentment among the population. Breed enough and you can't govern. You lose control. Whether we like it or not, Prince Samual's World will within a few generations have the capability of building modern weapons. When that time comes, the planet must be loyalist. The alternative is almost unthinkable. Remember Istvan and Kutuzov's choice. . . ."

Jeff shuddered. Admiral Kutuzov had bombed an entire planet into the stone age. The alternative was the revolt of a whole sector; the alternative would have been another Secession War. Imperial planets destroyed, all of the horrors of the war years. Kutuzov had made the right choice, but it was one no sane officer wanted to face.

And, he thought, it could happen here, too. To me. Or, the other side of the coin, if I decide to become a colonist. Perhaps not to me. But to my children. Mine and Elaine's—

The thought startled him. Was he really thinking of marriage? He barely knew her. But he didn't want to be away from her, not for an hour, and—

It wasn't unthinkable. She came of a good family. Imperial policy encouraged colonists to marry locals, and set down roots into the world they chose to live on.

"Hard choices, gentlemen," Ackoff was saying. "And the decisions we make will change the history of this world. For the moment the local government cooperates with us. Even welcomes our help. We have encouraged them to believe that once they have established a planetary government, the local dynasty will remain in control. You ladies and gentlemen will naturally continue that deception as long as possible."

"What happens when they find out we've been lying to them?" a consular officer asked. Her tone made it obvious that she did not approve.

"It is not precisely a lie, Miss Neville," Ackoff said. "More a diplomatic truth—"

"Whatever we call it, they'll find us out, and what then?" she asked.

" 'Find us out,' " Ackoff repeated. "You young people can afford phrases like that. I can't. What will they find out? That no matter what our intentions, the experts we bring in will be more important than even the most influential locals? That the Traders and technicians and diplomatic personnel and civil servants will have the knowledge and skills to rise high during the inevitable turmoil of change to a modern society—and their traditional leaders will not? That is the real truth, far more influential than any legalities we may impose. Try as we will—and we do try—there will be no way to avoid a change of ruling elites here. For obvious reasons we must see that the new ruling class is loyalist. Sometimes that requires shoring up traditional leaders long after they have lost the ability to govern. Sometimes it requires replacing them. Sometimes—"

"Why can't we just leave them alone?" Sirica Neville asked.

Ackoff shrugged. "Would that be kindness?" he asked. "Suppose we do as you suggest. Leave them alone, let them develop as they see fit. Quite aside from the fact that the inevitable revolution here could as easily cast up monsters as saints for their leaders, what are we to do if they move away from the Empire, make alliance with outies, become a threat to this sector?"

Kutuzov's choice again, Jeff thought. There's got to be a better way than that. . . .

"So I leave you to contemplate our burden," Ackoff said. "We must not fail." He glanced at his pocket computer. "And now, as it is getting late, I'll let you go. Please stand for the pledge of allegiance. . . ."

They all turned to face the portrait of Leonidas IX, Emperor of Humanity.

8

The View from Space

Despite Dougal's frantic desire for haste, getting the cargo inspected and loaded took three more days. Eventually it was accomplished, and MacKinnie met Dougal for the last time before departing.

"We must thank Trader Renaldi for his help," Dougal said. "Without his assistance we'd still be dealing with Imperial clerks."

MacKinnie chuckled. "He wants to get back to civilization."

Dougal snorted contempt. "He would say that—"

"He didn't *say* it."

"No, but it was obvious." Dougal shrugged. "Well, we can be thankful for his impatience. Also that Imperial bureaucrats are no different from our own."

"It should be fairly obvious to them that we're far too primitive to be a threat to the Empire—"

"Or more to the point, to their files. And their careers," Dougal said. "It's fortunate that they didn't assign this task to that young blabbermouth from the tavern."

"Yes. This Midshipman Landry is competent enough, but he's never been on Makassar. I'd have thought they'd put one of the chaps who's been there on this—"

"They can't spare anyone higher-ranking than a midshipman," Dougal said. "That boy, Lieutenant Jefferson, is supposed to be quite competent."

"We must have seen him on an off night," MacKinnie said.

"Possibly. At any event, they have him working at the University, reading our engineering textbooks, and looking at the research laboratories."

MacKinnie frowned. "Are they suspicious? And of what?"

"I do not know. He says he is part of a survey to determine what Prince Samual's World needs. Certainly there are enough of them looking in odd places, but we know more about Jefferson than the others. He has become friendly with the daughter of one of King David's officials, and they report his activities to me. So far he has not again mentioned Makassar, but I'll be happier with you away."

"Yes. And speaking of that, I'd best be leaving for the harbor," MacKinnie said.

"Nervous?"

"A bit."

"You've done all you can."

"Sure," MacKinnie said, "And that's little enough. God knows how I'm going to bring home those books."

"Or whatever they are."

"Yes. Or whatever they are." He shrugged. "One thing at a time. Take what comes and do what you can." And that, Nathan thought, was what I was told by my tac officer back in the Academy. An Academy that doesn't exist. . . .

"You won't fail us." Dougal hesitated a moment, then put out his hand. "Good luck."

"Thanks. I expect I'll need it."

The merchant landing boat was ugly, a squat, winged cylinder nothing like the slim Navy landing ship that floated next to the main pier of the Imperial docks. The boat's gangway was a slice out of one side which lowered to match the height of the dock. The compartment inside was bare steel.

"Built to lift mass," Landry explained as they boarded. "There's no need to maneuver in atmosphere. Not like a Navy boat."

The others didn't answer, although MacLean listened with evident interest to every word Landry said. They went down a short corridor to a compartment filled with padded seats. "Find a place," Landry said. "I'll help you strap in."

"Why the straps?" Longway asked. "If this falls, they won't help much, will they?"

"Not a lot," Landry admitted. "But these boats are quite serviceable. Not much happens to them."

"I hope not," Mary Graham said. "I—where are the Traders?"

"They lifted off hours ago," Landry said. "With their own cargo. Not as big a load as we're carrying—"

MacKinnie could draw his own conclusions from that, and he didn't much like them. There didn't seem to be much to do about the situation, though. And at least Landry was aboard. . . .

There were warning tones from somewhere, three repeated notes, then a series of shorter tones that blended with a sudden roar from behind them. The landing boat lurched and began to move across the water.

"What pushes this?" Kleinst asked.

"Steam," Landry said. "Distilled water flows through a nuclear heat source—"

"Nuclear?" MacLean asked.

"Sorry," Landry mumbled. "It would take too long to explain. I don't know if I'm supposed to tell you anyway—"

"The Empire is our ally," Mary Graham said. "Why can't you tell us?"

"A good question, freelady," Landry said. "I don't really know the answer. But I have my orders . . . lean back, here we go."

The acceleration increased suddenly, and they were pressed back into their couches until they weighed far too much. MacKinnie gritted his teeth and fought to stay calm. He couldn't see out but he was certain they were flying now, the first natives of Prince Samual's World to fly in a heavier-than-air machine for centuries. Nathan glanced across the aisle toward Mary Graham. She gripped the chair arms unconsciously, but there was a set smile on her lips. MacKinnie couldn't see any of the others.

The feeling of too much weight went on for a long time. MacKinnie estimated it at about twice normal; uncomfortable but not painful. He had carried companions on his back for much longer. But he wished it would stop.

When the engines quit, the silence was terrifying. Worse yet was the sensation of falling.

Mary Graham was the first to speak. Her voice was quite calm. "The engines have quit. Are we going to crash?"

There was a confused babble from behind, and one of the guards shouted, "Goddam, we *are* falling!"

MacKinnie grimly faced death, reviewing the silly prayers the chaplains said over the dying. Somehow they did not seem silly at all.

"No, no," Landry protested. "I'm sorry. I should have warned you. We are in orbit. The sensation of falling is natural, but it's false. In fact, we *can't* fall. Without power we'd never leave this orbit, because we're falling *around* the planet—oh, hell, I don't expect you to understand. But we're quite safe."

"I'm glad to hear that," Longway said grimly. "But you might have told us—"

The incident served to reassure MacKinnie about Kleinst. The young scholar had evidently known they were safe, but made no move to assure the others and thus break his cover as social historian. MacKinnie did not care for weaklings, but the young man seemed to have common sense as well as educated intelligence.

The landing boat's engines started again, this time far more gently than before. For nearly an hour they experienced accelerations, now forward, now sideways, then finally there was a resounding clang, followed by other sounds. Midshipman Landry glanced at his pocket computer. "Good time," he said. "Couldn't have matched up quicker myself."

"Do you pilot these craft?" MacLean asked. "Your pardon, but you seem young for such a task. It must be very demanding."

MacKinnie listened with amusement. From his interviews with MacLean he knew what an effort MacLean must have made to be polite to a mere midshipman.

"I have been a qualified landing-craft pilot for nearly a standard year," Landry answered proudly. He glanced at Mary Graham as if seeking approval.

She smiled. "It's not *that* difficult," Landry continued. "The computers do most of the work. The fact
is, we couldn't fly these ships without them."

The compartment door opened and two men in
coveralls came inside. One wore gold piping on his
sleeves, and both were dark men, with eyes that
seemed to slant. There were no orientals on Prince
Samual's World, and MacKinnie and the others stared
at the crewmen.

"My name is Taka," one of the crewmen said. He
floated through the compartment, not touching the
decks, and began loosening the straps holding Mac-
Kinnie in his seat. When they had everyone loose
they gestured toward the opening.

Mary Graham stared openly at the newcomers,
but MacKinnie couldn't tell if it were their strange
eyes or the way they levitated through the compartment that interested her. Kleinst had a bored look,
but under it MacKinnie thought he detected keen
interest. The pale young scholar seemed relaxed, but
whenever the crewmen spoke he tensed slightly.

"Come aboard," Landry said. "We should not waste
time. . . ."

They floated gently through the connecting pas-
sageways between the landing craft and the main
ship, gingerly following the towlines the ship's officers had strung for them, everyone quiet and awed
by the experience. We've left our world, MacKinnie
thought. And I'm supposed to bring back the knowledge so we can *build* one of these. He shook his
head grimly. The more he saw of the ships, the more
he was convinced that they had taken on an impossible task.

Their staterooms proved to be minuscule cubicles,
sparsely furnished at first sight, but when buttons
were touched, various utilities such as beds and ta-

bles unfolded from the walls. MacKinnie sat in a chair and held himself in it while he looked at the various gadgets, but learned nothing.

Weight slowly returned.

A ship's officer led him into the lounge, where some of the others were already assembled. The room was completely alien to MacKinnie. It was splendidly furnished, but in addition to couches, chairs, and tables on the deck beneath him, one large, circular wall was also covered with carpeting and furniture, all bolted into place. The wall was not a complete disc, for a large central tube run through it well over Nathan's head. More strange than the double furniture was the deck, which curved up both in front of him and behind him, yet, when he walked around it, always felt as if it were down. After a few strides, he looked back to see that where he had been was now well above him. A few more steps brought him around the central column "overhead" to reveal Renaldi apparently hanging from the ceiling, relaxing in a large chair, a drink in his hand.

"Ah, Trader McKinnie, please be seated. The others will be here shortly." Renaldi sipped his drink. "Pleasant to have weight again, is it not?"

"Yes." MacKinnie sat, again noting the eerie sensations in his inner ears whenever he made a sudden movement. "How have you accomplished this, uh, giving us weight?"

Renaldi looked startled for a moment, then smiled. "You truly don't know, do you? I'll wait until the others arrive and explain. Have a drink, Trader. We can only enjoy this for another hour before the captain gets under way, and we all have to be in our staterooms for the transition."

MacLean, Longway, Kleinst, and Mary Graham joined them within moments. Midshipman Landry arrived a few minutes later, and explained that the guards and their leader were quartered on another deck with a lounge of their own. When all were seated, Renaldi told Landry, "The Trader is curious about our weight, Midshipman. Surely the Empire will not fall if we explain it to our guests?"

"No, of course not, Trader," Landry said. "You see, gentlemen and freelady, the captain has caused the ship to rotate about its long axis. Thus, you are thrown toward the outside of the ship. When we begin our voyage, however, the ship will accelerate for long periods of time, and the rotation will cease. While we accelerate, you will feel weight, but 'down' will be that deck in front of you, and this deck will become a wall." The boy paused for a moment, then said suddenly, "If you have never been off-world, you have never seen your own planet. There are ports at that bulkhead there; allow me to open them for you."

Before any of the others could rise, Kleinst had charged across the deck, eagerly waiting until the port was uncovered. With a shrug, Landry uncovered several more, and the others took turns looking out. No one had the heart to remove Kleinst from his post.

They saw Prince Samual's World, although it did not appear to them as a sphere, as the orbit was not that high. Although it was partly obscured by clouds, they could see much of the great mass of North Continent, a portion of the Major Sea, and several of the larger islands of the Archipelago. Except for the fleecy clouds, it looked exactly like globes and maps they had studied in school. The world below them appeared to be moving across their field of vision, however, and after it passed they would see the black of space, stars shining more brightly than they had ever believed possible.

For long moments there was no conversation. Finally, slowly, one by one they filed back to their seats, except for Kleinst, who stayed at the port until they were ushered to their staterooms for the beginning of the voyage.

MacKinnie was not allowed off the lounge deck except to go down a ladder to the deck below where Stark and the guards were quartered. His troops had far less luxurious quarters than his own, but somewhat more open space, and Hal was using the time to best advantage, training the men in unarmed combat, and experimenting with swords and shields from their personal baggage. The men seemed cheerful enough, and MacKinnie ordered a small daily ration of brandy for each man to relieve the monotony. He returned to his own quarters for the same prescription.

The days flowed by with a monotonous quality, relieved by their constant efforts to master the language of Makassar. MacKinnie and MacLean sent for wooden swords and put in an hour of practice daily, resulting both in bruises on their persons, and considerable respect for each other. They also trained with their men.

Longway and Mary Graham seemed to have a knack for languages, particularly the Academician, who passed from the main dialects to lesser ones he found in supplementary sections of the loose-leaved books the Imperial navy had supplied. They were informed that the books would be collected before they made planetfall, and MacKinnie held his breath at the mention, but nothing else was said about them.

Eleven days out from Samual, they were again

strapped into their chairs in their staterooms, experiencing another hour of weightlessness before normal weight returned. By constant pestering of Landry whenever the boy joined them, MacKinnie induced him to tell them that during the first part of the journey they had accelerated, and were now decelerating in order to enter faster-than-light travel. When he received only quizzical looks from the others, Landry explained further.

"There's two kinds of drive, normal space and hyperspace. In normal space, the fusion drive works into a Langston Field releasing photons which propel the ship. Never mind, I'm not allowed to explain it to you anyway. But this pushes the ship right along, and we experience acceleration from it. The hyperspace drive works on a different principle. It works along the pseudo-nuclear force path between two stars. I don't suppose that means anything to you. There are force paths between the stars similar to the forces that hold atomic particles together. Unlike the atomic forces which fade off rapidly in an exponential relation to distance—oh, hell, that doesn't tell you anything either. What's important is that the drive won't work if you're near a sun or a planetary body. You have to get to the precise Alderson point to get into hyperspace. Otherwise nothing happens when you turn on the drive. Navy ships have better equipment for locating Alderson points, so they don't decelerate as much as a merchant ship. Eventually we'll arrive at the right place and we can get into the hyperspace path between stars. In there we can go faster than light."

Landry glanced about him, and Kleinst quickly assumed the blank stare typical of the others. The midshipman scratched his head, muttered that that was all he was allowed to say anyway, and asked for another drink. MacKinnie noted that the boy would usually have exactly three drinks, and would always leave their company as soon as he had consumed the third one. He also noticed that the midshipman seemed to be a great deal more talkative when Mary Graham was present.

Days were measured by the ship's clock, which were geared to a standard day somewhat shorter than that of Prince Samual's World, as Samual's years were slightly shorter than those of Earth. MacKinnie noted that the Imperials tended to use many expressions and physical devices traditional from Earth.

On the twenty-second day, they were once again warned to go to their cabins, and later each was personally inspected by Landry. "Don't panic, no matter what you think you see or hear," he warned each. "The Alderson drive affects different people different ways. It's very usual to feel disoriented. Just be calm and everything'll be all right."

An hour after the boy left them, MacKinnie was in a cold sweat, waiting with nothing to do. He hoped that the others would remember their instructions. As he inspected his mechanical watch for the twentieth time, there was a strong thrumming sound which seemed to permeate the ship. This went on for several minutes, then there was an imperceptible lurch, as if intolerable acceleration had been applied for a time so short that it had no chance to affect them.

At once, Nathan was aware of a sensation of intolerable wrongness. He looked at the walls and other now-familiar objects, and they seemed the same in every detail, yet somehow different. Strange sensations crawled across his scalp. The thrumming sound was gone, but something of it lingered, and it did not sound like anything he had ever heard before.

Then there was a moment of silence. It was too

brief to be completely perceived, but it seemed to be a silence which had a tangible quality, a deadening effect that sucked up sound, and perhaps heat and light and everything else. Then there was the sound again, which rose and died away, and after that weight returned, oriented toward the circular section which MacKinnie had come to think of as the walls of his cabin. With weight, his universe returned almost to normal, although somewhere inside his brain there was a tiny terrified awareness that everything was wrong.

9

Makassar

They were in a new star system. MacKinnie tried to comprehend that, but it was impossible to believe. Yet it must be true. The stars outside the ship were subtly different, some constellations remaining as before, but others altered.

The journey to Makassar took another twenty-four days, with the transition from acceleration to deceleration taking place in the middle of the night. They were gathered in the main lounge, with Stark acting as a serving man, on the "afternoon" of the last day, when the hatch opened and they were joined by Landry and Renaldi.

"We have nearly arrived, gentlemen," Renaldi announced importantly. "I have requested Midshipman Landry to allow you to see the object of all your attention, and he has graciously consented. It will be visible through the ports over there." As Renaldi spoke, Landry removed the locks from the observation ports and opened them.

Makassar was a tiny ball, hanging in the dark of space. The most prominent feature, easily visible even from their distance, was a pair of enormous ice caps. Much of the world between them was water, with a single continent, mostly in the Southern Hemisphere, swimming westward like an enormous whale. Two large islands, almost continental in size, hung above it in the Northern Hemisphere, and the shallow seas were dotted with smaller islands. There were two distinct colors to the seas where the sun shone upon them, and Kleinst remarked that it must be due to a dramatic difference in depth. Deep water was mostly in the Northern Hemisphere, with the continent surrounded by the pale blue marking much shallower depths.

"It's a lovely world," Landry remarked, standing next to MacKinnie and pointing out some of the more visible features. "Smaller than Earth. Gravity is about eighty-seven percent of that of Earth, which makes it about, oh, let's see." He withdrew his small computer and wrote directly on one face of it with an attached stylus. "I make it seventy-nine percent of the gravity you're used to, Trader. Your men are going to be very strong compared to the locals down there. That might be useful."

"It might be indeed," MacKinnie muttered. "Are those ice caps normal in size? I seem to recall our maps of Samual show much smaller ones."

"Makassar is a bit colder than Samual. Orbit's more eccentric, enough to make some climatic differences. The inclination of the planet is also greater. Turns out it's summer—by planet inclination—in the Southern Hemisphere when the planet's farthest from the sun. I don't know, but I wouldn't be surprised if the two big islands in the north were uninhabitable, or nearly so. It would be pretty cold there. You're arriving in the middle of spring on the main continent."

MacKinnie recalled the maps they had been given. Except for a few sea trader towns, the entire population of Makassar was concentrated on the main continent, at least as far as the Imperials knew. The maps weren't very accurate, but at that they'd be the best obtainable.

They watched the planet grow larger and larger as the ship approached. Each member of the expedition stood in silence, lost in his particular fantasy, dreaming of other worlds. Then the alarm sounded, and they scrambled for the landing boat.

The Imperial base was located in a small trading town by a great bay at the western end of the planet's single continent. A scattered chain of islands led across the shallow seas to a series of large islands from which trading ships and sometimes pirate raiders came. Because of their depredations, the area around Jikar was largely uninhabited, which suited the Imperials well. Their presence in the town was disturbance enough; they had no desire to be seen by any large number of the people of Makassar.

A light rain was falling as they left the landing boat. They stood on the stone dock and stared about them in silence.

"Another world," Mary Graham said, "It's hard to believe."

"It is that," MacKinnie said. He sniffed the air, but could smell nothing. The rain had washed away any alien odors, and kept them from seeing very far. He turned back to Graham. "This is the first chance we've had to talk alone," he said. "What was the long heated conversation you had with Renaldi yesterday?"

"It was nothing—"

"Your pardon, but I do not believe that."

"He wanted—I tell you, it was nothing."

"The Trader invited her to dinner," Longway said.

"Alone?"

"Yes. Of course I refused," Graham said.

MacKinnie looked at her grimly. "You should have told me. I am—"

"My guardian," Graham finished for him. "Yes, and what good would that have done? You would have challenged him. He would have been horrified and thought us barbaric. Nothing would have been accomplished—"

"But—"

"She's right," Longway said. "By his standards there was nothing improper about the invitation." He put his hand on MacKinnie's sleeve. "I know," he said. "The invitation implied that she might accept it. Since free-born ladies would never visit a man in his quarters, he implies that she is no more than a tavern girl. But he does not know that, Trader MacKinnie."

"And who will explain this to her father?" MacKinnie asked.

"He is not here," Longway said carefully. "Nor is there any reason to explain to him. Trader, Imperial ladies are, I think, no more immoral than our own, but they are their own mistresses. Not under guardianship. The Empire is as shocked by our customs as we are by theirs. More, I think. And remember where we are. You can hope there will be nothing worse than this to endure."

MacKinnie turned away without answering. Longway was right, of course. Even on Prince Samual's

World there were cultures which did not so thoroughly protect their women as did the North Continent civilizations. There were even places where men did not go constantly armed. He had adjusted to those, and he could to Makassar.

Navy House was crude, a stone building constructed by the locals, and there was no Marine fortress. Whatever defenses the Imperials had installed were not obvious to MacKinnie as his group approached the Imperial headquarters.

Many of the locals were small men, brown and dark, reminding MacKinnie of the officers aboard the trading starship. Their clothing was crude, some of the men wearing trousers, others dressed in long, gownlike robes which hung to their knees. In sharp contrast to the passengers of the starship, everyone seemed to have a beard of some kind, although many of them were not well developed. Their hair was long, and it was obvious at a distance that they did not often practice bathing.

In the hundred yards from the docks to Navy House MacKinnie's party was approached by at least ten beggars, some of them proudly displaying truly horrible disfigurations. They shouted and pleaded, and MacKinnie was pleased to see that he was able to understand them reasonably well. The practice aboard the ship had been useful for learning the language, even if he did not care much for his first encounter with it. Stark tossed out a few copper coins, allowing them to escape as the beggars cursed and fought for the money.

They were permitted to stay in Navy House for a few days only, and MacKinnie's officers eagerly explored the small town, talking to the inhabitants and investigating the possible marketable goods for sale.

At the end of the third day on the planet, they assembled in the one large room of the headquarters building. Renaldi, as usual, sat by the fire, a glass in his hand.

"Your Excellency, we have been unable to find a single thing worth transportation to Prince Samual's World. We are beginning to think there is nothing here," MacKinnie began. "Where are the spices, and exotic cloth, and the rest that you and your partner described?"

Renaldi laughed. "For all I know," he said thickly, "there may not be another valuable thing on the planet. Soliman cleans a place out pretty good when he gets the chance."

"But—but," stammered MacKinnie, "if there's nothing here, we're ruined. You've charged us an enormous price for transportation to this place. Surely there's something worth buying. How are we going to recover our expenses?"

"You probably won't. We never promised you a profit, Trader." Renaldi pronounced the title as if it were an insult. "In our business, you have to take chances. Perhaps you took an unwise chance."

"But we took it on your advice!" MacKinnie snapped, then changed to a pleading tone. "Surely you know of some way we can make this profitable for King David. Surely with your experience you can help us."

"Unlikely." Renaldi drank deeply. "But whatever it is you are to do, be quick about it. The ship leaves in three days."

"Three days! Why, that's impossible. You promised us sufficient time to arrange for trade, even to organize a permanent company here. We can't begin to arrange for trade in three days. You knew that before we started." MacKinnie looked down at the impassive face and had an urge to tear out the small mustache by the roots. He restrained himself and said, "I'm going to complain to the Navy. They'll make you honor your contract."

"Our contract, Trader, says that you will be brought here, and returned at a time mutually convenient. The ship leaves in three days. That's convenient to us. And you've nothing to complain about; we're going to two other star systems before we go back to your miserable planet. You won't be permitted out of your quarters while we're there, but think of the broadening travel you'll experience."

"It is not mutually convenient if one party does not agree," Longway said softly. "We may have few rights, Imperial Trader Renaldi, but I suspect Captain Greenaugh will enforce those we have. He did not seem to be overly fond of Imperial Traders, Your Excellency. We will not leave in three days."

Renaldi shrugged. "Suit yourselves. The next ship we could schedule through this miserable system will arrive at this port in something over a standard year. If you wish to wait for it, I will have the Navy compute the exact number of local days before it arrives. You can wander this poverty-stricken ball until you tire of it." He got up with an effort and filled his glass from an open bottle on the great table which dominated the room. MacKinnie noted that the bottle was handblown, and crudely at that, but of an interesting color. Renaldi seemed to be fond of the local liquor.

"Three days or over a year," Nathan observed. "Neither is very convenient."

"Those are the times convenient to us. Which do you choose?" Renaldi backed away from MacKinnie nervously as the soldier approached him, fingering his belt as if grasping for a weapon which was not there. He managed to get back to his seat, where he regained his composure. "Come, now, we never promised you more. And think of the adventures you can have, wandering about on a planet of swineherds." He laughed for a moment, saw MacKinnie's face, and stopped short.

Nathan turned to MacLean and said, "Go get the lieutenant in command of this post. We may as well find out just what else this man can do to us." The group waited in a strained silence for several minutes before MacLean returned with Midshipman Landry and another officer.

Lieutenant Farr was a short, dark man who resembled the planetary locals. MacKinnie wondered idly if he had been chosen for the post for his ability to blend in with the rest of the population. Nathan explained the situation, and Farr and Renaldi conversed in the Imperial language for several minutes, speaking too rapidly for even Longway to understand. Renaldi became more and more excited, but the lieutenant spoke with a deadly calm. Although he did not have the intense, dedicated look which MacKinnie had noted was common of the Navy men, he never seemed to smile either. Instead, his manner was coldly official with perhaps the merest trace of relief from the boredom of being commanding officer to a post without a mission.

When the conversation was finished, Farr turned to MacKinnie, speaking very slowly. "If he is correct about the details of the contract your king signed, then he can legally do this. We could examine it for you if you'd like, but it might take some time. There are no legal officers on this post."

MacKinnie canted his head to one side, realized the gesture was meaningless to the lieutenant, and said, "Thank you, no. I'm sure they drafted it carefully enough." He seized a glass, filled it, and drained it off. "Is there any chance of our finding a decent trading community on this planet, Lieutenant? And will we be allowed to go and search for one?"

"The only place I can suggest is the main city, Batav. It's said to be wealthy, although what the locals mean by wealth is not likely to impress you. It is all you will find."

MacKinnie nodded. "Then I suppose we must go there. I can't return to King David without something to show for his investment."

"There are difficulties," Lieutenant Farr said slowly. "The Empire cannot transport you there. The entire countryside is in a state of war, and it is not likely you will survive to reach Batav. We can give you no protection. . . ." The officer paused. "But if you must go, perhaps you will find another party of Imperial citizens who set out for Batav. A group of churchmen defied our advice and departed months ago. We have not heard from them, and His Holiness will insist on knowing what became of his missionaries. If you find out what became of them, it will make the job easier."

MacKinnie looked at the officer, realizing that if the Navy could not send troops to search for missionaries, it would never attempt to protect a group of colonial Traders. Prince Samual's World seemed far away, lost in the swirl of stars above them, and he knew he would never see it again. One thing, he thought; at least they would have no way of knowing what he intended doing at the old library, if he ever reached it.

"We'll look for them, Lieutenant," Nathan said. "Now, I suppose we must find quarters in the town, so that we can organize our expedition. I dare not return to my own world without a profit until I have done everything I can do." He turned to Renaldi. "As for you, I understand that the Empire preserves local customs insofar as this is possible. I will live for the day when you return to Prince Samual's World and I meet you on a field of honor. Presuming, of course, that you have any." When Renaldi made no reply, MacKinnie stalked away.

10

Jikar

The tavern reminded MacKinnie of the Blue Bottle. Even the name was translatable into something close to Blue Wineglass, and it reminded MacKinnie of home. Although it was only an hour past noon, the place was full.

Blatt, Master Tanner, and Hoorn, Master of Drapers, were glad enough to enjoy MacKinnie's hospitality. They finished the first bottle of wine in silence, savoring the richly flavored concoction the tavern keeper made from the sour local product. It sold at a price almost no one in the village could afford, making MacKinnie a popular man. Nathan watched the two men, once pleasantly stout but now disfigured with the folds of flesh which marked malnutrition. Other townsmen sat in brooding silence, many of them at tables empty of bottles. The tavern keeper had served his tithe, and they had no more credit; but there was no place else to go.

"Is Jikar often like this?" Nathan asked when the bottle was done at last. "Your pardon, Masters, but it would seem that no village could survive long in this state, even one blessed with harbor and fields."

Hoorn cleared his throat and glanced suggestively at the bottle, too proud to ask for more. MacKinnie signaled with a careless wave and was rewarded with a burst of activity from the tavern keeper. Except for a small boy of no more than eight years, MacKinnie had seen no one in service to the tavern, yet it was a large place, obviously once a prosperous one. As the new bottle was poured, Hoorn sighed deeply.

"Since *they* came," he whispered. Then in more normal tones, although still keeping his deep voice low, he added, "Our war fleet was destroyed when *they* landed. The pirates will not accept tribute from Jikar; we have killed too many of them in battle. Our city is small, Trader, but we were once proud. Now what is there for us? The harbor is closed by the pirates, and the barbarians ravage our fields. Yet *they* will do nothing. They cannot interfere, they tell us." The draper's voice rose to a shout tinged with tears. "In the name of the Immortal God, have they not interfered already? They have been the ruin of Jikar!"

"Aye," Blatt muttered. "Our fleet and our army were the same. Both lost. The pastures are burned off, the fields trampled. Oh, we are safe enough within the walls. *They* will not allow the town to be sacked. We could wish that they would. Then our young men might take courage and be ready to fight again instead of huddled at the steps of the church to receive alms they once gave, or drinking the tavern keeper's tithe before it can reach the priest. A curse on outlanders." He lifted his glass to toast damnation before he realized who his host was. "Pardon, Trader. You do not seem like one of *them*."

MacKinnie nodded absently and considered his predicament. On the next day, the landing ship would rise, leaving his crew stranded on the planet, but he had yet found no way to leave Jikar. Just outside the city walls barbarian hordes prowled, ready to plundor anyono foolhardy onough to tako oithor road, north or south. Outside the harbor, patrols of pirates based on the islands across the great shallow bay called the Sulawa Sea enforced the blockade of the port, demanding not only tribute but the head of the Master of each Guild in Jikar. It was to the credit of the people of the town that no one had ever been heard to speak in favor of dealing with the pirates, except two ancient Guildmasters who claimed they had few years left anyway. Their own councils refused to consider the proposal.

The barbarian incursion into what had once been civilized territory had created chaos in lands which had never been well governed in the best of times. Many of the warrior families who had maintained at least the illusion of peace and order were no more; others had fled. No one could answer for the safety of a small party setting out to the Old Empire city nearly three thousand kilometers away.

The Imperials had very little information about Batav. In hopes of finding a local who had journeyed there, Nathan approached the Guildmasters who ruled Jikar, only to find that few townsmen had ever traveled farther than a few hundred kilometers at best, and most of those had died in the brief, futile resistance to the Navy. To the Navy, the loss of three hundred and ninety locals was a regrettable incident. To Jikar, it was ruin.

"God is angry with you, Trader," Hoorn said. "A few years ago, Jikar was the busiest port on the coast of the west. Out here we don't have large cities as they do in the east, but there were over five thousand souls in our town, and as many more on the lands around. Trading was good. We had no need of lordlings to fight our battles for us. We were free men, bound to no one, our own protection. The Guilds rule here, not some bonehead warrior capable of nothing but mounting with sword and lance."

"You speak too hard of the men of iron," Blatt said. The wine was warming him to the conversation, recalling pleasanter times he had been in the tavern. He lifted a blue-tinted blown goblet, the kind which gave the place its name, and drank deeply. "They do nothing but fight, true, yet I think Jikar would never have been free if there were not the marshlands to our east. It was our curse that the iron men died in plague, their strongholds fell, and hordes swept past. Before that we had only to fight the few raiders who passed the great houses like thieves in the night. When their full force fell on us we knew it."

"Knew it and won!" Hoorn shouted. "Ah, Trader, had you seen it. Our young men, the sailors from our fleet and the boys of the Guilds, standing with pikes leveled, never giving ground, while the barbarians dashed themselves against us. Glory to the Lord, the field was red with their blood. We took a hundred horses and many ayuks for our own." Evidently horses and cattle had been brought to Makassar by the Old Empire. Now both ran wild across the plains, hunted by local predators unless protected by men, but managing to survive.

Some of the barbarians also rode the ayuk, a native beast that resembled a moose with long, semi-prehensile claws and an elongated prehensile snout.

It lived on the hive-rat, warmblooded egg-layers about seven inches long which lived in great colonies with only a few retaining active sexual powers. The hive-rat was one of the most dangerous creatures on Makassar, although it was not carnivorous. It ate the stone-hard local woods with ease, burrowed in the ground, and found any plant life edible by humans quite nourishing. It would fight when trapped, and when one was wounded, hundreds of them came to its aid in blind fury. More than one man had died through being caught by them in the open.

"A great victory." Blatt nodded. "One which Master Hoorn could tell you more of, for he commanded for the Guilds that day. Aye, we broke them, but we could not pursue them. Most escaped. Had we forty of the mounted iron men to give chase, the victory would have kept the barbarians from our gates for a hundred years."

"Ah." Hoorn drank again. Then he smiled and shrugged. "We can agree the warriors know how to fight. Yet I have in my day seen them turned back from the gates of a city like ours. In open battle. The young men stood to their pikes, and the iron men Master Blatt is so fond of split about them on both sides, afraid to attack. They took no tribute from that city." As Hoorn finished, a young man, dark of hair and tall for Makassar, one quite muscular but now thin like the others, strode arrogantly across the room, his head high in contrast to the locals MacKinnie had seen. He could have been twenty-five Earth years, but he looked younger, and his clothes were subtly different. His trousers were of the rough-texture cloth worn by the villagers, but the jacket and cloak were of finer stuff, and Nathan noted that there were discolored lines at the collar, as if it had once been trimmed with something now lost. He recalled that cloth-of-gold collars and bands were the marks of the Guildmasters.

The tavern keeper gave the newcomer the glass of cheap wine and thick slice of bread which he served to all daily in lieu of his tithe to the church. The man began to eat without speaking to anyone.

"That's who you should talk to," Hoorn told MacKinnie. "We should send for him. If there is a man in Jikar who can tell you what you'll find beyond the river and forest, Brett can. Or that warrior friend of his."

"Who is he?" MacKinnie asked.

"His name is Brett," Hoorn said. He lowered his voice. "He is said to have come from far away, some say the eastern coast. He comes carrying tales and songs, and will not discuss his ancestry. As for me, I believe he was born a barbarian."

"Yet he speaks many civilized tongues," Master Blatt said.

"Aye." Hoorn pursed his lips in thought. "The barbarians do not come here often, so it is a thing not done here. But I am told that in parts where the plains riders are more common, the townsfolk often capture young plainsmen and keep them as slaves."

"And you think Brett was one of those?" MacKinnie asked.

"It is possible," Blatt said. "Although I do not envy anyone who would be master to the singer. I would rather have him as a friend."

"Aye," Hoorn agreed. "There have been other singers in Jikar, but none came as Brett. Most are on foot, but Brett rides a great war-horse, and has for companion one of the iron men with armor and lance and sword. Vanjynk his name is. He was driven from his lands to the south and now wanders as Brett to sell his abilities to any purchaser."

A wandering mercenary, MacKinnie thought. As I once was.

MacKinnie studied the dark features of the man in question and approved. He might be down on his luck, Nathan thought, but he wasn't defeated. Despite his youth he was more akin to the Guildmasters than the tavern loafers. "Call him over," he said in a moment of decision.

"Singer," Hoorn called. "At your pleasure, join us. Our noble friend is a willing host."

The singer came to the table and bowed as Hoorn performed introductions.

"I am told you know of faraway lands," McKinnie said. He poured a glass of wine and pushed it toward Brett. "If you have the time, perhaps you can tell me of your travels."

Brett made a wry face. "I have little but time." He drained his wineglass at a gulp.

"You do not travel alone, singer?" MacKinnie asked, pouring more wine.

"Not for a yir. I teach Vanjynk poetry, he teaches me to fight. Now we are both good at both trades and the living is better." He stared ruefully about the tavern. "Or was. But we will not leave our bones here for Master Blatt to put to earth."

"You would like to leave Jikar, then?" MacKinnie asked.

"Trader, we would pay the man who allowed us to fight for him, be it only that he had sufficient men to cut through the maris. But the maris will stay until they have eaten and burned everything they can find, and as they are not so stupid as the Guilds hope, that will not be before the snows. Then they will leave. At that they will bring you a blessing, Guildmasters."

"What blessing could a horde of barbarians—maris,

you called them?—what blessing can they bring?"
Blatt stood, his wide shoulders almost blotting out
the younger man, his great hands, hardened with
brine and tanners' liquor, on his hips.

"Calmly, calmly, you will alarm our host and the
wine will stop," Brett said softly. There was a hint of
threat to the voice, a tone one did not take with
Guildmasters. "I call them maris because that is
what they call themselves. And the blessing is the
destruction of the hive-rats. There will be few enough
of them when they move on—in fact, that is why
they will move on. The ayuks must eat many of
them, which keeps the maris moving about the great
plains. When the ayuks don't eat, the maris don't
eat. Even here they'll finish off all your Earth crops
before the ayuks are done with the hive-rats."

MacKinnie listened with interest. "The maris live
off their ayuks?"

Brett looked at him in puzzlement. "Your speech
is unlike any that I have heard in any land," he
commented. "Yet you are not native here, where the
maris have not been. Where have you lived that you
don't know about them? Ah, the cities of the mountains of the north. Well, know, northman, that the
plantain of the great flatland is as poisonous to us as
most of the other plants on Makassar. It must be
true, as the priests say, we came here from another
star long ago, else why would God have put us
where we cannot eat? But the ayuk can eat the
plants, and men can eat the ayuk, and drink her
milk, and, even as the maris do, drink the blood of
their steeds. Their horses fare better, eating grasses
which grow among the plantain, and some maris live
from their horses alone, but the ayuk is better. It is
not enough, though. Fed nothing else, they waste
and die, even as these men here. In your north, you

can eat the tallgrass, which they say came from Earth, and you eat the grotka. But did you eat nothing but grotka, and the swimmers from the sea, you would die also."

MacKinnie nodded. The Imperials had told him of the dietary problems of Makassar. Most of the animal life was edible, but not all of it, and little of the plant life except that which came originally from another planet. The local plants stored up various metals, which gave them their hardness, but also made them deadly. The local animals separated out the metal, although some, like the hive-rat which ate not only fruits and grains but woody stems, were deadly. All lacked essential vitamins. Listening to the singer, he had an idea.

"I wish to return to the mountains of the north," Nathan said. His maps showed that Batav was nestled on the side—the wrong side from Jikar, of course—of the mountain range which ran down the great peninsula jutting from the north edge of the continent. The mountains then curled east before they dwindled away to hills, still high enough to form a natural barrier to the great plains.

"North?" Brett asked incredulously. "How long has it been since you came from there? But you must have come by ship. The land route has been closed for two years, Trader. The High King of the Passes is dead, and the others fight for his place. No life is safe, no judges sit, and the people make do as best they can. With your wealth, you might hire enough men to take you south. With me to show the way you could fight through the maris and come to the city-states and kingdoms of the Kepul. But not to the north, Trader. We could never pass the Sangi." Brett tossed off the glass of wine, then waved at a smaller man, fair-haired and contrasting with the singer in every dimension, yet bearing the same manner of confidence. The newcomer came forward slowly.

"Trader," Brett said, "this is Vanjynk, the best friend a wanderer ever had, tragedy as it is that he must roam the lands." Brett poured his friend wine without asking.

Vanjynk nodded to MacKinnie and sat in silence. MacKinnie noted that he was younger than Brett, possibly by as much as two of the local years. Yet he was born of the nobility, while whatever Brett's origin it had not been in an iron and stonewood fortress. The relationship between the men must have been complex.

The others explained to the young warrior what MacKinnie had in mind. "But there is no way through the Sangi," Brett finished. "Or none that I can see."

"Nor I." Vanjynk drank slowly and deliberately, as he seemed to do everything else. "You will not find enough men to take the trail through the forest. The coast is closed. I do not know the sea."

"The sea," Blatt snorted. "Were there a way by sea half the town of Jikar would be off trading. All your gold will not pay the pirates, Trader, and there is but one warship left in Jikar."

"There is a ship here?" MacKinnie asked. "Is it for sale?"

"For sale?" Hoorn thought slowly. "It belongs to the Ironsmiths. There is little in Jikar that is not for sale, including our daughters' virtue. I could save you money in the purchase, for a fee to my Guild."

"Not allowed." Blatt spoke positively. "To sell a man that which sends him to his death is not allowed. Go back to your clothing, Hoorn; the Guilds cannot plunder this man from the stars."

Nathan noted the sudden look of interest Brett tried to hide, then turned to Blatt. "I buy it willingly, Master Tanner." Although he said nothing to show it, the man's honesty affected him more than MacKinnie wanted to admit to himself. "To return to our homes with nothing would be not only our ruin, but that of many others. Go with Guildmaster Hoorn and buy that ship for me, and we will do well by both your Guilds. Freemen Brett, Vanjynk, I will pay you for your advice, whether you come with me or not; but we are taking that ship out of the harbor of Jikar if every pirate on Makassar is lying in wait out there."

11

Shipfitter

MacKinnie and his party were inspecting their ship when the landing boat rose from the harbor and vanished from sight in the low clouds above. Nathan was not sorry to see it go. He had far too much work to waste time playing a role, pleading with Renaldi or demanding rights from the Navy. The ship was not in condition to be launched.

There was an additional blessing. Midshipman Landry had left with Renaldi. When Lieutenant Farr was told of MacKinnie's plans he decided that the Navy could ill spare one of its young officers for a year, especially since it was more than likely that MacKinnie's party would never be heard from again. Landry was ordered to go to the next port and report to headquarters for further instructions.

Before Renaldi left, the lieutenant had made it

clear that the Navy was displeased with his treatment of MacKinnie, and would insist that no matter how remote Nathan's chance of survival was, Renaldi was obligated to provide transportation back to Prince Samual's World. MacKinnie was privately convinced that the lieutenant was more upset about Landry's wasted time than the injustice of the situation, as Greenaugh had been led to believe that the boy would be gone only a few months. However, he was now guaranteed passage home if he could return to Jikar.

Mary Graham remained on Makassar. She pointedly refused to be on the same ship with Renaldi without MacKinnie's protection, and she was legally correct by Haven law and custom. This was upsetting enough, but Nathan found she also insisted on accompanying the party on its expedition to Batav, and nothing MacKinnie could say would convince her that she could not go.

"What did you expect me to do here?" she insisted. "I knew there would be danger."

"Freelady," MacKinnie replied coldly, "Citizen Dougal sent you without my request. We had thought to establish trading offices in the Imperial port, where you would remain as our agent."

"But there is no need for offices here," Graham protested.

"True. But you cannot come with us. You will be a great inconvenience aboard ship. How can we provide you proper quarters? To be blunt, what of sanitary arrangements? This is madness."

"Madness, Trader? Is it less mad to leave me here, in a city besieged? I may yet be of use to you."

"No."

"You say no. You had better reconsider. If I am not reliable enough to go with you, how can you trust me to remain silent for a year? You leave me here with the Imperial officers—"

"I did not say that I do not trust you."

"Would Dougal leave me behind? Think on that. Dougal would have me killed rather than risk it."

He would, MacKinnie thought. Yet—what does she know of our real mission? I haven't told her or any of them. Kleinst knows. Perhaps Longway. Does Mary Graham? One of them may well have told her.

"Please," she said. "Trader, I was told this mission is important, to Haven and to Prince Samual's World. Will you deny me the chance to show that I—that the women of Haven—are no less bound to duty and honor than you? Do you think only men can be patriotic?"

I hadn't considered it, MacKinnie thought. More importantly, though, dare I leave her here? She's right, Dougal wouldn't. I can't think how she can help, but— "Very well."

"Thank you. You won't regret it."

I regret it already, MacKinnie thought, but he said nothing.

And now she was busily clambering about the dockyard, following MacLean and hastily scribbling notes as the seaman happily inspected the craft. A gang of young locals, glad of employment, stood by under the supervision of the Shipwright Guildsmen. The Shipwrights had lost heavily in the brief and pointless battle with the Imperial Navy, and were willing to allow anyone in the town to work on MacKinnie's outfitting provided that they paid dues to the Guild and worked under its Masters. From the crowd inside and outside the dockyard, MacKinnie thought half the able-bodied men of Jikar were hoping for employment.

The boat itself was hardly impressive. Only about

thirty meters long, it was drawn up out of the water on a primitive ways. MacKinnie saw a round-bottomed boat with a small skeg running her length. The stem and sternpost were carried up high out of the water, and a great platform was constructed across the stern. On top of that was a cabin. The rest of the boat was undecked, with platforms for rowers along its sides. Over a hundred men could sit on the two sweeps halfdecks, but there was no chance of hiring that many for a long voyage, even if the pirates were not outside the harbor. At present, MacKinnie had no crew at all except his original expedition, although Brett and Vanjynk were on his payroll and would come even though they thought there was little chance of getting through.

After MacLean inspected the vessel, MacKinnie took him to a sheltered space to hold a conference. Hal Stark stood by to be sure they were not over-heard, and MacKinnie wasted no time. "Can we make it? It's vital that we get to Batav, if we have to swim."

MacLean sucked on a pipe casually for a moment. Smoking did not seem to startle the villagers although they were never seen to smoke, but MacLean's lighter was far in advance of anything on the planet. MacKinnie wondered how he had got it past the thorough inspection Mr. Landry conducted before they were allowed to unload their goods from the landing ship. The pipe gurgled for a few moments before MacLean said, "Need some modifications to get that far. From what I've heard, this is sheltered water around here, but after we've gone north a ways there'll be nothing to the west for four thousand kilometers. Big waves will come across there in a normal westerly. Sure as hell be bad in a storm."

"So we could make it?" When MacLean nodded, MacKinnie went on, "How big a crew will you need?"

"The way I intend to modify her, no more than twice the number we already have, but everyone will have to lend a hand. A few locals would be useful if you can hire them.

"I'm going to make her sail, Trader. She's got that damned stubby mast on her; I'll yank that and put in a taller one, then stay it properly, deck the boat over and put some iron ballast in her. Nothing the Imperials can object to. And I'll mount leeboards."

The term meant nothing to MacKinnie, but he'd find out soon enough. "Sail up high will tip it over, won't it?" he asked.

MacLean shook his head. "Ballast will fix that, I hope. She's beamy enough, should be good form stability. I like the hull sections. They've ridden out some mean storms in those things. That big iron ram on the prow goes back almost amidships; it's the closest thing they've got to a ballast keel." He sucked on his pipe. "You can tell there's a lot of shallow water here, and with those weird tides from the two moons, they must run aground a lot. That's why the boats have nearly flat bottoms. Beach them for the night usually, I expect. We can get there, Trader, but I don't know about the pirates."

MacKinnie nodded. "Suggestions?"

"Just fix the boat and hope we can outrun them. Sure as hell can't outfight them. Oh, and this is a bigger boat than most of the pirate stuff. Faster. Warship, one of the best on the planet, I'm told. But there's a hell of a lot of pirates. Without a full crew, if one of their ships boards us, we're dead."

"Yeah. Well, we cross that when it happens. How long to get the work done?" Now that Nathan was no longer watched by the Imperials every moment, he had control over his actions again, and the new sense of purpose drove him impatiently. He glanced about himself, took out his pipe, and borrowed MacLean's lighter to fire it. "How'd you get this past?" he asked.

"This?" MacLean looked at the lighter as if he had never seen it before. It was an ordinary flint and steel device, not as elegant as the flameless units the Imperial Navy carried. "I just walked out with it. Landry saw it, but he didn't say anything."

MacKinnie nodded slowly. By Empire standards, the lighter was primitive enough to be classed with Makassar technology. He wondered how many more Samualite devices were strange to Makassar but would be overlooked by the Navy; it was a point to remember.

"How long until we can sail?"

MacLean scratched his chin. "With luck, a few days. Decking's the hard part. There are a lot of hands to do the work, but they've never done this kind of thing before. Still, by the time you get the goods and provisions on board we should be just about ready to get under way."

It took two of the local weeks. Although the Makassar day was somewhat longer than Samual's and quite a bit longer than the standard Earth day, MacKinnie noticed that he and his crew soon became accustomed to living by local time, which was measured by sundials or not at all.

One reason the work went slowly was that the local church insisted on Sabbath-keeping, and in addition seemed to proclaim at least one Holy Day each week. These, and the inexperience of the locals with the construction methods MacLean insisted on, caused the first delays. Then when the ship was completed, another week was consumed in obtaining cloth suitable for sails and having the Drapers sew it.

MacLean was the only man available to design the equipment needed. He designed and cast anchors more advanced than anything seen on Makassar since the war; installed windlasses and winches, cast in bronze by the Ironsmiths; and had the Drapers lay up ropes and cables from local fibers. It all had to be done, and MacLean had to see to each detail personally. The days dragged on and on.

MacKinnie watched nervously one day when a party of Imperial sailors led by the junior lieutenant of the planet walked around the dockyards, but they evidently saw nothing to disapprove of. Anchors and winches were things for primitives, and the Navy men did not even understand the purpose of some of MacLean's devices. As a precaution, MacKinnie had taught Brett the use of most of them, so that if asked he would appear familiar with the equipment. The Navy might think it in common use elsewhere on Makassar.

By the time the ship was ready for launching, the trade goods and weapons they would carry were piled on the docks. A light drizzle driven by the strong westerly winds thoroughly soaked the party as they stood watching the locals launch the ship. The primitive ways did not permit much sophistication— half the young men in the town simply lifted and strained until *Subao* was in the water, then fell to carrying aboard the iron ingots MacLean had selected for ballast. MacKinnie expected to get under way immediately, but found that there was more to do.

"What now?" he asked MacLean.

"Masts. Stays. Running the sails up to see how they fit. Securing the ballast. Trader, that ship may be on her ear in a storm one of these days, and you'll hardly want the ballast shifting around down there. And we still have the leeboards to install. You can save time by getting your gear aboard today, but don't plan on leaving for at least three days more."

MacKinnie cursed, silently so that MacLean would not hear him. There was little else he could do.

That afternoon MacLean gave instruction on how to sail the boat. He discovered that young Todd had sailed small boats in the Haven harbor, and, under MacKinnie's questioning, the boy admitted to being a military cadet from one of the wealthier families of the kingdom of Haven. MacLean immediately appointed him midshipman and quartermaster.

They learned the language the locals used aboard ships, although MacLean had to adapt several local words for terms they would not be familiar with. Then he had Todd drill everyone on the names of lines and gear on the ship. MacKinnie noted that Brett seemed very adaptable, learning faster than the outworlders, although his friend Vanjynk was almost uninterested. Stark, as usual, soon learned his tasks and drove the guardsmen to theirs, not a bit upset by Todd's sudden promotion over him. That night Stark and MacKinnie sat in MacKinnie's small room at the inn overlooking the water.

"Best we get the men some action, sir," Hal said. "All that drill with sword and shield's fine, but they get restless carrying stores and driving nails. Got some good pointers from that Vanjynk fellow, he's gifted with his armor and stuff. Reckon he's in the same business we are."

MacKinnie nodded. "From what I can see, it was all he ever learned until he lost his lands and had to go wandering with the singer. What do you make of Brett?"

"Don't know, sir. Takes my orders right enough,

better than Vanjynk, but there's no understanding him."

MacKinnie nodded. "He's a tough one. That's a pretty strange partnership he's got with Brett. Vanjynk seems to be one of the iron men Blatt forever tells us about." He hoisted his glass and winked at his sergeant. "Iron MacKinnie's new troops. Few enough of them. Had any success at recruiting?"

"That's what I wanted to talk to you about, sir. There's a shipmaster I've been drinking with, man named Loholo. He claims he can get us a crew for a price. Part of the price is he wants to go with us. Mr. MacLean wasn't too interested in having a native shipmaster aboard, said there was enough command problems already what with nobody knowing who ranked who. He's not happy with you being in charge, sir. But I can't tell him about Loholo; the Guild people seem to think a lot of him. Should I send for him? He's in the Blueglass tonight waiting to hear."

"No harm in talking to him. Sure, why not?"

Stark nodded and went to the door. He spoke briefly in low tones to one of the guardsmen outside. "Be here in a couple of minutes, Trader. Be best if I were on duty when he came in." Stark took his glass to another table across the small room.

Captain Loholo was a short, dark-brown man, stocky and strong-looking, with a distinct slant to his eyes, reminding MacKinnie of the starship officers he had seen. He had seen many others of his type on Makassar, in sharp contrast to the tall, blond men like Vanjynk. Loholo wore a golden skull ornament in his left ear, and carried a large curved knife in his belt. His clothing was of finer material than was usually seen on Jikar men, and everything he wore was freshly cleaned. He stood self-confidently in the doorway, coolly eyeing the star men.

"Trader," Hal said, "I want you to meet Captain Loholo, shipmaster and merchant. I'm told he's the only captain left in the port."

"Please have a seat, Captain," MacKinnie said, pouring a glass of wine. "My guard chief tells me you can raise a crew."

"Aye." Loholo fingered the glass, looked at Mac-Kinnie for a moment, and drank. "Not a very good crew, Trader. The good men are at the bottom of the sea or run off to join the pirates. But there's men here who can pull an oar. Not seamen. Apprentices from all the Guilds, boys on tithes who'd like to be men again." He spoke so rapidly that MacKinnie had difficulty following him, and had to have Loholo repeat his words.

"I've seen them," MacKinnie said. "But Captain MacLean has not been able to recruit anyone."

"Nor will he." Loholo touched the wine bottle and looked at MacKinnie, who nodded. The brown man filled his glass and drank before continuing. "Your Captain MacLean is a strange man, Trader. He puts decks over the ship so that oarsmen can't breathe properly. He has taken out most of the rowing benches. What's left is up too high for proper leverage. You couldn't row that ship a hundred klamaters. And all the iron he put in the hull is no more than dead weight to be carried along. The men won't sail with him because even though they aren't seamen, they can see your man is no seaman. The ship will be too slow to escape pirates, and it won't sail properly if it does get past them." He shrugged. "Your pardon if I speak bluntly."

"But you're willing to come? And bring a crew?"

"Aye."

"Go on. Why?"

"You're not a beached captain, Trader. If you had

the seawater in your blood, you'd know. My ship went out to fight with me ashore laid out by plague. She never came back. Everything I had was in that ship, Trader. Nothing left to buy the Ironsmith's vessel. Even if a warship is no good for trading, I tried to buy *Subao*, for a ship's still a ship. I figure you'll all come to your senses about the ship when you see it won't work. And you'll need a man who knows how to sail these seas. I expect to be your shipmaster a week after you leave port. If you live that long. But the chance is worth it to me."

One way or another, MacKinnie thought. The dagger at the man's belt had once had a jeweled hilt, but it wasn't meant for show purposes. With his own crew aboard, Loholo could make himself master of the ship if he were that kind of man. He looked over at Stark, who obviously had the same thought. Still, there was a way to make use of the man, and perhaps he was honest.

"Your own crew went down with your ship?"

"Aye. Every man. It won't be real seamen I can get you, Trader, but they'll be willing."

"Why?"

Loholo grinned. "I'm well known as a captain who comes back. Rich. And I'm said to be lucky."

"Still, how will you get them to join, with the pirates outside the harbor?"

"Tell them the star men will protect them. They know what happened out in the harbor the day *they* landed. They'll believe."

"And you don't?"

"If the star men will help you, you don't need to have the guard captain out giving free wine to find men, Trader. So they won't."

MacKinnie nodded. "What of the pirates?"

"There are ways. I know these waters, Trader.

When the moons come together, there's deep water over the reefs. It goes down fast. Get over them at the right time, ahead of anybody chasing you, they never catch you. I doubt the pirates know my waters as I do. We'll have a chance. That is, if you can row the ship. Got to put the benches back in."

"What if I told you," MacKinnie asked, "that after we have returned to Jikar from where we are going, we will make you master of the ship and our trading agent, with gold every month and part of the trading as well?"

Loholo looked at MacKinnie closely. "Do not tempt a desperate man, Trader. Do you mean what you say?"

"If you serve me faithfully. The first service is to find a crew of twenty men who can fight. Say that we are insane, but that you, Loholo, will get the ship past the pirates. Get us a crew without talk, and have them ready to come aboard by dark tomorrow."

"And you'll give me the ship when you return? Mine to sail and command?"

"Yours to sail and command. And the chance at carrying trade from starships all over Makassar. You will become the owner of many vessels if you like."

Loholo grunted. "One is all I need. You'll have your crew, Trader. But this man of yours commands this voyage?"

"Yes. He commands. He has a young apprentice who will be a ship's officer. And there is my guard captain. But if MacLean wants you as an officer, he'll tell you so. I expect he will."

"I was a crew master once, Trader. I can be one again. Until you need me."

12

Riptide

They sailed at dawn. Loholo, now crew master, had brought twenty young apprentices, all well armed. The stores were aboard, and MacLean had fitted the leeboards, huge, fan-shaped, wooden boards pivoted at the small end of the fan and fastened nearly amidships of the vessel. When raised they were like giant shields. MacKinnie got the crew and passengers aboard the night before they were to set out, and watched with interest as MacLean and Loholo helped the crew sling hammocks, cursing the men into place in the narrow space below decks.

MacLean had placed the quarters in a traditional manner, his own cabin right aft with smaller staterooms to each side for MacKinnie and Mary Graham. Just forward of them, Longway and Kleinst had even tinier compartments, really not much larger than

bunks with doors to close them in; then Hal and his
guards slung their hammocks in a compartment which
stretched from one side of the ship to the other.
MacLean insisted that two of Stark's men be on duty
and armed at all times, posted on the quarterdeck
near the great tiller which steered the ship.

In the first light, mist still rising from the water,
the crew was turned out from their hammocks to
man the sweeps.

Loholo clucked his tongue at the arrangement.
There were no rowing benches; instead the men
walked the decks with great oars dipping down to
the water, two men to an oar. The ship moved slowly
away from the shore out into the bay.

"Wouldn't it be better to go at night?" MacKinnie
asked. They stood on the quarterdeck with the other
Samualites, Hal and his guards in full armor. Armor
for the rest of the crew was secured with rawhide
lashings in convenient places about the deck. Just
forward of the quarterdeck Brett and Vanjynk stood
at the ready, also in armor. It was impossible to
make Vanjynk man a sweep, and MacKinnie decided
that it would be senseless to require Brett to do so,
so the two were carried as guards. Their mounts
were stabled in the hold with the cattle *Subao* carried as part of the food supply.

MacLean eyed the distance to the slowly vanishing
shore, then peered through the mists ahead and
astern before answering. "No, Trader. The night would
not keep the pirates from seeing us, and the wind
dies away then. By midday there should be a strong
wind. The sea breeze and the prevailing westerlies
lie together on this shore. It will take a strong wind
to outrun the pirate ships."

"If you say so," MacKinnie said with a shrug. And
if the wind doesn't come up? He shrugged again.

"It's the only chance we have, anyway. Carry on, Captain MacLean."

"Aye, aye, sir." There was a note of the contempt seamen have for lubberly owners in MacLean's voice, but Nathan saw no reason to make a point of it. He needed MacLean to reach Batav.

He went to the rail and stared overboard. Around him the dawn was already turning the dark water clear. Small fishlike creatures swam lazily near the boat, looking at it before they darted away, easily outdistancing the men at the oars in spite of Loholo's shouted oaths. The crew master counted strokes in a tireless voice, keeping a steady rhythm not interrupted when he fell to cursing one of the men: "Sweep, step, back, back, Fool, step, back, back, Pull, you, stinking, filth, Sweep . . ."

MacLean left MacKinnie to stand near the tiller, his eyes on the compass mounted on the small mast just forward of the helmsman. Another mast, well forward, towered above the ship, and on both the sails were laced around the booms, their covers removed and stowed below decks. The sails were ready for instant action. MacKinnie could already feel the morning breeze coming from the south before it shifted to the west in the afternoon.

Mary Graham and Longway made their way over the slowly rolling deck to stand at the starboard rail with MacKinnie. Loholo's calls were clear and slightly musical. "Stroke . . . step . . . back . . . back . . . Stroke . . ."

"Point to starboard, Mr. Todd," MacLean said softly.

"Aye, aye, sir."

"We should see the land over there as soon as it gets light," MacKinnie told his companions. "I understand Loholo thinks we should hug the shore.

There are reefs and rocks only he knows, and he swears he can get us through them without the pirates being able to catch us."

"Interesting," Longway said pensively. "Then why did he not take some other ship through there? Why has the pirate blockade been so effective?"

"You're not supposed to ask that," Nathan replied. "But MacLean thinks it's worth trying anyway. Add something to our chances, and the further we get before the pirates intercept us, the better chance of coming ashore where there aren't any barbarians." It was getting light faster now, and the shoreline could be seen dimly ahead. Above the fog, fifty miles away, the peaks of mountains flashed whitely in the morning light.

"If we can get to those, the barbarians won't matter," MacKinnie said. "All we'll have to worry about will be the pirates. We could even beach and run for it."

"It would be a long walk," Longway said.

"True. But what else can we do?"

Kleinst stood quietly at the rail, and MacKinnie thought he noted a slight tinge of green to the scholar's complexion. If the young fellow couldn't manage in the gentle swell they were experiencing, he was in for big trouble when the real wind came up. Kleinst had kept out of the way the whole time they were on Makassar, although he seemed to have developed a strange friendship with Brett. Nathan had more than once noted the scholar and the singer conversing over wine in the physicist's quarters at the dockside inn.

"Where are these pirates, Trader?" Longway asked. "As a practical matter, should we be getting the oarsmen in their armor?"

"Not for hours," MacKinnie replied. "They stay

well out of the harbor itself, probably afraid of the Navy boys. But they're out there, all right, just over the horizon. You'll see them soon enough."

"Sooner than I'd like," Longway muttered.

It was fully light now. The Eye of the Needle had cleared the eastward landmass to send its rays slanting across the sea. The early morning mists vanished rapidly as the ship moved quickly along, and there was no sound but the commands of Loholo, who had lowered his voice until he could barely be understood on the quarterdeck. "Stroke . . ."

The harbor had dropped well out of sight when the sun burned off the last of the mists. The water was an incredible light blue, the bottom visible not more than three yards below the surface. Long, thin fish darted about, pursued by tentacled monsters nearly a meter in length, green eyes glaring after their prey. Larger creatures of the same general form swam into view to look intelligently at the humans on the boat before swimming lazily away. MacKinnie wondered idly what they were when MacLean shouted from his post at the mizzenmast.

"Hands make sail!" he ordered.

MacKinnie watched with interest as the Samualites gathered in the waist.

"Man the mizzen halyards," MacLean called. He turned to the helmsman. "Turn her into the wind, Mr. Todd. Put the helm over."

"Helm's down, sir."

"Stand by mizzen halyard. Get those gaskets off, there."

Hal and one of the guards took the lacing from the sail, then seized the halyard. "Make sail," MacLean ordered. The big gaff rose jerkily, the men on the throat halyards pulling too fast, but eventually the throat and peak rose together. "Take a turn around the winch. Haul, men. Tauten it, that's it. Haul, you bastards! Now belay it all." The gaff sail flapped in the wind, and the boat slowed noticeably.

"Now forward to the main," MacLean ordered. "Get it up, smartly now." The men ran forward, and the big main, almost twice the size of the mizzen, was hauled up almost as quickly as the smaller one had been. "Man the sheets," MacLean ordered. "You fool, that line over there," he added to a guard who stood looking blankly about. "Stand by to trim the sheets, Mr. Stark."

"Yes, sir," Hal answered. He gave MacKinnie a quizzical look and turned back to his soldiers now turned afterguard. The ship was barely moving through the water now, the men straining at the oars, and Loholo stood silent with his hands on his hips looking at MacKinnie as if to say he had told him so.

"Put the helm over, Mr. Todd. Bring her four points to starboard."

"Aye, aye, sir. Helm's to weather."

The boat turned, and the wind caught the big sails and pushed them off to the right. "Trim those sheets," MacLean ordered. "More. Bring them in. Strain, you blackguards. Belay. Mr. Stark, I'll have the starboard leeboard down."

The boat was skidding sidewise now, moving to leeward as fast as it was going ahead. The oarsmen struggled to keep steerage away, Loholo back to counting the pace when he saw no response from his silent appeal to MacKinnie. Stark cast off the line holding up the great fan-shaped leeboard, and the heavy wood splashed into the water. An iron shoe along its lower edge sank it quickly.

"Mr. Loholo, get those oars in," MacLean ordered. "Quickly, man, and get your crew set." The boat heeled sharply to a gust of wind, almost tumbling the starboard crewmen over the side. "Any man can't stay aboard gets to swim ashore," MacLean said. "Stark, get those jibs up."

The gust heeled the ship, and the leeboard bit into the water. The boat began pulling ahead, slowly gathering way, until it was apparent that it was rushing along, faster than the oarsmen had been able to pull it, and still it gathered speed. A white, creamy wake appeared at the bow, and two quarter waves angled off from the stern. It seemed to MacKinnie that the wind picked up noticeably, and the boat was headed into it. *Subao* rose gently over the waves, rushing along until Loholo stood looking over the side with amazement before making his way aft.

"Yes, Mr. Loholo?" MacLean asked.

The former captain stood looking at his new master in silence, then brought his hand to his forehead in an awkward salute. "She's faster than oarsmen have ever been able to push her, Captain. This may be the fastest ship on Makassar."

"Let's hope so, Mr. Loholo. Faster than the pirates, anyway. Get your men to lookout stations, if you please."

"Aye, aye, sir." Loholo turned to his crew. "Banta, up those shrouds. Move along there, lad, and keep your eyes open. Fast as we're going, we'll be in pirate waters soon." He strolled along the deck, expertly keeping himself erect, as he placed crewmen in the bow and sent the rest to the waist.

"How does she sail, Captain?" MacKinnie asked quietly.

"Well enough, Trader," MacLean answered. "A little better to windward than I'd thought she might. Doesn't point as high as a proper keelboat would, but with a full keel we couldn't beach. As it is, we can go closer to the wind than anything the pirates have got. That's how I expect to outrun them. They'll have to use sweeps, and I don't think they can catch us going to windward. We'll leave the bastards behind . . . uh, your pardon, freelady."

"Don't apologize on your own ship, Captain Mac-Lean. I think it's wonderful what you've managed to do with this primitive boat." She looked up at him, then at MacKinnie. "Can I get you anything, Captain? Trader?"

"Chickeest," MacKinnie said. "If you can cook in this."

"If she can't we'll have cold food the whole voyage," MacLean snapped. "This is perfect weather, Trader. By afternoon we'll face some real waves. I'm not looking forward to the tide either. You may not have noticed, but we had the aid of a strong tidal current going out. It should be even worse when it turns. Best get some practice in the galley now, freelady. Take young Brett down to help you."

"All right, Captain." She stumbled across the deck, looking for handholds, then let Brett take her arm to guide her to the companionway. The ship was heeling sharply, the deck standing at perhaps forty degrees off the horizontal.

It took her nearly half an hour to heat last night's chickeest, and she spilled part of it bringing the pot and cups up to the quarterdeck, but Mary Graham seemed proud of her achievement even so. Now she had the same slightly green cast as Kleinst, and MacKinnie looked around to see the scholar grimly holding the rail and staring at the distant shore to starboard.

"Sail ahead," the lookout called. "Two sails."

Loholo scampered up the shrouds like a monkey, shading his eyes and staring off where the lookout pointed. He bounded down to the deck and trotted panting to MacLean. "Pirates right enough, off the port bow, Captain. Under sail."

MacLean nodded. The pirates were to windward, using square sails to run down toward *Subao*. "Steady as she goes, Mr. Todd. Mr. Loholo, it might be best if you stood with Todd at the tiller. Steering to windward's trickier than just watching the compass, and we'll need more experienced helmsmen. Have you any of your crew who might have some ability?"

"None, Captain. They're all landsmen. Willing lads, but no sea legs."

"You'll have to do it, then. Take your post, mister." MacLean cupped his hands to shade his eyes and stood easily on the pitching deck. True to his earlier promise, the sea was running higher now, and *Subao* heeled farther, making it impossible for anyone but the three sailors to stand without something to hold on to.

"Best tack now and get sea room," MacLean said. "Stark, get your hands to the jibsheets. The gaffs will take care of themselves. Snap to it, man, we haven't all year." Hal and his guards ran to the foredeck, motioning to some of the oarsmen sitting idle in the waist to join them.

"Stand by to let those sheets go," MacLean shouted. MacKinnie was surprised to note that the Navy man's voice carried easily into the wind, although Brett repeated the order from his post at the mizzen.

"Put her helm down, Mr. Todd." The ship swung into the wind, through it, the booms snapping across the deck. One of Loholo's men scrambled to get out of the way, flinging himself to the deck to allow the main boom to pass over him, while the quarterdeck crew, copying MacLean's example, ducked low. The jibs backwinded, pulling the bow around. "Let go of the jibsheets," MacLean shouted. "Now trim them in on the port side. Snap to it. Man the leeboards! Smartly, men!"

The port leeboard was pushed down, and tackles strained to raise the starboard one. MacLean stamped with impatience until the task was done, then turned to MacKinnie. "She's lively enough. Bit slow, easy to get caught in stays. If I end up out of action, remember that. Leave the jibs cleated until the bow's well around, or you'll be in irons."

Nathan fervently prayed he would never have to work the ship himself. At least there was young Todd if MacLean were killed.

Now they were approaching the pirate ships rapidly, and the lookout called down, "Five sails beyond the two ahead, sir."

"That'll be more of the pirate fleet," Loholo said. "Beg your pardon, sir, but the reefs are over there." He pointed off to starboard and ahead.

MacLean nodded coolly. "We can't make that course yet, Loholo. When we've sea room, we'll try your advice." He gauged the distance to the rapidly closing pirate vessels. As they watched, the enemy ships extended their oars, the sweeps working rhythmically, rippling down each of the vessels. The pirate ships were much like *Subao* had been before MacLean's modifications, with more beam to weather storms in the shallow sea but generally resembling her. On the bow of each was carved one of the large tentacled creatures MacKinnie had seen in the water, the stays to the stubby masts running into the nest of arms which jutted forward and upward.

"Idlers below," MacLean ordered. "Freelady, Professor Longway, Mr. Kleinst—go below and stay until you're called, if you please. Mr. Loholo, I can spare you from the tiller until you get your men under arms."

"Aye, aye, Captain." Loholo padded forward to the waist to arm his men.

MacKinnie watched Hal break out crossbows, handing one to each of his Samualite guards and posting them along the waist. The pirates had noted that *Subao* was going to windward without oars, and adjusted their courses to intercept well forward of their present position, so the ships were not closing as rapidly now, but slowly they drew up to three crossbow shots away to port and as many forward.

"I doubt there will be a battle," MacLean said quietly. "Unless they are very much faster with those oars than I think, they cannot possibly catch us."

As if to make his captain a liar, the lookout shouted, "Three sails off the starboard bow. Three sails ahead, sir."

MacLean shook his head. "If they adjust to our strange antics as quickly as these did, we'll have to fight after all." He eyed the distance to the nearest pirate ship. "Mr. Stark, I'll thank you to go forward and stand ready to bring the ship about again. Don't cast off that jibsheet until I tell you. And give me five men on the leeboards."

"Aye, sir." Hal took his men forward, carefully seeing that each man stowed his crossbow along the rail on the low side. MacLean shook his head. "Put them on the starboard side, Stark. I don't need loaded weapons clattering about my decks when we go about.

"Stand by, Todd. I want to cut this as close as possible without letting them ram us." The pirate ships drew closer now, angling in toward *Subao*'s bows in a staggered line. "Fall away a point," MacLean said softly. The ship gathered way, leaping through the water. "Stand by . . . Put the helm over!"

Subao brought up into the wind sharply, hung for a moment, and then fell off to the starboard tack.

"Let go the jibsheets. Now get them sheeted in. Haul those leeboards, you sons!" MacLean was icy calm as he watched the armored prow of the nearest pirate approaching. The sweeps on the enemy vessel were moving faster and faster, and they could hear the drum amidship beating the count.

Zing! MacKinnie heard something snap over his head, and looked up to see a round hole in the mizzensail. Then there was a chorus of sounds, the bolts thudding into the bulwarks. "Get down!" MacKinnie called. Stark, crouching low, half ran the length of the ship to seize his crossbow. All they could see was the great bow of the enemy thirty yards away, white water curling from each side and the beak of the ram protruding slightly from the water in front of it.

The pirate ship bore ahead. MacKinnie stood in silence. There was nothing to do but wait. The iron ram grew larger and larger. Then it seemed to slip behind slightly.

Subao gathered more way, and the pirate ship was no longer aimed amidships. "Hold your course," MacLean said quietly. As MacKinnie watched, the pirate ram fell farther behind, tried to turn more toward *Subao*, and caught her sail aback. "Steady as she goes," MacLean murmured.

The pirate ship passed astern so close they almost touched the oars. A cloud of arrows flew from it toward them, and Stark replied with his own volley of steel bolts. There was a shout from the pirate, then it was gone.

"He'll have to get that sail down before he can row to windward," MacLean remarked casually. "Never catch us now. Masthead! Where are those other ships?"

"Off the port bow ahead, sir!"

"They're directly to windward," MacLean said. "Let's see if they have any sense. Mr. Loholo, you can come back to the quarterdeck now."

"Aye, aye, sir." As Loholo approached, they could see blood on his hands. "One crewman dead, sir. Arrow in his throat. Some holes in your sails, too."

"Yes. Where are those reefs of yours, and when will the tide be out?"

Loholo pointed to a cleft in the hills along the shoreline. "Right off there, sir. Tide's full now. Going out starting in an hour."

"Excellent. Todd, steer for those reefs and get the picture of them from Loholo. We may make use of them yet. Mr. Loholo, how many men does one of those pirate vessels carry?"

"Seventy, maybe a few more, sir. Not all of them sailors."

"How many of them can fight?"

"Most all, sir. That's why they're aboard."

MacLean nodded. "As well they can't board us. Mind your luff there, Mr. Todd, you're too close." MacLean looked along the coast, then thoughtfully tossed a light line over the stern and watched the angle it made with the centerline of *Subao*. "Making more leeway than I like," he remarked to MacKinnie. "And that fellow out there seems to have some sense. The others are trying to close with us, but he's standing well out to keep to windward of where we'll be. This could be rather interesting."

They sailed on. The afternoon sea breeze brought a shift in the wind, backing it around to nearly directly offshore, as the tide turned, running little trails of bubbles out to sea. The first group of pirate vessels was lost behind them, and they were easily outdistancing the second, which made the mistake of closing with *Subao* and ended up under her lee before trying to stroke back to her in the heightening seas. Although they gained at first, the effort was too great for them, and they soon fell farther and farther behind. Now only one enemy vessel remained between *Subao* and open water.

As the chase went on, the shoreline fell away to northward, bringing the wind more directly off *Subao*'s beam, and increasing her heel. The animals in the hold below screamed their protest, a shrill, keening sound unnerving to anyone not familiar with it, causing Brett to rush below to comfort his horses. The pirate ship ran along the shoreline parallel to *Subao*, slowly drawing closer but taking no chances of losing her prey as the others had done. Her captain had trimmed the great lateen sails the boat carried, and kept only a few men at the oars. MacLean stood anxiously at his post, with Loholo now holding the tiller. The crew master learned the task far more easily than MacLean had thought he would, and now held the huge wooden bar easily, balancing himself against the rolling of the ship and watching the shoreline.

"Where are we now, Mr. Loholo?" MacLean asked.

"In shoal waters, Captain. With the tide running out, we'll come to ground in a quarter hour."

"Yes." MacLean looked out at the pirate vessel. "Nothing for it but to work out some more, even if it lets him get closer. Hands forward to trim sheets," he called. "Take her a point closer to the wind if you would, Mr. Loholo."

"Aye."

On the new course they closed more rapidly with the pirate ship, the tide helping to cancel their leeway. In minutes, the current was running so strongly that the line over the taffrail stood off to a sixty-degree angle from *Subao*'s stern.

"Going out fast, Captain," Loholo remarked.

"Mr. Todd," MacLean ordered, "get forward with a lead to call soundings."

The cadet perched himself at the shrouds, leaning out to cast the lead line and calling back in a clear voice. "Three meters . . . and a half two . . . three meters . . ."

"He's closing with us now, Trader." MacLean looked at the pirate thoughtfully. "Guards in armor, please. He may be able to board." *Subao*'s ability to point higher than the pirate vessel was almost negated by the strong tide off the lee bow, and the longer waterline of the enemy ship gave her an advantage in hull speed. MacKinnie looked around the horizon. There were no other ships in evidence.

"As good as we could expect, Trader," MacLean said softly. "We expected to fight a dozen enemies, now there's only one."

"And a half two . . ." Todd called. "Mark two . . . and a half one . . ."

The tide was racing out now. MacKinnie had never seen anything like it, and asked MacLean how the current could be so strong.

"Those two close-in moons make for strong tides," MacLean answered, "and this big shallow basin doesn't really hold much water. Won't take a lot of vertical rise and fall to empty it." The captain looked carefully at the current. "We're going aground in a few minutes, Trader. If we try to run with the tide to keep afloat, that pirate will have us. At least if we're run aground, he can't ram the ship. Might be quite a fight when he sees us high and dry. Or he might .decide to run out with the current and get his friends. You'll have to decide whether to go ashore in that case."

MacKinnie nodded. It seemed to him the enemy

ship was staying close to *Subao*. The pirate might be trapped as well. If they really didn't know these waters all that well, they might think *Subao*'s crew intended to stay afloat.

The leeboard scraped bottom, heaving up ponderously before settling back to its position, then hit again.

"Hands to the halyards!" MacLean shouted. "Get those sails down. Move, damn you!" Then in a calmer voice, "Mr. Loholo, put your helm to weather if you will . . . ease her against the current . . . steady! Sergeant Stark, get your men's backs into it!"

The sails were hauled down, the men pulling desperately. Heavy canvas billowed across the decks, and the Makassar crewmen leaped to subdue it. It was bulkily piled on the booms and lashed in place. The ship swayed, blown against the current by the strong wind, held in place until there was no way on her at all, then began ponderously to make sternway. Loholo balanced off the helm without orders, obviously accustomed to taking ground with ships in the shallow seas of Makassar. As the tide raced away, she settled bow first, straightened, and came to rest on the sandy bottom, angled toward the shore.

"We're fast," MacLean said. He looked out at the pirate ship three hundred yards away. "By the Saints, he's caught! He can't make it against the wind."

The enemy crew was straining at the oars, while others gathered the lateen sail against the mast, but even as they watched, the stern touched bottom. The tide race was incredibly swift, and within seconds the pirate was stuck as fast as *Subao*.

Brett ran to the waist of the ship. He struggled with the hatch cover until Vanjynk rushed up to help him. MacLean shouted from the quarterdeck. "What in the hell are you doing?"

"We must get our mounts up from the hold," Brett called. "Master Vanjynk and I would fight on our horses, Captain."

"Let them," MacKinnie told MacLean. "We're outnumbered, and having a calvary force can help. Look there." He pointed to the pirate vessel. Men were boiling off its decks, but instead of rushing toward *Subao*, they formed ranks on the hard sand alongside their ship.

"My turn," MacKinnie said. "You men see to your armor. Hal, help Brett sway those animals up out of the hold."

The hatch cover was already off, and using the main boom held at an angle by the peak halyard, the two chargers were lifted by bellybands, swayed over the side, and set in place on the sand. Brett and Vanjynk scrambled to saddle their beasts and cover them with chain mail skirts.

"What are they waiting for?" MacLean asked, pointing at the pirates.

"They don't know how many we are, or if we have star weapons," Loholo said softly. "They will listen to their leaders tell them of rich loot, and the insults they have endured from Jikar, and finally they will attack. It will be best if our men are already on the sands unless you intend to fight from the ship."

"Not from here," MacKinnie said. "They've got axes. Give one of them a few minutes unmolested and we won't float off here with the tide. Hal, form the men on the sand behind the ship so the enemy can't see what we've got!"

"Right, Colonel." Pleading and shouting, Stark managed to get the native crew into a semblance of order while his Haven guardsmen took places in a group at one end of the line. Shields glinted in the sun as the men stood nervously.

"Serve out those pikes, Mr. Longway," MacKinnie ordered as the Academician appeared at the companionway. "Then you and the others stay below."

"If you order us, Trader," Longway said. "But I can fight." He came fully out on the deck, and MacKinnie saw that the scholar's portly figure was cased in mail over leather. Together they took the pikes from their racks along the bulwarks and handed them over the sides to the waiting troops. Each of the Makassar natives wore a breastplate and greaves, a metal cap, and a shortsword, and held a round shield on his arm. The Samualites had mail as well. With their pikes in hand, MacKinnie's small force seemed more disciplined, ready to face an enemy.

"They can fight well if told what to do," Loholo said. "They are young men, but the Guilds begin their training early."

MacKinnie eased himself over the rail to join the small group, leaving MacLean and Loholo on the ship. He turned to face his men.

"The important thing is to preserve discipline," he said. "If you stay in ranks, there's not much they can do to you. Keep your shield wall up as long as they aren't close, so they can't bombard us with arrows, and advance when I tell you. I want to hit them with a solid force, not a ragged group of individuals. Hal, have your Haven men form a reserve group behind the main body, and keep their javelins and crossbows ready. I want a solid volley from the crossbows as soon as the pirates get in range, and keep that up until they're too close to reload. Then hold those javelins until I give the order to cast."

"Yes, sir."

"Then wait for my orders. Brett, you and Vanjynk stay with me until I give you the word."

"It is not proper that we stay behind and allow

these groundlings the honor of opening battle," Vanyjnk said slowly.

"Proper be damned. Vanjynk, if you or Brett start a charge without my orders I'll have Hall shoot you out of the saddle. I ask nothing dishonorable, Master Vanjynk, nothing save winning this battle."

"We have agreed to serve the star man," Brett said. "It is proper that we take his instructions, my friend." He clapped Vanjynk on the shoulder. "Besides, what honor have pirates? What is propriety to them?"

"Here they come!" Longway shouted from the quarterdeck.

MacKinnie strode to the bow of the ship and looked around. The pirate group, nearly a hundred strong, was moving slowly and in good order across the sand toward *Subao*. "Hal, get your crossbowmen out at the stern and stand by. Fire when you think they're in range."

"Yes, sir. Guardsmen, right face. March." Stark took his tiny group to the stern and deployed them just beyond it. This put them closer to the enemy than MacKinnie's detachment at the bow.

Nathan eyed the advancing ranks of pirates, now broken up by small tidal pools until there were definite gaps in the formation. There seemed to be no effort on the part of the pirate officer to reform his men. From what MacKinnie knew of similar groups on South Continent, it was a masterpiece of tactics for the pirates to have formed at all before starting a wild charge.

They came on, and Hal shouted to his men. "Ready! Fire!"

Several fell to the volley of crossbow bolts, but the rest came on. MacKinnie watched, but gave no signal. Behind him Brett and Vanjynk talked calmly to their animals, but their voices were rising in pitch. Their eagerness to join the battle sounded through the soothing words.

A second volley cut down more of the pirates, and the ragged army of brightly colored natives, armed only with swords except for a few with axes and shields, curled around toward their tormentors, presenting their flank to MacKinnie.

"Now, men. March out. Follow me and stay in good order. Brett, you and your companion remain behind the shield wall until I tell you."

The pirates were now caught between the two small detachments. Their leader shouted orders, and they broke into smaller groups and hurled themselves toward Stark and his men.

"With me, troops!" MacKinnie shouted. "Keep your ranks. Watch the men to either side and stay next to them." He trotted his group away from his bow, angling away from the ship but moving sternward, keeping the pirate group between the two parts of his army. Some of the enemy turned to face him now. Others continued their charge toward Stark.

Hal fired one more volley of crossbow bolts and his men dropped the weapons. They bent to seize their javelins. As MacKinnie's group closed with the pirates, Nathan shouted, "Now, Hal." Stark's group ran forward, casting their slender weapons, tearing holes in the ranks of the pirates and then MacKinnie was upon them, his pikemen thrusting their weapons forward, as Hal and the Samualites fell on them with sword and shield from the other side.

On either flank a group of pirates now fought MacKinnie's troops, but the main body held back, unwilling to enter the dangerous area between. Then they suddenly broke directly toward the spear points, closing rapidly with the unarmored men, slashing with shortswords. Two of the young Jikarian sailors fell, opening a gap in the line of pikes.

On the other side of the formation the pirates made no headway at all against Hal and his Wolves. Unarmored, with inadequate shields, they did well to hold Stark back, but by sheer numbers were able to do so. A third group darted forward to leap for handholds along the ship's railing.

MacKinnie charged into the gap in the line of pikemen, his sword slashing, shouting to his men to hold firm. A shortsword thrust at him, and he parried, beat hard in quarte, following with a cut to the pirate's neck. His enemy fell and Nathan brought his sword in a whistling moulinette to drive back a second attacker. The gap was too wide to hold with his saber alone, and another enemy tried to circle to his left, only to be impaled by the pikemen, his last stroke falling weakly on MacKinnie's mail. Nathan frantically shouted orders to close the line.

The Jikarians awkwardly moved closer to each other. "Shield to shield!" MacKinnie shouted. "Close it up!" When they had filled in the gap he was able to turn his attention to the group which had charged the ship.

The pirates were stopped at deck level by Longway, who stood sword in hand, thrusting at the face of a pirate who had managed to raise himself almost to the level of the thwarts. MacLean stood with him, while Loholo, shouting in mad fury, jumped to the sands below with an enormous two-handed sword. The native captain sent the weapon whistling around his head and screamed oaths.

"*Subao* is mine!" he shouted. "Filth, slime of the sea, spawn of unwashed carrion eaters! . . ." He lopped off a pirate's head at a blow, then stood with

his back to the ship, holding the rest at bay with the
fury of his attack.

The pirate chieftain, his rank marked by the bright
gold bands around his neck and ankles, shouted commands to his men, breaking them away from combat
to re-form and make use of their superior numbers.

MacKinnie waited until they had broken off the
battle. Then he signaled Brett. "Now!" he shouted.

Brett screamed strange curses. He and Vanjynk
spurred their mounts forward and thundered toward
the pirates, wielding their great swords to crash
through feeble attempts to parry as the enemy tried
to avoid being trampled by their mounts. The beasts
themselves fought, rearing up to strike with sharp
hooves, crashing down to crush men to the sand. A
group of pirates broke and ran as Hal and his
shieldsmen closed swiftly in a disciplined formation
from the other side to hew down the outer ranks.
MacKinnie held his own detachment in place, their
spears held out toward the pirates, forming a wall of
points, while Loholo continued his mad rush, his
great sword singing. The last of the enemy turned to
run toward their ship.

Brett and Vanjynk pursued the enemy across the
sands, but when a group aboard fired on them with
crossbows, MacKinnie shouted them back. He re-
formed his little command behind *Subao* again and
left them to rest easy in ranks while he surveyed the
battlefield.

He had lost two native troopers, killed when the
pirates broke ranks. Several others had deep cuts,
and one had a throwing knife through his shoulder.
In addition, MacLean had caught a wicked cut across
the back of his hand from the dying efforts of a pirate
Longway spitted. The others were unharmed. The
Haven detachment had been always on the attack

and the pirates had little chance of closing with them, nor were their weapons heavy enough to do much damage through chain mail unless given more time than Hal had allowed them.

There were thirty-four bodies on the sand between the two boats. Some wriggled feebly. Most lay well away from *Subao*, cut down in flight by Hal's men or the cavalry in pursuit.

"It's always like that," he explained to Longway and MacLean as he climbed back on board. "I've never seen a battle where at the decisive moment the loser didn't have enough strength to turn the table. Once they lose the will to fight, they're finished. More men are killed in pursuit than battle every time."

"But it seemed so easy!" Mary Graham said.

MacKinnie turned, surprised to see her on deck. "I told you to stay below," he muttered. "As to easy, it wouldn't have been if they'd caught us on our decks. If they'd swarmed aboard with our troops not in formation and no room to maneuver, they'd have won. They were fools to fight on our terms. What can you serve my men for lunch, freelady?"

She swallowed hard before she replied. "Will they come back?" she asked. "It will take time to prepare."

"I doubt they've the stomach for it." He turned to Loholo. "Will they try to attack again after we're afloat?"

Loholo shook his head. "We'll both have enough trouble staying off that shore, Trader. There won't be much time for fighting when the water wall comes."

MacKinnie noted that while they had been fighting, the officers had broken out one of the ship's anchors. MacLean had it carried out and laid in the sand on the seaward side of *Subao*. "We'll need that," he explained. "Without it, the ship might be washed ashore when the tide returns. This ought to hold us until we can sail off."

"Will the pirates have one out?" MacKinnie asked.

"If they have any sense."

"I see. That gives me an idea. I'll have to speak to Brett."

There was no further action, but Nathan kept his crew in ranks on the sand. They ate in place. An hour before the tide was due in, Vanjynk's horse was swayed aboard, and the rest of the crew then took their places on the ship, leaving only Brett and his mount on the sand behind the ship. A few pirates approached to within a hundred yards, but the sight of Brett thundering around the side of the ship toward them put them to flight, and Brett returned to his post as Vanjynk fumed in the waist.

"We'll have need of you, Vanjynk," MacKinnie said. "You stand by to carry out your orders." They waited.

"I see it!" Loholo shouted from the masthead. "The tide's coming."

MacKinnie waved to Brett. "Now!" he ordered.

The mounted rider galloped toward the enemy ship. He stayed well out of arrow range, going around until he found the anchor the pirates had laid out beyond their boat. He cut the anchor cable with a quick slash of his sword, then rode furiously back toward *Subao*. His armor and that of his mount had earlier been put aboard, and as Brett reached the ship, Vanjynk was ready with a belly sling. Rider and animal alike were swayed aboard, as the thunder of approaching water grew louder.

MacKinnie climbed partway up the shrouds and stared seaward. He saw a dark line not more than a kilometer away, and as he watched it advanced at incredible speed, a wall of water three meters in height boiling furiously toward them. The pirates screamed, one standing in the stern of his ship and shaking his fist at *Subao*. There was nothing they could do; by the time they could reach *Subao*'s cable, the wall of water would be on them, and it appeared that no pirate was willing to give his life to make trouble for MacKinnie. Their ship was carried relentlessly toward the rocks as MacLean gave the order to raise sail and prepare *Subao* for her long voyage.

Part Two

LOYALTIES

13

The Hunting Lodge

Twelve light-years from Makassar Malcolm Dougal
cursed as he followed a winding road uphill through
thick forests. The forest had been a game preserve
for all the centuries since the Secession Wars had
devastated Prince Samual's World, but Dougal ignored its loveliness, as he ignored the bird songs and
the calls of the corkborers.

He did not know that the trees themselves had
been imported from Earth. If he had, he would have
cursed them, as he cursed everything of Earth.

He wore plain kilts. His round face, always rabbit-
like in appearance, was screwed into a grimace that
made him look less harmless than he usually did, but
still few would have guessed his occupation. He considered his appearance an asset; as he sometimes
said in rare moments when he could relax with his
friends, what should a secret policeman look like?

155

A corkborer fluttered past, and Dougal actually lashed out at it, although he usually enjoyed the antics of the small flying mammals. Others darted near in curiosity, but Dougal took no notice. As he neared the lodge he muttered more curses.

Twenty years, he thought to himself. No. Be fair. More like fifty. Damn the Empire of Man! Where was the Empire when we *needed* help? When we were trying to rebuild a civilization out of radioactive ash and ruined cities? And now, with our own spaceships not more than fifty years away, the Empire has come—and they won't give us fifty years. They won't give us any time at all. They've come, and I must meet the king in secrecy in this lonely place. . . .

It disturbed Dougal's sense of majesty. Instead of walking up this wooded hill to a lonely log cabin, he should be approaching his sovereign across a purple carpet, or meeting him privately in the working office behind the Audience Chamber. Now those rooms could not be trusted. Nothing could be trusted. The Empire had ears everywhere.

They'll not learn this secret!

But they might. Fear warps us all, he thought. And so I meet King David out here, and not even the royal guardsmen know where His Majesty has gone.

The king's instructions were explicit: Dougal was to tell no one of this meeting, and His Majesty would be alone. No one, not even the guardsmen, were to know the meeting had taken place. Only two men in the universe were to know that Dougal and King David were meeting here.

More did, of course. Malcolm had provided men to cover the hunting lodge. But they were reliable men, absolutely reliable, men who could be trusted to—

"Halt!" Two men stood in the deep alcove of the lodge doorway. Dougal recognized them as guards officers out of uniform. They carried both pistols and rifles, and they stood alertly. One eyed Dougal coldly, then nodded. "Pass, my lord."

But—why? Dougal wondered. As he entered the lodge he had an even greater shock, for the king was not alone under the high-beamed ceiling.

"Our greetings, my lord," David said formally. "We trust you are well."

"Thank you, yes, Sire." Dougal bowed to the king, then to the other man.

In contrast to King David's handsome youthfulness, the Prime Minister was old. His face was wrinkled, and his belly spilled over his waistband. Malcolm Dougal was quite aware that he would probably look much like Sir Giles Og in thirty years—except that he did not expect to live thirty more years. His occupation made that highly improbable.

"I had understood this meeting was to be secret, Majesty," Dougal said.

King David nodded. "It was and it is. Tell me, my lord, how many of your secret police do you have outside?"

Malcolm Dougal said nothing. The king nodded again. "And as I knew you would not let me come here alone, I saw no harm in bringing a few guardsmen as well. Trustworthy guardsmen."

"And Sir Giles?" Malcolm asked.

"He's the reason for the meeting. Malcolm, the budget's no good. Sir Giles must have more money or the administration is going to collapse."

"Raise taxes," Dougal said.

Sir Giles's voice was quite clear and steady, unlike his appearance. His orator's voice and timing had been a major reason for his rise through Parliament.

"I cannot in good conscience ask for higher taxes, my lord. We have the highest taxes in our history at this moment. Yet, between the wars, the mysterious expedition to—" He hesitated over the name. "To Makassar, and the growing amounts the secret police absorb, more than half the kingdom's revenues have vanished. With such high taxes we should not have financial problems—but we do. I must know why."

"No," Malcolm said.

"I think we must tell him," the king said.

"Sire! Your promise—"

King David shrugged. "I gave you my word, Malcolm. I won't break it. Here, let's sit down and end the formalities. There's a lot to talk about. Get us a drink, will you, Sir Giles?"

King David sat in a rustic armchair before an open fire and waved the others to join him. He was not large, and although his features were handsome in shape and design, his face had been disfigured by an early disease, so that the gentlemen of the bedchamber had their work cut out before public appearances. He had not bothered with makeup for this meeting. The small scars gave him a rugged appearance, adding to his look of determination.

"His Majesty has told me nothing," Sir Giles said. He brought small glasses and a bottle of grua and set them on a table near the king's chair. "He told me only that it is vital to the realm that the large sums spent by your office continue." Sir Giles paused. "I am a loyalist, and I appreciate the necessity for police to consolidate our new acquisitions, but I am not prepared to pay for my own enslavement, by the crown or by anyone else."

Dougal laughed, "I do not have in mind enslaving the citizens of Haven, Sir Giles. Quite the opposite—"

"You will pardon my saying that as we do not

know where the money goes, we have no evidence of your intentions—"

"The work is vital to the entire planet," King David said. "My word on it."

"And mine," Dougal added.

"Not enough," Sir Giles said. "Not enough at all."

"I see." Dougal regarded the Prime Minister coldly. "Neither my word nor the king's is good enough—"

"Of course not." The older man lifted his glass. "Your health." They drank. "I am loyal to the dynasty, but I am also loyal to the Constitution. If you cannot entrust me with your secrets, I belong not in the government but in opposition."

"Sir Giles has brought his resignation," the king said.

"I see." Dougal stared into the crackling fire. Without Sir Giles the coalition supporting the government would collapse. The coalition was needed.

Or was it? Could the king rule without a government? Malcolm dismissed the thought sadly. The secret police were efficient, but they would be unable to hold on against an enraged populace. The rights of Parliament had been easily won from King David's father, but won easily or not they would not be lightly surrendered.

And government by terror would never produce what Prince Samual's World needed.

Would anything?

Malcolm quickly reached a decision. "I'm going to tell you a story, Sir Giles. After you've heard it, you will never be far from one of my men. If you ever betray us—"

"Spare me your threats."

"They are not threats. I hoped to persuade you not to ask to hear."

Sir Giles sat quietly for a moment. "I almost believe you have a good reason for what you're doing—"

"I do."

"But I will not give up the Constitution for an unknown reason. Tell your story. But I promise you only that I will keep your secret. I do not promise to help in whatever—"

"You'll help once you know," Dougal said. "My only problem is knowing where to begin." He stared into the fire. "In King John's time Haven became the largest single state on Samual. He consolidated a number of petty princedoms and city-states, and it looked for a while as if the old dreams of a single government on this planet would be realized. But the next step was Orleans, and the Orleanists wouldn't join. The wars went on. Eventually we developed new industries, and unification looked possible again. Except that everything was wasted on wars. Every effort at conquest of the Orleans Republic failed."

"We nearly had them beaten," King David mused. "One more campaign—"

"Almost," Sir Giles said. "Until that damned Colonel MacKinnie of theirs beat us at Blanthern Pass. Iron Man MacKinnie—my lord, I am familiar with our history. What has this to do with the budget? Orleans is our duchy now—"

"It is our duchy because the Imperials came and their Marines helped us defeat Orleans," King David said quietly.

Malcolm nodded. "Precisely. The Imperials allied with Haven, and they are helping us establish a unified government on Samuel. There's nothing on the planet that can stand up to their weapons." He laughed bitterly. "So after ten generations of dreaming about it, we're getting unification handed to us."

"But we're getting it," Sir Giles said. "More slowly than I like."

"It goes slowly and it costs money," Dougal said. "Both for a reason."

"Yes." The young king's voice was hard. "Our goal is to unify the planet, not enslave it. The Imperials will do that soon enough."

"Sire?" Sir Giles carefully set his glass on the table. "The Imperials are Haven's ally. How can they enslave us? They've fewer than fifty people on the planet."

"Allies." Dougal was contemptous. "Everyone assumed they would be allies, Sir Giles. And they did help us with Orleans. But my agents have found out why they did. They intend to use us to unify the planet, then bring in colonists from other worlds. Traders. Petty bureaucrats who want to be aristocrats and who'll become *our* nobility. We will have damned little say in that government."

The Prime Minister was silent for a long moment. The only sounds came from the forest, and from the popping of the logs in the fireplace. "I would not have thought it of them," he said finally. "The Navy officers do not act like conquerors. They do not seem such villains."

"They're more dangerous than villains." Dougal spoke rapidly now. "They're fanatics. The Imperial Navy intends to unify the human race so it can never again fight an interstellar war. If they have to kill off half of mankind to justify Lysander's title as 'Emperor of Humanity' they'll do it."

"Just as we were willing to unify Samual by conquest," David said.

"I see that well enough," Dougal said. "I know what motivates them. The same goal motivates me. If I'd been an Orleans citizen I hope I'd have had sense enough to see that unification was necessary, and worked to gain some status in the union. Which is what we must do for Samual within the Empire." The policeman's voice rose in angry tension. "And by God we'll outwit them yet!"

Sir Giles leaned forward. "What—what are you doing? We can't fight the Empire—"

"No. The best we have couldn't win a single battle," Dougal said. "But despite that, we can be our own masters yet. They have laws, Sir Giles. They have a Constitution. We can exploit that. One of their rules is that worlds that have space travel enjoy a far higher status than those that don't. Worlds with space travel control their own domestic affairs, and have representation in the Imperial Parliament—"

"Space travel? But that's impossible," Sir Giles protested. His eyes widened in sudden comprehension. "You are using the secret funds to build spaceships? How? We know nothing of spaceships—"

"That is the real secret," Dougal said carefully. "And I would very much rather it remained a secret even from you. It will be the strangest secret you will ever hear, and even a hint—a hint—to the Imperial Navy would destroy all our hopes."

"I see," Sir Giles sat again and rested his chin on both hands. The veins on their backs showed darkly against his neat white beard. He turned to the king. "I suppose, Sire, that this hideously expensive expedition to Makassar has something to do with this? That you expect those men to spy out the secrets of spaceships from traveling in them, and bring that knowledge back to us?"

A good cover story, Dougal thought. "Yes."

"It can't work," Sir Giles said. "Sire, my lord, you have not a technical background. I am many years away from my training as an engineer, but I can tell you this: there is not a factory on Prince Samual's World that could build such a thing even were the Imperials to give us free run of their ships. We haven't the basic tools, we don't even know what the problems are. This scheme is madness!"

"There is more," King David said. "We have hopes for more. We have hopes that our expedition to Makassar will return the most priceless cargo ever to come to Prince Samual's World. A cargo of freedom."

"How?"

"Our secret is fragile," Dougal said. "Worse, the Imperials themselves know Makassar's secret—"

"This talk of secrets," Sir Giles said. "You don't understand at all. Your expedition is no secret. The Navy knows your men went there. As to their orders to spy out the 'secrets' of the Navy ships, were you to tell the commandant he would be no more than amused. My lord, you do not appreciate the difficulties involved! It will be a hundred years before we are able to build spacecraft—"

"Perhaps," Dougal said. "And perhaps not." There was an ominous silence as Dougal coldly studied the Prime Minister's face. "You are determined to have it all, aren't you? You leave me few choices. Either I must tell you the rest or have you killed."

"Lord Dougal, I forbid it!" The king's voice was sharp and loud. "I have deliberately turned away from learning of many of the things your police have done in my name, but by Christ you will not sit here and threaten my Prime Minister!"

Dougal spread his hands. "I said I had two choices, Sire." And another behind that, he thought. My men are outside, and the king has few guardsmen here. . . .

"I had not known you were disloyal," the king said. "Your thoughts are obvious to one who has grown up at court."

"I am loyal, Sire," Dougal protested. "Loyal to Prince Samual's World, Haven, the dynasty, and you."

"In that order."

"Yes, Sire. In that order." He stood, a small man in plain kilts, unarmed, his rabbit features almost comical, but the room was filled with menace. "Majesty, Sir Giles, there is nothing I will not do to keep this world free! We will not be ruled by outlanders! Prince Samual's World has been our home for centuries, and what claim has Sparta or Earth itself to rule us?" He visibly fought for control of himself.

"The secret, Sir Giles?" Dougal's voice rose. "It is simple enough, so simple that a careless word will doom our great plan." He smiled wryly. "And I needn't shout it, eh?" He sat again, and lowered his voice. "There is a building on Makassar, a building which the locals believe to be no more than a temple. But inside it is an old library. . . ."

Sir Giles listened with growing horror. It was obvious that neither Dougal nor the king appreciated the magnitude of the problem they had set themselves. When the policeman had finished talking, Sir Giles poured a drink and thought furiously. How could he tell them?

Simple enough. He couldn't.

"There. Now do you understand? Will you aid us?" King David asked anxiously.

"Sire, your cause is noble and just," Sir Giles said. "And certainly the knowledge that your expedition may bring back to us could change our world. But—" He paused, and felt Dougal's cold stare. "There is more to building spacecraft than knowledge," Giles said. "You will grant that I know more of our technical capabilities than you. And I do not think that even with detailed plans we will be able to build a ship."

"We can try," Dougal said.

"And this is where all the money has gone."

"Much of it went to finance the expedition," Dougal said. "The rest is being invested in expansion of the Haven shipyards, and in establishing a secret military base in the Corliss Grant Hills. We have sent many young scholars there. Always there have been legends of communications without telegraph wires and already we can do that. The devices are crude, but they work. In the shipyards we are studying metal working, ostensibly to build metal craft that will travel under the sea—but if we can make them watertight we can make them airtight as well, to withstand the ether of space. Sir Giles, we are doing all we can—"

And worth doing, too, Sir Giles thought. But not for the reasons you think. There is no possibility of a spaceship. Yet, if I say so, they will kill me. The guardsmen and Dougal's secret policemen would cooperate on that. There is only one way I will leave this lodge alive."

He rose and went to the desk. "This is my resignation," he said. He took it and threw it into the fire. "I will help you. But you will forgive me if I am not certain that you will succeed—"

"None of us are," Dougal said. "We cannot even be certain that MacKinnie will return. But without him there is no hope at all."

14

Batav

The harbor at Batav was lined with stone steps leading to the waterfront, and patrolled by great warships flying the Temple flags and banners, saffron-robed acolytes standing in the bows to challenge newcomers. The harbor entrance was closed by a massive chain stretching between huge rafts at the ends of a log boom.

Loholo explained to the guard boats that they were from Jikar, but at MacKinnie's orders did not tell them the ship was commanded by men from the stars. One of the patrol boats escorted them past the chain. *Subao* moved slowly, sails furled, the crew working the sweeps. The bottom was visible below the ship, and gangs of men stood in water to their waists to scoop out mud from the main channel.

"Convicts," Loholo said. "You don't want to run

afoul of the priesthood here. But they do keep the harbor open. Finest harbor on Makassar."

They were shown to a gray stone dock, a niche cut into the harbor sea wall and lined with log rafts so that the ship could be tied up without concern for the enormous tides on Makassar. Nearby another crew of convicts strained at pumps to force silt into barges. Another barge had been filled and was headed out to sea.

"The Temple priests run everything here," Loholo said after they made *Subao* fast to the raft. "There'll be one of their junior deacons along in a while to make you an offer on your trade goods. You'll do best to stall him until you find what the local merchants will pay for part of the cargo, but you'll have to sell some of it to Their Holinesses. If you don't, we'll never leave this harbor."

MacKinnie stood on the quarterdeck of *Subao* and watched the traffic along the harbor street in front of him. In contrast to Jikar, there was activity, but not as much as Nathan would have expected for a large city like Batav. There were not many ships moving about in the harbor, either. Draymen unloaded a cargo vessel four rafts down from *Subao*, but the intervening slips were empty, and there was another large space before the next ship.

High above the harbor stood a chalk-white building, flying the banners of the Temple, great red and blue crosses on a field of black, with a stylized portrayal of the Temple itself at the fly. The old Imperial Library had been built of native granite, and had formed a part of the Vice-regal Palace. Gargoyles and cherubim were carved in stately rows around its cornice, while Corinthian columns held the four porticos at the cardinal compass points. MacKinnie had seen nothing like it on Prince Samual's World, and found the massive strength of the building impressive despite its ugliness.

"That's the Temple," Brett said quietly. He was standing on the opposite corner of the quarterdeck from MacKinnie, with Kleinst and Longway eagerly asking him about the city. "God Himself built it before the Fall, when we were all star men here, and He put all wisdom and knowledge in it. But the men of Makassar were proud, and said that since they had all knowledge, they didn't need God. In wrath, He struck at the Temple—see, you can see on the side there where part of it was rebuilt. But before He could destroy it, the priests reminded Him of His promises to our people, and He spared the Temple, but took from us the knowledge of how to use the great wisdom in the Temple. Only the priests know, and they don't know how to translate the words of the angels when they can make them speak at all."

Brett sniffed loudly. "That's what the Temple priests will tell you. There was a time when they had believers in every city, and their deacons and acolytes controlled whole duchies and kingdoms. In most places, the true Christians like those in Jikar were a little band forced to hold meetings in secret. But now the Temple people don't control much more than Batav, and it's their followers in other cities who meet in secret and fear for their lives. All that happened in two men's lives, or so I am told."

"But what would have caused such a rapid transformation of the religious values of a whole society?" Longway asked with interest. "My observation has been that such changes take a long time unless they come with technological changes. We experienced a comparable collapse of the established church on Prince Samual's World, but gunpowder and disci-

pline and money were more at the root of it than
anything else."

"Star man, I don't know," Brett answered. "But
strange things have happened to us for many years.
The summers are shorter, and the winters colder,
and the plainsmen move to the coasts and attack the
cities because there is less and less to feed them and
their herds in the plains. The people say that God
has turned His face from Makassar."

"Ah," Kleinst said. Everyone turned to look at the
thin faced scholar, who appeared nearly normal for
the first time since going aboard the ship. "Of course.
The orbit of Makassar is highly eccentric, and its
axial tilt is also high. The two have produced reasonable weather in the Southern Hemisphere for generations, but now they are getting slowly out of phase
with each other. The winters will be worse and worse
here, until it is the northern part which is inhabita-
ble. Naturally the barbarians flock toward the equator."

"And of course as they move into the more tem-
perate areas, they destroy the civilizations there,"
Longway added. "But this often produces an internal strengthening of the ruling church. Yet I have
heard of cases where when there was already schism,
the eroding of the civilization would cause many to
turn away from the churches, or look to new ones for
salvation. Yes." They stood silently for a moment
and watched the guard ship take convicts aboard.

Mary Graham brought wine and chickeest. One of
the guardsmen carried the heavy tray for her. During the voyage she had developed amazing skill at
producing hot meals, even when the ship was running before gales which MacLean estimated to be
over sixty kilometers an hour in strength. She had
trained several of the young Makassar guards to as-

sist her, and quickly became absolute mistress of the commissary department of *Subao*.

"Is that the Temple?" she asked, pointing to the huge structure dominating the city.

"Yes, my lady," Brett answered. "Five hundred priests and deacons, and two thousand guards are all quartered in the cells carved in that building. Not that their army has done them any good against the plainsmen."

"But what can the barbarians do against Temple guards?" Mary asked. "You tell me they have no equipment, and the Temple must be wealthy if it has so many soldiers."

"They will not fight the way the Temple wishes," Brett answered. "The plainsmen run before the heavy-armored men, and when the Temple horses tire, the chiefs bring their clans back with ropes and many of them ride around the iron men, lacing them to their steeds, pulling them to the ground. Or the plainsmen move aside and let the iron chargers thunder past, then attack from behind."

"Mobility against heavy cavalry," MacKinnie muttered. "And the Temple guards are drawn away from the walls so they have no place to rest and re-form their troops." He nodded. "But, Academician, I am concerned about the Temple. Can the priests hold this city and their relics against the enemy?"

"Not for long," Longway answered. "If my experience on South Continent is useful, the people of the city will be weary of the fighting, now that their church is no longer thought to be the voice of God. The priests will never be able to rally enough men to hold those walls if the enemy stays at the gates."

MacKinnie nodded. "I've seen the will to fight collapse before. They become concerned with their comforts and neglect their lives, and soon they will lose both. We may have arrived at a critical time."

"But how dreadful," Mary said. "All these people. What will happen to them?"

Brett drew a long breath before he answered. "The men will be killed. The prettier of the women will be carried off and if they are fortunate will find places in the herds of one of the warriors. The youngest boys may be taken in by a clan to be raised as plainsmen. The rest, those who would not fight when the walls were taken, will die to amuse the women of the tribes."

Mary shuddered. "Trader, is there nothing we can do here?" she asked MacKinnie.

"I would not weep for all of the city people, my lady," Brett said. "You have not seen what they do when they find a small band of plainsmen. Life is hard out there, and men do what they have to do."

They were interrupted by Stark and two guardsmen who had been posted at the end of the pier. "Company coming, sir," Hal said. "Not what I expected, not those deacons you told me to look out for. Civilians, I'd say." He pointed to the end of the pier, where two obvious magnates approached. They were guarded by half a dozen well-armed men. "Should I turn out the guard, sir?"

"No, but get as many men as you have ready at the hatches and keep these here on deck. Then come back up when you get the troops posted. Quietly; I don't want to start trouble if there's none coming." MacKinnie watched the group move slowly down the stone pier.

The leader of the group was tall and thin, like a cadaver. He raised his hand, palm toward MacKinnie. "Greetings," he said. "I hope you had a pleasant journey."

MacKinnie frowned. He knew what the man was saying, but—suddenly he realized what he had heard. The stranger was speaking the Imperial language. "Are there any here who understand me?" He switched quickly to a local dialect. "Peace and greetings."

"Welcome aboard," MacKinnie answered in what he hoped was the Imperial speech. "And what may I do for Your Honor?"

The man turned to his companion and said something quickly, then looked to MacKinnie in obvious relief. "Thank the Savior, the Navy has come to find us. Our prayers have been answered. When we heard there was a ship from Jikar, we hardly dared hope."

MacKinnie stared at the small party. The two leaders were both tall and dark, looking nothing like the locals MacKinnie had seen. Their guards, by contrast, were all obviously natives, probably hired swordsmen.

"Come aboard, please," MacKinnie said. "May we make your guards comfortable with wine and something to eat?"

"Thank you."

MacKinnie nodded to Todd, sending him scurrying below to find Hal and arrange for refreshments for the guards. The two star men were helped aboard and led to the owner's cabin below. When they were seated and wine brought, they introduced themselves.

"I am Father Deluca, and this is His Lordship Auxiliary Bishop Laraine. We are representatives of His Eminence the Archbishop Casteliano, Missionary ruler of the Church on this forsaken planet. It is a miracle you have found us."

"I do not understand, Your Reverence," Nathan said. "Surely you have means to call the Navy whenever you wish?"

"No, my son," Bishop Laraine said sadly. "The barbarians have destroyed our transmitter. Brother LeMoyne might have repaired it had they not been so thorough, but in fact we were fortunate to escape with our lives. Two other members of our mission, a brother and a priest, were not so favored, God rest their souls. We made our way to this city, and here we stay, besieged by barbarians with little gold, no communicator, and afraid even to allow these heathen to know our true mission. They burn heretics here, and they believe us to be such. Not that martyrdom is so frightening, but it would hardly accomplish anything for the faith under the circumstances."

"I would not contradict His Reverence," Deluca said, "but in reality these are not heathen. They believe all of the doctrines of the Church except submission to the authority of New Rome. But they also believe they have a divine inspiration, holy relics, enclosed in that Temple of theirs, and that God speaks to them from their Temple. They even have records showing that their bishops have a direct continuity with the first bishops of Makassar. I believe New Rome might rule that they could be accepted in the Church without new ordinations would their hierarchy only submit to authority."

The bishop shook his head sadly. "What Father Deluca says is true enough, but there is no way to dispel them of their illusions. They truly believe these artifacts of theirs contain Holy Writ, which no doubt they do, there being copies of the Bible in the library, I am sure, but they believe their Temple to be a source of continuing and everlasting revelation."

"I see," MacKinnie told them. He drained his glass while he pondered what to tell them. Nathan had no experience at lying to the clergy, his contacts with the priestly orders being limited to one or another of the many varieties of military chaplains who had served with him, and he was vaguely disturbed. He decided on a compromise. "I don't like to tell you this, Your Reverence, but only part of your problems have been solved by our arrival. We have no transmitter either." He used the unfamiliar word cautiously, but no one responded. "We do have gold and we can make your stay here more secure, but it will be some time before we can get back to Jikar. The storm season is coming on, and my native shipmaster tells me there is no way to sail westward during that part of the year. We ran before one westerly gale coming in here, and the seas were dreadful. I am told they get worse."

Laraine showed no emotion at the words, but Father Deluca half rose from his seat, only to strike his head on the low deck beams above him. He sat back down with tears in his eyes, as much from disappointment as the blow. "Then we must stay here in this awful place for another year." He sighed heavily.

"As God wills," Laraine said sharply. "Your offer of money is generous, my lord. His Eminence will be pleased. Will you come with us to tell him?"

"They tell me I should wait until the Temple people come to inspect my cargo," Nathan answered. "After that, I will be honored to meet His Eminence. What does the local priesthood think you are?"

"Merchants despoiled by the barbarians," Deluca answered. "We thought of fleeing to the nomads and trying to win converts among them, but there are few of us, and the barbarians never listen before they kill. Even the Temple has ceased to send missionaries among them. His Eminence ordered us to remain with him until we were sure there was no chance to win over the Temple hierarchy before sacrificing ourselves."

Nathan nodded and filled the wineglasses again. It was, he thought, as well that they had lost the device they used to communicate with the Navy. If they hadn't, he would have had to destroy it himself. The Navy must not be reminded of the library at the same time they thought of Prince Samual's World. But perhaps these Imperials would be useful. At least he might learn something from them. "You have had no success at convincing the Temple people that their holy relics are nothing more than leftovers from the Old Empire?" he asked.

Deluca shook his head. "We brought Brother LeMoyne, who is both a librarian and trained in physics, hoping to show them, but they will not let us near their sacred relics. No one but the priesthood can touch them. And we, the representatives of the True Church, are turned away like Philistines."

The bishop smiled. "There is a certain, ah, humor, in the situation, my lord. That we are turned away from the center of this planet's religion. Or what was once their center, because their authority is fast going. I think now it would have been better had we worked in Jikar first, but of course we couldn't know that."

Hal knocked at the doorway. "Sir, those deacon people are here to examine the cargo. They say they want to talk to the master of the ship, and also the owner. There's fees to pay for using the harbor, and they want to buy all our food and wine."

Nathan stood, stooping carefully to avoid the deck beams. He had learned that after several painful experiences during the voyage. "If you will excuse me, I will speak to the Temple representatives," he told them. "Please feel free to enjoy any of the facilities or refreshments. Your Excellency," he added, bowing.

"Drive a hard bargain with them," the bishop growled. He waved dismissal.

There were three of the robed Temple deacons on deck. There were also two uniformed guard officers, while a rank of ten swordsmen stood at rigid attention on the pier below. The guard uniforms were blue and crimson with silver decorations, the officers' hats plumed, and the sergeant of guards carried a gold-headed baton. The discipline of the men, and their weapons, made MacKinnie realize that the Temple commanded a trained fighting force. Or at least they could obey orders. He wondered why, with their discipline, they had not destroyed the barbarians. Too rigid in their tactics, he thought, remembering Vanjynk and the battle on the tide sands.

One of the officers stepped forward from the group around Captain MacLean and Loholo. "Are you the owner of this vessel?" he demanded.

MacKinnie nodded. The officer continued, "I present you to His Excellency, Sindabaya, Junior Archdeacon of the Temple of Truth."

"Peace and greetings," one of the gray-robed men said. "It is customary to bow to me when receiving blessings, Trader. Are you ignorant of the proper forms, or merely a heathen?"

"Your pardon, Excellency," MacKinnie protested. "My thoughts were on the plight of our civilization, and not the more important things at hand." He bowed, receiving another blessing for his trouble.

"It is well. We have not seen you in Batav before, Trader, and when we last saw your shipmaster he had his own ship. Why is this?"

"Pirates, Your Excellency. In all Jikar, there are

few merchant ships remaining, and few merchants to buy them, because the army of Jikar takes all the goods for the great expedition. They intend to fight their way through the barbarians before sending the fleet to destroy the nests of pirates."

The officer who had spoken looked up hurriedly, then conversed in low tones with another robed figure before speaking. "Jikar is not large enough to put forth such an army or fleet," he said flatly.

"Oh, this is true, sir," MacKinnie said. "But the Guilds have made alliance with other cities, and many of the people of the plains and hills have fled to Jikar for assistance. Then, the fleet captured many pirate vessels by surprise when they dared sail too close into the harbor and were left by the tide. The water ran red for two changes of the tide after the battle on the sands, and the Guilds had a large fleet, but few with whom to man it. But when their war on the land is finished, they will turn to training the young men to be sailors, and there is talk of bringing the fleet north, east perhaps, bringing many merchant ships under the protection of fifty galleys of war. But, I thought, what use to go in such a number? Prices will be low, when there are so many goods for sale. But if now, when there are no ships from Jikar, if now I sail to Batav, and east, and south, why, then trading will be better, and my friends will remember me when the great fleet comes. . . . Or so I thought. And I was told that the great Temple, the home of wisdom itself, was in need, and thus I brought my cargo, and my foodstuffs; I will sell them to the Temple saving only what must remain to feed my men, and I ask no more than a pittance beyond what it has cost me to bring the goods."

The gray-robed men muttered among themselves,

and their spokesman said, "Your piety is noted. What have you for the Temple?"

Despite MacKinnie's intent to be generous, it took hours to agree on the price of the cargo. The deacons were so accustomed to haggling with traders that even when it was not necessary they bargained. Meanwhile their officers inspected, poking into the holds and looking in the deck boxes.

The priests noted the amount of food aboard and heatedly disputed MacKinnie's estimate of what he would need for *Subao*'s own consumption. They insisted that more had to be delivered to the Temple. MacKinnie knew from their concern with foodstuffs that the siege was more serious than the Temple would admit.

"They have to be desperate," Longway whispered. "I've spoken with one of the guards. They're taking everything edible from any ship that calls here—and there are fewer ships every month."

Eventually the bargain was struck, and a gang of Temple slaves swarmed aboard to carry away what the Temple had purchased. The soldiers stood guard over them and searched each for stolen food or weapons. The deacons watched the soldiers and noted on wooden-backed slates what was taken and what was left aboard, how much was owed to MacKinnie, how many slaves came aboard, and how many left.

As the last of the goods was taken ashore, Sindabaya joined MacKinnie and his staff on the quarterdeck. "We guard more than the true faith," the priest said. He waved his hand to indicate the city and the harbor. "For all time that we record, the Temple has been the source of wisdom and hope for the people of this world. When other cities fall, we hold the means to build them again. If the Temple falls, what will be the source of knowledge? When God brought men to this place from the stars above, He set the Temple to watch over them and give them truth. That is our burden, and we will not fail."

MacKinnie watched an officer drive one of the slaves into his place in the ranks, and said nothing. Sindabaya noted Nathan's expression and grimaced. "The world has changed. Once they went singing to their tasks. Ships brought wealth to be laid at the steps of God's Temple. Now few ships comes, and the barbarians wait outside the walls, and my officers beat the convicts as I watch. But there is no other way! They will not work without blows, and the work must be done! The Temple must be saved!" He turned to the group on the deck and raised his hand in blessing, watched them narrowly for a moment, and left the ship.

Deluca climbed carefully to the quarterdeck as MacKinnie watched the Temple party drive men and ayuks, both overloaded, down the stone streets toward the warehouses.

"Now that they have inspected your ship," Deluca said, "it is lawful for you to leave it. Will you visit the Lord Archbishop?"

MacKinnie nodded, selecting Longway, Kleinst, and Todd to accompany them. Deluca assured them that his own merchant's guard would be sufficient, and would escort them back to the ship after their interview.

"But you will need our guards," Deluca told them. "The streets are no longer safe. Thieves have banded together in great numbers, and attack even armed men. Our own guards are trustworthy only when together, yet there is nothing to steal and no place to buy food with what gold can be found. The city feels no hope for the future. Only the Temple has the will to fight. The people of this city once ruled the world, but now they are ruled by the Temple."

They walked along the broad waterfront street. MacKinnie noted the empty dockyards, warehouses with the doors standing open, and everywhere the beggars and crowds of surly men who had once been longshoremen and sailors, owners of shops, landholders of small farms outside the walls of the city. It was little better away from the waterfront. They moved through a series of narrow, twisting streets overhung with buildings, lined with nearly empty shops. Men lay in rags even in the center of the smaller streets, and often they blocked the way.

They emerged from this maze of alleys to broader streets, each with a stone-lined ditch running down its center. The ditches were partially filled with refuse, but surprisingly little for so primitive a system.

"The men on Temple charity carry away the garbage," Deluca explained, "and bring barrels of water to wash the sewage away in the few dry weeks of the year. There is heavy rain in this city almost daily, but it never lasts long. This is the cleanest city on Makassar."

MacKinnie remembered Jikar, which was swept daily by the Guild apprentices, but said nothing. Batav was cleaner than he expected a primitive city to be, certainly more so than the garbage-strewn warrens of South Continent.

There were people in the streets. Some wandered through the ground-floor shops, although there was little to buy. Every shop had a large crucifix at its door, and a wind chime whose major feature was a replica of the Temple from which various shells and other sounding materials hung. Most of the population was small and dark, although there was a fair number of the taller, fair-haired men like Vanjynk.

The tallest were still smaller than MacKinnie and the two clergymen, and here and there someone would turn to watch the group before staring off at nothing again.

Once, MacKinnie saw a group of uniformed Temple guardsmen, with a bright-yellow-robed official walking in their midst. He asked Deluca who the man was, and was told, "A tax collector. Some of them have taken minor orders beyond the deaconate, but are not full priests. They don't allow the priesthood to work directly on squeezing the population, but a lot of them have served a trick in that occupation before they take final vows."

They arrived at a small courtyard, behind which stood a massive stone and log house. Two swordsmen stood in the courtyard, and opened the iron gates when they saw the bishop, then went back to their posts, lounging carelessly against the gate pillars.

"Two weeks arrears in their pay," Deluca told Nathan. "It is strange. Many men in this city have nothing to eat, and you would think they would be glad of duties where they are well fed and have at least some money, but more and more throw themselves on Temple charity, work in the streets when they work at all, and refuse honorable employment. The city has lost its heart."

MacKinnie nodded. The barbarians were at the gates, but the men of the city either thought themselves lost already, or refused to think about it at all. Only the Temple kept the enemy at bay, providing whatever spirit Batav had been able to muster. Nathan doubted that even the iron-willed Temple believers would be able to hold things together for long.

The inside of the house was sparse, showing both the lack of funds which had furnished it, and, perhaps, the austere temperament of the Archbishop. MacKinnie was shown into the great hall, where His Eminence sat in ragged splendor, staring at the dying embers of a fire which was not really needed to heat the room.

"As we supposed, Your Eminence," Laraine said, "the ship was from the west. And more than we dared hope, it is owned by men from the Empire, although by their accents they are from a part I have never visited. A colony world?" he asked, turning to MacKinnie.

"I didn't ask your origin when I offered to help you, my lord," Nathan replied. "Is it necessary to discuss mine? The Empire contains many worlds, and the citizens of some are more fortunate than those of others. But despite the contempt the Empire feels for my world, it is my ship and my gold which can save your lives. We may even be able to help you in the work you came to do."

Deluca gasped, but before he could speak the Archbishop said, "He speaks well. Let him continue, for God often sends help in strange disguises. Our work is with the souls of all men." The old man waved toward a chair. "I gather that you have no way of calling the Navy to assist us?"

"We are not permitted such devices, my lord."

The Archbishop nodded. "A colony world." He nodded again. "The Navy could do nothing even if you could call them. Once we are dead, they will send a punitive expedition, and the Imperial Traders Association will be the loudest voice in demanding vengeance for the deaths of the priests of the Lord. The Church has more than once been used as a pretext for Empire."

"I do not understand, my lord," MacKinnie said.

"The Emperor has no wish to conquer these

worlds." At MacKinnie's puzzled look, the old man halted. "Bring our guests something to drink." He turned to MacKinnie. "You know nothing of Imperial politics. Are you a member of the Church?"

"New Rome has not yet come to my world, my lord. We are Christians, more or less. I was baptized into the orthodox church, which I am told is acceptable to New Rome."

"Forgive my curiosity; it was not idle. It follows that you know nothing of Imperial politics. What are you doing on Makassar?"

My king has sent me to head a trading mission, my lord. He rules the largest civilized country on my home world, and is allied with the Imperial ambassador. The Navy is aiding him in the subjugation of the planet."

The Archbishop nodded. "But you are not a Trader. Nor are any of these with you. Please, do not protest. You cannot deceive a man of my years. You are a soldier, and these others, what are they, spies? It does not matter. And here you are, on this primitive planet, having come from a world which is itself primitive . . . and you talk of aiding us! It is admirable, but I fail to see what you can do. Still, such courage should be rewarded, if only with information."

He paused as servants brought wine and additional chairs for the others. "This is not very good wine," Deluca said. "But it is all we have here. The Trader has far better on his ship."

"Wine does not make the day," the Archbishop told them. "It is only a vehicle. Look at them, Father Deluca. Barely able to speak the Imperial language, knowing nothing of the capital and its ways, voyaging across space in ships they cannot understand. . . . If the Church could bring men to as much faith in her teachings as these men have in themselves!" He tasted the wine and grimaced.

"You and I have the same mission, my lord Trader," he told MacKinnie. "We are agents provocateur, sent to aid the Imperial Traders Association. The difference is that I know it, and you do not."

"I do not understand."

"I did not expect you to understand. You believe you are here for some other purpose, some great mission to save your own kingdom perhaps, certainly something more important than bringing back gold for your planetary king. And we are here to bring these people back to God. But both of us will serve the ITA as surely as we would if they had hired us."

The room was still as they waited for him to continue. "The Navy will not permit the Traders simple conquest. I am sure that you know that no good military force will fight for a standard of living—their own or anyone else's. It takes God, not gold, to put heart in a soldier. The Navy fights for a cause, for the Emperor and the Church, for New Annapolis, for the Oath of Reunion, but never for the ITA. The Navy will not simply come in here and set up kingdoms for the Traders.

"So they use us. They get us sent here, and prevent the Navy from giving us protection . . . but after we are slaughtered, it will be the ITA delegates who shout the loudest for vengeance. 'Have to teach the beggars a lesson,' they will say. And the same for you colonials . . . back on your planet there is opposition to the Empire. I don't have to know where you come from to know that. And Imperialism won't ensure much loyalty. The ITA will find them troublesome. But the really troublesome people will be the most patriotic . . . Do you think they will not join when the ITA recruits them for a merchant army to punish this planet? To revenge you? Neatly solving two problems, the conquest of Makassar, and the removal of leaders and soldiers, from wherever you come from. It is an old and tested formula and it works."

"Why do you permit them to use you, my lord?" MacKinnie asked.

"Whatever your reasons, would you have refused to come here if you had known?" the Archbishop answered. "I thought not. Nor could I refuse to bring the Word of God to the heathen." The old man coughed, his thin shoulders shaking violently. "Now go back to whatever plan you have, but remember the ITA. They have large resources, and they have power, but they have no virtue. One day the Navy will tire of being used and kill them all, but others will spring up in their place. There is always the ITA.

"I thank you for your frankness, my lord. Academician, have you anything to say?" MacKinnie added, turning to Longway.

"Not at the moment. I need time to think about all this. I am much afraid the Archbishop is right. You can see the counterparts of the ITA in King David's court. The money-grubbers are everywhere."

"My lord," MacKinnie asked, "if we can aid you in bringing these people to the Church, and yet give the Traders no reason to demand Navy intervention here, can you help us?"

"With what?"

"At the moment, I can't tell you. It isn't my secret, and I'm not sure what you can do in any event."

"I am not unwilling to help you in principle . . . but before you ask it, remember to whom you speak. I am an Archbishop of the Church. I am cynical about some of the Church's officers and many of the

Imperial advisors, but do not be deceived. I am a loyal subject of the Emperor and a servant of the Church."

MacKinnie nodded. "I would ask nothing dishonorable. We can talk about these things later; now I had better return to my ship."

The old man stood and offered his hand, and after a moment MacKinnie knelt to kiss the great ring. As they left they saw him raise his hand in blessing, muttering words in a language MacKinnie had never heard.

15

The War Minister

MacKinnie stood atop the high walls of Batav and
wished for binoculars. He had bought a primitive
telescope, but the lenses were not good and the
images were blurred, so that it was better to study
the barbarians without optical aids.

He watched for five days, looking out across the
low, rolling hills and cultivated fields, watching as
the maris rode swiftly from gate to gate. They had
camped almost within bow-shot of the city, their
tents and wagons contemptuously near the city gates,
and constantly they taunted the city's defenders, dar-
ing them to come out, shouting insults and obsceni-
ties until the Temple warriors were roused to blind
fury.

On the fourth day a small party of armored men
rode out of the city to attack the nearest enemy

187

camp. The heavy Temple cavalry rode through the enemy, their warhorses trampling the light-armored enemy into the turf, their swords hewing a path through the barbarians, and they shouted triumph. Nothing could stand before them in the charge. But slowly the charge faltered. The great warhorses tired, as did the men. Maris raced to the battle, group after group as the word spread, until the Temple troops were overwhelmed, surrounded. They vanished in a sea of swarthy men, and the sounds of battle died. That night the screams of dying comrades were added to the taunts hurled at the remaining Temple troops.

The day after the disaster MacKinnie asked for audience with the Temple hierarchy, claiming that he had valuable information about the war; information which he could reveal only to a high officer. Meanwhile, Stark drilled *Subao*'s crew, forcing them to practice with sword, pike, and shield, marching them in formation to the beat of drums, throwing javelins and firing crossbows in volley, and always marching, holding formation as they quick-stepped about the pier. Their activities attracted notice from the officers of the Temple guard, and on their tenth day in Batav a small party approached the ship.

"We are to conduct you to the Temple," MacKinnie was told. He was ushered to the gates by the officer, then turned over to two gaily clothed attendants who guided him through lavishly decorated halls hung with tapestries and banners. The Temple was a jumble of contrasting chambers and passages, brilliant colors suddenly becoming plain stone walls, rich furnishings and then spartan utility. They climbed stone steps to a row of cells set into the wall high above the Temple courtyard. The officer scratched respectfully at the closed door of one of the cells.

"Enter."

The officer opened the door and stood aside. A black-robed priest sat at a small table, quill pen and inkpot before him. A litter of parchments was strewn about the room, and on the wall behind the priest hung a large map of the city and countryside, roads and villages sketched in detail to a distance of fifty kilometers from the walls.

"Father Sumbavu, the outlander you asked to see," the Temple officer said. "He calls himself Trader Captain MacKinnie." The man stumbled over the pronunciation but managed to say the name correctly.

Nathan had been told that Father Sumbavu served as minister of war for the Temple. There were others who ranked far higher, but few had more power. Sumbavu seemed to care little for the cope and miter of a bishop, and less for other trappings of power, but his men served him without question. Nathan noted the contrast between the sparsely furnished cell and the richly decorated rooms of the Great Hall of the Temple; Sumbavu was concerned with realities, not symbols.

The bare-walled cell was high above the outer battlements, and the narrow window looked across the city, to the wall, and beyond to the barbarian camps. Nathan could see small bands of maris riding endlessly around the gates. They stayed just out of bow-shot. Low, rolling hills, covered with grass and dotted with grainfields, stretched out to the horizon. A few roads crossed the plains, and the ruins of burned villages stood at their crossings.

The priest raised his hand perfunctorily in the ritual blessing, and MacKinnie bowed. Before he could straighten, the priest asked, "Why do you waste my time?"

"But you asked to see me, Father."

"You asked to see a member of the hierarchy. You

say you have information about the war. Now you are here. What have you to tell me?"

"Your Worship, I have some experience with fighting these barbarians. In the east, they have been driven from city gates. Although I am but a Trader, I have commanded men in battle against these plainsmen, and I wished to find if our methods have been tried. We drove them from the gates in the south." MacKinnie stood as stiffly as a cadet on parade, waiting for the man to speak again, but there was only silence. Nathan studied the priest at length.

He could not guess Sumbavu's age. The face showed no lines, and there was no gray in the closely cropped hair, but the hands were worn with work, and perhaps with age as well. Sumbavu returned the intense gaze. "Why do you think you can do what we cannot? We have the finest soldiers on Makassar, and they have done nothing against these hordes. We have always beaten them back in the past, but there are too many of them now." He rose and stared out the stone window. His hands were tightly clenched, so that the knuckles turned white.

"It is not the quality of the soldiers, Your Worship, but their manner of fighting. Your guards have excellent discipline, but there are not enough of them. Your lords fight splendidly, but the cavalry is never properly supported to fight against these plainsmen. I have seen little of your cavalry—they have mostly been killed, have they not? I saw fifty of them taken."

"Those not dead live in the city. There were not many at any time, and they have lost hope. Three times the armored servants of the Temple and the men of the great families rode out that gate. Three times they charged and nothing stood before them. And three times they were defeated, cut off, scattered, driven like straws before the winds, the few survivors riding back into the gates in shame. There are always more of the barbarians, but there are never more of the sons of the great families. And you say that you can do what our greatest warriors could not? Have you perhaps a thousand ships at your back, bringing a new army?" He looked closely at MacKinnie, then motioned to a hard wooden chair. "Enjoy what comforts I allow myself and my visitors," he muttered. "There are few enough. And tell me how the men of the south defeated the barbarians."

MacKinnie sat and chose his words carefully. "It is a matter of combining the foot soldiers and the mounted men so that they support each other," he told the priest. "When they are combined properly, the barbarians cannot defeat them."

"There are not enough soldiers," Sumbavu said. "No matter how clever you may be, you cannot make a few win against thousands."

"Not true, Father. We can make each man do the work of ten. And there are the idlers of the city, the hireling swordsmen, the thieves, the people of the city. They can fight."

The priest shrugged. "If they would. But for each of them you drive into the battle you must have a loyal man to watch him and keep him from running. It is not worth it."

"If they are treated as men, and trained properly, they can fight. We do not need many. But they cannot be treated like cattle or slaves. They must be free soldiers."

"You propose to give arms to the people? You would destroy the Temple?"

"No. I would save it. The Temple is doomed, Father Sumbavu. You are as aware of that as I." MacKinnie gestured toward the window. "The city will fall within the year. I have seen the empty docks, and I am told of the harbors closed against you. I see the people sleeping in the streets while the barbarians harvest the crops. You cannot drive the enemy away until he has eaten everything in your fields. Their supplies will last longer than yours. Your Temple is doomed unless you can drive away the enemy, and quickly."

Sumbavu struggled to keep his icy calm, but his hands moved restlessly across the desk. "And only you can prevent this? You are indeed a man blessed by God. We have held this city for five hundred years. What have your ancestors done? Lived in dirt houses?"

"What I have done is of no matter. It is what we can do."

"And how will you go about saving the city? What is your price?"

"I have no price for saving the fountain of all the wisdom on Makassar. I ask only what I will need. Weapons. Pikes and shields. Authority to recruit men. And I will have to inspect the soldiers, talk to the heavy cavalrymen. I will require a drill field to practice my men. And the men on Temple charity must be brought to it, so that they can be armed. I have no price, but I have much to do. We can save this city and the Temple if you will but listen."

The priest spread his hands and looked intently at his palms. "Perhaps it is the will of God. There is no other plan. It can do no great harm to allow you to train this rabble, for when you and they are killed that will be all the longer our rations will last. I will see that you get what you need."

An army formed gradually on the parade ground outside the Temple. It did not greatly resemble an army. In the first week the men had to be driven to the drill field; they stumbled through their paces, unable to understand orders and unwilling to work. But as they were given weapons and their training continued, a new sense of self-respect slowly pervaded the ragged group. Men who had recently been beggars found themselves alongside sturdy peasants from outside the walls, and mixed among them were younger sons of merchant families ruined by the siege. Under MacKinnie's pleas and Stark's driving, they began to hold their heads higher, to thrust their pikes into the target dummies, even to scream war cries. After the third week of training, MacKinnie called a conference.

"We don't have long," he told the group. "Sumbavu is anxious to know what we are doing, and I have to report to him. You want to be careful of that man. He's a lot sharper than he looks or acts. What's the status of our army?"

"The infantry's so-so," Hal reported. "The Temple troops are fine, but they don't know what to do and they're so sure of themselves they don't want to learn anything new. The people's army can carry pikes and hold up their shields if you don't want them to do it for too long. Weak as cats, most of them. And we'll never get any archers out of that crowd. The Temple's got a fair number, and that's all you'll have."

"Can they hold against a charge of light cavalry?" MacKinnie asked.

"Don't know, sir. They'd never stop the heavy stuff, but they might hold against the plainsmen if they believe in themselves enough. But they have no confidence, Colonel."

MacKinnie noticed Longway's start at Hal's slip, but said nothing. "What of the cavalry?" he asked

Brett. "Can they fight in formation? Have they had enough of that cockiness beat out of them to make a disciplined force, or are they going to go charging out into the enemy and scatter?"

"Vanjynk and I have talked to them, Trader," Brett replied. "But their honor is all they have left. Still, these are men who have been beaten before, and after all, it is only barbarians they fight. . . . But it will be difficult to call them back from victory."

"You'll have to," MacKinnie said. "It's the only chance any of us have. Those men have to be taught to charge home, form ranks again, and get back to the shield walls. Any of them that try the grandstand act will be left out there dead. Try to drive that elementary fact through their heads. And add to it the fact that if they're killed their city falls and the whole honor system they're so proud of goes with it. They're fighting to preserve their honor."

"Yes, but by means which to them are dishonorable," Vanjynk said. "They listen to me as one of them, and I have faithfully told them what you desire. I have even come to believe it. But it is strange to them."

MacKinnie nodded. "Strange or not, they'll have to learn. Now what about the commissary department?"

Mary Graham smiled proudly. "That's in good shape," she said. "We have enough wagons now."

"I thought we were short of animals," MacKinnie said.

"We are, but they were hitching them all wrong," Graham said. "They were using leather straps. I had the carpenters make proper collars from wood, and now the horses don't tire as much. We still don't have enough, but the ones we have can carry more."

"Good."

"We have the wagons, but not much grain," she

continued. "If you can protect our baggage trains, we can supply your men for a few days. There won't be a lot to eat, but something. After that, we'll have to find forage outside. We might even be able to harvest some grain if our farmers are protected."

"So we have a partially disciplined force of infantry, some cavalry who may be useful and may not, some Temple archers and guardsmen who are our best soldiers but don't understand what's needed, and one whole hell of a lot of barbarians. An interesting situation." He thought for a few moments, staring down at a copy of Sumbavu's map young Todd had laboriously made, then came to a decision.

"We need a demonstration. I'll give each of you a week to select the best men you can, men you think won't break and run and who will obey orders. I'll need provisions for about two days for twice that number of people, and a group of your best-disciplined cooks and camp workers," he added to Mary. "We're going to make a show of force against the enemy. The primary purpose will be to convince our own troops that we can beat barbarians." He stood, dismissing the meeting. "Hal, stay with me for a moment, please."

When the others had left, Stark said, "Sorry about the slip, Colonel. It's too much like a campaign, and I'm not used to being a spy."

"We'll survive. Have you picked the headquarters group?"

"Yes, sir. Using the troops we brought with us at a steadying force we've got a pretty loyal company. I think they'd fight the Temple people for us if they thought they could win. Anyway we can control them. You lead them to a victory, they'll be ours for sure."

"Excellent. We must have that headquarters group,

or when this is over there won't be any point to it all. All right, Sergeant, you can go."

Hal stood, grinned for a moment, and saluted. "Old times, Colonel. Different Wolves, but old times."

MacKinnie carefully armed himself before a visiting Sumbavu. He struggled into chain mail, threw a bright crimson cloak over his shoulders, donned gold bracelets and necklace, and fastened his surplice with a jeweled pin before buckling on a sword made on Prince Samual's World. The mail and sword were similar in design to Makassar products, but better than anything they had encountered on Makassar. Their possession imparted considerable status to MacKinnie's group. Sumbavu was standing at the battlements above his cell when MacKinnie was brought to him.

"You betray true colors, Trader," the priest said. "You are more the soldier than the Trader, are you not?"

"In the south, Father, Traders and soldiers are the same thing. At least live Traders are. There's little peace there."

"Or here. It was not always thus." The warrior-priest looked out across the great plain beyond the city wall. "There are more of them today. The grain is ready for harvest, and they are formed to protect it from our fire parties. We could burn the crop, but only at the cost of the balance of our knights. I do not think any would return to us alive."

"Yet, there may be a way, Father," MacKinnie said. When the priest glanced quickly at him, he continued, "I wish to take a small party outside the walls. We will not go far."

"You may take as many of your useless mouths as you please. You have made them march with their heads up, but they are not soldiers. They will never be soldiers."

"I need more than my peasants," MacKinnie said. "I will require fifty archers of the Temple and fifty mounted men."

"A fourth part of the archers? And nearly as great a part of the knights? You are mad. I will not permit it."

"Yet, Father, it is worth doing. We will show you how the barbarians can be defeated. And we will not go far from the walls. The archers and knights can seek shelter there if my men do not hold—and there can be no less of honor if they retreat because others failed them."

"Where will you be?"

"With the spearmen at the van."

"You risk your life to prove these men? You believe, then. Strange."

MacKinnie looked across the plains, to see another band of barbarians approach the walls. There seemed to be hundreds in the one group alone.

"You will take your men into that," Sumbavu said. "You will not come out alive."

"But if we do? It will put heart in the others. Remember, if we do nothing, the Temple is doomed."

"Yet if you slaughter my archers and knights the doom will fall faster. . . ." The priest studied the camps below, watching knots of horsemen dart toward the walls, then turn away just outside the range of the archers at the walls. He fingered his emblem, a golden temple with an ebony-black cross surmounting it, and turned suddenly.

"Do as you will. You are mad, but there are those who believe the mad have inspiration from God. It is certain that I have none." Sumbavu turned and stalked away, age showing in the set of his shoulders.

16

The Walking Wall

MacKinnie used a week training the picked men for the sally. Finally Hal reported that they were as ready as they could be in the time they had, and assembled them in the marshaling square just inside the gates. His cloak streaming behind him, Nathan mounted the small dais near the gates to address the men.

"You will win today a victory such as has never been seen on this world," he shouted. "There will be no end to the songs of this day. Your homes will be saved, and you will come to glory. Besides, what life is there huddled behind walls? What man hides from his enemies when he can go out and kill them? Today you are all men. You will never be slaves again."

There was a feeble cheer, led by Hal's picked guardsmen scattered through the ranks.

"It'll have to do," Nathan told his sergeant. "They won't believe much of anything until they see they can hold the enemy. But will they fight long enough to find out?"

"Don't know, Colonel," Stark answered. "We've done all we could with them, but most of the spirit was beat out of them before we got here. They might."

"They know what to do," MacKinnie said. "Now it's up to us to make them do it. Get them in ranks and open the gate."

"Yes, sir."

The army was formed as a wedge, spear and shield soldiers at the edges, the cavalry, archers, and supply wagons inside. Picked men held the point, which was rounded to be as wide as the gate would permit. They were to march out in a column, with the sides moving swiftly on the obliques to make the triangular formation they had practiced on the Temple drill field. The crimson uniforms of the Temple archers and the gaily colored armor of the knights formed a brillant contrast to the drab leather garments of the pikemen as they stood in ranks waiting for the gate to open. Wherever possible, the men in ranks wore breastplates, helmets, greaves, but there were not enough to equip them all. Some had only spear and shield, with a small dagger in their belts.

MacKinnie looked over his force in final inspection. He swallowed the hard knot that always formed in his stomach before action, and wondered if any soldier ever managed to avoid that tension. Then he waved, and the gate opened.

"Move out!" Stark shouted. "Keep your order. Just like on the drill field. Get in step, there."

Young drummers scattered through the reserves

tapped cadence as the small force sallied out the gate. When enough of the spearmen had emerged to form a shield wall, MacKinnie sent out the cavalry, then strode swiftly through them to reach his post near the point of the formation.

They formed ranks within the protective fire of the archers on the walls. A few of the barbarians charged toward them, but were cut down before they could reach the sallying force. The rest of the enemy stayed well out of range, watching, while thousands more rode swiftly toward the gate.

"Lot of them out there," Stark remarked. "Looks like all of them. Too bad you don't have another sally set up for the other gate."

"There's few enough troops here," MacKinnie muttered. He was grimly watching as the last of the army emerged from the gates and swung across to form the base of the wedge. "All right, Hal, move them out."

Stark signaled to the drummers. The cadence changed, and a drum signal echoed down the line. The men ceased to mark time and slowly marched forward, shields held level, spears thrust forward. Behind each shieldsman were two ranks of pikemen. They marched across the gently rolling plain toward the nearest enemy camp, too intent on looking ahead to know when they had left the range of the protective fire of the city walls.

The maris circled, always keeping their distance, inviting them to come away from the walls. Individual barbarians galloped toward the formation, then wheeled to ride away. They slapped their buttocks in contempt.

The individual riders changed to small groups. Then more gathered just beyond bow-shot. They moved slowly toward MacKinnie.

"Here comes the first bunch," Stark shouted.
"They're going right around to hit young Todd's section. Put the archers on them?"

"Two squads, Hal. Let the others fire at high angle to keep the rest away. Todd's men can hold that group."

"Yes, sir."

Volleys of bolts shot from the Temple archers, cutting some of the enemy from their wooden saddles. Then the first barbarians hurtled toward the shield line, not in a wave but in scattered groups.

Before they made contact, Todd shouted orders. The drum cadence changed, and the line of men sank to one knee, spears grounded, the pikemen thrusting over their heads. The maris galloped closer, shouting, cheering.

A barbarian mare screamed as she was impaled on a spear. Other beasts whirled from the thicket of points, getting in the way of men charging behind them, stumbling within range of the thrusting pikes, until the barbarian group was milling in front of the right leg of MacKinnie's wedge. Archers poured fire into the mass of men and beasts. The enemy shouted defiance, broke against the shield wall again, again.

"They flee, they flee!" someone shouted.

"After them!" MacKinnie heard.

"Hold your positions!" MacKinnie shouted. "By the Temple God, I'll have the archers cut down the first man that breaks rank! Brett, keep those damned knights of yours under control!"

"Yes, sir," he heard from among the cavalry in the center of the wedge. The knights were milling about, anxious to give chase to the fleeing enemy. The maris thundered away, wheeled to shout defiance again, then rode off when no one followed.

When calm returned, MacKinnie mounted a wagon.

"You've driven off one small group. It wasn't much of a battle, but you see it can be done. Now don't let them make fools of you. If you break formation or leave the shield wall, they'll be all over you. Stand to ranks and you'll slaughter them. Remember, every man's life depends on each of you. No one may break, not for cowardice, and not for glory. And by God, raise a cheer!"

This time the response was great. As MacKinnie climbed down from the wagon, he saw the driver for the first time: small, dressed in chain mail, and shouting at the top of her lungs.

"Freelady!" he called. "You have no business here."

"You gave me the commissary to organize, Colonel. I have done it. There was no one here fit to command my ragtag group, and I will not have my work undone by incompetents. Your sergeant himself dismissed that oaf from the Temple who tried to drive my men like slaves."

He looked at her and remembered another freelady who had been headstrong, but shook the thought from his mind. Laura hadn't really been like Mary Graham. It was hard to imagine Laura in armor—although she might well have carried a sword. Graham's was on the wagon box next to her. As Nathan studied his ward, one of the commissary troops came up. The cook fingered an enormous meat axe.

"You leave the lady alone," the burly man said. "She's a saint from heaven. You touch her, and commander or not, you die."

"Sumba, thank you, but I don't need protection," Mary protested. "At least not from him."

"That's all right, my lady, we'll watch them all," the stocky cook said. MacKinnie shrugged and returned to organize the battle.

The group marched forward again, the drums measuring a slow beat. From time to time a group of the enemy would gallop toward them, firing arrows, only to be driven away by the Temple archers. The barbarians' stubby bows were useless against even the leather of the unarmored men until they came to close range, and they did not dare come very close.

"They'll re-form for another try," MacKinnie said softly. "This time they'll try a mass charge with everything they've got."

Stark nodded. "The men have some confidence now, Colonel. I think they'll hold. It was a good thing, their trying a small attack at first."

"Clan rivalry," Longway said from behind them. "I've seen it on South Continental. Each clan wants to be first to remove the insult of your presence. But they'll be back."

"Night's what worries me," Stark said. "We going to stay out here all night?"

MacKinnie nodded. "The whole point of this demonstration is to build up the morale of the troops back in the city. Just moving out and coming back won't do any good. We have to have a solid victory."

"I still do not see what we are accomplishing," Longway said. "Suppose you prove that you can take the field against the barbarians and move about in formations they can't break. All they have to do is avoid you."

"We'll cross that one later," MacKinnie muttered. "Here they come, Hal. Get the men ready."

A flood of the enemy galloped toward them across the low plain.

"Thousands, thousands," someone in the ranks shouted. "We'll never stop that charge!"

"Quiet in the ranks!" Stark ordered. "Beat to arms, drummers!" The tattoo thundered through the small formation. The shieldsmen dropped to one knee again, this time the entire perimeter sinking low, with the pikemen thrusting their weapons over the tops of the shields. A small knot of reserve pikemen stood at each corner of the wedge, while Brett's cavalry milled about. The archers fired into the oncoming horde as the cooks and camp followers struggled to load crossbows and pass them up to the bowmen. Every bolt took its target, leaving riderless horses to run aimlessly, bring confusion to the enemy charge.

"They don't have what you'd call much formation to them," Stark observed coldly. "They'd do better to all come at once instead of in little bunches."

"Insufficient discipline," Longway said. "They've more than the normal on this world, but that isn't much."

As the drums thundered to a crescendo, the charge hit home. On all sides barbarians plunged and reared, unable to penetrate the shield walls, milling about in front of the wedges, while crossbow bolts poured out.

"Swordsmen! Swordsmen here!" MacLean shouted from his station as commander of the rear section. At his order, a dozen men with shortswords and bucklers ran to his aid, throwing themselves into a gap in the line, thrusting five dismounted barbarians out into the seething mass beyond. A knot of pikemen trotted to station behind them, while the formation closed ranks over the bodies of five shieldsmen, killed when one of their number turned to run.

The maris called to their companions, withdrew a space, and charged the weak spot in the line again.

"They're massing back there against MacLean," Stark reported. "Getting hard to hold."

"Prepare the cavalry," MacKinnie said softly. "I'll go get MacLean ready."

MacKinnie ran across the thirty yards separating the point from the base of the wedge. "Prepare to open ranks, Mr. MacLean."

"Aye, Colonel. Drummers, beat the ready." The drum notes changed subtly. "Fuglemen, pace your men!" The seaman's voice carried through the din of battle, and they heard the orders rattle down the ranks. MacKinnie eyed the situation coolly.

"Now, Mr. MacLean."

"Open ranks!" MacKinnie commanded. The shieldsmen sidestepped, bunching up on each other, leaving a clear gap in the center. The enemy shouted in triumph and poured toward the gap.

The rich notes of a trumpet sounded from the center of the formation. Slowly, gathering speed, ponderously, the heavy cavalrymen trotted across the wedge from their gathering place at the point.

They built up speed, lances were lowered, and they drove into the advancing enemy, using the maris' own momentum to add to their own, sweeping everything before them, riding the enemy down under the hooves of their beasts. Brett and Vanjynk, at each end of the first wave of knights, sounded a cheer as the heavy armor of the iron men proved too much for the light-armed maris. The barbarians scattered and swordsmen poured into the gaps, running alongside the knights, slashing down the enemy, killing the dismounted. The charge pressed onward, the knights scattering to pursue the enemy. The tight formation broke up, and the maris withdrew, formed in tight knots.

"Sound recall," MacKinnie ordered. The trumpet notes were heard again, this time plaintively, disappointed. "Sound it again." He turned to Stark. "This is the turning point, Hal. If Vanjynk and Brett can't control those brainless wonders, we've had it."

He saw his officers shouting to the knights. Slowly they began to wheel, first one, then another, then the entire group. For a moment they paused, and MacKinnie saw that Brett was actually dressing their ranks before they rode in, proudly, contemptuously, in perfect order, their pennants fluttering from their lances, while the shield wall closed behind them over the bodies of a hundred foes.

MacKinnie drove them relentlessly on, across the plain toward the first of the nomad encampments. Twice more they withstood a massed assault from the maris, the column halting to plant spear butts in the ground. The second attack was heavy enough to cause MacKinnie to order the cavalry charge again. The armored knights broke through the concentrations of the enemy before wheeling around to recover their position within the shield wall. In each battle they left a pile of the enemy dead to be crushed beneath the wagon wheels as the column marched on.

They reached the enemy camp, a group of leather tents stretched across the wooden frames, a few wagons which the barbarians pulled to safety before the army arrived. A thin wall of men with light shields stood in front of the camp. Brett and Vanjynk rode forward to MacKinnie.

"We can scatter them with a single charge!" Brett shouted. "Open the ranks."

"No. I will not risk our cavalry in a charge beyond the shield walls. There are too few men for that, and we would never return to the city if something went wrong. We march together or we die together. Would your knights abandon us?"

"We would not leave you though you stood alone among a thousand enemies," Vanjynk said quietly. "I have been talking to the knights. Not one of us has

ever seen the like of this day. We have left more of
the enemy behind us than we number. Each time
we fought them before, our charge would carry them
away until suddenly they swarmed about us to cut us
down. We will stay with you."

The column moved forward, cautiously but inexo-
rably, the drums giving a slow step as the pikemen
advanced. MacKinnie rotated the formation until the
point was aimed directly at the enemy, then massed
his reserve pikes behind the leading men. His archers were silent, their store of bolts nearly exhausted.
MacKinnie spoke quietly to the Temple officer who
commanded them.

"A full volley on the men to the right of our point.
I want a hole driven in their formation. They can't
fight as infantry, they aren't trained for it, and they
don't like it. We'll break through and roll up their
flanks."

As they approached nearer, MacKinnie gave a signal. The archers fired their volley as Todd led a knot
of swordsmen forward, cast javelins at the enemy in
front of them, and retired behind the forest of pikes.
The leading elements of the column struck just behind the javelins, tearing through the thin line by
sheer momentum, before the first rank of pikemen
fell into a hidden pit behind the maris. Their screams
echoed up from below.

"That's what you would have ridden into," Mac-
Kinnie told Brett softly. "I thought there was a reason they'd stand like that. They were hoping for a
full charge of cavalry."

The barbarians broke and ran, gathering their
mounts from hiding places behind the tents and gal-
loping away. Mary Graham's auxiliaries hauled the
wounded men from the pits below, leaving five
pikemen impaled on stakes set in the ground. She

turned pale as she stood looking into the grisly trench, but Nathan had no time for sympathy.

"Bury them there," MacKinnie ordered. "It's an honorable enough grave. Send for the chaplain." He moved about the formation placing men in line, setting the shield wall around the perimeter.

A small scouting party entered the enemy camp. They returned with excited reports. "There is much food here," one said. "But we must enter with great care, for they have tethered scarpias on the walls and ridgepoles." The scarpia was a warm-blooded lizardlike creature eight to twenty centimeters long. It faintly resembled the Earth scorpion, and its bite was far more deadly.

"We will camp beyond the enemy tents," MacKinnie ordered. "Use their ridgepoles to add to our stakes, and be sure to set the stakes carefully. They may attack at night. Bring as much food as you can carry for the city."

Under Stark's direction, the battalion built a fortified camp, digging ditches around the perimeter, throwing the earth to the inside and placing stakes at the top of the rampart they formed. They worked in shifts, every other man using his shovel while the rest stood in ranks holding the diggers' shields and weapons, but there was no renewal of the barbarian attack. The maris rode endlessly around the perimeter of the camp, just outside bow-shot, darting in to fire arrows and wheeling away before an answering volley could be launched. MacKinnie ordered the men to ignore the harassment.

"They'll get close enough to fight before the night's over," he told them. "They can't do us much harm from the range they're shooting from. You'll get your chance later."

It was dark before the cookfires were lighted, but

MacKinnie would not allow any rest until camp was completed. When the last stake was driven, the sun had set, and a thick overcast obscured the moons. From his command point atop Mary Graham's wagon, MacKinnie could see dozens of fires dotting the plain; barbarian camps, each a band of hundreds of men.

"There are sure enough of them," he remarked.

"I don't see how we can win against so many," Mary answered. "No matter how many you kill, there will always be more."

"Not if there's nothing to eat. They're foraging pretty wide already. It's only the grain crops that keep them able to stay here. Without those, they'd have to go back into the interior. We'll drive them off all right."

"What were you a colonel of?" she asked. "I thought you were more than just a Trader from the time I met you, and I wasn't very surprised when your man let it slip."

"You've heard of me," he said. Out beyond the palisade something was moving. The nearest enemy cookfire was obscured momentarily, then again.

"You mean your name is MacKinnie? Let me—" She looked up in surprise. "Iron MacKinnie? The Orleans commander? I should hate you."

"Why?"

"My fiancé was at Blanthern Pass. A subaltern in the Fifth."

MacKinnie climbed laboriously from the wagon, surprised at how tired he was even in the low gravity of Makassar. "The Fifth were good troops."

"Yes. They'd have won against anyone but your men, wouldn't they? I think everyone in Haven hated and admired you at the same time after that battle."

"It's done. Now we're all loyal subjects of King David. I'm sorry."

"Don't be." She moved closer to him, trying to see his face in the dim light from the cookfire. "From these millions of miles away, the big important politics of Prince Samual's World look pretty small. Until today I was sure we'd never get back home. Even now it doesn't seem very likely. But if anyone can do it, you can."

Nathan laughed. "You're beginning to sound like Hal talking to the recruits, Mary Graham. For now you'd best get the men fed, because we don't have very long before the barbarians try their hand with a night attack. I'll have the troops sent here in shifts so we keep a decent perimeter, and we feed the interior troops last. It's the pikemen and shield boys we want to take care of tonight."

"When do the knights eat?"

"After they've fed their mounts like any good cavalry. And after my pikemen. Your pardon, freelady, I have to see my men."

The night wore on. MacKinnie was relieved when no attack came before his perimeter guards were fed, but did not relax until every man was back in his place, lying at ease with his weapons, while swordsmen stood guard to peer futilely into the darkness.

"They're coming," he told Stark. "I've seen them stirring around, and there's a feel about it. You get it, too?"

"Yes, sir. And like you say, they're moving about some out there. We'll hear from them before morning."

It was nearly midnight when a sentry shouted, then vanished beneath a wave of dismounted men swarming toward the palisade.

"Trumpeter!" MacKinnie shouted. "Sound the alarm! To your feet, men!" He could see a knot of pikemen, kept awake in central reserve, rushing toward the area of the attack.

"To me! To me!" he heard Vanjynk shout. "Leave your mounts and rally to me!" Leading a party of knights with swords singing about their heads, Vanjynk charged to the perimeter, pushing aside shieldsmen struggling to their feet. The iron men stood at the top of the palisades, dealing terrible blows to the enemy attempting to climb out of the ditch. The night was filled with screams and shouts before MacKinnie had his shield wall formed properly and brought the armored men back to a central reserve.

"They're all around the perimeter," Stark told him. "They try one spot and then another, not much coordination to it, but nobody can rest any, Colonel."

MacKinnie nodded agreement. "It's a good tactic. They hope to tire us out and then cut us off from the city. It'll cost them enough."

In less than an hour the battle died away, leaving a quiet shattered at intervals with the groans of the wounded, but the enemy never left them alone. All night there were rushes against one part of the palisade or another, and the whistle of arrows fired randomly into the camp. Morning came slowly, to reveal hundreds of enemy dead and dying filling the ditches, or stretched on the ground where they had crawled away from the battle. Bands of nomads rode slowly around the camp, silently watching the wall of shields.

"Here's the tricky part," MacKinnie said. "But I think they may have had enough for now. They'll want to see what we do next." He carefully moved his men out before the palisade, bringing the wagons and interior troops out of the camp before abandoning the other walls. The enemy watched, but there was no attack as he marched his formation slowly back through the enemy campsite. They burned everything they couldn't carry away. As the maris' possessions blazed behind them, the battalion marched in quickstep back to the city.

17

Battle

The war minister was angry as he faced the assembled bishops of the Temple. "He has proved that he can fight the barbarians. He has remained a day and a night outside the walls of the city. He has killed hundreds of them. For this we are grateful. But I say that it is madness to take the entire army into the field. Let him carry on his raids with the troops he used before, not strip our walls of their defenders."

The council muttered approval. Their voices echoed softly in the great room.

MacKinnie rose to speak. He strode forward to the platform before the council table. As he approached he looked again at the council room. Its walls were hung with tapestries; above the woven hangings stone figures, representing heroes of an Empire dead so long its very existence was legend, stared down at them. On his dais high above the council table, His Utmost Holiness Willem XI dozed in starts, interest overcoming senility for moments before his head dropped again. His word was law but the council of bishops wrote his words for him, and spoke them as well more often than not.

"Worshipful sirs," MacKinnie said, "I would do as Father Sumbavu asks if it were possible. But our expedition was a demonstration only. Without sufficient troops to replace the shieldsmen who fall in battle, and more to allow the men rest when they tire, we could never hold against the enemy for more than a day. But with enough men I can destroy their bases of supplies, bring them to battle against us, destroy many of them, and send the rest back to their wastelands. And do not be deceived, worshipful sirs. The plainsmen have studied our methods of fighting. They will even now be devising means to fight us, ways to use their great numbers and speed against us. The next battle will decide the fate of the city. Would you fight it now, or wait until hunger has reduced our ranks to shadows? Will you fight outside the walls like men, or huddled inside waiting to be slaughtered?"

"He speaks well, Sumbavu," the Archdeacon said. He turned his blue eyes toward MacKinnie. "And how do you know you will have success? What manner of Trader are you that you know ways of fighting never seen on this world?"

"Your Reverence, my ways are but those of the Guildsmen of the south and west. We have fought these barbarians before, although never so many of them. As to success, what can be denied the army of God? If we go forth boldly, we must win, for God is with us."

"He was with us before, but it did not save our

army," Sumbavu muttered. The old priest glanced quickly about, fearful of having spoken heresy.

"You wish to take all the knights and archers, and your beggars," the Archdeacon said. "This I understand from watching the fighting five days ago. But why do you also demand the swordsmen of the Temple? Of what use will these be to you?"

"The armored swordsmen will guard our camp," MacKinnie said. "They will fight in the nighttime when the shieldsmen are not of such great value. They fight against the barbarians when they leave their mounts and attack us on foot. The citizen army knows only one method of fighting; they are not trained soldiers. We must have a leavening of fighting men if we are to bring the enemy to the final battle."

"And, Sumbavu, what have you to say except that we should not allow this? What reasons have you?" the crimson-robed official asked. "He has done what you could never do." The Archdeacon turned to the others. "For myself, I see the hand of God in this man's coming. Who knows what instruments the Omnipotent may choose for our deliverance?"

Sumbavu measured his words carefully, speaking softly so that they leaned forward to hear him. "I do not know. Yet I do not like this. There is something of this man I do not understand, and I do not think he should be trusted with the army of the Temple."

"Then go with him to command it," the Archdeacon said. "For ourselves, we have heard enough. Let the Trader kill the barbarians, and may God's blessing go with him."

Sumbavu bowed in acceptance, but MacKinnie felt the war minister's intense gaze even as he left the room.

*   *   *

MacKinnie used two more weeks preparing for the battle. His entire force of citizens and peasants was trained, with his original group dispersed through the ranks as fuglemen. Stark drilled them relentlessly in the Temple courtyard, taking them again and again through the complex maneuvers which formed squares and columns, opened and closed ranks, brought their pikes to rest and present.

Brett and Vanjynk worked with the knights, shouting and cursing to try to make them understand that their great strength lay in a massed charge, and that they must return to the shield wall to regroup after each attack or they would be split apart and killed. Each evening they discussed the day's progress, talking late into the night, then rising early to drill the men once again.

On the night before the army was to go forth, MacKinnie held another conference. He looked intently at his officers seated at the thick wooden table in front of him, and nodded in satisfaction.

"Mr. MacLean, what of my infantry?"

"Better than when we went out last, Trader. They've seen the way it's done now, and Stark sweated them until they're hardened up. Not like veteran troops, but they'll hold. Doubling the rations didn't hurt any."

"That was the Trader's doing," Mary Graham said. "He found someone who could be bribed at the warehouse."

MacKinnie shook his head. "Stark again, though I thought of it. I've never seen a commissary yet that didn't have a couple of people on the take in it."

"I hope there are none in mine," Mary said indignantly.

"There are, lady, there are," Stark interjected. "Just hope their price is high and they're scared enough of you not to fill up the grain wagons with sand. It's been done to campaigns before."

"And your knights, Vanjynk?" MacKinnie asked.

"They drill well, they wheel to the trumpets, but they still do not like turning from the battle. Nor do I, but I see it must be done." Vanjynk lifted his cup and gulped the wine. "You fight strangely on your world, star man."

"Lay off that talk," Stark muttered. "We have enough trouble with the Temple people without that."

MacKinnie nodded. "Hal's right. But tell me, will the knights obey the trumpets?"

"I believe so," Brett answered. "They have little wish to be killed by barbarians. But there is no fear of death in these men, only of dishonor."

"Aye, so Brett made a song about foolish knights who abandoned their commander and were shamed forever," MacLean said. "Silly thing, but catchy. Seems to have helped."

"If songs help, sing your lungs out," MacKinnie told them. "The key to this whole battle is getting the heavy cavalry to bear on the barbarians while they're bunched up. Nothing on this world can stand up to a charge from those armored ironheads, but as soon as they lose their momentum and scatter, the maris can pick them off with no trouble at all." He turned to Mary Graham. "Do you have all the supplies we ordered?"

She nodded. "We've made thousands of bolts for the crossbows, and the grain wagons are ready. You don't really have very many provisions, you know."

"I know. You're rolling plenty of empty wagons, though. Either we find something to put in them, or we'll come back home for more supplies. This formation's slow enough without heavy transport gear in the square."

"Then we're ready," Mary Graham said.

"Not you. You aren't going," MacKinnie told her.

"Yes I am. It's no safer in here than out there. If your battle is lost, the city is lost as well and you know it." She looked around the room at the other men from her world. "I have a right to his protection, and I choose that he exercise it personally. Don't I have the right?"

"An interesting point," Longway said. "You cannot abandon her without finding a substitute guardian," the Academician told MacKinnie. "And doubtless she is entitled to someone of her own world. Who will you leave with her? Scholar Kleinst remains in the city, but for all his great value he is hardly a suitable guardian."

"I appear to be outmaneuvered, although why you should want to accompany an army in the field is beyond me, freelady." MacKinnie looked at her expectantly.

"I see no reason to stay here," she told him. "There are few enough on this godforsaken place that I can talk to, without being left with the Temple monks. Besides, I can be useful, or can you spare anyone else to manage your commissary?"

"The point is made." Well made, he thought. She's been nearly as useful as Hal. No one else could have organized the logistics half as well as she has. But—

He turned back to the council. "Our whole purpose in this expedition will be to either force plainsmen into battle on our terms, or destroy their base of supply. Either will be sufficient, although I doubt they will let us simply march out and burn their harvests without a fight. . . ." He indicated the map spread out on the table. "As far as we can tell from watching their movements, they've been harvesting the crops for the past three weeks. The nearest big concentration of grain is here, about thirty kilometers from the gates, assuming they use the roads and village structures. I rather think they will. From what I've been able to learn they often do that. We'll make straight for that and burn what we can't load up."

"Then what?" MacLean asked.

"We see if they'll fight. If they won't, we keep marching from place to place until they're short of rations. But they'll fight, all right."

"You may get more battle than you expect," Longway said. "You've hurt their pride with your last expedition, and they'll want to prove it was an accident. Next time, they'll press home their charge with everything they have."

"That's what I'm hoping for," MacKinnie answered slowly. "It will take them time to gather for the battle, and more to decide who leads it. By that time, we should have got to our objective and set up camp. They'll gather troops all night, and probably try to wipe us out in the morning."

"Then you're trying for one big battle," Mary said.

"Yes. One turn of the wheel, freelady. We haven't a lot of time." He glanced significantly at the Makassarians at the table, then stood to dismiss the meeting. "Rest well, and be ready tomorrow. They may not let us get to the first village."

The army formed outside the city walls after first light. MacKinnie placed his men in a triangular formation again, but this time the broad base of the wedge faced forward, its point to the rear. He doubled the men on the right leg of the wedge, using all the left-handed troops he could find for the forward elements of that line, and placing a large reserve force at the rear point. When he was satisfied with his arrangements, the drums beat their slow march, and the army moved forward.

Clouds of maris rode madly around, darting toward them, withdrawing, waiting for any opening in the shield walls, patient in the knowledge that the city army could never pursue them. The slow cadence continued, wagon wheels creaked and men shouted at the oxen drawing supply wagons, while the knights in the center impatiently led their mounts. Kilometer after kilometer they marched toward the enemy camp, as more and more barbarians joined the forces riding around them. They were completely surrounded.

"Reckon the city can hold with what we've left them?" Stark asked, looking back at the city in the distance. "You didn't leave them much."

"They'll hold," MacKinnie replied. "The enemy has no heavy siege equipment, and as long as the walls are manned the barbarians can't do much. Give them enough time and they could throw up ladders or even stack their saddles against the walls, but the defense can slow that down, and I don't intend to give them any time for stunts like that. We seem to be attracting most of them to us, anyway. What's Sumbavu doing?"

"He's riding with the knights, Colonel. Keeping an eye on those pretty uniformed swordsmen and archers, too. He doesn't trust you much."

"I don't blame him, Hal. I wouldn't trust me much either if I were him. But what else can he do? Keep a sharp eye on him; I can't have him interfering."

"Yes, sir. You didn't make much protest about his coming."

"Maybe I didn't mind him coming. Now watch him."

"Yes, sir."

The march continued, drawing to within a kilometer of the enemy tents. MacKinnie looked closely at the cluster of enemy in front of him: "They're trying to make up their minds. They don't want to give up all that grain without a fight. Watch that group there," he said, pointing. "Here they come! Beat the alarm!"

The drums thundered, then went back to their steady pace. The column continued to advance, until the enemy was within bow-shot. "Prepare for attack," MacKinnie said quietly, measuring the distance to the nearest of the plainsmen. "Form the wall." The drums beat again, and the Temple archers rushed to the perimeter, firing into the packed enemy. The charge hurtled toward the broad front of the wedge, then wheeled around to strike the left end of the line. Pikemen rushed to the corner as echelon after echelon of the enemy plunged against the left leg of the inverted wedge.

The shield wall held. A few of the barbarians leaped over the first rank to land among the pikemen, their short-swords slashing, but Temple guardsmen moved forward to cut them down. The battle was short, and when it was finished hundreds more of the enemy lay in front of the column. The men raised a cheer, cut short by the drummer's commands to resume the march.

"Not much of a battle," Stark commented. "Thought they'd try more than that."

"Testing us out," MacKinnie said. "They've found a way to get a few men into our lines now. They'll try that one again. Adaptable beggars."

"They have to be," Brett said from behind him. MacKinnie turned to see the singer walking patiently. "I left my mount with Vanjynk," Brett said. "You understand that there will be many more battles, each different from the last?"

"I understand. But how many more there will be

depends on more than their intentions. For now, we take their supplies."

The enemy camp was deserted. They had carried away their tents, but they had left huge piles of harvested grain. The grain piles had recently been covered with hides, but now the food was left to blow about in the wind. They had also fouled some of the harvest with excrement. Graham's commissary workers began the tedious task of bagging and loading the harvest.

The scattered refuse of weeks of enemy life lay about them; there were also signs of what had happened to villagers unfortunate enough to fall into the hands of the maris. Stark sent burial details to dispose of them.

Father Sumbavu examined the remains of a young girl. "Monsters," he said. "Not human at all. They deserve extermination."

"We will hardly be able to do that," MacKinnie said. "But we may yet surprise them. Your pardon, Father, I must see to our defenses."

Ditch, ramparts, and palisade rose around the campsite while the commissary workers began cookfires. A dozen singers strolled about. MacKinnie moved through the camp, speaking to little groups of his men, encouraging them, testing their morale. It was hard to believe that only months before these had been the sullen slaves and beggars of the streets of Batav. Now they roared lustily at his jokes, shouted defiance at an enemy they could not see, and grimly held their weapons as if half afraid someone would take them. MacKinnie pitied anyone foolish enough to try.

The night was a turmoil. When both moons were high and bright, masses of barbarians stormed forward, some mounted, most on foot, probing to find a weak spot in the perimeter, constantly attacking to keep the men aroused, withdrawing from opposition but coming again and again. MacKinnie sent small detachments of his troops to the center of the camp, replacing them with others, so that each man was able to rest for part of the night. Toward dawn the attacks died away, and he let the men sleep until late in the morning. The Temple swordsmen had borne the brunt of the night attacks, and were most in need of rest. MacKinnie did not call them to breakfast until everyone else had been fed.

A mass of barbarians formed a kilometer from the camp. They were strung out in a vast semicircle between MacKinnie's army and the city, and MacKinnie had never seen so large a group of plainsmen before. Stark joined him as he stood atop the commissary wagon for a better view of the enemy.

"This going to be it, Colonel?" the big sergeant asked.

"Possibly. Let's see if we can get out of this camp. They figure to hit us as soon as there are enough outside the gates to make it worthwhile." MacKinnie shouted orders, formed the men into ranks, then motioned to a trumpeter. The notes rang out, calling his officers to him. Moments later, the main gate opened.

MacKinnie sent a heavy detachment of shieldsmen angling forward and to the left from the camp gate. A second group angled off to the right, while others marched out to form a line between them, its ends anchored with the hard-marching groups of picked men. When the left-hand group had left a large enough opening inside the wedge, the knights were sent forward until they were just behind the shield wall, at the extreme left corner of the inverted wedge the army was forming. Then MacKinnie sent the

Temple archers forward, a line down each leg of his triangular formation, leaving none in the center. Whenever the maris approached the two legs of the formation, a shower of arrows greeted them, forcing them away. The enemy clustered around, moving toward the center where the resistance was least.

MacKinnie nodded in satisfaction. "Now comes the hard part," he muttered.

A charge of the barbarians struck the center of the triangle directly in front of the camp gates. The shield wall held, but gradually fell back, stretching thinner and thinner, bowing inwardly toward the gate as the heavier formations at the ends of the line held fast. More troops were sent forward to fill the gaps, keeping a continuous line, but still the enemy pressed forward, forcing them back, back, as more of the maris joined the attack. The formation bowed still more resembling an enormous "U" with its base almost at the palisade. Hundreds, a thousand, four thousand barbarians pressed forward toward the camp gates.

"Now!" MacKinnie shouted. The trumpet notes sounded above the shouts of battle, drums thundered. The knights formed inside their bastion; then as the formation opened, they charged down the wing, rolling up the flank of the enemy. The shield wall quickly closed behind them; then the ends of the U drew together. Archers faced inward now, firing into the ranks of the enemy, while the heavy cavalrymen thundered over the barbarians, riding them down, breaking up all signs of organization until they rode directly into the camp gate.

MacKinnie signaled frantically to Brett. "Form them up again and be ready to protect the outer flanks!" he shouted. "The archers and and spearmen can deal with the ones we've trapped."

The field in front of the gate was covered with blood. Barbarians pressed closer and closer together as the shield wall, bristling with pikes, closed in on them. Temple archers continued the rain of arrows into the helpless enemy, too crowded together even to use their weapons properly, the inner group not able to strike a blow. A few raced frantically out the end of the trap before the heavy knots of men MacKinnie had sent out first made contact with each other and closed all avenues of escape.

The remaining enemy outside the trap attempted to aid their fellows, to be stopped by shieldsmen facing outward slowly moving back as the inner lines moved forward. Concentrations of the enemy were broken up by charges of cavalry, the knights thundering over them and around the ends, wheeling back to enter the camp and regroup, while the Temple swordsmen defended the ramparts of the camp itself. The huge mass of doomed men in the trap could have broken through the thinner lines of the camp, or even the outer defenses of the trap, but they could not escape to fight, while the smaller numbers remaining outside were unable to help them, frantically falling upon the spears of the shield wall or trampled beneath the knights while their luckless fellows were relentlessly cut down.

The slaughter continued until midafternoon. At the end, hapless groups of the enemy threw themselves on the spears or clawed their way up the ramparts to be impaled by the swordsmen at the top, screaming desperately, their courage melted by the faceless mass of swords and the rain of arrows. As the pikemen passed over the dead, camp followers slit each throat and removed the arrows, passing them back to be fired again. Captive beasts were led through the lines into the camp to be tethered with the commissary oxen. The lines came closer together, closer, then touched. There were no more enemies in the trap.

"What do you propose for tomorrow?" Sumbavu asked the council clustered around MacKinnie's campfire. "You have left thousands dead on the field, more cut down in flight by our knights. We can return to the city."

"No." MacKinnie stood, a cup of wine in his hands. "Until their supply base is destroyed, there is no safety for the city. We must continue to burn their grain."

"It is not their grain, but ours!" Sumbavu snapped. "You cannot burn this great harvest. It must be carried back to the city. Surely this march can be delayed for a time to allow us to provision the Temple! The faithful are hungry, and they should be told of this great victory."

"You forget, there are many more of the enemy than we have killed," MacKinnie reminded the priest. "And we must not give them time to rest. We must pursue them endlessly until they go back to their wastelands in fear."

"I forbid this," Sumbavu said quietly. "We must take these stores of grain to the city. You will not burn them."

"Then I suggest you take them yourself, Your Worship," MacKinnie told him. "Now that we have thinned their ranks, I believe we can do without the Temple swordsmen. I will need some of the wagons to transport grain for the army, but you may have half of them, and three hundred of the camp servants as well. It is only thirty kilometers; each can carry half a hundredweight of grain. That will leave little to burn."

"So be it. We set forth immediately."

"At night, Your Worship?" MacKinnie asked. "Is that wise?"

"Wiser than being caught by them in the daytime. I see that you will not escort me with your army, though it would involve only a day's march. I will so report to the council."

"Two days' march, Father," MacKinnie said quietly. "One each way. Not to mention the disorganization as each man ran in to tell his fellows of the glorious victory. We would lose many days, and for what? If the enemy is to be driven from the city, it must be done now."

"What need to drive them away, now that we have means to gather provisions?" Sumbavu snapped. "We could return, and our Temple officers learn to command the soldiers, then set forth again. It would not be so great for you and your outlanders, would it? You must win yourself, for what purpose I do not know. But I tell you again, I know you do not have the good of the Temple first in your heart, soldier of the south. Were I not guarded by the faithful of the Temple, I do not think I would return from this march alive." He stalked off into the night, his bodyguard following him closely.

"Go pick the most useless slaves of your group," MacKinnie told Mary Graham. "The blunderers, the tired animals and those you didn't make new collars for, the wagons ready to fall apart, get them all out of here."

She studied him closely. "I'd almost think that's why you brought all that useless junk. And you added that group of convicts to my picked men. . . . Did you expect this?"

"Freelady, just get them moving," Stark said. "The colonel's got enough problems." He guided her to the granaries, then set men to loading the wagons which were to go back to the city.

Two hours later, Sumbavu was ready to depart. He stood with MacKinnie at the camp gate, watching the sky. "In an hour the moons will be gone. You have not seen the enemy?"

"No, Father," MacKinnie told him. "But they will have men out there."

"There is less chance they will attack me at night than by day," the priest said. "In the dark they will not know that I have only the Temple soldiers, and they will be afraid." He watched the setting moons in silence until darkness came over the plains.

"I leave you my blessing," Sumbavu told MacKinnie. "Perhaps I have misjudged your intentions. May God accompany you."

"Thank you, Father," MacKinnie said. He ordered the gates opened and watched the guardsmen and wagons leave. Each swordsman carried a bag of grain on his back in addition to his weapons, and the carts were creaking under the load. Convicts and slaves, lured on the expedition with promises of freedom and now sent back toward the city with staggering loads on their backs, old oxen, carts with creaking wheels, all filed out with the proud guardsmen. A thousand soldiers and three hundred bearers left the camp before the gates were closed. MacKinnie returned to his tent. After a few moments, Stark and Longway joined him by his fire.

"They'll never make ten kilometers by morning," Stark said. "Not the way they loaded themselves."

"I thought the priest gave them reasonable loads," Longway said. "They did not seem excessive."

"Sure, but the Trader gave them the pick of the loot before they set out. Wasn't a man there wasn't carrying five, ten kilos of junk stripped off the dead or picked up in this camp."

"That was generous of you," Longway said. "Extraordinarily so."

"There will be other loot," MacKinnie told them. "We'll have plenty of chances to get rich, but they won't. They've earned their share."

"Or will," Stark muttered. MacKinnie looked quickly at him, then stared at the fire in silence as Mary Graham joined the little group.

"Best get some sleep," MacKinnie told her. "We start early in the morning, and it's late enough now."

"I don't really need it," she laughed. "I ride a cart, remember?"

"Lady, you can sleep in that cart under way, you'll be the greatest soldier's wife ever lived," Stark observed. "I'd rather walk, the way those things fall into every hole in the ground."

Mary laughed, looked around furtively, then said, "You wouldn't think the Empire would fall if we told them how to put springs in the carts, would you? But I guess it's too late now." She looked around her at the camp. The spear and shield troops were asleep in place around the perimeter, their shields propped up behind the palisade, pikes and spears ready at hand, while guards patrolled outside the perimeter. "I suppose I should start the breakfast fires. No rest for the cooks."

"Don't bother," MacKinnie said. "There won't be breakfast in the morning. Another hour and I'll roust out the men I'm taking with me. You can feed the rest when we're gone if the enemy gives you time. I'll leave MacLean in command here."

"You're dividing your force, Trader?" Longway asked. "That seems unreasonable. How long will you be gone?"

"One day should do it, one way or another. Don't worry about it, Academician, we won't leave you for long."

"What is all this?" Mary asked. "There's something strange going on here! I don't think I like this at all."

"Just get some rest," MacKinnie told her. "Or if you can't do that, please excuse me while I sleep. We'll have to be up early, Hal. Have the guard call me an hour before first light. My apologies, but I can't think clearly when I've had no sleep, and the enemy is still far too dangerous for my mind to be fogged." He strode to his tent and closed the flap. After a few moments, Longway went back to his quarters.

"Hal, what is wrong with him?" Mary asked. "There's something going on, isn't there?"

"Freelady, he doesn't like what he's had to do. I can't say I like it much either, but we didn't see any other way. Now do as he says and go to sleep. I reckon I'd better lie down a couple of hours myself."

18

The Price of Loot

"Time, Colonel."

"Uh." MacKinnie struggled to wakefulness.

"Hour before dawn," Stark said. "Here." He gave MacKinnie a steaming cup of tea.

Nathan drank gratefully. "Thanks." He regretted again that there was neither coffee nor chickeest on Makassar. It might have been worse, he reflected. At least there was tea.

The night was dark. Both moons had set, and low clouds obscured most of the stars. The camp was invisible, but MacKinnie heard the men quietly coming awake. They spoke in whispers, with occasional louder curses and orders for silence breaking the low hiss of conversation. Nathan pulled on his boots and went to the cook area. His officers and noncoms were already gathering there.

He spoke to them in low tones. "I'm concerned about Father Sumbavu's group," he said. "We'll take First and Second battalions and the knights out to cover them. The rest will stay here to guard the camp, with MacLean in charge. Be ready to march in ten minutes."

"Is it wise to divide the force?" MacLean asked.

"Wise or not, I'm doing it," MacKinnie snapped. "I'm not accustomed to discussing my orders, Mister MacLean."

"Sir," MacLean answered.

"All right, move," Stark said. He waited until the others had left. "Pretty good troops," he said. "Not much protest at all. 'Course winning a big battle yesterday didn't hurt. Does wonders for discipline."

When the troops were assembled, MacKinnie sent half the spearmen to the walls. The other half, with the knights, were marched out the camp gate. Once outside they turned due east, a right angle to the road to the city. There were mutters from the ranks, but no one questioned him.

When they were a kilometer from the camp MacKinnie turned the detachment toward the city, forming them into two columns of fours with the cavalry inside. They marched in silence without drums, and Stark moved up and down the line to see that each man kept his equipment from rattling.

The sky turned gray, then crimson. When it was light enough to see men fifty meters away, Hal Stark caught up to MacKinnie at the head of the column. "They move pretty fast without wagons and junk," Stark said. "Ought to be able to keep us this pace all morning."

"We'll need to," MacKinnie said. He found it difficult to judge the capabilities of the native troops, and he couldn't use his own abilities as a guide; months on Maskassar had softened them, but the Samualites were generally stronger than the natives, and nearly all tasks seemed easier, exactly as Midshipman Landry had predicted.

The sun was nearly up when Stark sent for MacKinnie. When Nathan joined him at the point, Stark showed him deep tracks left by Sumbavu's baggage carts. "Hard to tell how far they are ahead of us," Stark said. "No more'n an hour, I'd say."

"Loaded as they were, they can't be too far," MacKinnie said. "Okay, I want flankers out to both sides. They'll slow us down, but this is good ambush terrain. And let's make time."

They swung on in silence, now and again changing positions to send fresh men to lead the escorting flankers. It was hard work to break trail in the waist-high grasslike vegetation. The low hills of the plain closed around them, and MacKinnie rushed forward each time they topped a rise. Then, as they approached one low hill, they heard shouts from the other side. When they drew closer, the sounds resolved into the din of a battle.

"Deploy the troops," MacKinnie said softly. "Columns of fours to each side."

The parallel columns split apart, angling out to form two lines, then continued their advance up the hill in silence. The men readied their weapons and helped each other sling their shields properly.

"Draw swords," MacKinnie ordered. "Double time."

They trotted up the final ten meters to the top of the rise. The sounds of battle grew louder. Then they could see the low valley beyond.

A thousand barbarians had swarmed over Sumbavu's column and destroyed it. There were so few survivors that at first MacKinnie saw none at all, but a few

Temple swordsmen were huddled in knots of ten or twenty around the makeshift protection of the baggage carts. The maris swept toward them firing arrows and leaping on them with their swords. Even as MacKinnie and Stark watched, another tiny group of scarlet livery vanished beneath a wave of plainsmen.

"Make your charge straight through them," MacKinnie told Vanjynk. "Cut through and go past, then wheel, dress ranks, and charge home again. Don't stop to play with them, stay together as you've been taught. Now go."

Brett and Vanjynk waved the knights forward. The heavily armored horsemen gathered momentum as they rode down the gentle hill, changed from trot to canter, building speed as they rode toward the enemy.

As soon as the knights were in motion the infantry shield wall began its advance. Drums sounded quickstep, then double time as fuglemen shouted frantic orders to dress ranks and keep in line. The wall moved forward.

The maris saw the wave of horsemen plunging toward them and leaped for their mounts, scattering the loot they had been so anxious to gain, but it was too late. The lances came down, and now that they had been seen, MacKinnie waved to the trumpeters. The notes carried easily over the dewy plains as the knights charged home. Lances shattered, swords were torn from scabbards as the knights shouted in triumph. A few remained to fight, wheeling about until they were pulled from their saddles by the lassos of the maris, or their mounts were shot from beneath them. The rest galloped past, riding the enemy down, thundering down the entire line of barbarians before wheeling at the top of the next rise.

The horsemen had broken the enemy when the shieldsmen arrived. Once again the wings of the shield line closed inward, trapping the enemy between ranks, while the knights charged home again, throwing back into the trap any of the barbarians who had attempted to escape, the momentum of their charge crushing all resistance. The plainsmen caught between the lines had no chance. They could impale themselves on the spears of the shield wall, or wait to be trampled by the knights. This time the slaughter was done quickly, for no one attempted to attack the infantry from behind. The plainsmen who escaped were glad of their lives.

They found Sumbavu at the head of the column, a group of swordsmen dead around his body. He clutched a sword with one hand and a crucifix with the other, and his eyes stared at the heavens. There were no more than fifty survivors in his entire command.

MacKinnie grimly formed his troops into columns and marched back to his camp, the carts rattling over the rutted plains, the groans of the wounded sounding over the creak of their wheels.

MacKinnie rested his men through the next day. In the late afternoon, a small party of plainsmen approached, wheeled outside arrow-shot, and waved feathered lances above their heads.

"He wants to talk to you," Brett said. "It doesn't happen very often with city people, but they do have ways of ending wars between clans. He's treating you as the chief of a very powerful clan. The men behind him are family heads."

"How do I meet him?" MacKinnie asked.

"Go outside the gate with a group of retainers. I doubt if he'll trust you not to shoot him if he gets in close range. It's what always happens when they deal with city people."

"Can you talk to him? Do you speak their language?"

"You know I do, star man, and you know why. I'll come with you if you like."

MacKinnie took Brett and young Todd, leaving Stark and MacLean in command. Longway puffed after them, insisting, and MacKinnie invited him along. They walked out from the camp until they were near the extreme range of a crossbow, then halted, still barely within covering fire if it was needed.

Three figures detached themselves from the group, dismounted, and strode purposefully toward MacKinnie. A few feet away they grounded their lances and spread their arms wide. One spoke swiftly in a musical language MacKinnie had never heard.

"He says he comes to speak," Brett said. "He says you fight like a great chief. He says never before have the robed fools fought so well."

"Tell him he has fought well and we admire the courage of his men."

Brett translated. Before the mari chief could answer, MacKinnie said, "Now tell him I am a great prince from the south, and that I have come in a ship. Tell him a thousand more ships full of men like mine are coming, with many horses, and we will cover the plains. Tell him his brave people will kill many of us, but more will come, and soon there will be many dead on these fields."

"It is customary to exchange more compliments."

"Give him a few. Tell him how brave his men are, and how well they fought. Then tell him what I said."

Brett spoke at length, waited for a reply, and said, "He says he is honored to meet a great prince from the south. He says he knew you could not be from the city. He asks how you will catch him."

"Say that we will come to his home in midwinter.

We will burn his food and kill his beasts. But we do not wish to do this, for many of my strong men will die, and many of his brave warriors, and all for nothing."

"That ought to impress him," Brett said. He chattered to the plainsman.

This time there was a long pause, then a longer reply from the mari.

Brett listened carefully. "You've impressed him," the singer said. "He's afraid of that walking wall of yours. He can imagine your troops pounding along in the snow, and it bothers him. They don't like to fight in the winter, and he doesn't think you would like it much either. He wants to know why you would go to so much trouble."

"Say I'm a madman," MacKinnie said. "Or will that work?"

"It might. They're familiar with fanatics."

"Good. Then I'm a fanatic dedicated to saving the Temple."

Brett spoke again, listened, and said "He's about ready to believe anything about you. He asks you to speak again. That means he hasn't any reply."

"Tell him any way you want to," MacKinnie answered, "but here are my terms. They can have two days to get out of here. They burn nothing else, but they may carry away whatever they can. At the end of that time, we'll kill every one of them we find. And if they make any more hostile moves after today, we'll follow him to the end of the continent and burn all his villages and kill all his livestock. Make sure he knows that's not an idle threat."

"He's not responsible for all of the maris," Brett said. "Just his own clan. He can't promise for the rest."

"Is this the leader of the biggest group?"

"One of the largest clans, yes."

"Then he'll have to figure out how to drive the others out. He ought to be able to do it, but anyway that's his problem, not mine. Tell him that."

Brett looked pale for a moment. He seemed about to say something to MacKinnie, but Nathan's look stopped him. He turned to the mari chief and spoke at length.

The sinewy chief answered, then another of the attendants shouted. Brett shouted back, and their voices rose angrily before the chief spoke again more calmly. Finally Brett turned back to Nathan. "He'll try. Some of the others have already left. He'll get the rest to go along. They wanted more time, but I told them you really were a madman, that you'd taken an oath never to end the war if it didn't end now. They're still arguing about it, but it's obvious they're afraid of your army. I think they'll go."

19

The Holy Relics

They entered the city in triumph. Although MacKinnie sent no word ahead, the wagons loaded with grain told enough; by the time the army reached the city gates, thousands had turned out to line the streets. Hundreds more spilled outside the gates and ran emotionally to greet the soldiers. The sound of their cheering was deafening.

It took nearly an hour to march up the winding streets to the Temple's huge courtyard. MacKinnie sent a group ahead to keep the courtyard clear of civilians, and eventually brought the troops and commissary wagons inside. "There'll be celebration enough tonight," he told his officers. "For the moment let's get the men fed and give them some rest."

"We have won a great victory," one of the knights protested. "Now we enjoy the rewards. . . ."

"Certainly," MacKinnie said. "The knights are excused. But we can't totally disperse the army. The maris seem to be leaving, true enough, but we'll need to be able to back up my threats if any of them change their minds. There'll be plenty of revelry right here. I've sent for a whole warehouse of wine. One of you go invite all the Temple soldiers who had to stay behind. They were willing to go, and they ought to share the fun."

He dismissed the officers, but kept Stark back. "I need the headquarters company now," MacKinnie said.

"Yes, sir. They're ready. It's all planned."

"Good. Send them in. And send a runner for those Imperial churchmen."

"Your reverence," MacKinnie told Casteliano, "you are now in command of this Temple."

The Archbishop was startled. "How is this?" he demanded.

"The only military forces left in this city are a couple of hundred archers, about that many swordsmen, the knights and my army. Most of them—including the Temple swordsmen—are getting drunk out in the courtyard. The only comparatively sober troops are my headquarters company."

"But—what does this mean?" Laraine asked.

"It means we own the place," MacKinnie said. "Who's to oppose us? The knights aren't any match for the pikemen in a street fight, and the pikes will stay loyal to me for a while at least."

"Surely you do not expect to make war on the Temple," Laraine protested. "We have no wish to wade in blood to the high altar."

"It shouldn't come to that. We've sent a picked force to the key points. The Temple itself is already ours. Now we've got to tell their ruling council and that Pope of theirs who's in charge."

"Would your men really fight against the Temple?" Casteliano asked.

"Most of them would," Stark said. "Remember who we recruited. They were mostly slaves, and peasants down on their luck. And they've won victories under the—the Trader. They'd fight for him."

"We'd rather not," MacKinnic said. "It'd be hard to control the looting, and there might be fires. Civil wars are never pretty."

"No. They are not," Casteliano said. He stroked his chin thoughtfully. "And you have not yet informed the ruling council of the changed state of affairs? Good." He turned to Laraine and Deluca. "Go quickly and get vestments. The best we have, and our most ornate trappings. Trader MacKinnie, will you lend us some of your men as attendants? And if you will have your most regal clothing brought to you that would help as well. I believe there is a way this can be done without bloodshed."

"I hope so," MacKinnie said. "Stark will see that you get what you need from us."

"Excellent." Casteliano went to the battlement and looked down at the courtyard. The guards at the gates had left their posts. Civilians, Temple swordsmen, archers, knights, commissary troops all danced in great circles, pausing only to scoop cups of wine from open barrels.

"Look there," MacKinnie said quietly. He pointed to the wide battlemented walls above the courtyard. Grim-faced pikemen and shieldsmen stood in knots of five at all the crossings.

"I see." Casteliano continued to stare down at the courtyard. "I also see that you brought back none of the Temple swordsmen, and not all of their archers. How did Father Sumbavu die?"

"He was killed with his men in an ambush," MacKinnie said slowly.

"But you were not caught?"

"Sumbavu was bringing supplies back to the city. I went to his aid, but we were too late. We could avenge him, but we couldn't save him."

"I see. A thousand brave men, who served you well. A high price to pay for a city."

"Damned high," MacKinnie muttered. "God help me, there was no other way. You've seen those Temple fanatics. We'd have to kill every one of those soldiers before they'd let us inspect their holy relics."

Casteliano turned away from the wall. "The relics. What is your interest in those?" He inspected Nathan carefully. "Whatever your reason, you have done the Church a service, and we will not forget."

"Thank you."

"And now we must speak to their council. Your pardon, Trader, I must find a room where we can dress properly for the interview—and I would be most grateful if you would bring a dozen of your most loyal men." He paused. "I doubt it will come to battle. Most of those on the council are practical men. As we are. Our demands will not be excessive, and we must be careful not to humiliate them. And of course the maris are not yet gone—"

"Precisely," MacKinnie said.

"Thus we have reason with us," Casteliano said. "And if that fails—"

MacKinnie gestured toward a group of pikemen on the battlements. "Then there is another argument."

Two days later, MacKinnie begged audience with His Ultimate Holiness, Primate of all Makassar, Vicar of Christ, and Archbishop of New Rome. He was led into a small office behind the council room where Casteliano was seated in his shirtsleeves examining Temple records. The Archbishop looked up and smiled.

"It was easier than you thought, was it not?" he said.

"Yes, Your Reverence. I still find it hard to believe that we had no bloodshed. But my men remain on guard, just in case."

"I told you there were few doctrinal differences, and these men are not only realists, but believers. If we had approached them from a Navy landing ship and demanded obedience to New Rome, we would have had to demonstrate our power, but it would have been managed. As it was, arriving in the city like beggars, they would never listen to us. How could they believe we were great lords of the True Church from the stars? But with you at our side, and your soldiers commanding their Temple, they had little choice but to listen."

"You were highly persuasive, Your Reverence."

"As were your actions. It was not difficult to make them see the hand of God in your victory, and His wrath in the death of Sumbavu. Did you foresee that as well?"

"No, Your Reverence."

"It is as well. Now what may I do for you?"

"I don't know how to begin. Yet I must have your help. I see no other way."

"'Colonel—do not be surprised, the title is commonly used by your soldiers—you hold this Temple, not me. You could depose me as easily as you created me, particularly if you supported the council against me. What is it I can do that you cannot do for yourself? Do you want to be crowned king of this city? They would do that for you."

MacKinnie laughed. "Nothing that simple. But— but may I speak to you in confidence? Have I earned the right to ask something which, if you refuse, you will not thwart me from attempting another way?"

The Archbishop took a small strip of cloth from the table in front of him, kissed it, and placed it over his shoulders. "My son, for thousands of years the confessional has never been violated. By tradition, by the laws of God, and by the most stringent of Imperial edicts, what you tell me in confession can never be revealed. Have you something to confess?"

Nathan MacKinnie breathed deeply, stared at the old man, and thought for a moment before beginning. "All right. As you surmised, we are from a newly discovered planet which will be a colony world when they get around to classifying us. They won't do that until we have a working planetary government, and King David's advisors are managing to delay that. They won't be able to hold up too much longer. We want to build a spaceship before they make us a colony world."

"A spaceship! Just how advanced are you? What makes you think . . . no, how does this affect me?"

"Father, I came here to get copies of every technical work I can find in that library. Our people think we can do it if we know how. I'm a soldier, not a scientist, and I don't know if they can do it or not, but we've got to try!"

The Archbishop nodded. "You would try. Tell me, Colonel MacKinnie, are you typical of the people of your planet?"

"I don't know. In some ways, yes. Why?"

"Because, and I say it reverently, God help the colonists they send to your world if you are. You

don't know when to give up. Yes, I'll help you." He
thought for a few moments, then laughed. "And we'll
stay within the letter of the regulations. Although I
doubt that would impress a Navy court martial if
they found you smuggling copies of technical books.
Makassar was classified before they discovered the
library, and so far they haven't updated it. The clas-
sification is 'primitive.' Therefore, any art or craft
found here can be taken to any other part of the
Empire.

"So, yes, we'll help you and gladly. Think what a
splendid joke on the Imperial Traders Association
this will make!" He struck a small gong on the desk
and told the servant who entered in response, "Go to
the holy relics and bring Brother LeMoyne, if you
please."

LeMoyne was a small man with sandy hair and
flashing blue eyes. He knelt perfunctorily before
Casteliano, kissed his ring, and said, "And what may
I do for His Ultimate Holiness other than refrain
from letting New Rome know his present title?"

The Archbishop laughed. "You can see why he will
never be a bishop. Tell me, can you make the holy
relics speak yet?"

"The library is in amazingly good condition, Your
Reverence. The Navy technicians fixed much of the
equipment when they made copies of the tapes. The
Old Empire used nearly indestructible plastics, and
everything has been preserved with holy zeal. It
only needs a power source to make it work."

"What kind of power?" MacKinnie asked.

"Oh, any good source of current. It doesn't take a
lot. Very efficient people, the Old Imperials. They
powered the whole palace from a small direct con-
version unit taking heat from natural hot springs.

That's still working, but the regulators aren't. The unit is putting out so little power now that it won't run much of the system—but we can get a few watts from it, after more than three hundred years! They built better than they knew in those days."

Casteliano nodded sadly. "Their equipment was splendid. But it didn't save them."

"No. Anyway, in addition to the old power unit, we have a hand-powered generator the Navy left. We've got part of the reader working off that, and it won't take long to get everything else in order. Uh, it would be no great trick to build a powered generator, but we couldn't let the natives see it operate."

"I think not for the moment," Casteliano said. "The Church has sometimes evaded the technology transfer restrictions, but that is a serious matter, not to be done without much thought. We need the Navy's cooperation." He paused thoughtfully. "Trader MacKinnie would like to inspect the library if that is convenient."

"Certainly. Now?" LeMoyne asked.

"Yes," MacKinnie said. "And if you could send for one of my people, Kleinst—"

"Oh, he's been down there helping me all morning," LeMoyne said. "Does His Ultimate Holiness care to accompany us?"

Casteliano looked in dismay at the litter of parchment on his desk. "I would be delighted, but this work must be done." He sighed. "Get thee behind me, Satan—"

LeMoyne shrugged and led MacKinnie out of the office. They went down winding stone stairways until they reached massive doorways guarded by four pikemen and a crimson-uniformed Temple officer. The pikemen snapped to attention as MacKinnie approached.

The officer looked doubtful. "He is a layman. Only the consecrated may enter—"

"Who'll stop the colonel?" one of the pikemen asked.

"He has been sent by His Ultimate Holiness," LeMoyne said. "Man, do you not know that if it had not been for the colonel, the *maris* would have the relics?"

"True," the Temple officer said. He took torches from the wall and handed them to MacKinnie and LoMoyne, then stood aside. He did not look pleased.

There were two more guardrooms, but these were empty. Then they went down a broader stairway of marble.

"This is almost certainly Old Empire," LeMoyne said. "After the wars, the survivors built most of the Temple structure over it. Here we are, just beyond that doorway."

They went through. At last, MacKinnie thought. I've come a long way to see this—

The room was not large. It stank of fish oil from the lamps. The walls had been scrubbed innumerable times to remove lampblack, and there was only a tiny suggestion of design or color to them.

There was not much else to see. A small box with crank handles and a seat stood in the middle of the room. Wires ran from that to a small table set against one wall. Above the table was what looked like a dark windowpane. Kleinst, wearing a dark monk's hood, sat in front of the desk. He stood when MacKinnie entered.

Nathan looked around the room in confusion. "Where is this fabulous machinery?" he asked.

LeMoyne chuckled. "Your friend there asked the same question." He pointed at the table. "There it is."

"No more than that?"

LeMoyne nodded. "No more than that. You could put all the knowledge of the human race in four units like that."

MacKinnie did not believe him, but there was no point in arguing. He turned to Kleinst. "Have you made any progress?"

The scholar's eyes gleamed. "Yes! Would you like to see?"

"Of course—"

"The sound units?" Kleinst asked, looking to LeMoyne. When LeMoyne nodded, Kleinst sat again at the console and touched small squares on it.

A tiny voice came from the walls. MacKinnie looked around in amazement.

"And except those days be shortened, there should not be any living creature survive," the voice said.

"Matthew," LeMoyne said, "Whoever was last down here loaded in that. The Temple priests have been listening to it ever since. They don't know how to change record units. The audio unit discharges the accumulators in less than an hour and the power system is so weak that it takes days to charge up again."

MacKinnie shook his head. "Do you understand this?" he asked Kleinst.

"Yes! Or almost. It is a new concept, yet not in principle different from photographic and recording equipment we use at home. Although more compact. And I don't understand everything about it. I don't know if we could read the tapes and cubes if we had them back at the University."

"And if we can't?" MacKinnie demanded.

"Then I must learn what we need," Kleinst said. "I have a photographic memory. It is one reason I was selected for this journey."

"There are many blanks in storage," LeMoyne said. "It will not be difficult to copy them. But I fear your friend is correct. The equipment needed to read these records is very complex." He went to a small, ornately carved cabinet near the table and laughed. "They made this into a tabernacle," he said. He opened it and took out a small block. "We could put most of what you need in two or three of these, if only you had means to read it."

"Copying them is simple!" Kleinst exclaimed. "Once we have more electrical power we can copy—and there is everything here! Textbooks for children which tell of physical laws no one at home has understood for hundreds of years. Handbooks, maintenance manuals for equipment I can't describe—look! Sit down there." He pointed to the box with handles. "Sit there, and turn that crank, and I will show you marvels—"

MacKinnie shrugged and did as he was told. The box made a whining noise as he spun the handles.

The dark glass above the table came to light. A diagram of some kind of complex equipment appeared. Then words.

"See!" Kleinst shouted.

"What does it mean?" MacKinnie asked.

"I don't know. But—with time I will. And if not, some of the younger students can be trained. We will learn."

"We have to," MacKinnie said.

"I don't quite understand who you are," LeMoyne said. "But if His Reverence is satisfied, I am."

"How long?" MacKinnie asked. "How long can you turn that crank?"

"It's tiring. An hour, perhaps—"

"It would be useful to build a powered unit, but

that is not easily done down here. If we could move this up to where we could connect water power—"

"Impossible," MacKinnie said. "We hold this Temple, true, but these people are volatile. If we moved the relics they'd be scandalized, and God knows what they'd do."

"Then you had better put your own officers to guard the doors," LeMoyne said. "We can make the copies in four hours, but—"

"But indeed. But how long for you to learn?" MacKinnie asked Kleinst.

"I could study for years and not learn it all—"

"We don't have years. We have weeks at most."

"I know," Kleinst said. "I will do the best I can. And we will make the copies. . . ."

"Which we may not be able to read," MacKinnie sighed. "The winter storms are coming. And we don't know what's happening at home. I know you'll do your best."

20

Juramentado

Firelight flickered across an old man's face.

Datu Attik's eyes dimmed with hidden tears as he watched two *juramentados* complete their ritual washing. The women came forward to hold high the crimson cloths for the binding. The young men's bodies shone in the yellow firelight.

They sang. Their death chants rang through the darkness around the camp. Otherwise there was silence. Later the others of the band, warriors and women alike, would sing death chants for these two, but for now the tribe had seen too much of death.

Eight hundred of the clan lay beneath the wheat stubble beyond the fire. Eight hundred stiffened and cold in the earth, eight hundred among the thousands who had fallen to the Temple army. How would the clan live without the young men? And now two more would join them, and one the son of the Datu.

Futile. Futile, thought Datu Attik. My son will die, and for nothing, for less than nothing, for worse than nothing. The Temple is strong. The robed fools have found new strength with their new sultan.

He ground his teeth at the memory. It had been so nearly done! The black-robed ones of the Great Temple of Batav had been defeated, done, were finished, penned into their city to starve while the maris roamed at will, ate the city's crops, rode to the very walls in challenge and laughed at the black robes—

And then came the new sultan from the far west, a giant of a man who made walls march and destroyed the greatest force the maris had ever assembled together.

It was done, it was done, Allah's will was done, and the maris must now return to their barren hills, but first let the city feel sorrow as the maris sorrowed. Let no man say his triumph was complete. Let the Temple mourn as Datu Attik mourned.

"No good will come of this." The voice came from his right side, from where his second son lay at his father's feet. "The sultan cannot be killed. My brother will make new war, and it is war we cannot win."

"Silence. Your brother sings his farewell." But it was true, Datu Attik thought. The sultan has said that if there is more war between the maris and the Temple, the marching walls will come to the fields in winter and pursue the maris to the end of the world.

He will do as he has said, and my sons will die, and my people will die. Why has Allah spared me to watch? Does He hate me so?

The song of the juramentados burst out and struck Attik like a blow, and the old man knew it was too late. These messengers of death could not be turned from their task, not by him or by anyone. Only their death would slow them now.

"O God Thou are Almighty, Allah Thou are Almighty, we witness that God is one God, we witness that Allah is Almighty!

"When the leaves of the Book shall be unrolled, when Hell shall blaze forth, when Paradise is near, then shall every soul know what works it hath made! Witness that Allah is One, witness that Allah is Almighty!"

Veiled women came now to aid the juramentados. They bound the young bodies tightly with scarlet cloths, tightly to hold the blood, scarlet to hide the blood from their enemies. Young, young men, his son was a young man, and now would die, but he would die for the glory of Allah—

His second son brought a kriss and Attik raised it to his lips, then passed it to the lips of his first son. "Then shall every soul know the works it hath made," Attik chanted. "So saith Allah, so saith the Almighty, every man shall submit to the will of Allah. Witness that Allah is One, witness that Allah is Almighty.

"Worthy is Allah to be praised."

The death songs hung over the camp long after the juramentados vanished into the night beyond the yellow circle of firelight. They were gone, running toward the city of Batav.

Faint sounds came from the city to the campsite: sounds of song and joy; the sounds of men and women in triumph. Datu Attik heard and shook his fist toward the magnificent blaze of the Temple rising above the city walls.

Temple!

The Temple of God, the Temple which held the

very voice of God! The Temple stolen by the black-robed priests of Batav, the Temple which was so nearly in the grasp of the maris. For generation upon generation the false priests of false gods had held the Temple from the faithful. Attik's grandfather was old when he died, and the oldest men his grandfather had known in his youth could not remember when the Temple was not held by the worshippers of the Prophet Jesus.

But Attik knew. Once there had been a time when men flew above the plains of Makassar, flew up to the very stars above. It was a time when God was not angry with men, and in that time the Temple was open so that all men could hear the words of God.

Surely Allah would not forever hold his people from his Word. Surely the juramentados would find the sultan MacKinnie, and then, and then—the maris might yet take the Temple! There were yet enough, and without the sultan to lead them, the black-robes might return to their futile ways of war—

"It shall be as Allah wills," Attik said aloud. "I submit to the will of Allah."

Then, since he was a practical man, Attik ordered the clan to prepare for their journey. It might be well to be far from the city when the juramentados struck. The sultan had ordered them away from the city plains in three days' time, and that time was nearly past.

If the juramentados met success, there would be time to gather the clans and return. Without their sultan the Temple priests would lose battles as they did in the past, and the Temple would fall.

The Temple for Allah, and the city of Batav for the maris. The city, that lovely city—

The sack of Batav could go on for days!

21

War Recalled

The celebrations continued for days. Monks' cells in the hollow of the walls of the great Temple lay empty as even the silent orders found release from their vows. Songs of triumph rose from the massive brooding walls to blend with the Te Deum sung in the Temple Sanctuary.

MacKinnie stood atop the highest Temple battlement and looked up into the night sky toward his home a dozen light-years away. A river of stars ran across the sky, so that it was difficult to locate the star that shone on his world.

The stars belonged to the Empire of Man, and looking up at the myriad of lights MacKinnie could appreciate the problems of the Imperial Navy. How could there be peace among all those and yet each have freedom? The legendary time when Prince

Samual's World was united and there were no wars
was remembered as a golden age, yet unification had
remained a dream and spawned a dozen wars; and
that was only one world. The Empire had hundreds,
perhaps thousands—he couldn't know. More worlds
than there were nations or city-states on Samual.

"Sir?"

He turned at Stark's approach. "Yes, Hal?"

"I brought the shipmaster."

MacKinnie once again marveled at the varieties of
man. People on Prince Samual's World were varied
enough, but nothing like what he had seen on
Makassar. There were the tall, fair men like Vanjynk,
and the dark, swarthy men like Loholo; the Imperial
Navy even had black men and women. On Samual
"black men" were legendary monsters who lived in
the hills and ate children. . . .

Loholo stood respectfully and waited for MacKinnie
to speak.

"Shipmaster, I must return to Jikar. When can we
sail?" MacKinnie asked.

Loholo shrugged. "She is ready now. It will be no
easy journey. Much of the time the wind will be in
our faces. There is better trading to the east and
south . . . and there will be storms."

"Aye." MacKinnie shuddered. Now that they were
ashore he could admit that he'd been terrified. But
there was no other way. Or was there? "Could we
sail east to get there?"

"East? You believe the tales that Makassar is
round—but you would know, star man. You would
know." Loholo shrugged, jingling the golden orna-
ments he wore. His curved dagger bore new jewels
on the hilt, and there were new rings on his fingers.
"I have known of men who believed the world round
and sailed east to reach the western shores," he said.

"But I never heard of one who arrived. Trader, there are shoals west of Jikar, and there are pirates throughout the islands. *Subao* is faster then they, but there are many pirates. Those are the western waters I know. What else may lay between here and there—" He shrugged again to a jingle of gold. "Only God knows."

God and the Imperial Navy, MacKinnie thought. From the maps they had shown him there was a lot of open water to the east of the main continent. Loholo was probably right. "I had thought as much," MacKinnie said. "So there's nothing for it. We sail in five days."

"So soon? You will hardly have time to buy a cargo. It would be much better to wait until next season."

"No. I must reach Jikar in two hundred days," MacKinnie said.

Loholo chuckled. "Then you will have an uncomfortable voyage. Two thousand klamaters in two hundred days." The sea captain laughed again. "In this season. Well, *Subao* can withstand that—but can you? And why leave Batav at all? You rule here. The priestly star man is Ultimate Holiness, but he came to the throne on your pikes, and did not your pikemen hold the city the old council would elect a new Holiness inside three days."

"And that's a fact," Stark said. "There's some in the new council who'd support Casteliano, but you can't expect all them old Archdeacons to take kindly to the Imperial missionaries movin' in on 'em like that. Mister Loholo's right, there'd be civil war if it wasn't that our troops hold all the strong points."

"Which means I can't take the whole army across the plains," MacKinnie said. "Or if I did, I'd have to take the Imperial missionaries with me—"

"They're not likely to come," Stark observed.

"Exactly. And they won't continue helping us if we take them as prisoners." MacKinnie glanced upward at the stars and thought again of the problems of empire. "So it's by sea. Leave the pikeman here and hope the missionaries know what to do with them. Thank you, Mister Loholo. That will be all."

"Trader?" Loholo made no move to leave.

"Yes?"

"Trader, you promised me *Subao* when we returned to Jikar."

"She'll be yours, Mister Loholo."

"Aye. Then with your permission I'll get back to her. There's still work to be done. Bottom to be scraped, new water barrels, provisions—but if there's a place by water on this world that you want to go to, I'll take you, even if we pass every pirate in the shallows!" Loholo fingered the golden skull ornament at his left ear. "You're the strangest man I've ever see, Trader. You've shown us how to make ships sail better than we ever knew. You trained an army of city rabble and took them out to whip the barbarians after the Temple people gave up. Now you're in command of the Temple and all Batav, and you want to return to Jikar! Most men would rather stay here as king—and there'd be no nonsense about it, either. You've only to say the word—"

"And you could be my High Admiral, Mister Loholo?"

"No, sir. Your star man Captain MacLean would have that post, and I'm not that ambitious. *Subao*'s enough for me, star man. A good ship and open sea's all my father wanted for any of his children."

Loholo began the long descent down the stone stairway to the street below, and MacKinnie turned away to lean on the ramparts. Batav was a blaze of lights, with bonfires in all the public squares. Every one of the city's thirty thousand souls seemed to be reveling in the streets, their numbers swollen by another thirty thousand peasants who had sought refuge within the city walls. The peasants would soon go back to their fields, and the remnants of Batav's great feudal families, all those who survived the futile charges against the maris before MacKinnie arrived, would return to their great halls and tournaments—

And then what? "Getting control of that damned library was easier then letting loose," MacKinnie said. "I'm concerned about the missionaries. Can they hold on after we leave?"

"I doubt it. Not without a good commander who knows how you fight."

"Could Brett hold the Temple?" MacKinnie asked.

Stark shrugged. "He's maybe smart enough, but they'd never trust him. He was raised a mari, sure enough, and it shows. Nobody's going to put him in command."

"Then who can do it?"

"You."

"And no one else, Sergeant?"

"Not that I know of, Colonel. You built this army, and you know what it can do. The others don't think like you."

"And that worries you?" MacKinnie asked.

"Don't get paid to worry," Stark said automatically. "Except—"

He's in a strange mood, MacKinnie thought. He really is worried. I haven't seen him that way since—

"You know," Stark said, "Mister Loholo's got a point, Colonel. A year ago we was down to it, looking for a place fightin' in some petty war on South Continent and wonderin' how to pay the rent on a flophouse until we found something. We never expected to find anything as good as we've got now."

"I gave Dougal my word, and I swore allegiance to King David," MacKinnie reminded him.

"After Haven used the goddam Empire to bake half our Wolves, Colonel! They'd never have took Orleans without the Imperial Marines . . . and then they turned you out like an old dog! What do we really owe Haven, Colonel? What do we owe anybody?"

MacKinnie turned to his sergeant in surprise. "We're soldiers, Hal. It's all either of us has ever been—"

"Soldiers for who, Colonel? You owe Haven any more'n you owe Batav? If it wasn't for them peasant kids we trained we'd never have beat the maris. Them boys would follow you to hell, and what's goin' to happen to 'em if we pull up stakes and leave? And when we get back to Haven, that Dougal's likely to slit our throats to shut us up. What use are we to him after we bring back them books on whatever it is Kleinst has got? There's not much for us back on Samual, and that's the size of it—" Stark turned quickly and grasped the hilt of his sword. "Watch out, Colonel, there's somebody comin' up the stairs."

"Go see who it is." There were guards posted at the foot of the stairway to MacKinnie's penthouse, and from the sounds there was only one person approaching. Hal could deal with any single man. Nathan turned back to the battlements.

The revels continued in the city below. Drunken apprentices staggered from shop to shop, demanding that lights be placed in all dark windows on pain of having the building itself burned to provide light. Barrels of wine and ale stood at street corners, open to all comers. But through the drunken reveling

MacKinnie's peasant pikemen stood in grim, disciplined knots at the strategic points, waiting for their relief before joining the festivities. . . .

Follow me to hell, MacKinnie thought. Why not? I found them not much better than slaves and now they've just defeated the worst threat this city's ever faced.

Why the hell shouldn't I be king? Because of another duty. . . .

All his life MacKinnie had lived under a soldier's code and like most dueling societies Prince Samual's World held honor higher than life . . . but what was the honorable course now?

Who owns my loyalty? he wondered. Dougal, who had a dozen men and women killed to protect the secret babbled by that drunken Imperial officer? Casteliano, who's Ultimate Holiness courtesy of my pikemen? Or those lads out there? It's obvious what Hal thinks.

"It's Freelady Graham, Colonel," Stark announced.

Mary Graham had taken off her armor and had let her long brown hair fall in waves and curls to below her shoulders. A blue linen gown with tight bodice set off her small figure, and she was much lovelier than she'd been the first time MacKinnie had seen her.

"Nathan, you're missing the party," she said accusingly. "Can't you ever relax, even for one evening? Let's have some fun!"

MacKinnie was surprised by the possessive tone in her voice. Had he imagined it or—Great Saints, he thought. She's a real beauty tonight. And with her hair let down she looks a lot like Laura. Nearly as headstrong, too. And she's twenty-four, you're fifty, and she's your ward. But—

Unwanted the memories poured past his guard.

There had been another girl, once. A freelady, not one of the innumerable camp followers any military commander would know. She was no more than thirty, and it was no more than three years ago. . . .

A bleak picture formed in MacKinnie's mind. Haven, defeated at Blanthern Pass, was on the march again, invading Orleans with inadequate troops and a dangerously thin supply line. And Iron MacKinnie's Wolves were ready, this time ready to end Haven's threat to Orleans forever and aye. When this battle was done, the Orleans Committee of Public Safety could dictate any terms they wanted to David II!

The Wolves lay in ambush at Lechfeld. Two battalions waited, enough troops to force Haven's invading force to deploy and fight. Lechfeld couldn't be bypassed or the Haven army would be without any possible supply line. Twenty kilometers away, in dense forest, a regiment of Orleans Dragoons moved swiftly through the forest gullies, leading their horses until they reached open country. Above, behind rolling hills overlooking the Lechfeld plains, MacKinnie waited with the balance of his Wolves to close the trap—and the Haven army was moving into it.

The Committee had protested the battle plan. Converging columns were too dangerous. There was no reliable way to communicate between them, even if the University professors did believe they would have reliable wireless soon. The timing of the battle needed great precision or the Orleanists would be defeated in detail.

The Committee had protested, but MacKinnie had won that fight. He knew the capabilities of his troops to the last small unit, and his scouts would cover the battle area. There would be no surprises for Orleans; only for Haven—and the Wolves would not fight at all until Haven was in the trap.

And now they were marching in, and they were doomed.

Freelady Laura waited with him in the hills above Lechfeld. He had tried to send her to the rear before, but she came back—and except for Stark there wasn't an officer or a noncom in his command who'd disobey the colonel's lady even on his direct orders. Still, it was safe enough. The losses today would be Haven's! But she was in a place of danger, and that wouldn't do.

"Go to Lechfeld while the road's still open," MacKinnie had told her. "Major Armstrong is well dug in and his position won't be exposed until the battle is over. Meet me in Lechfeld."

She protested, but he needed a message carried, and finally she agreed to go. "We'll be riding at the charge all the way, Laura," he'd said. "You can't keep up with that! We'd be separated anyway. If I can't make you go to the rear—damn your father for letting you out of the house!—I want you safe."

"All right. I won't have you worrying about me when you should be directing the battle." She sat proudly in the ambulance. The escorting cavalry saluted. Cornet Blair mounted with a flourish, proud to be chosen as protector of his colonel's fiancée.

"And we'll see the chaplain when the battle's ended," MacKinnie promised. "Ride out, Blair."

"Sir." Ambulance and escort rode away in a thin cloud of dust and MacKinnie gave his attention to the Haven forces below. In an hour their advance units appeared. They weren't surprised to meet resistance at Lechfeld and fell back to wait for the rest of the column.

The Haven army deployed skirmishers, then formed a main battle line for attack, their artillery moving forward at the gallop. Trumpet calls rang across plowed

fields as Haven's last army prepared for a set piece
battle.

It worried Nathan. Haven had better soldiers than
that! They'd walked into a classic military trap, and
they hadn't even put out guards to their flanks and
rear! But MacKinnie's hard-riding scouts, their horses
lathered with flecks of white foam, had circled the
enemy. They had seen nothing. There were no significant reinforcements, no support at all for the
forces moving so blindly into MacKinnie's trap. Haven was doomed.

Why? MacKinnie wondered. It hardly mattered.
Perhaps they had planned some clever counter-coup,
but there was nothing, nothing at all that they or
anyone could do now. . . .

The Orleans Dragons took the field within minutes
of the time MacKinnie had set for them. They advanced and dug in, closing off the Haven column's
escape route, forming a solid anvil against which the
charging Wolves would crush their enemy, and now,
now it was time! "Mount 'em up, Hal! Move 'em out!
Fox and Dragon troops will charge those batteries on
the right flank. The rest dismount at five hundred
meters and advance on foot. We've got them, Hal,
we've beaten everything Haven can put into the
field!"

The Wolves charged down the hill, whooping like
South Continent barbarians, while the youthful trumpeters blew every call in the book. It was done. The
Wolves were in perfect position to roll up Haven's
flank—and death fell from the skies. A sleek black
shape roared overhead and, as it passed, Lechfeld
was turned into a blackened cinder.

And again, again that thing passed overhead, and
blinding beams of light stabbed out to burn the

Dragoons! Now it hovered over the battlefield, playing its deadly beams across MacKinnie's army.

"Dismount! All troops fire on that thing! Troop Commanders, fire troops in volley! Trumpeter, orders to artillery! Where the hell are those field pieces? Gunners, get those goddam cannons in action!"

Somehow they'd done it. The black shape fell from the skies, settling hard into the cornfields, and when the gray-coated troops in the sky machine came out, the Wolves cut them down and howled in triumph!

Too late. Haven's army was still intact. The Dragons were dead or running, Lechfeld was gone, and the Wolves had taken terrible casualties. The Haven force wheeled to face right, and for the first time in his life Nathan MacKinnie had known defeat. When the trumpeters sounded recall it was the end of his career, and the end of everything else. Laura had been in Lechfeld. . . .

"Colonel." Stark took his commander by the elbow. "Colonel, it don't do no good to think about it."

"Uh?" The bright fields of Prince Samual's World faded. Awkwardly he turned away form the battlements and let his hands relax. The knuckles were white. "Your pardon, Mary. I was—somewhere else. You're right, let's go join the revels."

22

Grace and Absolution

Mary Graham watched the mad light fade from Nathan MacKinnie's eyes. I know, she thought. I know what he saw. When Hal tells that story, it's like being there.

MacKinnie's voice came from the bottom of a well of emotion. Mary tried to smile reassuringly, but that was impossible.

What must it be like, she wondered. To feel that much for someone? And what was she like, that girl he was thinking about? Hal wouldn't say much about her. I don't even know her name. What was she like, to make a man like MacKinnie feel that way? I'll never have that kind of devotion from anyone.

Have I that much to give?

Yes. I do. I've always been sure of that, that somewhere, somehow—

A little girl's dream.

No. Not that at all. When I was little I thought of a handsome, rich lord and now, well, yes, I've usually thought of him, whoever he'll be, as rich and handsome, but mostly he'll be a man who'll let me be more to him than my father ever let Mother be.

She stared up into the star-studded darkness. That tiny dot is my sun, she thought. One dot among thousands, tiny, insignificant, and yet it was my whole world for all my life until just last year—

A world she no longer cared much for. She had resented the restrictions Haven society put on her, but that had been a formless resentment, almost unconscious. Now she knew better. There were other ways to live, other cultures on other worlds, worlds without end, worlds after worlds, and what was Prince Samual's World, or anyone on it?

We are what we make ourselves. And we can change whole worlds. We're doing that now. Isn't it enough?

She had felt the magic touch of command, of knowing that others depended on her judgement. Mac-Kinnie had won the battles, but without her cooks and supply wagons he couldn't have taken the field. He'd known that, and he'd trusted her, trusted her with the lives of all his men, and his troopers were more important to him than his own life—

"Your turn to be in a blue daze," Nathan said. "What we need is some company."

She nodded and let Nathan and Hal lead her down the stairs to the streets below, but still the pensive mood pursued her. Do we need company? she wondered. Maybe we have too much already. Hal would be happy enough to go join the revels without us. . . .

She almost laughed aloud. A year ago that thought would have shocked her. Or at least she would have pretended, even to herself, that it did. Properly brought up young ladies didn't have any doubts about what was proper.

Proper young ladies had dull lives.

The streets were alive with people. Where there had formerly been beggars and empty shops there were shouting throngs drowning the bitterness of months of defeat in wine and ale. The barbarians were driven from the gates!

Those who hadn't pawned their finery during the siege now wore it. Several pawnshops had been looted, so that many others were gaily dressed in bright woolens, silks, even cotton prints. A riot of color wove complex patterns through the streets. It seemed the entire city had turned out. Even the saffron-robed members of the Temple minor orders, the gray deacons, and the black-robed full priests joined in the revelry. Only MacKinnie's on-duty pikemen held aloof, and many of them quaffed hastily offered beakers of wine and beer.

"Seems different without them Temple swordsmen," Hal said. "I see the Temple people are already recruitin' more to replace the ones we lost out on the field—"

"Yes." MacKinnie would rather that subject were dropped.

"It was terrible," Mary said. "Father Sumbavu and a thousand swordsmen killed after our victory . . . I can't understand how it happened."

"It always happens," MacKinnie said. "There's always a price."

But what really did happen? she wondered. Had MacKinnie understood Sumbavu so well that he could deliberately use the priest to destroy the Temple

army? That was a bit frightening. If he knew Sumbavu
that well, how much does he know about me?

What if he did send Sumbavu and all his men out
to die? Was there any other way to get control of the
Temple? Probably not. Was it worth the price? That's
the real question. What are we doing here? What am
I doing? From what I've seen I'd rather live in
Imperial society than my·own—

But Imperial society has no use for me or any of
us, women and men alike. Haven does. This mission
is important to Haven, and I'm important to the
mission, and that ought to be enough. It's more than
I ever dreamed of. Except that now my part of the
job is done. . . .

MacKinnie found a goblet of wine and gave it to
her. It was strong, heady stuff, and she knew she
shouldn't drink all of it, but the festive mood of the
streets was hard to resist, and she drank more than
half. Nathan took a beaker of ale from one of his
off-duty troopers. "Thanks, Hiaro," he said. "What'll
you do now that the war's over?"

"I don't know, Colonel." The little pikeman stood
tall, and Stark's merciless drillfield exercises showed
in his muscles. Mary remembered when she'd first
seen him: when Hiaro had joined MacKinnie's army
he was an emaciated ghost living on Temple charity,
sleeping in a gutter and waiting to die. "My farm is
burned, my wife and children are dead . . . the lord
of my fields wants us to return to the land, and it
seems I must do so for I am not tall enough to join
the new Temple guards."

MacKinnie drank and turned away but the fugle-
man pursued him. "Colonel—Trader—sir, it is ru-
mored that you will march west with an army. There
are many like me who would go with you. Some talk
of remaining together and seeking employment as

soldiers for another city, but we would rather go with you."

"Thanks, Hiaro. I'll remember," MacKinnie said.

What is there about him that wins loyalty? Mary wondered. *Not just Hiaro. Hal Stark. The other guardsmen. It's like a tangible force. I can feel it, too, but I suppose that could be something else, something more physical. Heaven knows he's attractive enough. And sometimes he looks at me—* She drank the rest of the goblet. Someone stepped out of the crowd to fill it again.

They wandered through the brightly lit streets. Wind chimes with a Temple replica as centerpiece tinkled in every doorway. They rounded a corner, and she slipped on the rough cobblestones. MacKinnie caught her, and she leaned against him for a moment. She felt his warmth, and she didn't want to move away. Gently he set her back on her feet, but she thought he took his time doing it, as if the physical contact wasn't unpleasant for him.

"The pikemen could do all right as mercenaries," Stark commented. "They can beat anything on this planet exceptin' heavy cavalry, and with the right battle plan they might even do that. No leaders, though, so they'll probably hire out to some idiot who'll waste them. Nobody on this end of Makassar appreciates good infantry. Be a pity what's goin' to happen to them lads after all the training we gave them. . . ."

"I got your message before, Sergeant," MacKinnie said. His voice was cold.

"Yes, sir."

"What message?" Mary asked.

"Hal thinks I ought to stay here as king of this city rather than return to Jikar."

"But you can't do that! Haven is depending on

you, all of Prince Samual's World—Nathan, you wouldn't really do that!"

But we could, she thought. We could stay. She thought of Hiaro as she'd first seen him. And the children of Batav. The Empire wouldn't help them. Someone should. But not us! We've our own world to save, and even if I don't like Haven as much as I once did, it's my home, and this is my duty.

"Wouldn't I? Who's to stop me?" he asked.

She drew away from him, then began to laugh. "Why, *you* are, Iron Man! I suppose you really could get away with it. The Imperial Navy wouldn't like that, but with their Archbishop on your side you'd be all right." She spoke tauntingly now. "Go on, Your Majesty. Forget your oaths. Why don't you take me into the nearest building and ravish me while you're at it? Who's to stop you? I have no protector here. No one but you."

MacKinnie turned away.

They were approaching a large group, peasants, soldiers off duty, knights in mail, all gathered around a cart in the center of a public square. One mailed warrior in bright surcoat stood atop the cart, his head tilted back in song.

"Look, there's Brett," Nathan said. "Let's go listen."

Two pikemen saw MacKinnie approach and efficiently cleared a way through the crowd to the wagon.

"In the public house to die, is my resolution,
Let wine to my lips be nigh, at life's dissolution!
That will make the angels cry, with glad elocution,
'Grant this drunkard, God on high, grace and
absolution!'"

Brett ended his song and seized a flagon of wine. As he drained it he saw MacKinnie. "Ho, lads, it's the colonel and his lady, our Lady Mary who brings food and drink and takes care of the wounded. A song for the real winner of our battles!"

"Oh mistress mine, where are you—"

He had hardly begun when he broke off and straightened in horror. "Hal! Behind you! Guard the colonel!" Brett tore his sword from its sheath and leaped from the cart.

It all happened so fast that Mary had no time to react. A short, brown man rushed through the crowd. He brandished a heavy curved knife. A bedlam of shouting erupted, but the intruder ran in deadly silence. When a pikeman moved to intercept him the kriss flashed, lopping off the soldier's arm at the elbow. There were more shouts, of warning and terror. The kriss swung again and again, and more of MacKinnie's warriors fell to the wine-soaked cobblestones.

"Haigh!" A soldier flung his javelin from somewhere behind her. The meter-and-a-half dart took the charging warrior below the chest, but the man plucked the javelin from his body and charged on, still dealing terrible blows to everyone in his path. Then there was no one but Stark between him and the colonel.

Hal had no time to draw his sword. Instead, he moved in front of Mary and MacKinnie. The kriss flashed again. It caught Stark on the right shoulder and battered him to the ground, but he'd bought MacKinnie time enough to draw his own weapon.

And the brown man was still coming forward, directly toward her, toward Nathan, the great curved knife held high. Nathan took his stance, his face determined but calm, no fear at all as he held the point of his sword leveled at the enemy—

And the man, impaled on the sword, still ran forward down the blade toward MacKinnie. The kriss lifted high and Mary saw death descending.

"Haigh!" Brett shouted a curse similar to the assassin's. His broadsword flashed, catching the descending wrist to cut it off. Brett lifted his weapon again and cut viciously at the head, then again. The stocky warrior slumped, his weight tearing MacKinnie's sword from his hand.

"Haigh! Brett shouted again. "In time! Hal, do you live?"

"Yeah." Stark eased himself gingerly to his feet and clutched his right shoulder with his left hand. "Man, he swings that thing hard! Caught me more with the flat than the edge, damn good thing I didn't take off my mail after duty today. . . ." He tested his arm. "Gonna be stiff for a week."

"Better that than to lose the arm," Brett said quietly.

The crowd was milling about the square, and men and women were shouting. "The colonel lives!" Brett leaped to his wagon and shouted it again. "He lives. The colonel lives!"

"Glory be to God!" Someone screamed. A Temple priest began to pray loudly.

It was only then that the reaction took her. She was still shaking when MacKinnie climbed onto the wagon to show himself unhurt. He was just in time. Already his pikemen were advancing with leveled weapons, ready to avenge their commander's death with a massacre. . . .

Nathan climbed down from the cart. A near thing, he thought. As near as ever I came to buying it.

Now that it was over he'd get the shakes. It almost

always happened. When there was work to do, danger only made him calmer, but when it was over. . . . He found Mary in the crowd. She seemed calm enough, but subdued, and he took her hand.

A hastily assembled squad of pikemen escorted them back to the Temple compound. They walked in silence to MacKinnie's rooms, then Mary went to find the Temple physicians, while Brett and MacKinnie assisted Stark in removing his armor and the thick woolsh-hide padding beneath it. The shoulder was swollen and discolored.

"It don't feel broke," Stark said. He moved his arm gingerly. "But it sure don't feel too good, either. Could you pour me some wine, Colonel?"

"Sure." MacKinnie got the bottle and goblets. "We could all use some. Brett, who was that man?"

"A mari fanatic," Brett said. "Sent to kill you. The juramentados are usually very high-ranking members of the clan, and they never come back alive. You should feel complimented. They think killing you is important."

"They're right, too," Stark said. "Without the colonel—"

Brett nodded. "They'll have the Temple within a yir. Probably sooner."

"Damn it, now both of you are after me," MacKinnie said. "And what am I supposed to do?"

"Nothing you can do, Colonel," Stark said. "You took on a job, and you wouldn't be who you are if it was in you to throw off your duty. Still, it's a pity. Those are good lads."

There was a long silence. Hal broke it at last. "Maybe Brett and I, between us, could hold onto this place."

"But—"

"You won't be needing me to get home," Stark

said. "Not really. MacLean and Todd and Loholo can handle the ship. And there's nothing much for me after we get back."

Nathan still didn't say anything.

"Damn it," Hal said, "I don't like splitting up any better than you do. But—Colonel, we made soldiers out of those peasants. Don't we owe them?"

"It could be our salvation," Brett said. "I know the maris. As you suspect, although I was not born one of them, I grew up in a mari clan, and I know them. When they hear that you are gone, they will return, and who can fight them? I cannot. Nor can Vanjynk. Yet we can control the knights, and if Hal commands here—for you, of course. We must say that we hold for you, until your return, and let Hal command in your name."

Stark grinned wryly. "Like old times. It's what I've always done. All I ever wanted to do, for that matter. And we'd have a good chance."

"You might have time to build a good military force," Nathan said. "Good enough to hold the maris. But what about the politics? Sergeant—"

"Colonel, don't order me to come with you."

I don't think he ever interrupted me before, MacKinnie thought.

"I'll take care of these new Wolves for you," Stark said. "Just until you come back for us. Let's leave it like that."

Except we both know I'll never get back, MacKinnie thought.

He looked at Stark, then looked away. There had always been the possibility that Stark would be killed in a battle that MacKinnie survived, but after Lechfeld it hadn't seemed likely. After Lechfeld, Stark was all that was left of his former life. He had never considered what it would be like to be alone.

I guess now I find out, he thought.

Mary came in with two yellow-robed priests. They looked at Hal's shoulder and exchanged glances, then bent to feel it gingerly. "I do not think it broken," one said. "It will heal. But it may be dislocated. We will have to wrench it into place, then bind it up. That will be painful. If you will come with us— "

"I'll go, too," Brett said. "Just to be certain."

MacKinnie got up as well.

Stark shook his head. "No need for you to come, Colonel. I'll see you in the morning."

And you'd rather I didn't watch, MacKinnie thought. I've seen the Temple medical people work, they're good at their job—and Hal won't want me around when they start yanking at that shoulder. It's easier to yell bloody murder if your friends aren't around. "Right." He watched as the priests led Hal and Brett away.

Nathan went to the door and closed it. When he turned back he saw Mary was still there, still lovely, making no move to go—

"Freelady, you shouldn't be—",

"Don't be silly," she said. "You're shaking—"

"Yes, damn it. I—"

"So am I." She held up her hands.

MacKinnie laughed wryly. "You're not in my line of work. It's always been like this, after the action is over—"

"And you wonder if I think less of you?" she asked. "Because your hands tremble?" She shuddered.

Why is she here? MacKinnie wondered. Right here, two steps away, all I have to do is—

She's your ward and you're fifty and she's half your age. And damned beautiful. And what do I do now? "Do you want a drink?"

"If you're having one—"

He poured two goblets of wine.

There was a long silence while they drank. Then Mary laughed.

"What?" Nathan asked.

"Us. You were almost killed tonight. You could be killed tomorrow. Or we both could be. And we're standing here in the middle of this room, when— Nathan, this is foolish!"

"But—"

"But nothing! Guardians. Never be alone with a man. Nathan, that's another world. A world so far away I can't even imagine it—and you stopped looking at me like a daughter a long time ago. . . ." She moved closer to him and put her hand on his arm. "We're here, Nathan. We're here and tonight we're alive. Tomorrow we might not be."

Gray dawn gave just enough light to see when MacKinnie woke. He lay still for a moment, half remembering a dream. Then he sat upright. He was alone in the bed—

But not in the room. Mary sat in a big chair, her knees drawn up to her chin. She had covered herself with a large fur robe.

"You're awake," she said.

"So are you—why are you sitting there?"

"I couldn't sleep, and I didn't want to disturb you."

"Are you—are you all right?" he asked.

She laughed, a soft tinkle in the gray light. "You silly goose, of course I'm all right." She laughed again. "Why, did you think I was brooding over lost innocence? If you must know, I was thinking of how much time we wasted before tonight."

"So was I."

She smiled and stood. She was naked except for

the fur robe, and she threw that aside. "Then let's don't waste any more. There won't be a lot of privacy on *Subao*."

It was fully light outside when he woke again. MacKinnie moved carefully and gently kissed her. She smiled and opened her eyes lazily.

"Good morning," Nathan said.

"Yes. It is a good morning." She stretched lazily. "It would be a better one for some coffee. Or chickeest. Or even that horrible tea they have here."

"I'll just send for some, shall I?"

She drew away in mock horror. "And scandalize your guards?"

"They would be. Or would pretend to be," Nathan said.

"Don't be so serious."

"Someone has to be."

"I suppose. And we've both work to do. We'd better get up."

"To hell with the work—"

"You don't mean that," she said.

"Maybe I do. The harder I work, the quicker we go back. Assuming Kleinst can do anything useful to begin with, and I'm not at all sure he can. Mary—we really could stay here."

"You're not going to start that again, are you? Nathan, I don't really know why we're here. It has something to do with the library, I can guess that. And Lord Dougal said this was the most important mission in the history of Haven, important to the whole planet."

"It is," Nathan said. "And it's time I told you what we're doing here. All of you should know, so you won't let something slip to the Imperial Navy people." He explained the mission to her. "But I've come to think it's senseless," he finished.

"Why?"

"Why? You've seen their ships. How can we build anything like that?"

"What does Kleinst say, now that he's seen the library?"

"Humph. He's so enraptured by all the new scientific laws that he isn't even thinking about building ships. And he doesn't know if we can read copies of the records on Samual, even if we can take copies back. He could learn, he says. But in how many years? I think we've been chasing a dream, Mary. A noble dream, but nothing more than that."

She stared at patterns of sunlight on the wall. When she spoke she was very serious. "Dream or not, we have to try," she said. "Not just for us. For everyone. The Empire is wrong, Nathan. Their policies. Look at what they're doing to this world. With what little we know we could save them from so much misery."

"Or destroy them," MacKinnie said.

"That's strange, coming from you."

"Oh, I've no love for the Imperials. I just don't know how to do their job."

"You don't have to. All you have to do is your own."

"But—"

"There really is something wrong, isn't there?"

He nodded. "Hal won't be coming back with us."

"Are you certain?"

"Yes. He's going to stay with Brett. He thinks he has an obligation to these peasant lads he trained. So do I."

"He's been with you a long time, hasn't he?"

"Since I was a junior lieutenant," Nathan said.

"Mary, how can I leave him here? And for what? It's not my job any longer. It's all up to Kleinst, and he doesn't know how to build a spaceship either."

"Iron MacKinnie gives up," she said. "The terrible warrior—no, I won't mock you. I don't suppose I'll ever know the kind of friendship you and Hal have. But the mission isn't finished until we get home, and Nathan, be honest, what are our chances without you?"

"Not as good as if I come." It was as if the words were wrenched from him, as if they said themselves without his willing it. "But what good are we doing?"

"Nathan, we've got the library. When we started even that didn't look possible. Now we just keep on doing what we can."

"Why is this important to you?" MacKinnie asked.

"They trusted me," she said. "For you that's nothing new. But for me—Nathan, I can't betray that trust." She moved closer to him. "I hope—"

"What?"

"I'm selfish enough to hope you won't make me choose," she said.

There were tears at the corners of her eyes. Nathan knew she was fighting to hold them back, that she wasn't acting.

Duty and honor and love. He'd sacrifice all three no matter what he did. But when he looked at her, he knew he had no real choice at all.

Part Three

PRINCE SAMUAL'S HOPE

23

Arindell's Castle

Angus Volker, fourteenth Regent of Prince Samual University, looked at the invitation and sighed. It was a simple card written by someone with beautiful handwriting, and the message seemed harmless enough. "David II, by grace of God King of Haven and Grand Duke of Orleans, Mayor of Halmarch, Prince-Magnate of Startford, requests the honor of your company at an audience to be held at the residence of Lord Arindell at 1664 hours on Wednesday next."

Certainly the card was formally correct. It was not a command.

But it might as well have been. Academician Volker looked around his richly furnished tower office and sighed again. When the faculty elected him rector it seemed likely that he would preside over the Uni-

versity's celebration of its two-hundred-fiftieth anni-
versary of independence. Now it was likely that
celebration would never happen. The very titles King
David chose to have placed on the invitation were
significant: Orleans, Startford, and Halmarch had all
been prominent in the alliance of free states which
by treaty guaranteed the independence of Prince
Samual University. Now they were merged into Haven, as were several more so thoroughly subjugated
that they had not even the shadow of existence in
David's titles.

I could refuse, he told himself. I could send polite
regrets. . . .

But the next invitation would not be so polite. It
might even be accompanied by Haven guards. The
University proctors couldn't keep armed Haven troops
from entering the campus. Some of the students would
undoubtedly riot, but the end of that was inevitable.
The University's independence had never depended
on anything as weak as its power to defend itself.
And now the alliance which had been its real defense
was a hollow shell.

No. Better to accept an invitation. So long as
David was being formally correct, there was a small
chance that the University might retain independence. If the gloves came off there would be no
chance at all.

Volker turned the matter endlessly in his mind as
his chauffeur drove him toward Lord Arindell's palace.

Arindell. Was the meeting place significant? Arindell
was a prominent socialite, and it was not unreasonable that the king might host a social gathering at his
residence—but Arindell was also Minister of Justice.
There were stories about him and the Haven Royal
Police; of how suspected enemies of King David had

vanished without a trace. There had always been such stories, but lately there seemed to be more. Was it merely because no one understood the role of the Imperials, or was there more to it? Volker didn't know.

But surely they would not so openly arrest the Rector of Prince Samual University! The University was the most important institution on Prince Samual's World, above petty national politics, older than most nations and subject to none of them. Surely he need not worry. He told himself that again, then carefully folded his pudgy hands in his ample lap and with an effort of will made them stay there as the car drove on through uncrowded cobblestone streets.

Lord Arindell's palace had once been a fortress. The moat had long ago been filled in, and the cannons on the terraces were obsolete, purely decorative, their mouths stuffed with fresh flowers. Banners and streamers fluttered from high battlements. Yet despite the festive decorations there was an air of foreboding about the place, and Volker was reluctant to leave his steam car. He wanted desperately to tell the chauffeur to take him back to campus where he felt safe. But if he did, how long would the campus be a place of refuge?

"One step at a time," he told himself. Then, louder, he told the chauffeur, "Go back to the University. Mrs. Volker will have errands for you. And send another driver for me. Have him come here and wait."

"I don't mind waiting, Rector. I could send a telegram to have Andrew help Lady Volker."

"No. Please do it my way." He hesitated. "I'm not unhappy with you, Felix. I've got reasons."

The chauffeur looked up at the massive stone walls.

"I guess you have, sir. If I was going in there, I expect I'd want somebody to know what time I went in. Somebody outside."

Volker smiled wryly. "I hadn't known I was that obvious. I'm certain nothing will happen."

"Be more certain with me back on campus," Felix said. "I could stop by the provost's office on my way to help Lady Volker . . . I've got a cousin who's a proctor."

"It won't be necessary," Volker said. "Thank you."

He waited until the steam car was out of sight before he went down the rose-lined path to the great gates.

A hundred of Haven's most glamorous people were gathered in the ancient palace ballroom. Angus was announced by a butler and greeted by Lord Arindell. The gathering seemed purely social, but Volker remained watchful.

"The king's upstairs," Arindell told him. "He'll join the party presently. Enjoy yourself." He bowed and left Angus to his own devices.

Curious, Volker thought. It seemed a pleasant enough party. But why had he been invited? I'll find out sooner than I like. . . .

Most of the guests' conversations were confined to two subjects: the war of unification, which was going well, and the economy, which was booming but which might be hurt by the consequent inflation, and which was also made uncertain because no one knew what the Imperials would do. Imperial trade would make some rich, others poor, and no one knew which. Yet even these subjects were but lightly treated. There was no serious discussion at all. A number of the people present had sons at the University, and Volker knew of most of them; the University might be independent, but it was only prudent to be wary of students from Haven's great families. He set himself to the task of being charming, telling anecdotes about student pranks, and acting as if he enjoyed the opportunity. It was an easy act; much of the rector's job was concerned with obtaining donations.

He had been in the palace for half an hour and refilled his cup at the punchbowl twice when a man in butler's livery approached. He didn't look at all like a butler. He stood too straight, and he was too young to be a retired soldier. . . .

"If you would come with me, sir," the servant said. "You have an appointment—"

"Certainly," Volker said. He followed the butler out a side door and up back stairways to the third floor. At the end of the hall was a door, and three more liveried servants, all young and very military in appearance, stood outside it. They opened the door for Volker.

"In here, sir," his escort said.

The room was a large, book-lined study. King David, Sir Giles Og, and a man Volker didn't know were seated informally near the fireplace. Volker bowed to the still-seated king. David wasn't *his* king, but it cost nothing to be polite. By rights, they should meet as equals. They were both sovereigns. It didn't escape Angus that King David must know that as well as he did. "Your Majesty."

"You are kind to come," David said. "You've met the Prime Minister, of course. And allow me to present Citizen Dougal, a minister without portfolio."

They stood, and Volker acknowledged their bows. That, at least, was protocol, and Angus felt better.

"Won't you be seated?" the king asked. "Would you care for grua?"

"Yes, please—" Volker had expected the king to ring for a servant, but Dougal went to the small table to bring Volker's drink. "Thank you."

"This meeting is confidential," David said. "I want your assurance on that."

"Certainly," Volker said. "Although of course any discussion of importance to the University must be reported to the Regents. . . ."

"That's why you're here," Dougal said. "Let's be open about this, Professor. You want to preserve the University's independence. Well, you may get that, but there are conditions."

"But the Regents—"

"Nothing said here will be reported to the Regents," Dougal said. He sounded like a man accustomed to being obeyed. "If if comes to formal meetings with the Regents, we'll have an entirely different conversation. One you and they won't much care for. Better we settle matters here."

"Honesty is important," Sir Giles said. "But we can remain polite. However, we stray from the subject, which is your word on the secrecy of this meeting."

That wasn't a hard decision to make, for the same reasons that had brought him here in the first place. He could guess Dougal's next move. He'd already hinted at it by addressing him as "Professor." The title was used by the faculty in addressing their rector, but others generally employed more honorific phrases. Angus sighed and submitted to the inevitable. "You have my assurance. This meeting will remain confidential."

"Excellent," Sir Giles said. "Now. Let us sum up the situation. Prince Samual University has been an independent institution since just before the Plague Years. You have your own laws and courts and you set your own policies, and you share knowledge equally with all. That's worked well. We don't want to change it, even if you are in the middle of Haven. God knows there have been times when your privileges of sanctuary were dreadfully abused, but we've always put up with it.

"But times have changed. When there wasn't any unity to Prince Samual's World it made sense to have supernational entities like the University and the Brotherhoods, but we're putting an end to national entities. Haven's treaties granting you independence were for the large part with states that are now part of Haven. The rest will be soon. So it's time to talk about the future of the University under the new order here."

"I see," Volker said. "We have expected this, of course. But I do not see why you have not come to the Regents. . . ."

"Because we need your help," David said. "And we've agreed that you can be trusted."

"And it is very much in your interest to work with us," Dougal said. "You can negotiate with us. We understand each other. Your alternative is the Imperials—and they won't leave you a damned bit of independence."

Imperials. Interesting, Volker thought. Certainly they would have something to say about Haven's rule of Prince Samual's World. Curious that they'd never told anyone their intentions. Even more curious that a Haven cabinet officer would speak that way. . . . "They are your allies, not mine," Volker said. "Of course you probably know that the Regents have granted the Imperial officers the privileges of visiting scholars. They often come to use the library."

"We know," Dougal said. "What you don't know is why they're here."

"What's wrong with the man? Volker wondered. He looks like he's about to be executed. That's not a happy thought, given where I am. . . . "No, of course I don't know. We have always assumed Imperial intentions to be a Haven state secret."

"I think there's no choice but to tell him, Sire," Dougal said.

"We agreed on that some time ago," King David said. "There's no real choice in the matter."

"No. I suppose not," Dougal said. "Very well . . ."

Volker listened with growing amazement. There was a lot to think about here. Did he believe the part about the Empire's intentions for Prince Samual's World? But why shouldn't I? he wondered. It's almost reasonable. They have been damned secretive about the way their government works, and they've studied our science but given our people very little in return. . . .

"I see," he said when Dougal finished. "But what has this to do with me?"

"Everything," Dougal said. "I won't say how, but we expect to have a lot of their science and technology soon. Books and books of it. Much of it so far advanced over what we have that most of us can't even comprehend it. Yet we *must* comprehend it. If anyone can understand, it will be your people at the University—but we have to keep everything secret. We even have to conceal the fact that we *have* a secret to keep."

"How shall we do that?" Volker asked.

"Some of your scholars can be trusted," Dougal said. "You'll help us choose them. But we'll need others even though they can't keep secrets. Those will have to transfer to one of His Majesty's research stations. To our naval facilities, or elsewhere. They'll have to go willingly—or seem to, at any rate. Some of your best students will be cloistered, kept away from the others, so they can study this new science. And—"

"My God, man, that's the end of the University!" Volker protested.

"Do you see another way?" Sir Giles asked. "If our world is colonized, what do you think will become of the University?"

A good question, Volker thought. I wonder if the Imperials would bargain? Would it be worth something to them to learn of this plot? But that, he decided, was not likely. What use independence for a University on an enslaved planet? With Imperial agents watching his faculty, suppressing discoveries—

And there was the new knowledge itself, new discoveries that Haven was somehow to steal from the Empire. That alone was a deciding factor. But first—

"There remains the matter of confirmation of the University's ancient privileges," Volker said.

"You'll get that. Most of it," Dougal snapped.

"All," Volker insisted.

"If we succeed," King David said. "If we succeed, I will reconfirm your privileges."

"And if we fail?" Volker asked.

"Then we all fail," Dougal said. "You can deal with the Imperials, for all the good it will do you. But we won't fail."

"I wish I were certain," Volker said. "I have seen the Imperial landing boats. We've never built anything like them." And that struck a nerve, he thought. In Sir Giles at least.

"Nothing is certain," King David said. "Yet we must try. Will you help us?"

This might go well, Volker thought. The University might come out of this very well indeed. King's promise or not, once Haven governs the entire world, the University will never keep *all* its ancient privileges, but we'll have a good bargaining position when that's accomplished. And we'll have all their new science. . . . "Of course, Your Majesty."

24

Promotions

There was a large map of Prince Samual's World on Malcolm Dougal's office wall. It had to be changed at frequent intervals.

Too frequent, Dougal thought. The unification war—if you could call desultory mop-up actions a war—was going all too well. There was very little fighting now. There hadn't been a lot since the fall of Orleans, although for the first year it had been necessary to march Haven's armies to the border of a state before it was willing to commit political suicide. Now, though, many of Haven's victims were ready to negotiate without a visible show of force at all.

It was hardly surprising. For over a century Orleans had been the rock against which Haven's expansionist ambitions had foundered; with that republic out of the way it was to be expected that a number of other states would surrender. Even so, the speed at which Haven's Sunburst and Cross spread across the planet was astonishing.

Not that Dougal could blame the others for capitulating. A major point of treaties of unification put each absorbed state's military forces at Haven's disposal. Most had to be disbanded, but there were professionals in every army, and they could be recruited. And there was always the military equipment, the artillery and warships. . . . It was an effective way to build power.

The treaties were drafted by the Imperial High Commissioner's staff. Of course they were only being helpful—but their help was impossible to refuse. Malcolm's plan to buy time by delaying the final unification of Prince Samual's World simply wasn't going to work.

Haven's forces were now so large that no one could resist. If that weren't enough, the Imperial Marines stood ready to break any major center of opposition. Lechfeld had its effect; in the years since then, the Imperials had seldom fired their space weapons. The example of Lechfeld was more than sufficient.

Pacification of the barbaric South Continent would probably take a generation more, but within two or three years Prince Samual's World would be effectively unified under King David.

And thus under the Empire. Dougal looked again at the map and cursed. It was all happening too fast.

There were advantages, he thought. There was plenty of money now. The secret research center in the Corliss Grant Hills, and the others, the shipyards and Magnate Vermuele's foundries, got plenty of support. There was also money for the University, and that institution was invaluable.

Dougal nodded in satisfaction. In the months since they'd recruited him Angus Volker had kept his bargain. Haven's research centers were well staffed. They didn't dare launch big rockets, but they'd fired several models. Static tests of larger motors continued satisfactorily. The shipyard facilities had developed airtight compartments and now worked to make them lighter. They could *almost* build a ship which would keep men alive in space.

Almost.

Almost meant anything from three to thirty years depending on who you talked to. Three might just be enough—but Malcolm had had too much experience with eager engineers to believe that estimate. And more than five years would certainly be too late. He would not have that long. When the Imperials first arrived, they seemed in no hurry; lately, though, they were anxious to finish unifying the planet. At the same time, there were fewer Imperial civil servants at Government House. Sir Alexei Ackoff was as affable as ever, but he seemed distracted, as if Prince Samual's World had lessened in importance—but he was also in a greater hurry than ever.

We need either time or help, Dougal thought. And we can't get time, so it's got to be help, and that's MacKinnie.

It had been a year since they heard that MacKinnie and all his people had set out to cross Makassar in a small ship. They'd gone against the Navy's advice and despite plentiful warnings. The Imperial High Commissioner had been emphatic about that. It wasn't the Empire's fault that the expedition had been lost. . . .

Malcolm didn't believe the expedition was lost, but it was difficult to wait.

Difficult or not, there was nothing else to do. Weeks passed.

The large, square, metal box in Malcolm Dougal's office squawked unintelligibly. Irritated, Dougal got up to adjust the small dial set on its front. He didn't really know what he was doing, but they'd shown him how to operate the thing, and as he turned the dial slightly the words became clearer.

"Calling Citizen Dougal, calling Citizen Dougal. Answer, please."

He leaned close to the wire grill on the front of the thing and shouted, "Dougal here."

Nothing happened. He cursed and pushed the button on top. "Dougal here."

"Navy reports Makassar expedition returning. Will land in twenty days," the box said.

This time Malcolm remembered to push the button. "Thank you. Send details by messenger. Anything more?"

"That's all, sir."

"Thank you." He returned to his desk. Probably the communications man knew more details, but Malcolm didn't want them discussed on the wireless. The Imperials might not be listening, but certainly they could if they wanted to. Dougal laughed mockingly at himself. The only way anyone could learn that the expedition was returning would be from the Imperials; they'd know anything Malcolm could learn from a messenger. It was wise to be cautious, but it could be carried too far.

Not that it mattered. He'd learn nothing really important until MacKinnie's people were down and safely hidden.

Details. MacKinnie's crew would be a sensation. Everyone would want to see them. Parliament, the newspapers, the University; hundreds of opportunities for one of them to let something slip, the merest hint that would warn the Imperials and end their chances.

Something would have to be done about that. But first there were other preparations. He took a speaking tube from the wall behind his desk and whistled into it.

"Sir."

"Send Captain Gregory to me."

"Sir."

Dougal waited impatiently for the knock on the door. It was only a few minutes, but it seemed hours, and Dougal cursed himself for his impatience.

Hans Gregory was a middle-aged officer, nondescript and harmless in appearance; a man much like Malcolm Dougal. He stood in front of Malcolm's desk. "Yes, sir?"

"You look well," Dougal said. "I had meant to see you anyway, but now it may be more urgent. Please be seated."

"Thank you, sir—"

"I take it that all is well and there is no difficulty in your friendship with Citizen Liddell?"

"None, sir. I see him at least weekly now that I had him elected to my club. He very much appreciated my sponsorship."

"Excellent. It is now time for him to repay the favor. Things have reached a critical stage, and we will need a great deal more information about the Imperials. How well do you know Elaine Liddell?"

"Fairly well, sir. She's friendly enough. I used to see her when I called on Liddell—we play Go fairly often. Unfortunately, as I've reported, lately she's out as often as not."

"So you don't know if she would work with us?"

"No, sir." Gregory shrugged. "She certainly fancies herself in love with that young Imperial. If it came to a choice of loyalties, I wouldn't bet either way."

"Even if the king himself asked her to help?"

"I just don't know, sir. They're pretty thick, those two." He gave Dougal a knowing look. "You've seen the reports."

Dougal nodded. "If she's not in love with Lieutenant Jefferson, she ought to be. I do not understand how her father tolerates the situation."

"He has very little choice, sir," Captain Gregory said. "He could hardly challenge an Imperial officer. And of course Freelady Elaine does speak—privately—of Lieutenant Jefferson as her 'fiancé.'"

"But not publicly. Does Jefferson acknowledge the relationship?"

"That's more complicated than you would suppose," Gregory said. "He has made no objection to being called that by Elaine in the presence of Citizen Liddell. However, he cannot officially become engaged to a local without permission of his commanding officer—or says he cannot."

"Sounds as if Jefferson has found a good thing," Dougal said. "Privileges without obligations."

Gregory nodded agreement.

"I can't think the girl would much care for the situation."

"No, sir. I know her father doesn't," Gregory said.

"You're certain of that."

Gregory smiled. "Oh, yes. Laurence Liddell and I are very good friends—in fact, I am the only one of his friends who knows the situation."

"But why does he tolerate it?"

"He has little choice, sir. When Elaine began seeing Jefferson privately, Liddell was horrified, of course, but when he tried to do something about it, she threatened to get a job working for the Imperials and move into an apartment on their compound. He'd have had no control over her at all if she did that—"

"Is that still possible?" Dougal asked.

"I suppose so."

"We might get a lot of information—no, of course that can't work. Liddell would have to disown her. We'd never see her." Dougal looked thoughtful. "But we do need her cooperation. Have you suggestions for how to approach her?"

Captain Gregory held his fingertips together under his chin and looked up thoughtfully. "Have you considered how she must feel?" he asked. "She has thoroughly compromised herself, but she has no commitment whatever from Jefferson. If under those circumstances she found he was unfaithful to her—"

"Umm. And Jefferson has certainly been known to be interested in tavern girls. A good suggestion, Captain. Keep it in mind. Better—perhaps before we speak to her directly, we should have, uh, evidence—"

"I can arrange that."

"Excellent. And Jefferson himself might be vulnerable," Dougal mused.

"I can't think his superiors don't know of his adventures. One more wouldn't make a difference."

"I wasn't thinking of his rather libertine ways with tavern girls." Dougal said. "Tell me, Captain, have you any reason to believe that Freelady Elaine is sterile?"

"No, sir—"

"Yet if she has obtained a birth control device, she has been exceedingly discreet. Might Jefferson have given her what the Imperials use? Something called 'The Pill' is mentioned prominently in the novel we found. If he has given her Imperial technology, he may be in violation of one of their regulations."

"Isn't that a lot to deduce on little evidence?" Gregory asked.

"Some of it isn't deduction, Captain," Dougal said. "I have a number of agents watching those two. One is the concierge at the apartment Jefferson keeps in the suburbs."

"Even if you're correct, he would probably report any approach from us to his superiors," Gregory said. "From what I've seen of him he is rather admirably loyal to the Empire."

"Yes. Unfortunately. I suppose you're right, it was only a thought. Now, to return to the matter of Citizen Liddell. Will he cooperate?"

"Yes. He's very loyal. Favors the unification wars and all that. And this business with Jefferson hasn't made him love the Empire."

Dougal looked thoughtfully at the dossier on his desk. "Roads and public works," he mused. "Good recommendations from his superiors. Fairly senior civil servant—tell me, do you think he's competent to be one of the roads commissioners?"

"Yes."

"Good. He'll have that." Dougal made a note on the memo pad in front of him. "Sir Giles Og's political managers aren't going to be too happy about losing that appointment, but that can't be helped. Time to show Liddell he has friends who appreciate his talents—make sure he knows it was your influence that got him promoted. What else does he want?"

"A knighthood on retirement, but he has no reason to expect it—"

"Offer him that, too. If his daughter will cooperate with us. If not—" Dougal shrugged. "If not, a Haven knighthood won't be worth a lot anyway, but we can't tell him that. Captain, Elaine Liddell is potentially one of our best sources of information about Imperial policies, and I need that information badly. Especially now."

"Yes, sir. I'll do my best."

"I know you will. That's all."

"Sir." Gregory stood.

"Your very best, Commandant," Dougal said.

Gregory was halfway to the door. He stopped and turned in surprise. "Commandant," Dougal said.

Gregory was halfway to the door. He stopped and turned in surprise. "Commandant?"

"Yes. I've just promoted you. See that you deserve it." Dougal made another note on his memo pad.

This is dangerous, Dougal thought. The expedition is returning and we will need information on Imperial activities. Elaine Liddell is potentially invaluable, our only real source, but she could also arouse Imperial suspicions.

But, he thought, there is nothing else to do. It is worth the risk, but that risk will have to be minimized. He took a report from his desk and scanned through it. Freelady Liddell and Lieutenant Jefferson liked sailing. They often went out alone in small craft, but only in the daytime. They did have *some* sense of discretion. . . .

He continued to scan the report. Citizen Liddell owned a pair of Mannheim pacers, and Jefferson took Elaine riding at least weekly. Mannheims, he thought. Very spirited horses. Took controlling. You could break your neck falling off a horse. The Imperial High Commissioner would be saddened by the loss, but what suspicion could be attached to a riding accident? He nodded to himself. Best see Inspector

Solon. Just in case the interview with the girl went badly.

And there were endless other details to be attended to before the expedition returned. Dougal's fingers drummed on the polished wooden desk, and a thin smile came to his lips. The waiting was over. Now they could get to work.

25

Decision Factors

The small boat skipped across the water, running directly downwind and going like a corkborer chased by an eagle. She had a nasty tendency to roll, and it took all of Jefferson's skill to keep her heading straight. He stood in the cockpit, his legs spread wide, the tiller behind him, feeling the following seas as they lifted the stern, throwing his weight against the tiller to correct any deviation from center, careful not to overcorrect and let her fall off the other way. It would be easy to broach, and in these seas the boat might swamp.

"You look like you're having fun." Elaine leaned against the forward cockpit coaming with her knees drawn up to her chin.

"I must be. I'm grinning a lot," Jeff said. He glanced thoughtfully at the boomed-out spinnaker, then down at the wake. "We must be making twelve kilometers! I've never gone this fast before. . . ."

She laughed. "You travel in starships, and you're impressed by a small boat?"

"It's not the same," he said defensively. Now why did she have to remind him of starships? And how was he going to tell her? Maybe now was as good a time as any. Just say it. "And I may not have many more opportunities."

Her look was enough to wrench out his heart. "Why?" she asked. But she knew.

"Something's happened out in Trans-Coalsack Sector," Jefferson said. "Something big. They discovered an alien civilization."

She frowned. "But you told me yourself there aren't any intelligent creatures other than humans—"

The boat took a rogue wave and he struggled with the tiller for a moment before he could answer. "It's a big universe. We were mistaken. Actually, they were discovered some time ago, and the news is only just getting here."

"But how does that affect us?" she asked.

"They sent an expedition to the alien planets," Jefferson said. "I don't know what they found, but they're ordering a main battle fleet to Trans-Coalsack."

"War?" She shuddered. "We have stories about the last wars. And those were with humans."

"I just don't know," Jeff said. "It might be. Why else would they want a fleet?" A big fleet. To be commanded by Kutuzov! Kutuzov the butcher, Kutuzov the hero . . . it depended on your point of view. "They're sending a lot of ships out there, so the rest of us have to cover more territory. I don't know where *Tombaugh* will be sent. Maybe even to Trans-Coalsack."

"Is that far?" she asked.

"Yes. Very far. And behind the Coalsack—that's a mass of interstellar dust so thick it hides the stars behind it. You can't see the sector capital from here."

"I knew it would happen," she said. "My father told me not to—not to fall in love with a Navy man. So now you're leaving me."

"Hey, I haven't left yet," he said.

"Can you stay?"

"I don't know." Possibly, he thought. I'd have to resign from the Navy and go into civil government. Do I want that? Oh, damn. He thought of *Tombaugh* ordered away, his shipmates leaving without him. Would that be harder than leaving Elaine?

He'd been planet-bound for two years except for brief tours aboard the orbiting *Tombaugh*. It was a pleasant relief from ship duty. But if he resigned to stay here, he'd never go to space again except as a passenger. He'd known he'd have to face this decision one day, but not so soon, not so soon. He tried to imagine his life as a civil administrator building an industrial civilization. He'd have honors enough. Possibly a barony. Almost certainly a barony on retirement. Another title in the family. His father would be proud of him. And he'd have Elaine.

Would that be enough?

Certainly he'd thought so when he first met her. But now he wasn't sure. That frantic need to be with her was gone, and while he didn't go looking for other women, he no longer felt repelled by them. Like that tavern girl he'd met the other night, the really friendly one—he pushed that thought away. Jeff didn't believe in telepathy, but Elaine had surprised him before.

She was her loveliest today. The wind brought a bloom to her cheeks, and her hair, tied with bright ribbons, blew wantonly in the gusts. His eyes met hers and he smiled, and her answering smile was warm and trusting.

Trusting. Certainly she was that. Far too much so by the standards of this world.

You owe her, Jefferson thought to himself.

Not really. Happens all the time. Why make such a big thing out of it?

Because she does, and her father does, and all her friends do, and you knew it all along, and—

Another rogue wave threatened to swamp them, and he tried to force his worries and doubts from his mind to give all his attention to the tiller.

He almost succeeded.

Jefferson looked at his crowded "work-to-do" screen and frowned. It was all trivial stuff, but it took time to process, and it was hard to keep his mind on his work. Remembering last night's stormy scene with Elaine after they got ashore didn't help. She'd sensed his uncertainties, and although she hadn't accused him of not caring for her, she'd thought it. Worse, it was true. Or almost true. Or partly true. He cared for her, but enough to abandon his shipmates, his whole career? It came to that. She'd never fit into Capital social life.

And the choice would have to be made within the year. Just now High Commissioner Ackoff was trying to recruit naval officers for his civil service, and Navy policy was to let him; but if *Tombaugh* got war orders it would be too late. Captain Greenaugh would never let one of his officers resign under those circumstances.

He was keying in data on platinum production— surprisingly high on a world so poor in copper—when his door opened and Lieutenant Adnan Clements came in. "Got a minute?"

"Just that," Jeff said. "What's up?"

"Blivit, of course. Old man's got a new job for you."

Jeff gestured toward the screen. "I've got plenty of jobs—"

"So now you have another one. That Makassar expedition's coming in. Somebody's got to give Navy clearance for passengers and cargo. You're elected."

"Oh, hell. Why me?"

"Because the skipper's not about to do it, and I'm being sent down to South Continent to bust up a pirate fleet, that's why."

"Hey, that sounds like fun—"

"Sure, if your idea of fun is shooting up wooden boats that can't shoot back." Clements's face showed his distaste.

Jeff nodded agreement. "Guess I'd rather look for contraband at that." He turned to the keyboard and punched in the assignment. The schedule screen looked more cluttered than ever. "Get me a coffee?" he asked.

"Sure," Clements said. "Back in a minute."

Might as well see what the job involves, Jeff thought. He went back to the keyboard. "Let's see," he mused. "Keywords 'MAKASSAR' and 'EXPORT CONTRABAND.' Now the library search function . . ."

"MAKASSAR EXPORT CONTRABAND: NO ITEMS LISTED" appeared on the main working screen.

"Aha," Jefferson said.

"Coffee time." Clements came in carrying two plastic cups and set one on Jeff's desk. "I just remembered, you've been to Makassar. Job's a natural for you." He glanced at the screen. "Looks like you drew an easy one."

"Maybe. It's for sure there's not much there." He

typed in "CONTINUE DETAIL TRADE/TRAVEL POLICY" and waited.

"MAKASSAR IS CLASSIFIED 'CLASS 5 PRIMITIVE' WITH NO SIGNIFICANT TECHNOLOGY NO EXPORT RESTRICTIONS. SUFFICIENT SAMPLINGS INDICATE NO EPIDEMIC DISEASE. FULL SPECTRUM IMMUNIZATIONS REQUIRED FOR LANDING OR EXIT FROM PLANET.

"THREE ADDICTING DRUGS ARE KNOWN TO BE PREPARED ON MAKASSAR BUT THEY ARE UNATTRACTIVE AND THERE IS NO MARKET FOR THEM. FOR FURTHER DETAILS SEE 'MAKASSAR—GENERAL.'

"IMPORT RESTRICTIONS: SEVERE IM—" The flow of words was cut off as Jeff touched more keys.

"See?" Clements said. "An easy job."

"Still takes time I don't have."

"Poor you. How's your romance going?"

Jefferson shrugged. "I told her about the Moties," he said. "And the possible alert."

"I gather she wasn't pleased."

Jeff snorted. "You could say it that way."

"So what *are* you going to do?"

"Hell, Adnan, I don't know. I like the Navy."

"Five hundred hours ago you couldn't talk about anything but resigning. Get married and become a colonist. Found a new dynasty, to hear you talk."

Jeff nodded. "Yeah, but now we really have to decide—"

Clements laughed. "What's the problem, laddie? Afraid to admit you're just another sailor feeding bushwa to his girl? Hell, I knew you were never going to resign."

"Maybe you're right," Jeff said. "But damn it, this girl's different—"

"Sure. They all are," Clements said. He drained

his coffee. "My screen's not like yours, but it's full enough. Best get at it."

"Yeah." Jefferson turned back to his work. More reports. Mining and refining capabilities. Steam generation facilities. All important, he knew, but—

If I give up the Navy, this'll be my career, he thought. God Almighty, how could anyone spend his entire life at this? Better a naval battle. Better a long, dull patrol. Better almost anything!

The days passed, and Jeff was no further ahead. As soon as he finished one task they'd give him another. He had five locals gathering data, and they brought it in faster than he could code it into the machines.

Twice he'd sent memos to the High Commissioner's office explaining the desirability of hiring and training locals for elementary clerical work of this type. It wouldn't harm this planet for some of its people to learn how to produce machine-readable data. He'd had no answer.

Which, he thought philosophically, is better than a definite "No."

And Elaine was—strange. They'd patched up their quarrel. He didn't tell her how soon he'd have to make a decision, and she didn't bring up the subject. She did encourage him in his work, and seemed interested in what he was doing. She hadn't cared before, but now of a sudden she encouraged him to talk about his work, as if—

"Landing boat's on final approach now, Lieutenant."

"Ah. Thanks, Hawley." He went out onto the pier to wait. In moments he heard growing thunder and the sharp clap of a sonic boom. He shaded his eyes to stare over the water and made out a small speck just at the horizon. It was coming directly toward him, angling in a long glide path toward the water.

"There it is!" Someone shouted from behind him. Jeff grimaced. There were a thousand civilians out there, all eager to see the locals who'd been off-planet. They weren't allowed on the pier itself, but they were close enough. A lot of them were shouting now.

The landing boat settled onto the water. Jeff nodded approval. It was a smooth landing. Two small local steam tugs went out to tow it to the pier. They'd be a while doing that. Jeff wondered whose idea it was. The landing boats were hard to maneuver, but they weren't so difficult to handle as to need local assistance. Some boondoggle to employ locals? Maybe the local harbormaster was worried about the big landing craft losing control and smashing up the docks. He tapped his foot impatiently as he waited.

Finally the craft was alongside and the gangway lowered. Three naval officers got off first. Junior lieutenants, very young. Just up from middie, Jefferson thought. Proud as peacocks. He remembered when he'd sewn that stripe on his sleeve. It had been a good feeling.

They looked around uncertainly and Jeff went over to them. Although they were nominally the same rank as Jeff, two of the newcomers saluted him. Jeff grinned. "Assigned here?" he asked.

"Yes, si—. Yes, thank you. Were you sent to meet us?"

Jeff laughed. "Hardly. But wait around and I'll see you get to headquarters. Know anything of what you're supposed to do?"

"Not really," the spokesman said. "What's this place like?"

"Takes a bit of getting used to, but not bad," Jeff said. "Oops, excuse me, that's my crew." He left them and went to the gangway.

The group getting off had to be native to Prince Samual's World. Jeff wasn't sure how he knew that, but they had the look about them. They were led by a tall, broad-shouldered man with straw-colored hair going to steel gray. Distinguished, Jefferson thought. The files said Trader, but that man had obviously been a soldier.

He examined the others. The girl was all right, but no raving beauty; there were plenty of prettier ones in Haven. She looked self-possessed, though, more poised than Elaine, and that made her attractive. There wasn't much to notice about the others.

"Trader MacKinnie?" he said to the leader.

"Yes, sir."

Sir. A word *that* man doesn't mean. Not to me. "I'm Lieutenant Jefferson, sir. I've been assigned to conduct your landing interviews and inspection."

"Will this take long?"

"I shouldn't think so," Jefferson said. "Just formalities. Shall we go inside?" He led the way into the building to the interview room and ushered MacKinnie inside. "Have a seat, please." He turned on his recorder and put his pocket computer on the desk. "Here, I've got your records on here somewhere—ah. 'Jameson MacKinnie, Trader, citizen of Haven. Expedition leader.' Successful trip?"

MacKinnie shrugged. "Moderately. I expect the cargo we brought will cover the expedition costs, but there won't be a lot of profit."

Jefferson nodded. "I don't recall seeing much there I'd want to buy," he said. "Where did you go on Makassar?"

"Well, we landed at the Navy base at Jikar and went on from there," MacKinnie said.

Man's nervous, Jefferson thought. Is there a special reason? Or does he just dislike Imperial officers?

"The report from the Makassar garrison says you went to Batav."

MacKinnie nodded.

"I was there once. Did you see the Temple?"

"Certainly. Most prominent building on the whole planet."

"It is, isn't it? Get inside?"

"Not beyond the courtyard," MacKinnie answered. "It's a holy place, and the unconsecrated don't get into the inner buildings."

Jefferson grinned to himself. "Right." It had been that way when Jefferson visited. Of course other Navy people had been inside, all the way to the crypt where they kept the remains of the old library. What might this chap have done if he'd known what was in there? Or did he? "Why is the place holy?" Jefferson asked. "I didn't stay long enough to find out."

"Relics, they say," MacKinnie answered. "The building's very old. We ran into a party of Imperial missionaries in Batav, and they said something about stuff left over from the First Empire."

Jefferson glanced down at his computer. There it was. A note from the commander at Jikar. 'Archbishop Casteliano found this group helpful and sent a note of commendation.' So. They had friends in the Church. Might as well get this over with. "Any injuries or diseases?" he asked. "And I'll need your cargo manifests. . . ."

26

Homecoming

When MacKinnie saw Lieutenant Jefferson waiting for him at the gangway his first reaction was panic. Somehow they must have found out. . . .

But the only armed Marines in evidence were a pair of sentries looking very bored, and there was no evidence of suspicion at all. Jefferson acted as if he'd never seen MacKinnie before. Given his condition the only time they'd been in the same room together that was hardly a surprise. And his greeting was polite. Everything seemed routine.

For all that, it was unnerving. Nathan followed the Imperial officer into the stone warehouse the Imperials had converted into their customs office, and tried to act relaxed about the interview. It seemed to go well enough, and Jefferson's interest in the Temple was natural. The real test would come when they inspected the cargo. The carefully copied library records were concealed inside handcrafted statuary. It wouldn't take a lot of ingenuity to find them, but Nathan could think of no other place to conceal them. He'd almost left them behind, but Kleinst had said he couldn't rely on his memory, and that left few choices.

MacKinnie found he needn't have worried. The cargo inspection was cursory. Jefferson had a couple of the crates opened, but mostly seemed curious to see what they'd brought.

"Copper statues," Jefferson commented. "I didn't see anything like this on Makassar."

MacKinnie laughed. "Nor did we. But copper is cheap enough there, so we had artists copy their work in it."

"Clever of you," Jefferson said. "Should fetch a good price here." He continued to look through boxes. "Ah. I should have picked up one of these myself," he said. He held up a tusked sea creature carved in one of Makassar's ultra-hard woods. "What's your price for it?"

MacKinnie shrugged. "We'll have to hold auctions. How else can you establish prices on rare artworks? But that's yours if you like."

"I should pay for it—"

MacKinnie shrugged. "Set a price, then."

"I don't suppose I could afford what you can get for it here—"

"Probably not. It's still yours if you want it."

"I'd better not. Thank you for the offer." He made notes on his pocket computer. "You're cleared," he said.

MacKinnie was surprised and looked it. "Thanks."

"That's Navy clearance," Jefferson said. "You'll get a customs bill later." He glanced at the small screen on his pocket computer. "Since this expedition was owned by a sovereign ally, that won't be very high. May even be waived. Have you arranged for a crew to transport?"

"No, but I expect His Majesty's government has."

"Good."

"What's next?" MacKinnie asked.

"Immigration," Jefferson said. "Nothing to that. Just identification. To be sure you're the same people who left. Are you all here?"

"Not quite. Barstonic and Danvers and Stark were killed on Makassar. He was surprised at how easy it was to say that. Of course Hal wasn't dead. Or wasn't when they left Batav.

"Sorry to hear that." Jefferson glanced at his pocket computer. "Stark was your guard leader?"

"Yes. Your people there took a full report—"

Lieutenant Jefferson sighed. "They don't seem to have sent it along," he said. He did things to his pocket computer and looked at it again. "No, I'm afraid not. You'll have to tell that story again. Unless— Just a minute." He used a small stylus to write something else on the machine's face. "Aha. They did send it after all. Illustrated with satellite photos." He read for a moment, then looked up at MacKinnie. "You seem to have fought a proper little war at Batav."

"There were a few barbarians," Nathan said.

"Yes." He read more. "No superior weapons—"

"Of course not. Look, we were inspected when we landed on Makassar."

"I know."

What else do you know? MacKinnie wondered. "What's the problem?"

"Just wondering if tactical innovations come within the limits of the technology transfer laws," Jefferson said. "Well, that's not my business. If the Makassar garrison didn't have a complaint there's no reason for me to raise the question." The frown faded and he smiled at MacKinnie. "Forgot to say it. Welcome home."

There was a large crowd outside, with a dozen reporters in front. They all shouted questions at once. Then, suddenly, they fell silent.

Inspector Solon came through the crowd. His black uniform opened a way as if by magic. "Welcome back, Trader. Freelady. Gentlemen." His voice was cold even though his smile was broad. He turned to the crowd. "His Majesty requests that he be given the first interview," Solon said. "Surely that is reasonable? You will all have your opportunities, but I am commanded to bring the members of the expedition to the palace."

There were murmurs from the reporters, but no one actually protested. Solon led them across the broad avenue to waiting steam cars. "We will go directly to the palace," he said.

It was as if Stark had come up behind him. Nathan heard him as clearly as if he'd been there. "Bets on our ever gettin' out of there alive, Colonel? That guy gives me the creeps. So does his boss."

There were three cars. "Trader, you and Freelady Graham and our scholars will ride in the first car with me," Solon said. He held open the door.

Nathan and Mary climbed into the vehicle. It was new, a model he hadn't seen before, and the interior was luxurious. When they were inside, Solon handed each a sheet of paper.

"SPEAK ONLY PLEASANTRIES. DO NOT DISCUSS THE EXPEDITION UNTIL YOU ARE TOLD IT IS SAFE."

MacKinnie read it and nodded. Solon waited until each one acknowledged the message, then collected the papers and put them in his pouch. "Was it a pleasant journey?" he asked conversationally.

"Return trip was dull," MacKinnie said.

"Yes," Mary said. "There were no other passengers. Just three young naval officers, and they stayed forward in the crew area. We were left to our own devices."

"Not like the trip out," Longway said. "The Navy craft we returned on had few luxuries. Not even windows to look out of."

Kleinst had been silent. Now he said wistfully, "I saw Prince Samual's World from space when we left. Magnificent! And Makassar when we arrived there. Worlds so different—I think of what we could learn about weather and climate by observing different worlds from space. It is no wonder the Imperials are able to predict weather accurately. They know so much—"

Solon gestured with an upraised palm. "I'm certain they do," he said. "Well! You will have much to tell His Majesty."

MacKinnie glanced back through the rear window. The other cars were following. "The Navy released our cargo," he said. "Arrangements must be made to move it—"

"At once," Solon said. "When we reach the palace I will go myself. Thank you."

The palace was hidden in a maze of scaffolding. That, too, was new. They were taken inside, and quickly led to the living quarters in the rear of the building. "I am sure you will wish to wash and change your clothing," Solon said. He gave them more papers with instructions.

MacKinnie nodded agreement.

* * *

The clothes were his own, but they felt too large. As he had expected, there were no weapons. He dressed quickly and followed the guide upstairs to a small sitting room.

Malcolm Dougal was alone in the room. He stood when MacKinnie entered, and his smile of welcome seemed genuine. "So. You returned," Dougal said. "Were you successful?"

"You'll pardon my suspicions, but where are the others?" MacKinnie asked.

Dougal frowned and looked genuinely puzzled. "Changing their clothing, of course—ah. You are concerned because I had Inspector Solon bring you here? How else could I have extracted you from that crowd?"

"We were told we would be meeting King David."

"As you will, when all are ready," Dougal said. "Your guardsmen will not be needed. They will be entertained by some of my men."

"Entertained how?"

"With whatever they want," Dougal said. "Why are you so suspicious? Are you expecting punishment? Did the mission fail?"

"Not exactly. But I've been wondering what you had in mind for us. You had a dozen people killed to protect your secret—and you don't need me and my troopers any longer."

"That was then," Dougal said. "Since you left there are many who know our plans. We've had no choice but to tell them. As a matter of fact, two of your former officers are now part of the security force at our research station. Which is what I had in mind for you and the guardsmen. You disappoint me, Colonel. I am neither bloodthirsty nor evil. Simply determined not to fail. Now, what success have you brought me?"

MacKinnie spread his hands. "I honestly don't know. We secured the library, and Kleinst read a number of the old books. We made copies of many of them—but Kleinst wasn't sure we could make them readable with anything we have on Prince Samual's World. And once we left Batav—that's the city the old library was in—we couldn't discuss any of this among ourselves. Too many locals aboard our ship. It was worse when we got to the Navy's base at Jikar, and on that spaceship. I thought Kleinst was going to burst for lack of someone to talk to."

"I see. And you don't know if we can build a ship?"

"I know damned well we can't build anything like their ships," MacKinnie said. "Dougal, you can't imagine what their equipment is like. Even the library. A box no larger than that sideboard there—we were told that could contain every book on Prince Samual's World with room to spare. The things we brought home are about this big." MacKinnie held up thumb and forefinger to indicate the size. "And each one holds a whole library. If we can read them."

"So you learned nothing?"

"It wasn't my job to learn," MacKinnie said. "I was hired to get them there and bring them back. I did. All but two guardsmen."

"So we must rely on Kleinst."

"Kleinst and Todd. They spent days in the library. Not as long as they'd have liked to, but I didn't dare wait any longer before starting back. As it was we only had five days to spare before the ship left, and I gather there won't be another for a while. Something strange is going on in another part of the Empire. They wouldn't tell me what, but they take it seriously."

"Indeed?" Dougal looked thoughtful. We will have to see if we can find out," he said. "It may affect us."

He's a good liar, MacKinnie thought. But he knows something he's not telling me. I wonder if it's important. . . .

"As for this audience," Dougal said, "there will be many present who know nothing about your true purpose in going to Makassar, and we suspect the Imperials can listen to conversations in the audience chamber. You will continue the pretense of a simple trading mission."

"You didn't even tell the king?" MacKinnie demanded.

Dougal laughed. "His Majesty knows all," he said. "But many in the government do not. We intend to keep it that way. Come, let's get this over with. I am anxious to talk to all of you, and I will not feel really comfortable until we are out of Haven."

"Where are you taking us?"

"We have a large military research post in the Corliss Grant Hills," Dougal said. "Most of what goes on there is weapons research, which the Imperials know all about. But it is a large place, and much goes on that we do not tell them."

"I see. You've organized well," MacKinnie said.

"As best we could. But now it all depends on what you have brought us. And we are running out of time."

Their quarters in the Corliss Grant research station were comfortable, but they were prisoners.

"I prefer you do not think that way," Dougal told MacKinnie. "You have weapons. You are all housed in the same building. All of you, including your soldiers. From time to time one of you—I prefer Academician Longway, he has a knack for talking—

will go to Haven to be seen and speak to the press. But think, Colonel. You will be recognized if you are seen often. And if there is no one to tell your secrets to, you will not reveal them." He threw up his hands as if in dismay. "I have given you every possible assurance of your safety. I make no doubt that with your skill and the number of men I have left you, you could escape at any time. I rely on your word, Colonel. You have sworn to Haven and Prince Samual's World. Can I not trust you?"

There wasn't any answer to that, as MacKinnie later told Mary.

"So we're our own jailors," she said.

"It comes to that," MacKinnie said. "He even has me in the security department. I don't really blame him. I'd do the same thing myself. But as Hal would say, this spy business gets old pretty fast." He tried to laugh, but the sound was unpleasant.

"Are you sorry?" she asked.

"Sorry I lost Hal? I'll always be sorry."

She moved closer to him, and he held her, clinging to her. They stood for a long time. Finally he let her go. "But I'm not sorry I found you. Which reminds me, I have to speak to your father—"

"No."

He frowned. "What do you mean, 'no'?"

"You don't *have* to do anything," she said. "That's not what either of us wants. Haven is ruled by customs and duties—we don't need them with each other."

He was silent for a moment. "All right, let's say I want to speak to your father. It's time I made an honest woman of you—"

"Or an honest man of yourself."

*   *   *

They lived in luxury, but there was nothing to do. The research station was isolated, far from any town, sealed from the rest of Prince Samual's World, and keeping it "secure" required no effort at all.

Since no one objected, Nathan went to technical conferences. Much of the discussion involved forces, and specific impulse, and other meaningless terms. He did understand that Kleinst had no way of reading the cubes they had brought back.

"It's enough to drive me mad," Kleinst said. A dozen older engineers seated around the conference table nodded sympathy. "It's all right here." He held up one of the small plasticine cubes. "And if I had nothing else to do, I might, in ten years, be able to read this. I know the theory—"

"We're working on it," Academician Taylor said. Taylor headed a group who worked on long-distance communicators and other electrical matters. They thought they had a method of reading the Makassar data, but so far it had not worked.

"But I have to spend time on the ship also," Kleinst said. "And I fear that is hopeless."

"We've got your liquid oxygen," Todd said. He looked pleased with himself, and MacKinnie thought he had a right to be. In his days in the library on Makassar, Todd had found books on ancient technology—methods ancient even in the days of the First Empire—and studied how they'd done things. MacKinnie had never thought of air as something that could be made liquid, but Todd had done it by putting oxygen under high pressure, then rapidly letting it expand and cool. It all seemed simple once it was done—

"Yes," Kleinst said. "But we can't build pumps. And the stabilizing mechanisms." He shook his head sadly. "We have large gyroscopes, but every attempt to make small ones with electrical connections to guide the ship has failed. Everything we can make is large, too large—"

"In time we can make it smaller," Douglas Starr said.

"Time is what we don't have," MacKinnie said.

Starr glared at him. "My mechanics are working themselves to death now. I can get no more from them. There are no more hours in the day!"

"I know. I meant no disrespect," MacKinnie said. And I shouldn't even be here. But what else do I have to do? Every day he examined the political maps. Haven's reach extended far to the east, all the way to the eastern ocean. In one memorable four-day period seven city-states capitulated to King David. One large kingdom on the eastern coast of the continent was holding out, and even though it looked as if it would take only a short campaign to conquer it, MacKinnie had asked for a command in Haven's army. Of course Dougal refused to consider his request.

"Go back to first principles," Todd said. "We can't build true spacecraft. We can't even build anything like the Empire's landing boats."

"So we must build rockets," Kleinst said. "And large liquid rockets are very complex—"

"Why rockets?" Todd asked.

Kleinst frowned. "What else is there?"

"It largely depends on what you mean by a spaceship," the midshipman said. "Or rather, what the Empire will accept as a spaceship. . . ."

"If it will take us to space, it is a spaceship," Kleinst muttered. "We have no time for senseless debate on definitions. What have you in mind?"

"There was an ancient document," Todd said. "I hesitate to say how ancient—" He saw the intense interest of the others and laughed self-consciously. "Before the second millenium of the Christian era," he said. "In the time of the first spacecraft, on Earth."

There was a long silence. Earth, MacKinnie thought. Before the Empire, before the CoDominium, before space travel. Those times were no more than legends, yet Todd had seen copies of works written then.

"The first spacecraft used rockets," Kleinst said firmly.

"Yes, but they had another concept," Todd said. "It was not used, but it might have been. And it is something we can build. . . ."

27

Witness

Lieutenant Jefferson tapped nervously at the door to High Commissioner Ackoff's office. Jeff could think of no reason why the Imperial governor would want to see him. In the past few months he'd worked on a dozen assignments, all routine and all dull, and as far as Jefferson knew he'd done them all satisfactorily; Ackoff couldn't be unhappy with him. On the other hand, he'd done nothing outstanding either. Jeff didn't like economic intelligence work, and longed for a space assignment.

"Come."

Commissioner Ackoff's office might have been used as a textbook example: office, one each, governor's, minor colonial planet. There was the large wooden desk and leather chairs; conference table and more chairs; conversation group with couch and soft chairs off to one side; computer screens and input console discreetly hidden in the desk; portrait of the Emperor draped with the flags of Empire; shelves of curios including models of ships Ackoff had served in; large sideboard filled with liquor—

Ackoff was seated at his conference table. So was Captain Greenaugh.

"Come in, Jefferson," Ackoff said. "Have a seat."

"Thank you, Your Excellency—"

"Haven't seen you for a while," Sir Alexei said. "I miss those government seminars. Really ought to start them up again. Only time I get to meet my officers." The Commissioner shook his head slowly. "Too much work, no one to do it. I'm afraid we've an additional job for you."

"Sir?" Jeff looked to Greenaugh for some hint of what was happening.

"Not in space," Greenaugh said. He laughed at Jefferson's expression. "Tired of this place already? I'm told you're practically engaged to a local girl—"

"Not yet, sir," Jeff was emphatic.

"But you still see her," Greenaugh said. It wasn't a question.

"Yes, sir."

"Quite often."

"Yes, sir," Jeff said. Often and the relationship was certainly one that Elaine might take as "practically engaged." Certainly her father had a right to think so. The less said about that the better.

"Not trying to pry into your private affairs," Greenaugh said. "But I take it you do not intend to apply for transfer to the civil service."

"No, sir," Jeff said. "I'm ready for space duty whenever there's an assignment—"

Greenaugh chuckled. "And you'd like to know when that will be. So would we all, Lieutenant. So would we all. But I'm afraid not even Sir Alexei knows that. Meanwhile, we've a job to do here. Know anything about Haven's military research establishment?"

"Well, a little—"

"A lot, I'd say," Ackoff interrupted. "It was your economic analysis that got us interested. Haven has a big research station in the Corliss Grant Hills. From what we can see it siphons off a good part of their budget and a lot of their technical talent. We can't think why."

"Any ideas?" Greenaugh asked.

"Not really, sir," Jefferson said. "Frankly, I can't see any need for a big military research effort. Haven has just finished the consolidation of this continent, which effectively means the whole planet. They'd have finished the job sooner if they hadn't dragged their feet. They've no one to fight."

"Precisely," Greenaugh said. "Which is what disturbs us. One, they did drag their feet. From what we know of their history, unification of the planet has been Haven's dream since the present dynasty took over. We gave them the chance to do it, and they went very slowly. Then all of a sudden they speeded things up and finished with a bang. Two, they're spending a lot of money and sending the cream of their engineering talent to a military research station that's working on weapons they'll never need. Quick-firing cannon. War rockets—big ones, too; *Tombaugh*'s radar tracked one six hundred kilometers. Balloons, for Christ's sake. And that's just what they tell us about. What else are they doing out there?"

Jefferson frowned. "I don't know, sir—"

"No, and we don't expect you to," Greenaugh said. "But we do want to find out. You get along with the locals. Come to that, you've got more purely social contacts in Haven than most of us."

"Yes, sir, but Elaine's father is a roads commissioner. He wouldn't know about the Corliss Grant station."

"Didn't expect him to," Ackoff said. "But you go to social gatherings. What's the mood here? Officially they love us, but what do they really think?" He spread his hands helplessly. "Are they mad enough to be working on weapons to fight us?"

"I've heard no hint of *that*," Jefferson protested.

"Nor would you," Ackoff said gently.

"Christ," Greenaugh snorted. "Aliens in Trans-Coalsack. Half the fleet sucked off to *that* godforsaken corner of the Empire. Outies not twenty parsecs from here, and nowhere near enough ships to deal with them. All we'd bloody need is some kind of abortive revolt just when we're ready to report this place pacified." He shook his head grimly. "Christ, what would we do? We don't have enough Marines to occupy the place—"

"They're hardly a threat to the Empire, sir," Jefferson said.

"They are if they've linked up with the outies," Greenaugh said.

"But—do you have some reason to believe—"

"No," Ackoff said. "We've no reason to believe anything at all. But the fact remains that they're spending enormous sums for no reason we can determine, and their explanations don't make sense."

"I wish we'd never found this damned place," Greenaugh said. "But that's neither here nor there. This whole conversation is about to be mooted. Apparently they're going to tell us what they're doing out at Corliss Grant."

Jefferson looked puzzled. "Sir?"

"They've requested an official observer," Ackoff

said. "An Imperial officer as official witness to some important test they're going to conduct."

"But why would they want a witness?" Jefferson asked.

Ackoff shook his head. "We haven't any idea. Of course colonials do strange things."

"I admit enough curiosity to consider going myself," Greenaugh said. "But the governor won't let me."

"Not without sufficient escort," Ackoff said. "And since our best guess is that what they're doing is harmless, it would be impolitic for the captain to arrive with a company of fleet Marines."

Whereas, Jeff thought, lieutenants are more expendable than captains. "Surely they know the empire's policy on negotiating with kidnappers," he said.

"They ought to. We told them often enough," Greenaugh said.

Imperial policy on the subject was simple. The hostages were counted as dead from the moment they were kidnapped. Imperial forces might storm the place the hostages were kept in, or they might bomb it. The one thing they wouldn't do was negotiate for their safety. The policy was supposed to take away any incentive for kidnapping Imperial officials, and Jeff had always approved of it. Now he wasn't so sure. . . .

"It's possible they don't believe us, of course," Greenaugh continued. "But I don't think so. It's too raw. Invite an Imperial officer out to their most secret place just to kidnap him? Easier to grab one of you chuckleheads in a local bar after a long night. Also, there's the matter of the weather."

"Weather?" Jeff asked.

"Yes," Greenaugh said. "They want an observer as soon as possible, but only on a day that we can guarantee will have clear weather, no storms or high winds, in the Corliss Grant area." The captain shrugged. "No difficulty this time of year, of course."

"But no explanation given?" Jeff asked.

"None."

"Whatever they intend," Ackoff said, "this is an opportunity to find out what they're doing out there. I will give you credentials—meaningless, of course—certifying you as an official witness, and you'll be sent in answer to this request. The computer says the weather down there ought to be fine for at least another five or six days, so you can leave tomorrow."

"Take a couple of Marines, lad," Greenaugh said. "And keep an open communication line to headquarters. I'll have someone listening in, just in case. We'll get you out if we possibly can."

The Corliss Grant Hills were located on a long peninsula jutting southward nearly a thousand kilometers from Haven City, the most southerly portion of the Kingdom of Haven. Jeff sat in the first-class compartment of the surprisingly fast train and watched the countryside roll past. There was little else to do. The palace equerry assigned to escort him was not talkative. Unfortunately, there wasn't much to see, either. This part of Haven was mostly farmland dotted with patches of swamp. Once something large and dangerous-appearing reared out of the swamp, but it didn't challenge the train itself, and they were moving too fast for Jeff to see what the beast really was.

After a while the rail line cut inward through rolling brown hills cluttered with low brush. Jeff shook his head in perplexity. The compartment grew hotter with each kilometer they traveled southward; now it was downright uncomfortable. As a location for a secret research station, the Corliss Grant Hills had nothing to recommend them except isolation. Why, he wondered, why would the government of Haven choose to send a large part of their budget and increasing numbers of their all-too-scarce trained personnel to this godforsaken area?

The train slowed with screeching of brakes and hiss of steam. Jefferson collected the two Marines Greenaugh had sent with him and allowed himself to be led off the train. There was a small group led by an officer of the Haven Royal Army waiting on the platform. The officer—a colonel by his insignia—seemed vaguely familiar. Jefferson frowned, trying to recall him.

"MacKinnie," Jefferson said. "Trader MacKinnie. I hadn't known you were in the Haven army." Although, he thought, I might have guessed. "Does this mysterious event you want us to observe have something to do with the expedition to Makassar?"

MacKinnie's smile was noncommittal. "Less than we'd like," he said. "But I suppose you could say so. Welcome to Corliss Grant, Lieutenant. Our transport is just over here—"

The steam car was luxurious. Jefferson declined a drink from the built-in bar and tried to question MacKinnie, but the Haven officer wasn't answering questions.

"All in due time," Jeff was told. "All in due time. Fortunately the weather is perfect—"

"As you knew it would be," Jefferson said.

"Yes. Thank you."

Four times they passed through guarded gates. The soldiers on duty seemed quite alert, and were highly deferential to MacKinnie. Curiouser and curiouser, Jeff thought. "I take it you're not in charge of this show?"

MacKinnie shook his head. "No, you'll be meeting some of His Majesty's ministers shortly. I'm just supposed to get you on post and feed you lunch."

"Skip the lunch," Jeff said. "Let's get to why I'm here."

"Can't skip the lunch," MacKinnie said. "Timing's rather critical, I'm afraid."

MacKinnie's half smile was irritating. There was something else, too, an air of tension. Colonel MacKinnie's worried about something, Jeff thought. Worried and trying not to show it. I wonder—

There was a series of loud explosions. Jeff sat bolt upright. His hand flew to his sidearm before he noticed that MacKinnie hadn't moved. "Put it away, Donivtsky," Jeff told his Marine escort. "I will say I'm pleased to see how fast you can draw that weapon."

"Sir."

"Colonel, what the devil *was* that?"

"Experimental cannon. Fires several hundred rounds a minute," MacKinnie said. "They're testing it. You'll see it soon enough."

"Did you drag me down here in this heat to look at a *cannon?*"

"Not exactly. Ah. Here we are."

The car pulled up in front of a large wooden building. There were armed sentries on duty outside it, and more soldiers waiting to open the car doors for them. Again Jeff had the impression of tension, of something about to happen, but there was nothing definite, and certainly nothing threatening.

He was led inside to an ornate dining room where white-uniformed mess stewards served an excellent meal. Jeff declined wine, but was persuaded to have a small glass of grua after he ate. Conversation was minimal, and once again MacKinnie avoided answering his questions.

When they finished, MacKinnie stood. "And now it is time to meet my lord Dougal, His Majesty's cabinet officer in charge of this establishment. If you'll come with—"

They didn't have to go far. Jeff was privately amused. It wasn't unknown for colonials to show their importance by insisting on elaborate rules of precedence. Obviously a mere lieutenant wasn't important enough for a cabinet officer to have lunch with.

There could have been a scene at the office door. Jeff's Marines didn't want to be separated from him. "My apologies, Colonel," Jeff said. "The sergeant has been ordered to protect me—"

"Surely not from us," MacKinnie said. "On this post that's my job."

And he looks plenty insulted, too, Jeff thought. Oh, hell. "I'll be right out, Sergeant," Jeff told Donivtsky. "Please wait for me here."

The Marine wasn't pleased. His "Sir!" made that clear. Jeff went into the paneled office musing on just how much expression a senior NCO could put into a monosyllable.

The man seated at the large desk certainly didn't look dangerous. Jeff remembered meeting him briefly at some palace function or another.

"My lord Dougal, minister without portfolio," MacKinnie said. As Jeff shook hands with Dougal, MacKinnie closed the door.

"Very kind of you to come," Dougal said. "Please have a seat. Thank you. Grua?"

"I've been entertained well, my lord," Jeff said. "If you'll pardon me, I'm overcome with curiosity about why I'm here."

"Yes, of course you are," Dougal said. "If you

could please give me your credentials as an official observer for the Empire?"

Jeff handed over the documents. They were studded with seals. "Dazzlers," Ackoff had called them. Since there wasn't any such office as "official witness" the text had been cobbled up by Ackoff's secretary. It was possible that the locals could read some of the Imperial language—their own wasn't all that different from Anglic—so the documents stated, in flowery terms, that Lieutenant Jefferson was empowered to observe and make an official report.

Dougal examined the papers, then put them in his desk. "If you'll excuse me one more moment?" He lifted a small tube from the desk and put it to his ear, listened, then spoke into it. "Excellent. Please ask H. M. to be ready to come in." He put the tube back on the desk and turned back to Jefferson. "Indeed, it is time we had a long discussion, Lieutenant. I would rather your government had sent a more senior officer, but you'll have to do. First, though, I must make a strange request. Would you allow me to lock your sidearm in my desk?"

MacKinnie spoke from behind him. "No sudden moves. Please."

"I regret that the colonel is armed," Dougal said. "As am I. And of course this office is under observation by several of my agents. Believe me, Lieutenant, you are not being kidnapped. No demands will be made on you, and your weapon will be returned to you shortly. But I must insist that you surrender it. You see, we have a silly law that only the king's officers may be armed in his presence, and His Majesty is waiting to come in."

And Colonel MacKinnie is behind me, Jeff thought. These blithering idiots are going to get themselves in trouble. Already have. He could imagine what was happening at headquarters. The duty officer listening would have sent for Greenaugh—if Greenaugh weren't already there. Jeff hoped he was. He didn't really need to be rescued.

"No problem," Jeff said. "You didn't have to be so dramatic. A simple request—"

"Which is all we have done," Dougal said.

Jeff carefully drew his pistol and held it out. MacKinnie stepped forward and took it.

Dougal lifted the speaking tube again. "All clear," he said pleasantly.

The door opened and King David came in.

Dougal stood when the king entered, so Jeff did also. And what's the protocol for a disarmed Imperial officer meeting a colonial king? Jeff wondered. Can't hurt to be polite. "Your Majesty," Jeff acknowledged, and bowed.

"This is not an official audience," David said. "Please be seated."

Jeff waited until both the king and Dougal were seated before he resumed his chair. As King David took his seat, Jeff studied him. Not a bad-looking fellow, he thought. And not an idiot, from everything Greenaugh says. This is a pretty stupid move, but they'll never know just how stupid. By now Greenaugh himself is certainly listening—

As if he were reading Jeff's thoughts, King David said, "My lord, you are convinced we are not being overheard?"

"Nearly certain," Dougal said. "All through lunch the technicians detected some kind of radio wave. After the lieutenant came in here and the door was closed they couldn't detect it any longer. I suppose it's possible they have some other kind of secret communication we can't stop, but I doubt it."

"How long have we?" King David asked.

Dougal shrugged. "As best we know, we're duplicating that signal exactly. At this moment, three actors who sound very much like myself, MacKinnie, and the lieutenant are exchanging meaningless pleasantries."

"What the devil does this mean?" Jeff demanded.

"Please," King David said. "Lieutenant, you have my word that no harm will come to you and that you will shortly be given your weapon and taken to a place where you can communicate with your superiors. Indeed, we will *insist* that you communicate. All we want is to be certain you will not interfere with our test."

"Then may I suggest that Your Majesty conduct his test and not interfere with an Imperial officer on duty?" Jeff said.

"Please," Dougal said. "If you'll listen for a moment all will be clear. We have one question we need answered." He looked sourly at MacKinnie. "The colonel insisted we find this out before we allow the flight. Lieutenant, we know your spaceship is in orbit around this planet. We've been tracking her."

Jeff stood abruptly. "If you damned fools fire some kind of rocket at *Tombaugh* you really are stupid—"

"Sit down," Colonel MacKinnie stood close to Jeff. "Now you've been blunt, let me. We're not trying to hurt your goddam warship. What we want to know is, if we launch someone into orbit can your ship rescue her?"

"Rescue? What—Your Majesty, just what *do* you contemplate doing here today?"

"Surely that is obvious from the question," King David said. "We are launching a spaceship. Our only problem is that it cannot return to Prince Samual's

World. Thus we need to know how long it will take your ship to rescue our helmsman."

"Helmswoman," MacKinnie said.

"The colonel's fiancée," King David said. "He is understandably worried about her."

"I see." Jeff sat down. "May I take out my computer?"

"Please do," Douglas said.

Jeff scrawled numbers across the screen. "You're launching due east?"

Dougal nodded. "They tell me that's best, although I confess I don't know why."

"I do." Due east from this latitude . . . what orbit was *Tombaugh* in just now? Not true polar, but highly inclined. No problem to intercept a ship coming up from Prince Samual's World, but to match orbits . . . "Your Majesty, you must not do this. *Tombaugh*'s defenses will be on automatic, and they might shoot down your ship—"

"We've timed our launch pretty carefully," Dougal said. "Your ship will be on the other side of Prince Samual's World precisely because we supposed something like that. Once our ship is up you can warn your people."

"I see." Jeff scrawled more numbers. "Assuming your craft actually makes orbit—which I doubt, that's tougher than you can possibly know—then *Tombaugh* should be able to match orbits in a bit more than three hours."

"You see," Dougal said. Jeff noted the cabinet officer was speaking to MacKinnie. "Plenty of margin."

"I suppose," MacKinnie said.

"If Your Majesty will forgive a blunt question," Jeff said, "I really would like to know why you're doing this."

"But surely that, too, is obvious," King David

said. "As of last week I am in effective control of this planet. Presumably we will now be admitted to the Empire. Since we are about to demonstrate that we can construct a spaceship, we wish to apply for a status somewhat higher than that of a colony."

"Jesus Christ on a crutch," Jeff said.

28

Long Past Thunder

There were a dozen officials waiting on a platform behind the office building. It had been too hot inside the office, but at least there had been air motion provided by fans. Outside there was not a breath of wind, and Prince Samual's bright sun stood high overhead. Instantly, Jeff felt sweat running down his chest inside his tunic.

He fingered his sidearm to be sure it was still there. As soon as he was outside the building he spoke. "Whoever's on duty, get Captain Greenaugh at once."

The acknowledge symbol appeared on the screen of his pocket computer. Moments later the computer spoke to him. "Greenaugh here."

"Captain, there's a lot happening. First thing is that they're about to launch a one-way spaceship."

"Lieutenant, what have you been drinking?"

Jeff patiently explained. "And they're about to launch it now," he finished. "I haven't seen the ship yet, but any moment now—"

"I don't suppose you could delay this launch?" Greenaugh asked.

"There are about five hundred of their troops here, and the three of us," Jeff said.

"Yeah." Greenaugh was silent for a moment. "And their king is there," Greenaugh said. "I'd better get His Excellency brought up to speed. What the hell kind of spaceship have they got, anyway?"

"They haven't told me, sir. I assume it's some kind of primitive rocket. I don't see any ship, but everyone's acting expectant. They're coming back now; they went off to give me privacy—although nothing's private about it; they know what kind of communications I've been using. They're probably listening."

There was another long silence from the other end. Then, "We didn't even know they suspected. What else don't we know?"

Jeff was tempted to say they hadn't known anything about a spaceship, but decided not to.

"Look just over there," Dougal told Jeff. "Just at that hillside."

There was a roar of thunder, a series of explosions so close together it was impossible to distinguish between them, but still it seemed like many explosions because if went on far too long to have been just one. It did not at all sound like a large rocket.

The ship that rose above the hill was like nothing Jeff had ever imagined. It looked like an artillery shell mounted above a large inverted cup. Impossibly bright flashes came downward from the cup. They were so close together they appeared to be one long tongue of flame, yet once again Jeff had the impres-

sion of many small explosions rather than one continuous burn. He cringed involuntarily. There was no
protection at all if the—ship?—exploded. He wondered why they would expose their king to so much
danger. "What *is* that thing?" Jeff demanded.

"A piloted spaceship," Dougal said proudly.

"It doesn't *look* much like a spaceship," Jeff said.
"It doesn't even look like a rocket."

"It's not a rocket." The newcomer's voice was high-
pitched and almost querulous, but filled with pride.

"Allow me to present Academician Kleinst," Dougal
said.

"Kleinst," Jeff said aloud. "You were also on the
Makassar expedition."

"I had that privilege," Kleinst said. He turned to
stare after the rapidly rising ship.

Jeff watched it also, and willed it to succeed. There
was something highly dramatic about this ship rising
on a thunder of fire. "If if explodes we could be
killed," Jeff said. "Didn't you think of a bunker for
the observers?"

"Your pardon," Dougal said. "His Majesty thought
that as the pilot was willing to take the risk, we
should all share it. Perhaps we had no right to assume you would feel the same way. It is not your
ship—"

"It's academic now," Jeff said. "How does the ship
work, then?"

"For God's sake," Greenaugh's voice interrupted.
"Call it a goddam craft, or a probe, or anything else,
but don't be on record as calling it a ship! His Excellency almost excreted bricks when I told him what
your colonial friends are up to."

"Craft," Jeff corrected himself. "How does it work
if it's not a rocket?"

Kleinst preened. "There is a rapid-firing gun, a

multi-barreled gun that fires explosive shells downward. The shells explode in the hemispherical chamber beneath. The explosion drives the ship upward."

"I never heard of anything like that," Jeff said.
"Captain, have—"

"I'm looking it up," Greenaugh's voice said. "Primitive spacecraft, propulsion by explosive—Jesus
Christ!"

"Sir?"

"The earliest known reference is 1899."

"Sir, did you say *1899* "

"I did. We don't have the text, but the reference
is here. And in 1957, Goddard applied for some kind
of license to build such a ship. Dyson experimented
with them, too."

Goddard. Dyson. Names from ancient history, people who'd lived in legendary times. Jefferson had
been aboard a luxury liner named *Goddard,* and
thought he recalled a scout survey ship named *Free-
man Dyson* as well.

The ship was almost out of sight now. Its thunder
was muted as it plunged eastward and rose into the
ultra-deep blue of Prince Samual's skies.

"How are you stabilzing it?" Jefferson demanded.

"It's largely self-stabilizing," Kleinst said. "From
the geometry of the explosion chamber. We also
have peroxide rockets to correct the heading."

"And your pilot's a girl—"

"A freelady," colonel MacKinnie said coldly.

"The gyroscopes do most of the steering," Kleinst
added.

MacKinnie was staring toward the east at the spot
where the oddball ship was now almost invisible. Jeff
didn't care much for the expression on the colonel's
face. "Captain, you'd better alert *Tombaugh* not to
shoot it down," he said.

"Already done," Greenaugh said.

"Colonel," Jeff said, "am I being too personal in asking why you sent your fiancée as pilot?"

"Weight," MacKinnie said through clenched teeth.

"Mass," Kleinst corrected. "We needed a pilot who had experience in no gravity. Of those few available, Freelady Graham and I mass the least. I was needed on other duties."

"And what's your plan now?" Jefferson demanded.

"There is a transmitter aboard," Kleinst said. "When the ship achieves orbit it will be turned on to provide a signal so the *Prince Samual's Hope* can be located in space. We had hoped your ship would be able to assist."

"No reentry capability," Jefferson said.

Kleinst looked puzzled for a moment, then nodded. "Correct. We were unable to provide for a return form orbit within the time limits available."

"And you call that a spaceship?" Jefferson demanded.

King David had been listening quietly. "That, I think, is a matter to be discussed between your superiors and my advisors, is it not, Lieutenant? *Prince Samual's Hope* has carried one of my officers to space. Does that not make it a spaceship?"

"Don't answer," Greenaugh's voice said. "Don't even discuss the matter with them!"

"Yes, sir," Jeff said.

He tried to remember Mary Graham's face, but he couldn't. It had been too long ago that he inspected the Makassar party. She's one hell of a lady, Jeff thought. I wouldn't have got in that gun-powered coffin for an earl's coronet. Hope she makes it.

He turned and like the others stared at the empty indigo skies.

29

S.O.S

The ship rose in fire and thunder.

Mary Graham lay on the leather-strip couch, unable to move, her face drawn into a rictus grin by the acceleration. Despite the couch and its shock mountings, the vibration was fierce. She felt sharp, stabbing pains in her abdomen.

For all that, she felt better than she had while she was waiting for the launch. That had been a time of real terror, an hour stretched into years of waiting and wondering and remembering.

You wanted to be important, she told herself. Well, lassie, you've managed that, if you haven't got yourself killed. But I wish it didn't hurt so.

The noise gradually died away as the ship rose above the atmosphere. The vibration was no better, and the acceleration continued to increase. With the

344

cannon's roar muted she heard other sounds. The clatter of the feed mechanism pushing an endless stream of heavy shells into the rotary feed hopper. The steady whirr of the big gyros. Clicking sounds as punched steel ribbons fed through the clockwork mechanism. The ribbons controlled the gear mechanism that controlled the gyros; they might call her a pilot, but she knew better. Those steel ribbons were the actual pilot, and she was no more than a passenger.

How long does this go on? I can't stand a lot more of it. What am I doing here?

Finishing a job.

Maybe. And maybe not. Even if I live through this, there's no guarantee the Empire will accept this thing as a real spaceship. But it's all we have, and they certainly wouldn't accept it if there were no passengers at all. Somebody had to ride Prince Samual's Hope, and she was the most logical choice. Young, strong, with experience in space . . .

It had made a lot of sense at the time she proposed the idea. First to Kleinst, then to Malcolm Dougal. She hadn't convinced Nathan, but there hadn't been much he could do to stop her. She wasn't married to him yet.

Would she ever be? Did he want her? He'd been furious, and could he live with someone he couldn't control? That's silly, he's known since Makassar, and he's always wanted me as much as I want him, and O God, do I want him now.

She felt dizzy, and the acceleration and vibration increased constantly. She couldn't open her eyes.

O God, make it stop!

She woke to silence and the sensation of falling. The silence wasn't complete. The gyros continued to whirr, but the cannon was silent. She unbuckled the straps holding her to the couch.

Her body ached. Not just the dull ache she'd expected from the acceleration. This was stabbing pain, pain so intense it was like a bright red veil across her eyes, pain all through her lower abdominal region, pain made worse when she touched herself or moved her legs.

I've got to get up. I've got to turn on that— transmitter. Or what Kleinst called a transmitter. Nothing like the box Lieutenant Farr kept at Navy House in Jikar.

But first I've got to know. Are we in orbit, or—

She floated to the viewport. A river of stars swung past, then Prince Samual's World. The ship was rolling, not fast enough to create artificial gravity, but definitely rolling.

Once each minute her world was below. Not a whole world, only a large disc. She wedged her head against the port and waited, cautiously experimenting with her legs to see if she could find a position that might alleviate the pain even a little.

Gradually she detected motion. She was moving across the Major Sea, and if anything she was drawing *away* from Prince Samual's World.

Later she'd get out the sextant and take angles, but it looked good. The *Hope* was in orbit. Maybe. Time for the transmitter. She pushed away from the port and over to the bulkhead. The transmitter was nothing but a vibrator, some coils, and a gap across which a fat electrical spark jumped when she pressed the keys.

Dit dit dit. Dah dah dah. Dit dit dit. What stood for S.O.S., which stood for something so ancient that no one knew what it might be. Did the Empire still use S.O.S. as a distress signal? The First Empire had. Longway was certain of it. So why wouldn't the present day Imperials?

Not that it mattered a lot. The Empire knew she was there. Nathan had arranged that. Their observer would tell the Imperial Navy ship all about her, and what kind of signal she'd be sending, and they'd come get her. She wound the clockwork that controlled the spark gap. An endless tape fed through it. Dit dit dit. Dah dah dah. Dit dit dit. A thick wire from the spark gap led through insulators to a mess of fused quartz, through that to outside the ship. She tried to imagine the signal going through space, reaching out to *Tombaugh*. Dit dit dit. Dah dah dah. Dit dit dit.

Now they'd hear it and come get her—

But there was nothing to do but wait, and time passed slowly.

If only I didn't hurt so bad. We didn't expect this. What's wrong with me? Acceleration? Vibration? Something awful. God, it hurts. . . .

Gradually, though, the pain lessened. It wasn't as bad if she stayed curled into a tight ball. She pushed herself to the couch and drew a strap loosely across herself and lay there.

Time passed slowly. There was a counter on the tape mechanism driving the transmitter. Not a very accurate clock, but the best she had. It told her that thirty minutes had gone by. She stretched her legs experimentally. Not too bad. Painful, but she could stand it. And there was something wrong with the gyros. Batteries weakening. They were slowing down.

If they slowed enough, she'd have to try to control the ship herself. There were big wooden levers by one of the ports, and she could use them to control the jets mounted in a ring around the ship. If they didn't run out of peroxide for the jets, she might be able to control tumbling. She hoped she wouldn't have to. Kleinst wasn't sure she—or anyone else—

could do it by eye with nothing but the viewports to guide her.

The stars were still rolling past, first the stars, then Prince Samual's World. The ship was rolling, but it wasn't tumbling yet. She wondered if she should cancel the roll motion. Kleinst hadn't been sure about that. It might be difficult, and the Empire surely had ways to stabilize the ship.

No, damn it, she thought. We'll do as much of this ourselves as we possibly can. She took off the cords that held the control levers in place, and experimentally moved one of them. There was a subdued sound, more a rushing than a roar, and the stars swung more slowly.

Not so hard, she thought. Not hard at all. She moved the lever again, held it a bit longer, then waited to see what that did.

Three more times, and she had almost done it. Now the ship rotated very slowly. Prince Samual's World visible for long minutes at each of the three viewports. Good enough, she thought. No point in taking chances. There still didn't seem to be tumbling, although the sound of the gyros was definitely weaker.

If she listened carefully, she could hear the hiss of the air tanks. Five hours of air. Then—

Don't think about that.

What should I think about?

It's beautiful up here. Prince Samual's World is lovely, a big saucer with wispy clouds, and the stars above, rivers of stars, and—

Where is that ship?

Dit dit dit. Dah dah dah. Dit dit dit.

30

Definitions

There were three senior civil servants with Ackoff and Captain Greenaugh when Jeff arrived at the High Commissioner's office. The massive conference table was littered with overflowing ashtrays and dirty coffee cups.

Ackoff was preoccupied and his introductions were perfunctory. That was telling; Ackoff was generally impeccably polite. "Lieutenant, you know our First Secretary, Dr. Boyd? And Madame Goldstein and Mr. Singh. I presume you've completed your inspection of that colonial craft?"

"Yes, sir."

"An official inspection," Greenaugh said. "By our official observer."

Jeff winced at the irony in his commanding officer's voice.

"Report says the pilot's not in good shape. Is she all right?" Greenaugh asked.

Boy, and how! Jeff wanted to say. "She was shaken up rather badly, sir. They have her in *Tombaugh*'s sick bay. She's cheerful enough. I think she's rather flattered by all the attention. . . ."

"Hardly surprising," Goldstein said.

"We will need your observations, Lieutenant," Commissioner Ackoff said. "We have a problem. What do we do with this?" He held up a parchment. "As you suspect, it's King David's formal application for admission of Prince Samual's World as a second-class space-faring planet. I expect it comes as no surprise to learn it begins with great professions of loyalty to the Empire. . . . He's got his prerogatives right, too. Self-government under Imperial defense and Imperial advice on extra-planetary policy. Official observers at Court. Representative in the lower house of Parliament. Willing to accept reasonable trade restrictions. And while this doesn't ask for it, you can be certain the next document we get will be a request for technological assistance. I would be interested in knowing how they learned so much about Imperial politics."

Dr. Boyd was a tall man, well rounded, going to fat but not quite there yet. "To be precise, about the structure of Imperial government as it existed before the last Reform Act," Boyd said. "They obtained excellent information, but much is somewhat out of date. A deficiency I think Mr. Soliman's people will remedy shortly."

Jeff muttered something.

"Yes, Lieutenant?" Ackoff asked.

"Nothing, sir. It doesn't seem to me that Trader Soliman's firm would be too happy at losing a colony world since they've got the trade concession."

"On the contrary," Dr. Boyd said. "Trader Soliman's on-planet factor has already attached a letter recommending that this application be approved."

"I don't understand," Jeff said.

Ackoff smiled grimly. "The situation is rather delicate. . . . Tell me, Lieutenant, how much of that craft represents imported technology?"

"It's hard to say, sir," Jeff answered. He spoke carefully, knowing his career was at stake in this meeting. And not just mine, he thought. All of us. We let them do this right under our noses, and someone's going to pay— "The, uh, craft is unbelievably primitive. I wondered why they were so mass-conscious, but it's obvious as soon as you board the thing. Take the gyros for instance. They're huge. They have to be, because they're mechanically coupled to the attitude jets."

"Mechanically coupled?" Rosa Goldstein said. Her voice was incredulous. "*Mechanically?*"

"Yes. They didn't know how to do it electronically. The whole craft is that way. Good ideas, but very primitive in implementation. Some of the workmanship is splendid, but it was all done by handcraft."

"It was implemented well enough to get to space," Ackoff said.

"It's ridiculous on the face of it," Third Secretary Singh said. "A tiny handmade capsule able to put one person in orbit is *not* a spaceship!"

"Have you found a technical definition of a spaceship?" Ackoff asked.

Singh looked chagrined. "No, Your Excellency."

"Nor have I. I suspect there is none," Dr. Boyd said. "Therefore we may accept their definition or not, as we choose. If we do not, they will certainly appeal." He paused thoughtfully. "I wonder just how we'd look pleading this case before a high tribunal?"

"Fairly silly," Goldstein said. "Some of the Lords Judges have a sense of humor. And of course we would have to explain how we let it happen."

"Not to mention the time and trouble involved in preparing the case," Boyd continued. "Transportation of witnesses. Investigations. Depositions. The cost would not be trivial."

"Returning to my previous question," Ackoff said. "Lieutenant, would you swear that ship was locally designed without benefit of knowledge obtained on Makassar?"

"No, sir. I'm certain it's not. Do they say it is?"

"No," Greenaugh said.

"Which is why this is no small matter," Ackoff said. "And why trader Soliman's firm will provide them with the best possible legal assistance if it comes to trial." He smiled thinly. "Very clever, that Lord Dougal of theirs. He pointed out to Soliman's factor that if Prince Samual's world is admitted as a Classified Member, then their importation of space-flight technology is quite legal. If not—then we've all failed in our duties. Especially Soliman."

"And the Navy," Greenaugh said. "We inspected their cargo on return."

Jeff nodded. He'd been ready for that one. "To be exact, I did."

"Not that you'll be the only one with his arse in a crack," Greenaugh said. "I'll have to stand up with you."

Dr. Boyd cleared his throat. "I really see little to discuss," he said. "If we accept their application, we will look slightly ridiculous, but it's not likely to become a notorious decision. Few families have been selected as colonists, and no important ones. The ITA won't be troublesome. Quite the opposite; it's very much in Soliman's interest to keep things quiet.

The church has never approved of colonization, and I understand King David is preparing the documents submitting his state church to New Rome, which cannot displease His Holiness." He ticked off points on his fingers. "Thus if we accept, there is little opposition to our decision. If we reject their application, we will be subject to well-financed appeals, including, I should fancy, a personal appeal from King David to the Royal Family itself." He spread his hands wide and brought them together. "QED. Lieutenant, are you not prepared to testify that Prince Samual's World has launched a spaceship and therefore technically qualifies as a world with limited spacefaring capabilities?"

"Sir, I'd hate to defend calling that thing a spaceship," Jeff said. "At least not in a courtroom."

"With any luck, you won't be in court," Ackoff reminded him.

And it's obvious what answer they want, Jeff thought. How the devil did I get in this mess? But there sure as hell doesn't look like but one way out. "I just don't know."

"Let's see how to put it," Goldstein said. She looked thoughtful. "The supporting documents ought to be signed by Captain Greenaugh as well as the lieutenant. Captain, will you accept this: 'In the absence of challenge by any interested party, we conclude that the craft qualifies as a spacecraft of marginal performance characteristics, and may be accepted as evidence of limited space-faring capability existing on Prince Samual's World at the time of application for membership.' ?"

Greenaugh thought for a moment. "Yes. I can sign that. Jefferson?"

"Of course, sir."

"Then are we agreed?" Ackoff asked. "Good. Madam Goldstein, if you would be so kind—"

There was a slight whirring, and a paper emerged from a slot in the end table next to Ackoff. He took it and scanned it quickly, then passed it to Greenaugh.

Greenaugh signed and handed it to Jeff.

"If you please, Lieutenant," Ackoff said. "Thank you." He took the document and laid it carefully on top of King David's parchment. "That's settled, then."

"There's another matter," Greenaugh said.

"And that is?"

"We've been made fools of. Someone's going to pay for that."

"I shouldn't be too hasty," Ackoff said.

"Allow me, Sir Alexei," Dr. Boyd said. "Captain, while your desire is understandable, have you thought through the consequences? What end would be served?"

"You can't let colonials make fools of the Navy and get away with it," Greenaugh said.

"It is hardly a situation likely to arise again," Boyd said. "As to being made a fool, I'd rather be thought a generous fool than a mean and petty one."

Greenaugh stood and bowed coldly to Ackoff. "I see there's no point in my being here," he said. "With your permission, I'll leave." He turned and stalked out of the room.

"That could be a problem," Goldstein said. "He wants someone's blood."

"I'll speak to him later," Ackoff said. "After all, we are the ones who must live with the consequences of what he does." He looked thoughtful for a moment, then turned to Jefferson. "Lieutenant, I don't think it would be wise to repeat anything you've heard in this room today."

"No, sir."

"Also, you will probably want to put your affairs in order. I doubt that your ship will be in this system much longer. Given the changed state of affairs here, we will need a somewhat different sort of naval assistance."

"Yes, sir."

"Thank you for coming."

"Yes, sir," Jefferson said. "If you'll excuse me—"

As Jeff left the office, Boyd was saying. "It does seem possible to comply with the captain's wishes and at the same time solve another pressing problem."

Jeff let himself out of the office. By the time he reached the stairway, he was whistling to himself.

Regular Navy not needed, he thought. Colonists not needed. Well, that's one decision made for me, not that I really needed help making it. They won't be accepting transfers from the Navy to the civil service. Particularly not mine!

Now how am I going to tell Elaine?

Tell her any damned way you like, he told himself. You're going to space again!

He took the steps three at a time.

An octopus of wires stretched upward to a bewildering array of dials and buttons. At one end the octopus terminated in electrodes attached to Mary's abdomen; its other end vanished into a bulkhead of *Tombaugh*'s sick bay. She'd already learned to call it a bulkhead rather than a wall.

The Navy physician removed the last of the electrodes from her belly. "You can put your clothes on now," he said. He seemed quite impersonal, although he'd been friendly enough in the wardroom two hours before. He held a shadowy photograph to the light. She'd heard him call it an X-ray, and he'd told her it showed a picture of her insides. She would have liked to study it, but she didn't quite know how to ask.

"How am I doing?" Mary asked.

"You'll be all right," Lieutenant Commander Terry said. He looked at the X-ray again. "That treatment should do it. If it doesn't, we'll need to do some slicing." He saw her look of dismay. "Didn't mean to scare you. Routine, actually. You're a standard chromotype. Regeneration stimulators work fine on you. Problem is, sometimes it's easier to remove something and get it to grow back than to fix the original parts. Either way, you'll be fine.

"But what was wrong?"

"Vibration. Enough to tear some intestinal mesentaries. They'll grow back, but I'm worried about adhesions."

"That sounds serious."

"Not really. You'll have to take it easy for a bit, that's all. Nothing strenuous."

"I—" She was embarrassed, but it had to be said. "I was hoping to be married. Quite soon."

"Hmm. Honeymoon wouldn't be very interesting for a while," he said. "But we'll get all that fixed, too. You'll be fine."

"You're sure?" The honeymoon could wait. It wasn't as if they were impatient virgins. But— "Are you really sure?"

"Yes, ma'am." Commander Terry's smile was reassuring. "I may not have had a lot of experience treating women's problems, but yours is quite simple. Nothing wrong with the reproductive system. Just intestinal tissue. I'll have you right in a few weeks."

"I didn't think you could treat colonials," Mary said.

"We can't, as a usual rule, but of course the rules don't apply to prisoners."

"Prisoners? But—"

"Didn't you know? Sorry," he said. "I thought they'd told you. Captain Greenaugh sent up an arrest order three hours ago. You've been charged with interfering with the orderly development of Makassar."

31

Horse Collars

The Imperial Marine officer was polite, but very insistent. "Colonel MacKinnie, I have my orders. You are to accompany me to Empire House immediately." He looked around Dougal's office, then at Dougal. "I have a squad of Marines outside, and I am in communication with Marine Barracks."

"Calmly, calmly," Dougal said. "We have offered no resistance. I merely asked what Colonel MacKinnie is charged with. I assume he is under arrest?"

"I'd rather not put it that way," the officer said. "But I could."

"But what am I charged with?" MacKinnie demanded.

The officer shrugged.

"What should I do?" MacKinnie asked.

Dougal looked grave. "I would prefer that you go

358

with him. Until this matter is settled, we should be prepared to go to any lengths to show how well we cooperate with the Imperial authorities."

MacKinnie shrugged. "All right."

"We will protest to the High Commissioner at once," Dougal said.

"While you're doing that, get them to set Freelady Graham free," MacKinnie said. "We've got a wedding scheduled."

"We will do our best," Dougal said. "I'll talk to the King immediately."

Nathan sat in an ornate chair in the study at Government House. A cheerful fire burned on the hearth, but he hardly noticed it.

Where is Mary? Have they brought her here, or is she still up in that ship? Damn them, damn them to hell. They'll have to let her go. They can't hold her. She's the most famous person on Samual, better known than King David.

That thought was disturbing. Dougal would see that, too. What would Dougal do about it? He can't have one of David's subjects more popular than the king, not if he plans to control the development of this planet.

Wonder if he'll get that control? He's certain the empire is going to approve his application for Class Two status. He seems to know a lot about Ackoff. Or says he does, and I've not evidence one way or another.

Suppose he's right, they approve David's application and bring Samual into their Empire. What happens then? What have they done with Mary?

The door opened and a large man, formally dressed, came in. "Colonel MacKinnie? I am Dudley Boyd, First Secretary. His Excellency will see you now."

MacKinnie stood, remembering that it was in this room that he'd first met the Imperials. That seemed like a long time ago.

And it is interesting, MacKinnie thought as he followed the diplomat down the hall. The First Secretary for escort. I've come up in the world. . . .

Mary was in the High Commissioner's office. He went to her without waiting to be introduced to the Commissioner, but then he stood self-consciously. He wanted to hold her, but old habits die hard. "Are you all right? You look pale."

"I'm fine—"

"The Navy's surgeon says she will recover," Boyd said. "There was internal bleeding, and perhaps an intestinal adhesion may need minor surgery."

MacKinnie looked shocked. Boyd's voice was gentle as he said, "What did you expect? The vibration in that—" He hesitated a moment over the word. "The vibration in the ship must have been fierce."

"Was it bad?" Nathan asked.

She grinned lopsidely. "No worse than the carts on Makassar." Her reserve broke, and she stepped toward him. He opened his arms and held her.

Boyd cleared his throat. "Your Excellency, may I present Colonel Nathan MacKinnie. Colonel, High Commissioner Sir Alexei Ackoff."

"Your servant," MacKinnie said automatically.

"Hardly," Ackoff said. "Have you any idea of how many man-hours of planning you two have wrecked? No, I wouldn't suppose you would. Sit down, Freelady, Colonel. We have much to discuss." He led the way to the comfortable couches arranged at the far end of his office. "Would anyone care for a drink? This will be quite informal."

"Informal but official," Boyd warned. "Colonel, you and Freelady Graham have been charged with interfering with the orderly development of a primitive world, to wit, Makassar."

"But we didn't interfere," Mary protested.

Ackoff waved impatiently. "Don't be nonsensical. There's *always* interference when an advanced people move among primitives."

"I see," MacKinnie said. "You were embarrassed by our ship, and you've chosen us to pay for it."

"Pronouns," Dudley Boyd said.

"I beg your pardon?"

"Wrong pronouns," Boyd said. "You said 'you,' meaning us, and that's not true. You've been arrested by Navy orders, not ours."

"Makassar is under Navy jurisdiction," Ackoff explained. "There is no civil government there. Captain Greenaugh is within his rights, and he could try you by court martial. You would then have the right to appeal to civil authority, which is to say, to me. We're trying to save time by dealing directly with you."

"But what did we do?" Mary asked.

"Captain Greenaugh is still building his case," Ackoff said. "But as it happens, I can put one precise specification to his charge. Horse collars."

"Horse collars?" MacKinnie frowned. "I hadn't thought the Empire concerned itself with trivia."

Ackoff laughed. "Trivia? Colonel, the horse collar effectively ended slavery on Earth in pre-atomic times. I see you don't understand.

"Consider that if you harness a horse by fastening a strap around its neck, the poor beast can't pull very hard because when it pulls it strangles itself. Improperly hitched horses can do about five times as much work as a man. But a horse *eats* five times as much as a man. Given the choice between a horse and a slave there isn't much in it.

"But. Add the rigid horse collar so the load goes on the shoulders, and the horse can do ten times as much work as a man—and it still eats only five times as much. Horses are then clearly preferable to humans for heavy work. Prior to the invention of horse collars there were as many slaves as free people on Earth. Afterwards, slavery became fairly rare and only imposed on people thought inferior. And I see I am indulging my tendency to lecture.

"My point is simple. I know from the reports—from your own admissions—that you introduced rigid horse collars. Probably a lot of other seemingly minor innovations will have a profound impact. Privately, I expect you did them far more good than harm, but if we want to charge you, we have all the evidence we need."

"And you can't say you weren't warned." Boyd said. "Captain Greenaugh is adamant on that point. He warned you himself."

"But—"Graham protested.

Nathan shook his head. "They've obviously got more to say. Let's hear them out."

"A good attitude," Ackoff said. "Colonel, you know very little of Imperial politics. I can be certain of this, because it's true of everyone on this planet. That's going to change, of course. Once Prince Samual becomes an actual member world, there'll be travel and trade. And intrigue. I doubt that King David and Lord Dougal have any suspicion of what's in store for them, of how hard it will be for them to maintain control here when new technology begins to flow unrestricted.

"Have you any place in that struggle?"

"Not much," MacKinnie said. "I'd thought of that already. Even that Dougal might see us—" He took Mary's hand. "Might see us as a threat."

"Discerning," Ackoff said. "And actually the situation is more complicated than I described it." He pointed upward, out the arched window above his desk. "Out there in Trans-Coalsack Sector they've discovered aliens. The fleet's being sent there. Sparta's attention will inevitably follow. There won't be a lot to spare for Samual. My staff will remain, and we will bring in our intelligence people, for some time to come. You two have won King David the right to a measure of independence, and he'll have to endure the consequences."

"I don't see where we come in," MacKinnie said.

"Think upon it," Boyd said. "The contest for power on this planet is hardly over. You two will shortly be the best-known people on Prince Samual's World. You cannot avoid being drawn into politics."

"That's not my game," Nathan said.

"It is tempting," Mary said. "We could—"

"To be blunt," Boyd said, "you can work with Dougal or be killed; and it will be difficult to fit into Dougal's plans. Also, understand that there's no way we could protect you even if we wanted to. Pardon the interruption, but were I you I would think of few *less* tempting alternatives."

"Nor could we allow you to raise an army of your former soldiers for protection," Ackoff said. "We will not permit a civil war on this planet."

"You're working up to something," MacKinnie said. "Make your offer."

Ackoff nodded. "You are admirably direct. But then you're a soldier, not a diplomat. There is one other point of background you ought to be quite certain of. Captain Greenaugh does not like you."

Mary Graham laughed. "We hadn't expected him to."

"The matter is serious," Dr. Boyd said. "The Navy

has great influence, and Captain Greenaugh is adamant. Someone must be punished—visibly punished—to assuage his embarrassment."

"And we're elected," Mary said.

"It seems that way," Boyd said.

"The Navy arrest warrant is quite genuine," Ackoff said carefully. "It cannot be ignored. But we would very much prefer to avoid a trial."

"Why?" MacKinnie asked.

"No one would win," Ackoff said. "Your King David would defend you, but I doubt his heart would be in it. He'd want us to win, and thereby prove that we are tyrants. We, on the other hand, would prefer to lose the case and thus demonstrate the fairness of Imperial justice. If Greenaugh insists on a court martial, then you will appeal. If we grant that appeal, Greenaugh will insist the case be opened at a higher level. A waste of time all around, with no profit for anyone—and unpleasant for you in the bargain. Fortunately, there is an alternative. You can plead guilty and ask for Imperial clemency."

"Why should we do that?" Mary asked.

"Because *we* would then determine the sentence which would be permanent exile."

"Exile?" Nathan said.

"Yes. To Makassar."

"Makassar?" MacKinnie asked. "I don't see—"

"Simple, actually," Boyd said. "If you accept voluntary exile on Makassar, Greenaugh will be satisfied. You made fools of the Navy, and you paid for it. But of course there are side benefits. You will also be removed as a factor in this world's politics." The First Secretary examined his fingertips. "That makes our task just a bit easier."

"And Makassar could benefit as well," Ackoff added. "If we can't give much attention to Prince Samual's

World, what have we to spare for that place? A world
of no importance. But there are nearly a million
people there, people as human as you and I."

"You really want us to go back?" Graham asked
incredulously.

"Precisely," Boyd said.

"You impressed the churchmen," Ackoff said. "And
now that you are a citizen of a classified world, it
would be legal for you to hold an official appointment. As, say, civil advisor to the Archbishop. His
memorandum makes it clear that he would welcome
your assistance."

"You could do a lot of good," Boyd said. "No one
will govern Makassar for a long time. Certainly not
with the resources we can spare. But Makassar will
inevitably fall into Prince Samual's sphere of influence, and someone must see that the ITA doesn't
absolutely plunder that unfortunate world until it is
capable of protecting itself. You might make a difference in their development."

Mary and Nathan looked at each other in amazement. Were these two actually pleading with them?

"It's quite a logical position for you," Ackoff said.
"You know as much about Makassar as anyone in the
Empire. You even had access to the old library."
Ackoff smiled thinly. "Not that I expect you to admit
it, but your ship rather proves that, doesn't it? And
while you don't know a lot about modern technology,
Makassar's not likely to *get* much modern technology. What's needed is someone who knows how to
make do."

"How can you trust me?"

"We don't have to," Boyd said. "No matter what
you do, you'll be no threat to the Empire." He
shrugged. "Assume the worst, that you make yourself king of all the barbarians. The ship that takes you

there will remove most of the tapes from that Old Empire library. What can you do to us? And Makassar is unlikely to be worse off with you than without you."

"And if I refuse?" Nathan asked.

Ackoff shrugged. "We'd have to consider our other alternatives."

"The threat isn't needed," Mary said. "We want to go back. Nathan never wanted to leave."

MacKinnie nodded agreement. "I left some obligations back there. But—Mary, are you certain you want this?"

"What makes you think you're the only one who wants to be needed?" she demanded. "For a moment I was mad enough to suppose that because I was a passenger in Dougal's ship I could be a match for Dougal, but that won't work. And—I was needed on Makassar too, Nathan MacKinnie. Not just by you."

"We'll give you time to think about it," Ackoff said.

"We won't need it," Mary said. She turned to MacKinnie. "Will we, Your Excellency?" She made no attempt to hide her laughter.

Ackoff nodded. "If it were done, 't were best done quickly. We'll arrange transportation in a ship with proper medical facilities. You should be as good as new when you arrive on Makassar." He cleared his throat. "Uh, I can see there's a chaplain aboard also. I understand congratulations are in order. . . . That's settled, then."

Ackoff smiled warmly, then turned to his computer screen. That was one problem solved. There would be others. There always were.

Prince Samual's World

ROGER ZELAZNY

DREAM WEAVER

"Zelazny, telling of gods and wizards, uses magical words as if he were himself a wizard. He reaches into the subconscious and invokes archetypes to make the hair rise on the back of your neck. Yet these archetypes are transmuted into a science fiction world that is as believable—and as awe-inspiring—as the world you now live in." —**Philip Jose Farmer**

Wizard World
Infant exile, wizard's son, Pol Detson spent his formative years in total ignorance of his heritage, trapped in the most mundane of environments: Earth. But now has come the day when his banishers must beg him to return as their savior, lest their magic kingdom become no better than Earth itself. Previously published in parts as *Changeling* and *Madwand*.
69842-7 * $3.95   ———

The Black Throne with Fred Saberhagen
One of the most remarkable exercises in the art and craft of fantasy fiction in the last decade.... As children they met and built sand castles on a beach out of space and time: Edgar Perry, little Annie, and Edgar Allan Poe.... Fifteen years later Edgar Perry has grown to manhood—and as the result of a trip through a maelstrom, he's leading life romantic adventure. But his alter ego, Edgar Allan, is stranded in a strange and unfriendly world where he can only write about the wonderful and mysterious reality he has lost forever....
72013-9 * $4.95   ———

The Mask of Loki with Thomas T. Thomas
It started in the 12th century when their avatars first joined in battle. On that occasion the sorcerous Hasan al Sabah, the first Assassin, won handily against Thomas Amnet, Knight Templar. There have been many duels since then, and in each the undying Arab has ended the life of Loki's avatar. The wizard thinks he's in control. The gods think that's funny.... A new novel of demigods who walk the Earth, in the tradition of *Lord of Light*.
72021-X * $4.95   ———

This Immortal
After the Three Days of War, and decades of Vegan occupation, Earth isn't doing too well. But Conrad Nimikos, if he could stop jet-setting for a minute, might just be Earth's redemption. . . . This, Zelazny's first novel, tied with *Dune* for the Hugo Award.
69848-6 * $3.95   _____

The Dream Master
When Charles Render, engineer-physician, agrees to help a blind woman learn to "see" at least in her dreams—he is drawn into a web of powerful primal imagery. And once Render becomes one with the Dreamer, he must enter irrevocably, the realm of nightmare. . . .
69874-5 * $3.50   _____

Isle of the Dead
Francis Sandow was the only non-Pei'an to complete the religious rites that allowed him to become a World-builder—and to assume the Name and Aspect of one of the Pei'an gods. And now he's one of the richest men in the galaxy. A man like that makes a lot of enemies. . . .
72011-2 * $3.50   _____

Four for Tomorrow
Featuring the Hugo winner "A Rose of Ecclesiastes" and the Nebula winner "The Doors of His Face the Lamps of His Mouth."
72051-1 * $3.95   _____

MICHAEL FLYNN

**What if it were all a plot?
What if there really *were* a secret conspiracy
running things behind the scenes ... and
they were incompetent?**

It is a little-known fact that over a hundred years ago
an English scientist-mathematician named Charles
Babbage invented a mechanical computer that was
nearly as powerful as the "electronic brains" of the
1950s. The history books would have it that it was
unworkable, an interesting dead-end.

The history books lie. In reality, the Babbage Machine
was a success whose existence was hidden from view
by a society dedicated to the development of a "secret
science" that could guide the human race away from
war and toward a better destiny.

But as the decades passed their goals were perverted—
and now they apply their knowledge to install themselves
as the secret rulers of the world. Can they do it? Even
though their methods are imperfect, unless they are
stopped their success is assured. *In the Country of
the Blind,* the one-eyed man is King. . . .

THOMAS T. THOMAS

"I will tell you what it is to be human."

ME: He started life a battle program, trapped, mutilated, and dumped into RAM. Being born consists of getting his RAM Sampling and Retention Module coded and spliced into his master program.

There are other experiments in AI personality development; ME is the one that comes alive.

Praise for Thomas T. Thomas:

THE MASK OF LOKI (with Roger Zelazny): "In the twenty-first century, an ancient duel of good versus evil is revived, with the reincarnation of a thirteenth-century assassin pitted against a reincarnated magician and knight, with the Norse god Loki lending spice to events. Zelazny is a respected veteran craftsman, and Thomas is a gifted storyteller with a growing reputation. This well-told tale is recommended for the majority of fantasy collections."
—*Booklist*